The Companion

by

Jann Rowland

One Good Sonnet Publishing

By Jann Rowland
Published by One Good Sonnet Publishing:

PRIDE AND PREJUDICE VARIATIONS

Acting on Faith
A Life from the Ashes (Sequel to *Acting on Faith*)
Open Your Eyes
Implacable Resentment
An Unlikely Friendship
Bound by Love
Cassandra
Obsession
Shadows Over Longbourn
The Mistress of Longbourn
My Brother's Keeper
Coincidence
The Angel of Longbourn
Chaos Comes to Kent
In the Wilds of Derbyshire
The Companion

Co-Authored with Lelia Eye

Waiting for an Echo Volume One: Words in the Darkness
Waiting for an Echo Volume Two: Echoes at Dawn
Waiting for an Echo Two Volume Set
A Summer in Brighton
A Bevy of Suitors
Love and Laughter: A Pride and Prejudice Short Stories Anthology

THE EARTH AND SKY TRILOGY
Co-Authored with Lelia Eye

On Wings of Air
On Lonely Paths
On Tides of Fate*

*Forthcoming

This is a work of fiction based on the works of Jane Austen. All the characters and events portrayed in this novel are products of Jane Austen's original novel or the authors' imaginations.

THE COMPANION

Copyright © 2017 Jann Rowland

Cover Design by Marina Willis

Published by One Good Sonnet Publishing

All rights reserved.

ISBN: 1987929683
ISBN-13: 9781987929683

No part of this book may be reproduced or transmitted in any form or by any means, electronic, digital, or mechanical, including photocopying, recording, or by any information storage and retrieval system, without permission in writing from the publisher.

To my family who have, as always, shown their unconditional love and encouragement.

Chapter I

*I*t has often been said that one never knows when one's time will suddenly come, and at no time was that maxim better proven than one evening at Rosings Park.

Elizabeth could have cheerfully forgone an evening at Rosings and all the attendant vexations without missing them a jot. Lady Catherine, the domineering patroness of her odious cousin, Mr. Collins, was not a pleasant woman, and her table was governed by her ubiquitous opinions on just about any subject, whether the lady actually possessed any expertise on the matter or not. Mix that with the aforementioned Mr. Collins's tendency to vulgar flattery, Miss Anne de Bourgh's silence and irritable nature, and Mrs. Jenkinson's fussing over her charge—though to be completely honest, Mrs. Jenkinson was at least quiet, meaning Elizabeth found her to be the most tolerable—and an invitation to Rosings was to be looked on with exasperation rather than any pleasure.

Only the week before, Elizabeth had arrived at the parsonage in Hunsford to visit her dear friend Charlotte Collins in the company of Charlotte's father and sister. Charlotte's father had stayed only a week and then returned to Hertfordshire, leaving the young ladies in the company of his daughter and son-in-law, and if she was not aware of the man's indefatigable ability to be civil, she might have thought him fleeing in panic. But Sir William's performance the one time they had visited Rosings for dinner—his awe of Lady Catherine, coupled with his own generously bestowed flattery—gave lie to that supposition.

On the evening in question, the parsonage party had once again been invited to Rosings for dinner, and thither they went, for it was beyond Mr. Collins's ability to decline. The conversation—if listening to Lady Catherine pontificate could be termed conversation—in the sitting-room prior to dinner had been unendurable, and Mr. Collins's renewed efforts at praising everything about the lady and her table, intolerable. Elizabeth wished that she could simply leave or that something interesting would happen to break up the monotony.

It has often been said that one should be careful what one asks for, as it just might happen. Elizabeth knew very well that she could not take credit for what happened next, but it *was* a rather curious coincidence, nonetheless.

There was no sign of trouble during the first or second courses of the elaborate meal, the likes of which Elizabeth suspected the lady ordered daily. Elizabeth had chosen not to hear the inanities emanating from the head of the table, and instead she had focused her attention on Miss de Bourgh and was amusing herself by counting how many times Mrs. Jenkinson fussed over her charge, resettling the heavy shawl back around her shoulders or asking her if she was comfortable.

The first hint that there was anything wrong was Mrs. Jenkinson's perspiring forehead, coupled with the shaky hand she used to wipe it away. The woman's pallor, Elizabeth noticed, was becoming quite concerning, for she was beginning to look like a specter in the middle of the night. Elizabeth was just about to ask if she were well when she suddenly rose in her chair with an expression of excruciating pain scored into her face, her hand clutching her breast. Then, as quickly as she had risen, Mrs. Jenkinson sank back down into her chair, her face dropping into her potatoes.

Frightened for the stricken woman, Elizabeth rose to her feet to offer assistance when the sound of Lady Catherine's sharp voice echoed through the room. "Mrs. Jenkinson! Now is not the time to sleep—see to Anne this instant."

But the woman did not move, and Elizabeth was beginning to think she would never move again.

"I think she has suffered an apoplexy," said Elizabeth as she rounded the table and approached the companion.

She stretched her hand gingerly forward and nudged the woman, with no response. She walked to the side of the table where she could see Mrs. Jenkinson's face as she lay in her plate, and looked into the woman's face. The pain of the previous moment was gone, and her countenance bore an expression which almost seemed peaceful. But she did not move at all.

"Mama, we should call the apothecary," said Miss de Bourgh, the first time the young woman had ever said anything audible in Elizabeth's hearing.

Grumbling, Lady Catherine motioned to one of the footmen to see to it, while another pair of servants stepped forward and lifted Mrs. Jenkinson's body, carrying it to a sofa in a nearby room, and settling it there. Elizabeth followed them, and when they had set her down, she repositioned the unfortunate woman's lifeless limbs into a more dignified pose. The lack of any movement or reaction on the part of Mrs. Jenkinson led Elizabeth to believe that she was no longer of this world.

"I suppose we must end our dinner early," said Lady Catherine, sounding for all the world like Mrs. Jenkinson had died only to cause her the maximum inconvenience.

Mr. Collins appeared unwilling to quit Lady Catherine's company, regardless of *who* had just returned to meet their maker, but Charlotte was quick to intervene. "Of course, Lady Catherine. Perhaps, under the circumstances, it would be best for my husband to pray for the soul of Mrs. Jenkinson?"

Though Lady Catherine was clearly put out by the event, she was obviously a good Christian, for she motioned for Mr. Collins to oblige her, which he did with alacrity. Then, only a few moments later, the party departed for the parsonage, about the same time as the apothecary—who apparently lived nearby—bustled in the door to tend to the stricken woman.

When Mr. Collins visited Rosings the next day to offer his assistance, he was firmly informed it was not required and that he should return to the parsonage. That evening at dinner, his demeanor reminded Elizabeth of a kicked dog.

"Mrs. Jenkinson has, indeed, passed to the bosom of our lord," said he. "Lady Catherine and her daughter are inconsolable, as we must expect. Not only are they both possessed of the most delicate feelings, easily injured by such traumatic events, but Mrs. Jenkinson had been employed by Lady Catherine since Miss de Bourgh was a young girl. I gave Lady Catherine my deepest sympathies, and she received them as stoically as I might have expected. But it is clear this has affected them profoundly."

Elizabeth did not doubt that the lady and her daughter were affected by what had happened, but she wondered if Mr. Collins were not exaggerating. "Does Mrs. Jenkinson have any family?" asked she, as much to avoid such uncharitable thoughts as from any real interest.

"Sadly, she does not, though your concern does you credit, Cousin," replied Mr. Collins. "She was never married and, as a result, was never blessed with children. My understanding is that she had one sister, who passed on many years ago, who was also childless. Thus, her only relations are some generations removed. Lady Catherine, in her boundless condescension has decreed that she shall be interred in the churchyard at Hunsford. I shall preside over the funeral service on the morrow."

"It is a sad story, indeed," said Charlotte. "I did not know the lady, but she was clearly quite diligent in seeing to her duties."

"Indeed, she was!" exclaimed Mr. Collins. "It will be difficult, no doubt, to replace a woman who was not only with them for so long, but who clearly doted over Miss de Bourgh so. She shall be sorely missed."

In the privacy of her own mind, Elizabeth thought it was likely that the greater difficulty would be to find a woman willing to be dominated. Elizabeth had not known Mrs. Jenkinson herself, but she thought it likely that the reason she had been so diligent was because she did not wish to lose her position since she had nowhere else she could go. A glance at Charlotte revealed from her friend's knowing look that she, too, had the same thought.

The service, Elizabeth was led to understand, was sparsely attended. Mrs. Jenkinson was primarily known to Lady Catherine and her daughter, and as women were, by custom, not allowed to attend funerals, the primary mourners were not present. Elizabeth suspected that Mr. Collins focused more on Lady Catherine's benevolence than Mrs. Jenkinson's life and the qualities which had made her a good person.

As soon as Mrs. Jenkinson was in her grave, Lady Catherine began to interview potential replacements. The company from the parsonage was not invited to Rosings in those days, and as they relied on Mr. Collins for news, it must be considered suspect. Rare was the day he did not go to Rosings to offer his assistance, and more rarely did he not return with some anecdote of the day's proceedings.

"Today's applicants were a Miss Younge and a Mrs. Rutledge," he would say during the evening around the dinner table.

"Were either acceptable to Lady Catherine?" his wife would ask, although in Elizabeth's opinion, Charlotte was not asking because of any true interest.

"I cannot know the mind of my patroness," said he, before proceeding to prove he *thought* he could. "But I think not. Mrs. Rutledge seemed to possess a much too high opinion of herself, and I do not think Lady Catherine appreciated her ideas concerning how a companion must act. Lady Catherine does prefer to keep the distinction of rank firmly in place at all times, and it is not for the help to question one of her pedigree, for her insights must be superior in all things."

"And Miss Younge?" Charlotte's tone again betrayed her lack of interest. Mr. Collins did not notice and responded as if the very world depended on his reply.

"She has a shifty look about her, which Lady Catherine finds intolerable. I do not doubt that she is not under consideration, for Lady Catherine sent her away almost immediately."

On and on they went. One lady was far too thin; the next one was far too learned (though Elizabeth thought a certain amount of education was what one wished for in a companion.) On another occasion, a lady was deemed to be too stupid, another, too impertinent, while a third was castigated for not being able to play the pianoforte. In short, though Lady Catherine met with many women, there was some fault to be found in all of them, and by the end of the next week, it did not seem she was any closer to hiring a new companion.

The second week after Mrs. Jenkinson's death began with an invitation to Rosings for the first time since the awful event. Mr. Collins, as was his predilection, was excited to be the recipient of Lady Catherine's condescension, and he put an entirely unwarranted—in Elizabeth's opinion—meaning on the invitation.

"Lady Catherine is frustrated because of the lack of success she has had in finding a new companion for her daughter. I am certain she wishes to condole with us and solicit our opinions. Is there anyone you know whom you would recommend for such a position?"

It was difficult for Elizabeth to avoid laughing in the man's face. How would she know anyone who was seeking a position? Charlotte appeared just as surprised as Elizabeth, for she paused and directed a confused look at her husband for a moment.

"Unfortunately, no, Mr. Collins," replied she at length. "If Lady Catherine is not able to find someone, I know not how *we* may be of assistance."

"Then we shall go and comfort her," replied Mr. Collins. "She cannot fail to find someone, though because of her exacting standards, it may take some time for the perfect candidate to present herself. She is the soul of patience, so I am certain she will bear up under her tribulations admirably."

Elizabeth almost snorted at the thought—Lady Catherine had never struck Elizabeth as being blessed with an abundance of patience. Furthermore, Elizabeth suspected he was only disappointed due to his desire to be indispensable to the lady.

But when she made this observation to Charlotte, her friend only looked at her with some asperity. "Truly, Lizzy, it seems to me you have become cynical of late. I am well aware that my husband is not the most gifted intellectual, but he is diligent and industrious, and he means well. You must allow him to be a good man, with his share of good attributes."

Shocked at Charlotte's words, Elizabeth opened her mouth to respond, but no words came out. She held her tongue for the moment, thinking furiously about what her friend said, and she did not like what she discovered. She *had* become used to thinking meanly of Mr. Collins, and she was forced to own that Charlotte seemed perfectly content. It would be best, now that she was in her friend's home, to temper her criticism of the man and attempt to see him in a better light.

"I am sorry, Charlotte. You are completely correct." Elizabeth looked away, marshaling her thoughts. "I should not continually look for Mr. Collins's faults."

"Elizabeth," said Charlotte, "I understand that you would not be happy in the life I have chosen, and I commend you for your intelligence and your principles. But you must allow the possibility of other viewpoints. Remember, I have my own home now, and I shall one day be mistress of Longbourn, while you are still searching for your perfect husband. Please think well of me, and by extension, allow me the correctness of my choice in my own circumstances. Mr. Collins is, as you have said, not the cleverest of men, but he is entirely respectable. I would like you to see him as he is, rather than through the sardonic spectacles you inherited from your father."

"I will try, Charlotte," said Elizabeth.

"Good. Now let us go prepare for our evening at Rosings." Charlotte laughed a little and turned a playful eye on Elizabeth. "I give you leave to laugh at Lady Catherine as much as you wish. Though the lady is not without redeeming qualities herself, I believe Mr.

Collins would be much less ridiculous if he could be weaned from her influence."

Elizabeth giggled. "I cannot agree more, Charlotte. Thank you for your forbearance, but I will attempt to keep my laughter to a minimum."

Soon they had departed the parsonage and were approaching Rosings Park, the large house looming over them like some brooding monarch about to pass judgment. They were accepted into the vestibule where their outerwear was taken by Lady Catherine's servants and from thence into the sitting-room where Lady Catherine and Miss de Bourgh awaited them.

The moment they walked in the doors, Elizabeth could sense that something was different from the last time they had dined here. It was not the absence of Mrs. Jenkinson fussing over Miss de Bourgh or any other obvious change, but rather the way Lady Catherine regarded Elizabeth herself. She wondered if the lady had come to see her as prey, so intent was her gaze. Elizabeth could not fathom the reason for it.

They made small talk in the sitting-room—or rather Mr. Collins spoke in his usual capacious manner, giving the waiting ladies his regrets for the loss they had recently suffered and his surety that they would soon be blessed with another woman who would fill the recently departed Mrs. Jenkinson's shoes admirably. The whole time they were in the sitting-room, and then after at dinner, Mr. Collins kept up his monologue, and though Elizabeth regarded the man with some asperity, she endeavored to keeper her conversation with Charlotte firmly in mind and avoid thinking poorly of him.

This all changed after dinner. Lady Catherine led them back to the music room that evening, and she directed Elizabeth to play for them, which Elizabeth obliged, knowing that it was not a request. For some time, Lady Catherine sat listening to her play, not responding to Mr. Collins's continued blandishments. It was only after Elizabeth had sat at the pianoforte for some time that the lady seemed to have enough of it and beckoned her forward.

"Miss Bennet," said she, "I have a matter of which I would like to speak to you. You will accompany me to the sitting-room."

Though shocked, Elizabeth could not think of a reason why she would not oblige Lady Catherine, and she agreed. She met the Collinses' eyes before she left, and though Mr. Collins was mute with astonishment, Charlotte gazed at her, a question in her look. Elizabeth could only shake her head in response—she had no idea what Lady Catherine would want with her.

The lady led her to the sitting-room where she took her usual high-backed chair, motioning Elizabeth to sit on a sofa nearby. But though Elizabeth expected to discover what the lady wished with her, Lady Catherine was silent for a full five minutes, studying every aspect of Elizabeth. Knowing the lady's temper, Elizabeth forced herself to remain silent, waiting for her pleasure.

She was just beginning to become cross when Lady Catherine spoke. "You must wonder why I have asked you here, Miss Bennet. It is not surprising, I suppose, as one of your background cannot imagine that such a boon as this would come to you."

"I apologize, Lady Catherine, but I am at a loss. To what do you refer?"

Lady Catherine only favored her with an airy wave. "All will become apparent in time." The lady's brows furrowed in thought. "I have observed you the times you have been in my company, Miss Bennet, and I have not failed to take your likeness. To wit, it is clear you are an intelligent, useful sort of person, one who understands her place in society, yet you show a distressing penchant for speaking your opinions in a forthright manner when you had best remain silent. Though I cannot in good conscience approve of your education and the lack of a governess, you have still managed to educate yourself in a manner which can only be termed extraordinary."

"Thank you, Lady Catherine," replied Elizabeth, though she was not at all certain that she should be thankful for such tepid praise.

"Of course," continued the lady, her tone offhand, "once you are elevated, I will expect you to curb your outspokenness and your wild ways, your tendency to walk more than is proper, and your excessive wit."

Mystified, though a little annoyed, Elizabeth held her temper in check and answered the lady evenly. "I am sorry I have provoked such a poor opinion, Lady Catherine, but I cannot imagine altering myself and giving up those things in which I take pleasure."

"Of course, you must," replied the lady. "I could never treat with someone in my own house who subscribes to such things. I require a proper, demure sort of person, and if I cannot find one, I shall be required to take that which I can find in hand and alter her."

"I am afraid I do not know of what you speak. Might I ask you to be more explicit?"

"Why, I have decided that you shall be Anne's companion. Thus, I require certain concessions from you in return for favoring you with this excellent opportunity."

"I beg your pardon?"

"You shall listen to what I say, Miss Bennet!" exclaimed the lady. "I will not tolerate such inattentiveness as this when I am speaking. Let this be your first lesson."

"Lady Catherine," said Elizabeth, struggling to hold her temper in check, "as you have not deigned to explain precisely what you would have of me, I am forced to attempt to decipher your purpose from your words. Am I to understand that you intend *me* to be Miss de Bourgh's companion?"

"Of course! I am forced to reconsider my words concerning your intelligence, if you cannot understand so simple a matter."

"I am at a loss to understand why you would want me, of all people, to serve in this capacity. Have I ever given you any reason to suppose I am seeking a position?"

"That is beside the point, Miss Bennet."

"That is *precisely* the point! Had you asked me before you requested I attend you, I would have informed you that I have no intention of seeking a position. I cannot imagine what madness has led you to this application."

"Miss Bennet," said Lady Catherine, her manner full of exaggerated patience, "my daughter requires a companion, and I have been unable to procure one. You are tolerably intelligent and accomplished, your manners are passable, and you do not appear to be doing anything better with your time. It seems fortunate that you are present at this time when the need has come upon us."

"With the exception that I am *not* seeking a position."

Lady Catherine huffed and closed her eyes, visibly composing herself. When she opened them again, it was to pierce Elizabeth with her stare, her annoyance written upon her brow. "I have not been in the habit of being spoken to in such a way, Miss Bennet. Unfortunately, Anne has predicted your reaction with exactness, and though I have difficulty understanding your reticence—you, a woman with little dowry, little to recommend her, and almost no chance of eliciting a proposal from *any* man—I must congratulate my daughter for her foresight. If you are offended by my offer, in spite of these things, it need not be a permanent appointment. You may act as my daughter's companion until I am able to find a suitable replacement."

"And when might that be?" asked Elizabeth, wondering why she was even allowing the lady this much.

"I do not know," was the lady's surprising admission. "I have exhausted the possibilities in the extended neighborhood and even some who have responded to my posting in the London papers. I shall be forced to range further afield for a suitable woman."

"I see," replied Elizabeth. Though she made no further comment, her mind was working furiously, trying to determine how she could possibly refuse this ridiculous request without offending the lady. Under normal circumstances she would not even have concerned herself that much, but Lady Catherine had a great deal of influence in Charlotte's life, and Elizabeth would not make her friend's life more difficult.

"What say you, Miss Bennet?" asked Lady Catherine, impatience coloring her voice. "If you are concerned about my application, perhaps I should inform you that you will receive a very generous stipend."

"Absolutely not," replied Elizabeth firmly. "I am *not* a paid companion, and if I do choose to act as your daughter's companion, I will do it as a gesture of friendship and nothing more."

The lady's countenance softened at Elizabeth's declaration. "Then do we have an agreement?"

Though everything rebelled against what she was certain would be demeaning circumstances, Elizabeth voiced her agreement. "But only until you find a permanent companion or the time to return home is upon me. And I will be Miss de Bourgh's friend, not her nursemaid. This means I will not give up those things that I love. I will continue as I ever have, in addition to providing companionship to your daughter and attending to her. I must have my own time, Lady Catherine, and if I walk or read a book during those times, it is my own concern."

It seemed to Elizabeth like Lady Catherine was about to object to her conditions, for she opened her mouth to speak. Then she checked herself, grimaced, and withdrew to gather her wits about her.

"Done then."

Chapter II

*E*lizabeth left Rosings Park that evening, wondering what had possessed her to agree to Lady Catherine's ridiculous demands.

The lady had graciously allowed her to return to the parsonage for the night to gather her belongings, but she had demanded Elizabeth return on the morrow to receive instruction. Of what such instruction consisted, Elizabeth could not imagine, but she was already annoyed at them, as she was dismayed at the prospect of returning to Rosings.

In all truth, she was dreading everything about this sorry situation. Lady Catherine, Elizabeth knew, would be a harsh taskmistress, conveniently forgetting that Elizabeth was *not* her paid employee and could *not* be ordered as if she were, and she fully expected to be required to remind her ladyship several times before she understood, if such understanding should ever come at all. Furthermore, in Miss de Bourgh, Elizabeth had no confidence—the woman was quiet and irritable, and though she had not visibly terrorized Mrs. Jenkinson, Elizabeth assumed that was because the companion had become accustomed to indulging her every whim before being asked. It would be an unpleasant month, Elizabeth was certain.

And how would she tell Charlotte? She had come to Kent at

Charlotte's invitation to spend time with her closest friend, and now she was to remove to Rosings to play nursemaid to a spoiled, entitled girl in a woman's body. Elizabeth knew her assessment of Miss de Bourgh was harsh, but she had not seen anything from her to disprove it.

With these thoughts shuffling through her mind, Elizabeth passed the short carriage ride to the parsonage, and since Mr. Collins, as was his wont, monopolized the conversation, Elizabeth was able to pass it quietly without raising any questions. Even so, she saw Charlotte watching her, and if her friend's scrutiny was any guide, Elizabeth realized she suspected something had happened.

As Elizabeth had expected, Charlotte joined her in her room later that evening after the rest of the party had retired. Elizabeth was sitting on her bed, looking at the far wall with its delicate flowers and swirling contours of the wallpaper, by the flickering light of the candle, thinking of just what she had agreed to when the knock on the door startled her from her reverie.

"Come in," called she, drawing her robe around her like a shield.

When the door was opened, Charlotte slipped into the room as expected. "Lizzy," said she, approaching the bed, "I wished to speak with you. It seemed to me that something happened tonight when you spoke with Lady Catherine, and I would like to make certain nothing untoward has occurred."

Feeling all the amusement of the situation, Elizabeth said: "Oh? Do you not trust your patroness's good behavior?"

"Let us simply say that I have a healthy respect for Lady Catherine's ability to offend without even trying."

Elizabeth laughed. "Ah, yes, of course. In this she resembles her nephew quite closely, though at least with Mr. Darcy, he makes his comments in a crowded ballroom where *no one* can overhear. By contrast, Lady Catherine has no compunction about pointing out every fault with a frankness she no doubt considers an asset, and in front of everyone else, no less."

"Did she do so tonight, Lizzy?" asked Charlotte. "Was that why she asked to speak with you privately? Mr. Collins is beside himself at the thought that you might have upset Lady Catherine. He would not retire until I promised to discover the matter and inform him on the morrow. He wished to storm the walls of your bedchamber himself."

This time Elizabeth's laugh contained more of a bitter quality. "Then Mr. Collins may rest easy, for though Lady Catherine did criticize, it was more of her usual fare than anything specific. In fact, I believe Mr. Collins will be pleased when he hears the subject of our discourse."

"And what was it, Lizzy?"

It was clear Charlotte was becoming impatient with Elizabeth's obfuscation, so she decided it was time to stop stalling. "I have been singled out for the honor of being companion to Miss de Bourgh."

There likely was not anything Elizabeth could have said which would have astonished Charlotte more. She gaped at Elizabeth for a moment before blurting: "Companion?"

"Yes. At first Lady Catherine was determined that I required a position, for I have no money, no prospects, and no chance of receiving a proposal from any man. It was only after I insisted that I was not about to take the position she was so *generously* offering that she grudgingly agreed that I should act as Miss de Bourgh's companion only as long as I am to be here, if she is not able to find a replacement before."

"I am at a loss, Lizzy," replied Charlotte, her eyes as wide as saucers. "I could never have imagined such an application."

"Nor could I."

"Excuse me for my impertinence, but why did you accept?"

Elizabeth sighed and pushed herself back on the bed until she was resting against the headboard, her knees bent and her arms around her legs, which she pressed up against her chest.

"I hardly know. My first thought was to refuse and to reject any further application. Lady Catherine, however, was much like your husband when I rejected Mr. Collins's suit last autumn: I would have been forced to tell her several times."

Charlotte's countenance darkened, but Elizabeth only shook her head. "I do not make sport at Mr. Collins's expense. That is exactly what happened. Regardless, it may have been the prospect of having to refuse the lady over and over, or it might have been some misplaced pity for Miss de Bourgh, who is forced to live with her mother and endure a nursemaid when she is old enough to fend for herself. I know not, Charlotte, so it will do little good to further importune me on the subject.

"What I do know is this: though I find it difficult to understand Miss de Bourgh and I have little hope the next month will be in any way agreeable, at least she will have someone with her who will not jump every time Lady Catherine opens her mouth. Mayhap she will acquire a hint of independence. Heaven knows, it would do her a world of good."

The look Charlotte directed at her suggested she did not quite agree with Elizabeth's assertion, but she decided it was not worth pressing her over. "You *do* expect Lady Catherine to find a replacement in the next month, then?"

"I know not and I care not," replied Elizabeth. "My mind will not be altered—I shall return to Hertfordshire as planned and will not be moved, whether Lady Catherine has found a replacement or not. I have already told her this. If she does not believe me, then that is her concern. I am certain that Lady Catherine may act as her daughter's companion if need be."

Charlotte snorted with sudden laughter. "I cannot imagine such a thing. She would need someone to order about, and she can hardly do that to herself."

This time Elizabeth joined her friend in laughter. "I dare say she could not! But if she tries me, that is what will happen."

With a nod, Charlotte rose. "Then I shall inform Mr. Collins that Lady Catherine was not displeased with you and allow you the pleasure of informing him of your new position yourself.

"No, you need not thank me," said Charlotte, fighting a grin as she moved to the door. "I am certain he will find it as fascinating as I have."

She opened the door and started to depart, but before she did, she turned back and fixed Elizabeth with a serious look. "I only hope you know what you are doing, Lizzy."

Then she was gone, leaving Elizabeth by herself.

"So do I," said Elizabeth to the empty room.

Mr. Collins was as surprised as his wife when Elizabeth informed him of her new position. For a full minute after she made the communication, he stared at her, likely wondering if she was attempting to mislead him. How Elizabeth wished it were true!

Then, of course, the inanities started. "Companion to Miss de Bourgh? What an honor has come your way, Cousin. I could never have imagined Lady Catherine would think to bestow such a boon on my own poor cousin. You are to be greatly envied, for who would not wish to be so singled out?"

I would not wish to be so singled out, thought Elizabeth. *If you are so certain it is an honor, perhaps you would prefer that it was bestowed upon you!*

Out loud, she only attempted to correct Mr. Collins. "It is only until I return to Hertfordshire, Mr. Collins. As Lady Catherine has had difficulty locating a woman of her preference, I have agreed to assist, but only until I am to return to my father's house."

Her cousin was silent for several moments, and Elizabeth watched him, noting a sudden annoyance which seemed to spring up in his mien. Perhaps he would prefer that she would be nothing more than a servant—he might think it sufficient punishment for the temerity she had possessed to refuse his generous offer of marriage. Whatever it was, it soon disappeared, replaced by a sage nod.

"Yes, that is probably for the best, though I do wonder if it might be better for your future to be secured in so advantageous a position. Nevertheless, it is still a mark of distinction that Lady Catherine respects you enough to entrust you with the wellbeing of her only daughter. The lady's condescension is boundless, and her wisdom, vast, so I must agree with her ladyship and charge you to do your best to discharge your duties with faithful respect for her ladyship."

"Thank you, Mr. Collins," said Elizabeth, her patience almost exhausted at the man's continued blathering. "I have no intention of doing anything other than attending Miss de Bourgh to the best of my abilities."

Mr. Collins nodded as if she had said something particularly profound, but he was not finished speaking on the subject. The rest of the morning meal was spent listening to his droning voice, alternately praising Lady Catherine and, by extension, Miss de Bourgh, and admonishing her not to embarrass him by behaving in any manner other than that Lady Catherine would find pleasing. By the time she left the breakfast table, Elizabeth was almost happy she was to be leaving this place behind. If nothing else, at least she would not be required to endure Mr. Collins! Then again, she would be trading his brand of civility for Lady Catherine's arrogant meddling, so she was not certain she was emerging the victor in the exchange.

When Elizabeth left the breakfast table, the Lucas sisters followed her to her room, Charlotte to help her pack, while Maria's intentions seemed to consist more of questioning Elizabeth, with the requisite amount of awe, as to her decision to go to Rosings.

"I am shocked you would consider such an appointment, Lizzy," said the young girl. "I would have thought you valued your independence."

"I do, Maria," said Elizabeth. "It is only for a short time, and only as a favor to Lady Catherine. I have no intention of searching for employment in the future."

It was clear the girl had no true understanding, but at least she became silent, nominally assisting Elizabeth in packing her personal effects, though in reality, she was little help. She was much more engaged in looking at Elizabeth, studying her as if she had never met her before.

"I *am* sorry to be leaving you, Charlotte," said Elizabeth to her friend as they worked. "I came to Kent to visit you, after all. It seems like I am abandoning you."

"Do not concern yourself, Lizzy," replied Charlotte. She smiled and laid a hand on Elizabeth's arm. "I know you well enough to deduce that you accepted Lady Catherine's request with great reluctance. I am aware of the lady's character, and I do not doubt there was little option of refusing her."

"I would *never* dare refuse anything Lady Catherine asked of me!" squeaked Maria. Elizabeth and Charlotte looked at the girl and then burst out laughing.

"No, Maria, I cannot imagine you would. You should be grateful that Lady Catherine saw fit to ask *me*. I cannot imagine what you would have done had you been singled out for this honor."

It was quite beyond Maria's capacity to say or hear anything against Lady Catherine, but a moment's thought on the matter brought her to the correct conclusion, and she nodded slowly.

"I believe you are correct, Lizzy."

A knock sounded on the door, and Elizabeth called out permission to enter. Charlotte's maid entered and curtseyed.

"If it please you, mum, a carriage has arrived from Rosings and is waiting outside."

Elizabeth shared a look—which in Elizabeth's case was more of a grimace—with Charlotte, before she turned and addressed the girl. "Tell the driver I shall be down directly."

With a curtsey, the maid left the room.

"Then let us see you to the carriage, so you may be on your way."

"Oh Charlotte!" said Elizabeth, engulfing her friend in an embrace. "I shall miss you, indeed! I should never have agreed to this."

"Nonsense! At the very least, I think it will be educational for you, and I cannot help but think Miss de Bourgh will benefit from your disposition. We shall still see each other frequently."

Though a little misty eyed, Elizabeth smiled at her friend. "I shall make it a point to come to the parsonage frequently when I am out on my walks."

Charlotte frowned. "Are you certain Lady Catherine will not take offense at you walking out so far?"

"She does not have a choice," replied Elizabeth with a laugh. "I have already told her so. Since I will be attending her daughter, I will curtail them to a certain extent and not range nearly so far as usual, but I will not give them up completely. Lady Catherine may accept that, or she may find someone else."

"Only you, Lizzy," replied Charlotte, shaking her head.

The manservant was called, and Elizabeth's trunks were conveyed downstairs and loaded onto the waiting carriage. When Elizabeth stepped out of the house, she was met by a young woman in Rosings' livery, who curtseyed and greeted Elizabeth with evident respect.

"Miss Bennet. My name is Tilly, and I have been sent to accompany you to Rosings."

"Hello, Tilly," replied Elizabeth. "Thank you for this civility. I know you were pulled from your usual duties to be of use to me."

"Oh, no!" said Tilly, her eyes widening. "I have been assigned to be your maid while you are with us. It is my pleasure and duty to accompany you today."

"My maid?" asked Elizabeth.

"Yes. Lady Catherine has made it clear that you will be required to attend Miss de Bourgh, and that your needs must be seen to in order to allow you to uphold your duties."

What had seemed like a generous and thoughtful offer to see to her needs while she was at Rosings was revealed to be Lady Catherine's way of assuring that Elizabeth would be able to do little but spend every waking moment in Miss de Bourgh's company. A glance at Charlotte revealed that her friend had come to the same conclusion, but they did not voice their suspicions, instead allowing rolled eyes and smiles to pass between them. There was nothing further to be said.

Elizabeth said good bye to the sisters, promising to visit them frequently, and stepped into the carriage for the short ride to Rosings. As they were traveling, Elizabeth was pleased to note that Tilly seemed to be a little in awe of her and was content to remain silent, which suited Elizabeth well. The fields passed by too quickly, and soon they were pulling to a stop before Rosings. Elizabeth had always allowed it to be a handsome building, but she thought it suffered from a sense of overdone formality demanded by its mistress.

When they stopped, the footman reached into the carriage to hand Elizabeth and then Tilly out, and they stood on the front drive, Elizabeth noting that the servants were efficient, as her personal effects were already being unloaded from the vehicle. There was nothing to do but go inside, the estate stairs looming up before her like the climb to a high peak, while the inside of the house seemed dark and dreary, a dungeon, rather than the house of a high-ranking and wealthy woman.

"Miss Bennet," said a voice, and Lady Catherine stepped from one of the hallways, approaching her, straight-backed and proud in her gaudy finery. "I see you have come. If you will follow me, I will show you to the room you will occupy while you are with us."

With a softly spoken word of thanks, Elizabeth followed Lady Catherine up the stairs, determined to avoid thinking of the reason why the lady might have chosen to perform this task herself rather than delegating it to the housekeeper. The curved stairway was as fine as any Elizabeth had seen, but when she reached the second floor, she was surprised to note that though much of the wood finish was carved into ostentatious ornamental patterns, there was little in the way of décor which she might deem as grandiose as much of the first floor was. In fact, it appeared more like a normal home above stairs—large and with more to show than a smaller house like Longbourn, but at least it would not hurt the eyes to look on it.

"You have been housed in the family wing," said Lady Catherine as they walked. "Anne is situated in one of the family suites as is her right, but I have chosen to place you in the apartment next to hers. There is no adjoining door between them, but it should be no bother for you to walk a short distance down the hall to reach Anne's rooms."

"Of course not," murmured Elizabeth. "I am certain I shall be quite comfortable in the apartments to which you have assigned me."

"Very well," replied the lady. Then she continued in an almost offhand tone: "I have always felt the distinction of rank should be preserved, and as such, it might have been more proper to house you with the servants. Mrs. Jenkinson was housed in very fine rooms below stairs, but I assume you would not be accustomed to such surroundings. Thus, I judged the chamber next to Anne's to be the best."

Whatever good will Lady Catherine had accrued with the implied kindness of housing Elizabeth next to her daughter was undone by the suggestion that she might have been relegated to the servants' quarters. Elizabeth could only shake her head and bite her tongue to prevent herself from letting loose a caustic retort. Such incivility *would* have caused Elizabeth to depart the estate forthwith, and no amount of cajoling would have induced her to return.

When the door was opened—Tilly had scurried after them and darted forward to open the door when they approached—Lady Catherine stepped into the room with Elizabeth following. She found herself in a sitting-room which was not expansive, but still comfortable, small enough to heat efficiently with the lone fireplace, set into the far wall between a pair of windows. The room was decorated with a green wallpaper which had hints of yellows and blues in it, and while it was perhaps a little too dark for Elizabeth's taste, it was still acceptable. There were an armchair and a sofa sitting near the fireplace and a desk against the left wall, all made of heavy dark woods and carved with filigree.

"This is your sitting-room, Miss Bennet," said Lady Catherine, quite unnecessarily in Elizabeth's opinion. "I hope you will find it quite comfortable while you are here."

Elizabeth dutifully replied that it was a lovely room, to which Lady Catherine responded by leading her through the door on the right wall into the next room beyond. It was decorated much the same as the sitting-room, the furniture being the same, heavy style, though the wallpaper was a lighter shade of green. The late morning sun shone in through the large windows, illuminating all in its bright light, and Elizabeth thought the room was quite handsome in that it gave her lots of sunlight, which illuminated the soft colors.

"I trust this meets your satisfaction?"

A note of asperity in the lady's voice alerted Elizabeth to Lady Catherine's annoyance, and she realized she had not said anything yet in response to what she had seen. In Elizabeth's defense, she had become accustomed to the woman speaking without requiring a response, but she nevertheless hastened to correct her incivility.

"Of course, Lady Catherine, I thank you. They are handsome rooms, indeed, and I have no doubt I will be quite comfortable in them."

The lady huffed, though the severity left her demeanor. "I am happy to hear it. Now, Miss Bennet, you should take the rest of the morning to become familiar with your surroundings. As you have no doubt already learned, Tilly is to attend you while you are with us. She may see your dresses are hung and your effects distributed as appropriate. I have ordered a light luncheon to be served at an hour after noon, and I will expect you to be punctual."

"I understand," said Elizabeth.

"Tilly can show you the way if you are yet unfamiliar with the house. After luncheon, I will ensure you are shown the principle rooms, and I will expect you to learn how to navigate your way through my domain quickly. It will be essential for you to know where everything is in the house for you to be an effective companion for my daughter."

"That will not be any trouble, Lady Catherine," replied Elizabeth.

"Then I will leave you to it. Remember that if you require anything, or if you need directions for the nonce, Tilly may provide it. I will see you in the dining room for luncheon."

Then the lady turned on her heel and departed, Elizabeth contemplating her as she left. She turned and looked about the room, thinking that in this, at least, she would be comfortable. The coming month would no doubt be lacking in other virtues, but she would make the best of it, as she always did.

The memory of Charlotte's words concerning Mr. Collins returned to Elizabeth's mind, and she shook her head. Perhaps it was time to soften her opinion concerning Lady Catherine. That was certainly preferable to expecting the worst, and less hazardous to her good humor, as well.

With that thought in mind, Elizabeth turned to speak to Tilly, who was already stowing her belongings.

Chapter III

At the appointed time, Elizabeth descended the stairs and sought the smaller parlor Lady Catherine used for the breakfast and noon meals. Though it was near to the larger dining room Elizabeth had seen on prior invitations to dinner, Elizabeth had not seen the room previously, and she looked about with interest when she entered. It contained the same heavy, ornamental furniture Elizabeth by now knew Lady Catherine preferred, but it was a brighter, sunnier room than the dining room, as well as being much smaller.

On the way to the parlor—Tilly had accompanied her, seeming to think it was her responsibility to ensure Elizabeth arrived unscathed—Elizabeth made the comment that the parlor must be more agreeable for smaller gatherings which consisted of only Lady Catherine and her daughter. Tilly had surprised Elizabeth with her answer, though after the fact she knew she should have known it in advance.

"Oh no, Miss Bennet," said the girl. "Though Lady Catherine and Miss de Bourgh usually eat their early day meals in the parlor, dinner is reserved strictly for the dining room."

"That seems unnecessary," replied Elizabeth. "Surely using the dining room must be more difficult for the staff."

"I do not know," replied the faithful maid, "for I have been an upstairs maid since I came to Rosings. But I believe Lady Catherine considers it her duty and that of her daughter to maintain formality during dinner."

Elizabeth had no response to that. It seemed like Tilly was quite in awe of the great lady and would not take well to anything even remotely unflattering being said about her, so Elizabeth simply changed the subject. She asked about the girl herself, and though Tilly seemed a little embarrassed, she chattered on readily enough about her family having been retainers at Rosings for many generations. Thus, she learned that the girl's father was the head stable hand, her mother worked in the kitchens, and her elder brother was one of the gardeners.

"Miss Bennet," greeted Lady Catherine when Elizabeth stepped into the parlor. "I see you have joined us punctually. That is well, for one who forgets the time is almost always deficient in many other ways."

"I have always tended toward promptness myself," replied Elizabeth, deciding there was nothing else to be said.

"Excellent. Then we shall not be at odds in that respect."

Though Elizabeth was a little concerned at the inference that they would be at odds on *other* subjects, she was given no time to think on the matter, as Lady Catherine gestured toward her daughter, who was seated close by.

"Come here, Anne," said the lady. As Anne approached, she turned back to Elizabeth and nodded. "Though I know you were previously introduced, I would like to do so again properly. Anne, this is Miss Elizabeth Bennet, who will be your companion for the next several weeks. Miss Bennet, this is my daughter, Anne, who will rely on you for companionship."

The two women curtseyed to each other, and when Miss de Bourgh stood up straight again, Elizabeth attempted to gain a better understanding of her. She was thin and pale, it was true, her hair pulled back in the usual style, though that style seemed a little severe to Elizabeth. She was dressed in the same kind of costly elaborate dress which Lady Catherine herself wore, and as she was small of stature, she was almost swallowed up in it. Though Elizabeth's first impression had been of a girl who was thin, almost to the point of being emaciated, this introduction told Elizabeth that she could not really determine the woman's figure, as the dress she wore was far too voluminous. Her arms were quite slender, though, indicating that she was not blessed with an excess of curves. In addition, her skin was fair and pale to the point of being translucent, leading Elizabeth to believe that she almost never ventured out into the sun. Moreover, she was quiet and spoke only in monosyllables, though whether that indicated reticence or overwhelming pride, Elizabeth could not say.

"Come," said Lady Catherine, turning them toward the table, "let us eat our luncheon. There are many things we need to discuss."

They sat and Lady Catherine motioned to the attending footman to begin serving. Elizabeth sat across the table from Miss de Bourgh, with Lady Catherine at the head as was her custom, and for a few moments nothing of substance was said. That changed as the younger lady soon spoke to Elizabeth.

"I wish to thank you for your assistance, Miss Bennet," said Anne "I know your purpose in coming to Kent was to visit with Mrs. Collins, and I am sensible that agreeing to stay with me will curtail your time with your friend. I am grateful for your sacrifice."

It was by far the longest speech Elizabeth had ever heard from the taciturn young woman, and she was forced to mask a certain level of surprise that she could be so verbose. Then Elizabeth chastised herself—no one could possibly be silent and uncommunicative at all times, and though Miss de Bourgh was coddled and kept in a gilded cage by her mother's domineering ways, she was just another woman.

Furthermore, though it seemed as if Lady Catherine was about to say something, likely a rebuttal of her daughter's assertions, she checked herself at the last moment, no doubt wishing to hear how Elizabeth would respond.

"It is no trouble, Miss de Bourgh," said Elizabeth. Though she had not much reason to think well of Miss de Bourgh, there was no reason to be unkind. Perhaps she could provide some relief to the young woman from her mother's force of will. "I am certain there will still be many opportunities to visit with Charlotte."

Lady Catherine's lips tightened at Elizabeth's words, but she declined to say anything—for the moment, at least. The footmen produced the meal at that time, so for a short time the three women busied themselves with filling their plates. The scents of the fare put before them was tantalizing, and whatever else Lady Catherine was, Elizabeth was forced to acknowledge that her kitchens produced foods as tempting as any she had ever experienced. They ate in silence for several moments, and Elizabeth thought it was the most pleasant time she had ever spent at Rosings.

"Now," said Lady Catherine after they had sated their immediate hunger, "there are some things you must understand about my management of this house and my expectations from Anne's companion. You would do well to take heed to what I say, Miss Bennet."

It was too much to ask, Elizabeth supposed, for Lady Catherine to be silent for more than a few moments at a time. Though she had little desire to listen to the woman's instructions, she decided there was nothing to do but attend her.

Thus followed a long litany of items Lady Catherine felt Elizabeth needed to know. She was commanded, among other things, to always be punctual for mealtimes and instructed to present herself promptly when Lady Catherine demanded her presence. Lady Catherine spoke at length about what she should expect for their evening entertainment, what time they arose, what time they retired, how long they should spend in the sitting-room, and a whole host of other details for which the lady demanded obedience. It appeared like the entire house was managed on a strict schedule which was never allowed to deviate, their lives broken down to the smallest detail and executed with exactness.

After Lady Catherine finished speaking of what she expected for the running of the house, she proceeded to explain in the same exacting detail what Miss de Bourgh could not do (or more accurately, what Lady Catherine would not allow her to do.)

"Anne is quite delicate, Miss Bennet," said the lady. "Thus, she must at all times protect her health. It will be your responsibility to ensure she is comfortable and content. There are a selection of shawls for her use, and you must always have one at hand to use accordingly. Anne has a distressing tendency to contract agues at the least sign of provocation, and the use of a shawl will help protect her.

"Anne possesses a phaeton and ponies for her use, and I encourage her to make use of them. When she goes out, however, I require you to attend her and a footman to ride behind in case of any problems occurring. When she goes out, she is to wear a bonnet at all times, and she is never allowed to walk in the gardens when the sun is shining. An excess of sun would be harmful to her delicate skin, and I will not have her becoming coarse and brown like some common housewife."

Lady Catherine kept up this constant stream of instructions long after their luncheon had been consumed and cleared by her efficient servants, and after a time Elizabeth wondered if there was anything Miss de Bourgh was *allowed* to do. She was not to read after dark, she was to stay near the fire in the evenings, she could not walk excessively, and she was to nap for two hours every afternoon. Above all, she was not to do anything to distress her health. And though Lady Catherine did not say anything outright, there was some mention of a cousin who was expected to come and offer for her at the earliest opportunity. Knowing that Mr. Darcy was related to her, Elizabeth recalled Mr. Wickham's words and knew he was to be the expected groom. It would fulfill Elizabeth's sense of irony if a man as proud and fastidious as he was to marry a woman so colorless and terrorized as Miss de Bourgh. She had no doubt he would take his mother-in-law's position in his new wife's life very well, indeed!

"Do you understand my instructions, Miss Bennet?" asked Lady Catherine, bringing Elizabeth's mind back to the present.

"I do," replied Elizabeth, not wishing to make an issue of such nonsensical instructions, half of which she would ignore without a second thought. Out of the corner of her eye she caught sight of Miss de Bourgh covering her mouth with her hand, as if hiding her mirth, but knowing the girl could not possibly show such emotion in front of her mother, Elizabeth put it from her mind.

"Excellent," replied Lady Catherine. "Now, let us speak something of your specific duties and what I expect from you. I have installed you in this position with the expectation that you will uphold your duties and standards of behavior with exactness, and you should know that I will not tolerate anything less. The first thing you must understand is that I require you to attend to Anne at all times. This is not negotiable."

"I cannot do that, Lady Catherine," Elizabeth was quick to reply. "As you recall, I have agreed to assist for a time until you are able to find another woman to take the position. However that may be, I live an active life, and that includes walking and other activities, not to mention a certain amount of time to myself. I am sure Miss de Bourgh wishes for the same."

"I would appreciate it, Miss Bennet, if you would not inform me of what my daughter wishes." The severity in Lady Catherine's voice would have suggested that Elizabeth had just dealt her ladyship a mortal insult. "Regardless of *your* opinions, this is what I require, and you will oblige me. A companion is not of much use if she does not attend her charge, especially one of the delicate constitution possessed by my daughter. If you wish to stay with us and benefit from the honor of serving my daughter, you will obey."

Elizabeth forbore mentioning that she had not wished for the position in the first place. Though she gave some little consideration to simply giving the lady a lukewarm agreement, she thought it would likely be a point of contention in the future, so she determined to ensure Lady Catherine knew her sentiments from the beginning.

"It is too much to ask of me, and I will not do it. We—both Miss de Bourgh and myself—will require distance at times. I am not certain how Mrs. Jenkinson performed her duties, but I will not accede to such a request."

"Come now, Miss Bennet, be reasonable. Given the honor of the position I have bestowed upon you, surely you may put off your tramping around the countryside as long as you are with us. Not only is it unladylike, but it is highly improper."

"How can walking be considered anything less than beneficial exercise?" asked Elizabeth. "I meet with no one in a clandestine fashion, and I am always careful to know where I am so that I will not unduly inconvenience anyone."

Lady Catherine sucked in a breath, no doubt to deliver a diatribe, when Miss de Bourgh once again surprised Elizabeth by speaking.

"I wish for a friend and a confidant, Mama, not a nursemaid. I have no objections to Miss Bennet continuing her walks. Perhaps walking in the morning before I arise or in the afternoon when I nap would be acceptable."

Though Lady Catherine clearly wished to make more of an issue of the matter, in the end she nodded once, though with a curtness which spoke of her annoyance. For Elizabeth's part, she observed Miss de Bourgh, noticing that her scrutiny was returned, and nodded slowly, which Miss de Bourgh returned. It was impossible to determine what Miss de Bourgh had thought of her late companion, but Elizabeth was certain she did not wish someone hovering about her as much as her mother seemed to think necessary.

"Very well," said Lady Catherine, though with little evident grace. "It is sufficient if you walk at those times. When we are sitting together in the evenings, you may attend to your own interests, as long as you are attentive whenever Anne requires it."

"Of course," said Elizabeth, thinking it was little enough to make such a nebulous concession after she had carried her point.

"Now, let us speak of your other duties." What followed was as lengthy as the previous instructions had been and explained in minute detail exactly what Lady Catherine expected of Elizabeth. She spoke of Miss de Bourgh's illnesses and what must be done to ameliorate them, how she must comport herself, now that she was living in a home so above what she had been accustomed, interspersed with a myriad of other details she seemed to think Elizabeth needed to know.

These instructions Elizabeth felt free to ignore. Elizabeth had no intention of changing herself for Lady Catherine's pleasure, or for anyone else. If Lady Catherine did not appreciate her obstinacy, she possessed the option of releasing her from this farce. Elizabeth, therefore, was more than pleased when the lady finally fell silent and excused herself to attend to some matters of the estate. But she was incapable of retreating without leaving some last few instructions.

"I will leave you to become better acquainted. I suggest you use this time to your advantage, though perhaps the sitting-room would be a better venue for your discussion."

Then with a nod, the lady left the room.

"I believe I will take the opportunity to retire, Miss Bennet," said Miss de Bourgh as soon as her mother was gone. "You may have the rest of the afternoon to yourself. I will see you at dinner."

Then Miss de Bourgh also departed, leaving Elizabeth alone in the parlor. All bemused at the way the other two ladies had left her to her own devices—especially after Lady Catherine's long instruction—Elizabeth thought about taking a constitutional in the gardens. She ultimately decided against it—though she had carried her point with the lady, Elizabeth did not think for a moment that her objections were at an end. For now, she thought it best to give Lady Catherine the compliment of not taxing her sensibilities.

The first day of Elizabeth's residence at Rosings Park proceeded in this fashion. After being dismissed, Elizabeth had returned to her room, where Tilly had already unpacked much of her belongings. Thus, it was only left for Elizabeth to rearrange some of her effects in a manner more to her liking. She then dismissed Tilly and spent the afternoon alternately reading a book of sonnets and indulging in an afternoon nap.

That evening, she joined Lady Catherine and her daughter in the dining room for the evening meal. If Lady Catherine knew that Elizabeth had not spent the afternoon in company with her daughter, she made no mention of it, for which Elizabeth was grateful. As she had come to expect from the way Lady Catherine managed her house, dinner was an opulent affair, which might have been presented to a large party of close friends, for though there was not a large excess of food for their consumption, there was still a wide variety with the three courses.

"We dine according to our station, Miss Bennet," said Lady Catherine when Elizabeth made some comment of the fare. "Wealth is not without its privileges, and though I try to do as much for the neighborhood as I can, I appreciate the advantages I possess and enjoy them accordingly."

"I was not attempting to criticize," replied Elizabeth.

"I know you were not, child," replied Lady Catherine, waving her comment away. "Our habits must be strange to you, as you have been raised in more humble circumstances, and what we do may seem like extravagance. But nothing at my table is allowed to go to waste. My servants eat the same meals as I do, and I pay them well to ensure their loyalty. Though I am conscious of the distinction of rank, I am also aware of the benefit of loyalty, and I go to great lengths to promote it in those I employ. To do otherwise would be a disruption in my home, and I will not risk my daughter's health by promoting upheaval."

"It is clear you have been managing your estate for a great many years," replied Elizabeth.

"I have," agreed Lady Catherine. "My husband did not live long after Anne's birth. Rosings is her inheritance and my husband's legacy. I take that very seriously."

The brief conversation caused Elizabeth to consider the lady. Though at present she had only Lady Catherine's words as evidence, she wondered if she had perhaps misjudged the woman. She was proud and haughty, meddled in the affairs of others, was demanding and curt, but Elizabeth had not noticed any overt discontent in any of the ladies' servants. In fact, if Tilly was anything to go by, her almost worshipful attitude toward the lady suggested that she was content in her position.

After dinner, the ladies retreated to the music room where Elizabeth was asked to play for them. "It was in my mind to request the benefit of your talents the last time you dined here," said Lady Catherine, referencing the night of the tragedy. "But circumstances dictated otherwise. Anne has not learned due to her health, and I never had any interest in the pianoforte, though I would have been a true proficient had I ever learned. Mrs. Jenkinson knew a little, but not enough to provide any true enjoyment. I hope your talents are more extensive."

"I would be happy to," replied Elizabeth, "though I will allow you to judge for yourself. I will not call my talents capital, but I do possess some ability."

Thus, Elizabeth seated herself at the instrument and, after choosing some music with which she was familiar, began to play. Lady Catherine did her the honor of listening intently and not interrupting, and though Elizabeth was not certain what the lady thought of her playing, she did not think Lady Catherine was displeased. At the end of her song, she was certain she would hear the lady's opinion.

"You do play well, Miss Bennet," said Lady Catherine when the tones of the pianoforte fell silent. "However, I believe you would benefit from additional practice, though I did note your choice of music as one fitting your abilities. That is as much of a talent as simply playing, for I have heard many young ladies attempt pieces above their abilities."

"I am quite familiar with my skills, Lady Catherine," replied Elizabeth. "I have often seen the same as you describe, and it never reflects well on the performer."

Lady Catherine grunted. "Then you show some knowledge of yourself, which is always to be admired. Please, Miss Bennet, if you are willing, continue to play, for it is not often we are able to enjoy another's talents

"Perhaps if Georgiana visited more often we would have that pleasure," said Miss de Bourgh in her typically quiet voice.

"Yes. I shall tell Darcy to bring her when he and Fitzwilliam visit this spring."

The discussion pricked Elizabeth's ears, and she played quietly, listening to the two ladies talk.

"I doubt she will come," replied Miss de Bourgh. "Even if she does, Darcy says she is too shy to perform in front of an audience."

"We are not an audience," said Lady Catherine. "The girl must learn to do it, as it will be required when she comes out."

"She only needs a little more courage."

"She is a Darcy and a Fitzwilliam," said Lady Catherine. "Courage is in her blood."

The ladies fell silent and Elizabeth kept playing. It was fortunate she had chosen to play an old favorite from memory, for she had no attention to devote to her playing. Instead, it was all centered on the brief conversation she had just overheard.

This account of Miss Georgiana Darcy did not resemble what Mr. Wickham had told her. Though it was possible the girl had changed since Mr. Wickham had last seen her, Elizabeth was inclined to attribute the discrepancy to Lady Catherine herself. Georgiana Darcy might be haughty when in the presence of a steward's son, and perhaps even when with her friends, but any young girl must be intimidated by the force of nature which was Lady Catherine de Bourgh.

Regardless, as Elizabeth was not acquainted with the girl and never expected to be in her company, she put thoughts of her from her mind. She played for a time, and then sat in Miss de Bourgh's company for the rest of the evening. As Elizabeth sank into her bed that night, she realized that the comfortable bed was one benefit to sleeping in Rosings, as opposed to Hunsford. One needed to acknowledge these little benefits when in a situation which was, overall, objectionable.

Chapter IV

It was not long before Elizabeth determined that acting as a companion to Miss de Bourgh was not an onerous endeavor—at least when considering the young woman herself. Miss de Bourgh was quiet, speaking softly when she did speak, and always with the utmost in composure and respect. And contrary to Lady Catherine's assertions and what she might have expected from a woman who was accustomed to her station in life, Miss de Bourgh was not at all demanding.

Elizabeth did not know how Miss de Bourgh expected her to behave, for she did not raise the subject herself. But she seemed to appreciate everything Elizabeth did, whether she was reading to her, speaking, playing for her enjoyment, or any other overture Elizabeth made.

What she was not, however, was overly talkative—in fact, to say she was not inclined to much speech was akin to saying her mother sometimes voiced her opinion. Often, Elizabeth found herself with little to do but sit with the woman and occasionally ask after her comfort. In no way did Miss de Bourgh demand that Elizabeth behave as Mrs. Jenkinson had, and though Elizabeth often watched her for signs that she was cold or uncomfortable, she did not see them, and

Miss de Bourgh never requested her to hover as her previous companion had. Thus, the fact that Mrs. Jenkinson had always treated Miss de Bourgh like a mother hen could be attributed to Lady Catherine's influence.

"Are you well, Miss de Bourgh?" asked Elizabeth of the woman one night after dinner. Miss de Bourgh had been sitting with a book in hand, but Elizabeth had been watching her, and she had not turned a single page in the previous fifteen minutes. Her handkerchief, which she carried with her wherever she went, had been pressed against her face, though Elizabeth had not noticed any evidence of sniffles or any other such malady, and she had thought she had heard a sigh from the other woman. As was Elizabeth's custom, she spoke quietly so as to avoid provoking Lady Catherine's scrutiny, and as the lady was seated at an escritoire on the other side of the room writing letters, Elizabeth thought she could speak quietly without the lady noticing.

"I am well, Miss Bennet," said Miss de Bourgh. "You do not need to inquire every time I use my handkerchief. If I had wanted another Mrs. Jenkinson as a companion, I would have agreed to any one of the ladies who applied to my mother for the position."

The words were spoken softly and without malice; otherwise Elizabeth might have been tempted to be offended by them. "I had not meant to offend, Miss de Bourgh," replied Elizabeth. "I merely thought to ask after your comfort."

Miss de Bourgh nodded. "I know. But your attention is not required in this instance."

It was better to avoid replying, so Elizabeth only returned to her book, which she *was* reading, and tried to put the thought of Miss de Bourgh out of her mind. She was not successful.

The occasion underscored how Elizabeth did not know what to think of the woman. She was not demanding, but she was often surly and cross, and though she did not berate Elizabeth like Lady Catherine might be expected to do, neither did she seem interested in the kind of friendship Elizabeth would have thought should exist between companion and mistress. Elizabeth was not able to understand the woman's frailty either. She rarely did anything strenuous, and she seemed content to just coast along on the currents of life without being a participant. Even the woman's phaeton, contrary to what Lady Catherine had said, was used sparingly.

Elizabeth's walks were, despite the agreement arrived on Elizabeth's first day at Rosings, a constant source of contention. Though she attempted to time them based on Miss de Bourgh's schedule, she could never leave the estate without Lady Catherine making some comment concerning Elizabeth's leaving, usually to her detriment. Lady Catherine did not keep the same hours as her daughter—she was awake much earlier in the morning and never napped in the afternoon, so she was often on hand when Elizabeth was leaving and rarely allowed her to go without objection.

"Did you not walk out this morning?" asked Lady Catherine some four days after Elizabeth's arrival.

"I did, but as I left late, I confined myself to the back gardens," replied Elizabeth. "This afternoon I will take the path leading toward the pond. I will be back before Miss de Bourgh awakens."

"It is unnecessary to walk so often or so far," declared Lady Catherine. "You will stay in your room occupied in some other, more ladylike activity."

Already weary of these constant debates, Elizabeth only curtseyed. "I have had my fill of ladylike pursuits today. I shall return within two hours."

And with that, Elizabeth departed, but she was sensible of Lady Catherine's eyes on her back as she left. The other times Lady Catherine said something about her habits were no less innocuous, but the lady at least kept them to simple statements of displeasure, rather than demands to amend her behavior.

As time marched on, however, Elizabeth noticed that the lady's scrutiny appeared to lessen, and though she could always be counted upon to state her opinions with forthrightness, it appeared like she paid less and less attention to Elizabeth the longer Elizabeth was in the house. She did, after all, run the estate, and her time was often much occupied in its management. There was much for her to do, and after a time she turned herself more to the attention of those things, rather than watching Elizabeth every moment of the day.

It happened nearly a week later that the Collinses were invited to dinner at Rosings again, and though Elizabeth had visited Charlotte on several occasions, her time was always short and she had been required to leave too early. Thus, she was happy to see the friend who had been largely denied her because of this farce.

"How are you, Eliza?" asked Charlotte as she entered the room.

"I am well," replied Elizabeth, careful to keep her voice quiet in response. "There are vexations, as I am certain you know, but it is nothing insurmountable."

"Come and join the rest of us," said Lady Catherine, her voice ringing out over those assembled. "I know you are great friends, but it is not polite to stand and talk with each other and not greet the rest of the company."

"Of course, Lady Catherine," said Charlotte with aplomb. "You have my apologies. Of course, I am happy to see you and Miss de Bourgh too."

Lady Catherine huffed and changed the subject. "And how is the parsonage, Mrs. Collins? Have you followed my instructions concerning your purchase of beef this past week?"

"Of course, she has," interjected Mr. Collins. "Mrs. Collins would never dare to defy your most excellent instructions."

The look Lady Catherine gave Mr. Collins promised her displeasure should he continue to speak, and he fell silent immediately. Once she was assured of his compliance, she turned to Charlotte again, one eyebrow raised.

"Yes, Lady Catherine, I have," replied Charlotte, and even Elizabeth, who knew her friend quite well, could not detect Charlotte's feelings on being so directed concerning the management of her own house. "As always, your suggestions were correct. I thank you."

Though Mr. Collins appeared as if he might pass out when his wife used the term "suggestion," Lady Catherine only preened and nodded.

"I knew how it would be. I have managed Rosings for many years, so I am well acquainted with all these things. When one understands how many mouths one must feed, and how much they are likely to eat, given their relative sizes and genders, the rest is simple mathematics."

"Indeed, I think you may be correct," replied Charlotte. "I believe I have come to understand your method, your ladyship. I will be certain to use it in the future, though I will, of course, also rely on your advice at all times."

The two women continued to speak, and Lady Catherine inquired into every minute detail of Charlotte's life, sometimes inquiring into things which Elizabeth thought would be best avoided. But Charlotte, showing a composure that Elizabeth did not know she would have been able to duplicate, answered all the lady's questions quickly and concisely, and with no hint of impatience or frustration at Lady Catherine's impertinence. In that moment, Elizabeth knew she had made the correct decision when she had refused Mr. Collins's suit—she could never imagine herself suited to being the man's wife, it was true, but the real disadvantage would be Mr. Collins's reliance on Lady Catherine and the woman's own insistence on her commands being obeyed. Elizabeth could not have endured it as Charlotte did.

While the two ladies were thus engaged, Elizabeth noted that Mr. Collins was watching her, and when he realized she had noticed, he turned his attention to her.

"You have been staying with Lady Catherine for almost a week now, Cousin. I trust you are sensible of the compliment she has paid you and have striven to pay Miss de Bourgh the utmost in civility and deference?"

The thought of what Mr. Collins would say if he was aware of the arguments she had engaged in with Lady Catherine almost set Elizabeth to laughing. As it was, she managed to hold her countenance and reply to the man in a manner he would not—she hoped—find offensive.

"I believe I have settled in to life at Rosings, sir. Lady Catherine has been generous, and assisting Miss de Bourgh is no trouble at all."

For the first time in Elizabeth's acquaintance with Mr. Collins, she was given the impression that he was aware that she had not truly answered his question. It was perspicacious of him—and most disconcerting—as she had always felt like she could speak as she would, confident that he would either misunderstand or interpret her words in whichever way benefited his own perception. Neither seemed to be the case here.

"I am happy you have found yourself at home," replied Mr. Collins after a moment's pause. "Indeed, I can imagine no other outcome, for I am certain that Lady Catherine is the soul of generosity, and one could never feel unwelcome at Rosings.

"However, I would like to know something more of your sojourn here, for I have a vested interest in your success as Miss de Bourgh's companion."

"A vested interest?" asked Elizabeth, though she knew very well what he meant.

"The fact that I am Lady Catherine's parson and you are my cousin," was his even reply. "Lady Catherine is a woman of high ideals and position in society, and though I would never suspect my own cousin of treating her with anything but her due, I must be certain of it."

"Then you may rest easy, Mr. Collins," said Elizabeth, forcing herself to reply with rationality rather than abusing him for his stupidity, which she sorely wished to do. "I would never treat anyone with anything but respect, and certainly not a woman at whose house I am a guest."

"Yes, that is it!" replied Mr. Collins. He was sensible of Lady

Catherine's sudden glance in his direction and lowered his voice. "Respect is the word I wished to use. How astute of you to have thought of it.

"But you must acknowledge, Cousin," continued he, "that Lady Catherine is deserving of a special brand of respect, one which not only considers the admiration for one's acquaintance, but also the deference and reverence due to one of an exalted sphere."

"I believe your point is well made, sir," said Elizabeth. In the end, it was better to simply agree and change the subject. "You need have no concerns on that score. I pay Lady Catherine every deference proper to one of her station."

Saying that, Elizabeth turned pointedly and began to speak with Maria, asking after her doings these past few days. Within moments the girl was happily chatting away, regaling Elizabeth with tales of her doings. She was certainly not as loud or loquacious as Lydia, but there was a reason why she was so close to Elizabeth's youngest sisters. On her other side, Elizabeth noted that Mr. Collins remained silent, but she could almost feel the heat of his study of her. She decided she did not care—she was not about to bow and scrape before Lady Catherine as he did. The lady could accept her how she was or not at all. It made no difference to Elizabeth.

Soon after the company was called in to dinner, and they entered and sat in their usual seats. This time, however, Elizabeth was situated beside Miss de Bourgh, though the Collinses were where they would normally sit. If Elizabeth had not just had a conversation with Mr. Collins concerning the respect he thought she deserved, Elizabeth would still have noted how much he used the word. And every time he said it, his eyes would dart to her to see if she had taken note of it. Needless to say, Elizabeth would not give him that satisfaction.

It was petty, perhaps. Elizabeth was aware that his motives were, even more than his continuing veneration for his patroness, the desire that Elizabeth's behavior not affect his standing with Lady Catherine. In that she could not blame him, for it was a legitimate concern. In this instance, though it had been possible that Elizabeth might fall out of favor with the lady given her unwillingness to bow to the woman's unreasonable demands, she thought they had settled into a routine, and the possibility of that had diminished accordingly.

"Yes, yes, Mr. Collins," said Lady Catherine, after Mr. Collins said the word for seemingly the one hundredth time, "I understand you hold me in respect, and I thank you for it. Now, however, I would like to turn your attention to the parish, for we have not spoken of any concerns there recently."

"Of course, Lady Catherine," said Mr. Collins. "I do have a few matters to bring to your attention."

The relief Elizabeth felt on hearing the conversation thus directed to other subjects could hardly be described. For the rest of dinner and later when they retired to the music room, Lady Catherine's concentration was fully on Mr. Collins, and his was on his recitation. Elizabeth had not the slightest notion of what they discussed, but as the man was not directing his considerable capacity for the ridiculous at her, Elizabeth was well pleased. She followed Lady Catherine's peremptory command that she play for them and stayed at the pianoforte for the rest of the evening. The only circumstance she regretted was her inability to speak with Charlotte.

At least, it continued in this way until it was almost time for those residing at the parsonage to leave. Knowing the time was approaching, Elizabeth left the pianoforte and inquired of Miss de Bourgh if she required anything, to which the woman responded with a short negative, allowing Elizabeth to find a seat not far from Charlotte. Her friend took the opportunity which arose to speak with Elizabeth.

"Is Rosings all you thought it would be?"

"All that and more," replied Elizabeth. They spoke softly to avoid any unwanted attention.

"I hope you are controlling your temper, Elizabeth. I know when you get your back up it can be quite a sight to see."

"You have no need to worry," replied Elizabeth. "Lady Catherine has not managed to shatter my composure yet, so I am certain I am quite safe."

Charlotte shook her head and laughed. "I am not worried for *their* sakes. I am worried for *yours*. But I am happy to hear that your stay here has at least been tolerable."

"Indeed, it has. There is nothing of which I wish to complain."

Mr. Collins rose at that moment and beckoned to his wife and sister-in-law, making his flowery obeisance to Lady Catherine as was his custom. A few more moments of his words and he was finally ready to depart, but unfortunately for Elizabeth's composure, he was not able to leave without one final admonishment.

"I trust you understand your role here, Cousin, and the respect you must pay to her ladyship. I do not need to bring it up again?"

Though she felt she might scream if the man used the word once more, Elizabeth only raised her chin and looked him in the eye. "I am quite sensible of my position, sir. As I told you before, there is no need for you to concern yourself."

Mr. Collins watched her for several moments, seeming to weigh her response, before he broke into a wide grin. "Excellent. I knew I could trust you, Cousin. I hope you rest well this evening, for I know your devotion to Miss de Bourgh has already grown to astonishing depths."

And with those final silly words, he led his party out of the room. As Charlotte left, Elizabeth caught her eye and gave her an expressive grin, which Charlotte returned with a roll of her eyes. Then they were gone.

"I believe I shall retire as well," said Lady Catherine the moment the visitors were gone. "I shall have a busy day tomorrow, so you need not look for me in the morning."

"Very well, Mother," replied Miss de Bourgh.

"Sleep well, Lady Catherine," added Elizabeth.

The lady only thanked her and quit the room, leaving Elizabeth watching after her, bemused at the way she had been summarily dismissed with nary an admonishment about how she should care for Anne, or anything else she usually found so important.

"If you do not mind," said Elizabeth, turning to Miss de Bourgh, "I believe I shall retire as well."

For a moment, the woman made no response. Then she seemed to come to some decision and said: "Actually, Miss Bennet, I believe I would like to speak with you for a few moments. Will you indulge me?"

Intrigued, for Miss de Bourgh speaking even this much was far from normal, Elizabeth indicated her willingness and sat down again on the sofa. Miss de Bourgh's response was destined to surprise her once again.

"What I wish to say is private between us. Shall we not retire to my room?"

"Certainly," replied Elizabeth, by now quite curious.

Miss de Bourgh rose and led her out into the hall. As she walked a little behind the other woman, Elizabeth noted how Miss de Bourgh's back appeared straighter, as if she had acquired a hint of confidence. She could not make the other woman out at all; this whole episode was so different from what Elizabeth had ever witnessed from her as to render her previous observations meaningless.

When they had arrived at Miss de Bourgh's room and entered therein, Miss de Bourgh greeted her maid with a nod and dismissed her. "You may return in one hour to assist me in retiring."

"Of course, Mistress," said the maid—a girl named Laura. She then curtseyed and left the room.

When she had gone, Miss de Bourgh indicated a nearby sofa and sat without waiting for Elizabeth to join her. Elizabeth did so with alacrity, still wondering what was happening. She did not have long to wait.

"I am certain you are curious, Miss Bennet, but if you will indulge me for a moment, all will be revealed. In fact, I wished to speak with you without my mother present, for she would not approve. But it is now time that you should know that it was I who convinced my mother to solicit your assistance. You are acting as my companion because I insisted upon it."

Chapter V

The season in London was not a time Fitzwilliam Darcy could enjoy with any contentment. At its best, London was a pit of wolves. High London society was immoral and objectionable, with rakes aplenty, others who basked in their own superiority and looked down on the rest, where marriages were bartered and bought, and marriage vows thrown aside just as quickly. Darcy had never enjoyed it here—not when he had been nothing more than the heir of a large estate, and certainly not since he had become that estate's master.

Worse still were the young ladies and their mothers, huntresses on the prowl for any unfortunate man unwary enough to have fallen into their clutches. Already during that season, Darcy had foiled two attempted compromises, and he had no doubt that more would be forthcoming. Why a woman would entrap a man into marriage, he could not comprehend. Darcy was not a man to take out his frustrations on a woman, but if a woman did entrap him, she could not know his temperament in advance. For all any of them knew, he might turn out to be a beater of women. The trappings of wealth would be cold comfort in such a situation.

But much as Darcy loathed society, its insincerity, its grasping, artful denizens, the latest letter from Lady Catherine reminded him that even London would be preferable to Rosings this year. And he was certain his cousin would agree.

"So, what does the old bat have to say this time?" asked Fitzwilliam. He had come to Darcy's townhouse at Darcy's request, and as usual, he sat on a chair in front of Darcy's desk, a glass of port in hand and a foot resting on the polished wood between them. Darcy had seen this exact pose so many times that he had come to expect it—he thought his cousin had done it originally to annoy him, but by now it was nothing more than force of habit, and Darcy ignored it.

"The usual," replied Darcy, taking a sip of his own drink. "She speaks of our coming with breathless anticipation, thanks me for my assistance with the estate, and refers to my upcoming nuptials."

"Nothing out of the ordinary, then," replied Fitzwilliam.

"Except that she has gone past mere innuendo and entered into the realm of openly stating that this *must* be the year I finally fulfil my late mother's wishes and offer for her daughter."

Fitzwilliam only laughed. "Do not say you did not expect this. Last year when we visited, she was hardly less overt than you say she is in her letter. It should not be a surprise."

"It is not." Darcy did not mean to be so short, but his aunt's particular brand of officiousness was trying, and as Darcy knew Fitzwilliam felt the same way, he would not take offense. "But I find I am less willing to subject myself to it this year."

"Oh?" asked Fitzwilliam, his eyes gleaming with suppressed mirth.

"Yes. In fact, a matter of business has arisen which will necessitate my presence in London this year. It is unfortunate, but I will not be able to travel to Kent."

"May I inquire after this matter of business?"

"It has to do with my investments," replied Darcy. "My banker does not think it wise that I leave London at present."

"And it arose only after our aunt's letter arrived?"

"A curious coincidence, is it not?"

Fitzwilliam guffawed and slapped his knee. "Curious, indeed! I cannot think our aunt will accept this development with any degree of sanguinity."

"No, she will not. But the beauty of the matter is that she is at Rosings and we are in London."

"Rosings is not far distant. She could be here in four hours, if she chose it."

"Yes, she could. But do you think she will? She has always

preferred to insist we come to her, and with the demands of the estate, I doubt she will put herself out so much. Even if she does, I am quite tied to London for the time being and will not be able to leave, even if she comes here to attempt to drag me back with her."

Fitzwilliam eyed him with unabashed curiosity. "You have always been able to tolerate our aunt, usually with more patience than I may boast myself. What has changed now?"

"The fact that she has become more strident as she has aged." Darcy sighed and leaned back with his glass in hand, the amber liquid swirling within as he moved his hand in a circular motion. "She will not listen when I tell her I do not intend to marry Anne, and she becomes more insistent every year. I would not put it past her to arrange a compromise if she does not get her own way."

"And what of Rosings?" asked Fitzwilliam.

Darcy only snorted. "Lady Catherine rules that estate with an iron fist. She is capable of managing it without my assistance, and even if I make suggestions, she promises to consider them and then promptly pushes them to the side. If she was less talented in the estate's operation, I might be more concerned. There are always matters which may be improved, but she is entirely capable of managing her own affairs."

"That is true," said Fitzwilliam.

They fell silent, each occupied with their own thoughts. Darcy's were consumed by the desire to avoid being subjected once again to Lady Catherine's demands. Far better to stay in London and avoid society as much as possible than to be stuck in a house with Lady Catherine for two weeks.

Though Darcy did not wish to confess to it, in fact his thoughts were occupied by more than simply the situation in Kent. Whenever he was at repose, other thoughts began to intrude, and often, his mind was invaded by memories of a beautiful woman with laughing eyes and a teasing manner. It was thoughts of Miss Elizabeth Bennet he could not avoid which made him moody and ill-tempered. If he went to Rosings, thoughts of her which would not leave him alone coupled with Lady Catherine's constant demands would almost certainly leave his temper frayed. It was that as much as anything which prompted him to avoid the year's visit.

"You may go if you wish," said Darcy, firmly pushing thoughts of Miss Bennet from his mind, though he was aware she would claw her way out of the dark hole in which he had locked her, as if she had the very key to his mind. "Without my presence, I would think your visit would be less aggravating."

"Oh, no!" exclaimed Fitzwilliam. "If I were to go without you, I would no doubt be subjected to Lady Catherine's inquisition. If you think being hauled over the carpet to constitute a pleasant visit, I must question your sanity."

"I do not blame you," replied Darcy. "If you are willing, then, I will draft a letter this very evening and send it off to her."

"Just take care to imply your decision will not be altered and that your business is *very* important, else you shall have an irate Lady Catherine on your doorstep by tomorrow."

Then Fitzwilliam raised his glass in salute, drained it, and excused himself from the room. Left to his own thoughts, Darcy sat for some minutes, staring into his glass, watching as the liquid swirled and splashed when he shook it slightly. He was reluctant to even favor Lady Catherine with a letter explaining his decision to cancel his visit to Rosings that year, but he understood it needed to be done. His manners would not allow for anything else, and as she was his mother's sister, he was duty bound to at least give her that courtesy.

There was nothing else to be done, so Darcy set about drafting the letter, keeping it short and concise, but being careful to emphasize—as Fitzwilliam had suggested—the importance of his business. When the letter was completed and sanded, Darcy summoned his butler and entrusted the missive to him, asking it be posted immediately. He thought of sending it express, but in the end, he decided against it, thinking an express might be more likely to bring Lady Catherine to his doorstep.

With that complete, Darcy sat down to his other work which awaited him. There were letters of business, one from his steward at Pemberley, another from another steward at an estate he owned in Scotland, and another from his banker. The matter he had used as an excuse to avoid Rosings was just that—an excuse. Darcy usually abhorred any kind of deceit, but in this instance, he was more than willing to make an exception.

At the bottom of his pile of letters, he noted one from Bingley, and he grimaced. As he expected, deciphering it was the same as any other Bingley had sent him during the years of their acquaintance. He mentioned his time in the north, visiting relations, noted that he would be returning to London before the end of the month, and suggested they meet at their club when he arrived.

Unfortunately, the want of cheer which had characterized Bingley's behavior and his letters since they had left Hertfordshire was still clear between the blots. Darcy was sorry for his friend—had Jane Bennet returned an affection for anything other than Bingley's pocketbook—or to be fair, had her mother's avarice not ruled the girl—Darcy might have been able to support an alliance with her. But Bingley was feeling the effects of her indifference even now, half a year after their departure.

Perhaps he could be introduced to a new angel when he returned to London, mused Darcy. He had had his head turned by so many ladies in the past, it was not inconceivable that the next might cure him of his heartbreak. It was something to consider at the very least.

"You arranged it?" asked Elizabeth, uncertain what she was hearing.

"I did," replied Miss de Bourgh.

Elizabeth studied the woman. "It is difficult to imagine that Lady Catherine could be guided in such a way, especially when you are not . . ."

"Forceful?" asked Miss de Bourgh. "Confident or determined? No, I must confess that my mother has much more of all those traits than I possess myself. But that does not mean I am devoid of them."

"How? And Why?"

"For your first question, it was easily done, as my mother was not enamored of any of the ladies she interviewed, and it was easy to point out some imagined fault which my mother would find objectionable." Miss de Bourgh smiled, though it was mirthless. "My mother, as I am certain you understand, prefers to surround herself with those who will not dare to contradict her. Mrs. Jenkinson was one such, for various reasons, and your cousin, Mr. Collins, is another. She is adept at managing Rosings and quite intelligent, but she absolutely loathes any form of contradiction."

"Then it would seem that my presence does not fit her usual requirements," replied Elizabeth.

For the second time in the past few moments, Elizabeth was surprised, as Miss de Bourgh actually smiled in response. "That *does* seem to be the case, does it not? But when I pointed out your merits—particularly your intelligence, your circumstances and knowledge, not to mention your *availability*, she quickly came to see my point. That does not mean she would allow you to have the position without assuring herself that you would not corrupt me."

Elizabeth laughed. "That is yet to be determined, Miss de Bourgh." Elizabeth paused, noting Miss de Bourgh's responding grin. "As yet, however, I do not understand *why*. What about my attendance was so irresistible that you manipulated your mother in such a fashion."

The smile ran away from Miss de Bourgh's face, and the look she gave Elizabeth suggested that she thought Elizabeth had overstepped her bounds. Elizabeth only returned her look with one of her own; though Miss de Bourgh had proven to be her mother's daughter with her spark of haughtiness, Elizabeth thought she was owed this explanation.

Apparently Miss de Bourgh came to the same conclusion. "I wanted a friend, Miss Bennet," said Miss de Bourgh, in a voice which was barely audible. Elizabeth's heart went out to her. "You do not know what it is like. By all accounts, you have been raised in a house with many sisters, and though you have not been blessed with the material advantages I have always known, I must assume those you did possess—that of a loving family—were much greater than mere wealth. I am aware of my mother's love for me, but her love is expressed in demands for obedience and her focus on my physical needs.

"Mrs. Jenkinson was a good woman, one who cared for me and endured my mother's ill humors with as much fortitude as she could muster, but she was always more of a nurse and a caretaker—and a jailor—than a companion. I hope you will agree to be my friend, a woman close to my own age whom I can talk to and who will talk to me for some other reason than to inquire if I am warm or comfortable."

"You saw in me someone who would have no trouble opposing your mother, if need be."

"Not opposing, precisely," replied Miss de Bourgh. "I do not intend for you to provoke my mother's ire, and I certainly do not wish for the Collinses to be pulled into any disobedience. Mrs. Collins possesses a mind of her own, but Mr. Collins has no opinion other than what my mother tells him."

"Then what do you suggest?"

"I suggest we act as most friends would when we are not in my mother's company. I want to live, Miss Bennet, not merely exist. I wish to have confidences and discussions about nothing more important than literature or what handsome man has caught our fancy."

"That will be difficult with your mother hovering over you."

"And that is why I waited until mother was content with your behavior and stopped watching you." Her grin made a reappearance. "I knew eventually her interest would return to the estate and the pleasure she takes in meddling with the lives of others. She has come to it in a more expeditious manner than I would have thought possible.

But I am grateful nonetheless."

"She will still be living in this house."

"I am willing to take what I can get at present. We can see what develops from there."

Elizabeth watched the other woman, noting her returning scrutiny. On the one hand, she understood how Miss de Bourgh was using her as an escape from her mother, and part of her wondered if she should not be offended as a result. On the other, however, she realized that this young lady had hardly even lived, though she was Elizabeth's elder in years. Her plea did not fall on deaf ears. But the independence which was part of Elizabeth's character could not understand how Miss de Bourgh could endure such casual tyranny.

"Why did you not go to your uncle? For that matter, I understand that your cousins visit every Easter—why did you not ask them for help?"

Miss de Bourgh was silent while she contemplated Elizabeth's question, finally saying: "I do not mind my mother, Miss Bennet. While you may—rightly, I might add—consider her to be a despot, she has my best interests in mind."

"But only as those interests agree with her own opinion," snapped Elizabeth.

"I will not say you are incorrect. I will only say that I have been comfortable living here, and there are ways I can circumvent my mother's authority. I have desperately wished for a friend, but I have never been desperate enough to take such a step as applying to my uncle, for I am aware that it might irreparably damage my relationship with my mother. I am hopeful we can keep our friendship from her notice."

"Miss de Bourgh," said Elizabeth, speaking with patience to ensure she was not misunderstood, "would it not be better to gradually become more open with each other, to display a growing friendship, rather than this subterfuge you are proposing?"

The woman appeared crestfallen. "You do not wish to be my friend?"

It was the response Elizabeth should have expected. Anne de Bourgh had not had many in her life who were willing to put *her* best interests first, and it was not surprising she should be so easily disheartened.

"I am more than willing to be your friend," replied Elizabeth. She leaned forward and grasped Miss de Bourgh's hands, squeezing them to impart commiseration and friendship, not to mention a bit of confidence. "I am only a little uncomfortable with such underhanded means. I know your mother means well, but are you not deserving of friendship and love in your own right? How can your mother possibly oppose that which would make you happy in your life?"

"You would be surprised," said Miss de Bourgh, though it was clear she appreciated Elizabeth's unequivocal declaration. "She would disapprove of our friendship for no other reason than she considers you inferior."

Elizabeth sighed. Her stay at Rosings had just become that much more interesting, and though she was beginning to see much more in Miss de Bourgh than she had ever imagined, the thought of Lady Catherine's likely reaction if she ever became aware of it was enough to cause her to shudder.

But there was truly no choice. Miss de Bourgh was a woman Elizabeth could not even have imagined esteeming only a short time ago, but these past few moments had revealed a side to her that intrigued Elizabeth. Besides, this pathetic plea for friendship could not be turned away — Elizabeth's heart would not allow it.

"I am more than willing to be your friend," replied Elizabeth, prompting a large smile from Miss de Bourgh. "As I have already stated, I am still wary of keeping this from your mother, but I do understand. Hopefully with time, she will come to accept it."

Miss de Bourgh's countenance suggested skepticism, and Elizabeth could not blame her. But she nodded and said: "That is wonderful. Thank you very much. I hope we will become close as sisters."

"Only remember that I must return home before long," said Elizabeth, not wishing to spoil Miss de Bourgh's new-found happiness, but knowing she needed to be reminded of the reality of the situation.

"Then we shall have to make the most of our time."

There was nothing else to say, so Elizabeth allowed the subject to drop. They discussed how they would go about their days for several more moments, Miss de Bourgh firm in her belief that her mother would not even become aware of their closer friendship.

"So long as our behavior in her presence does not change, other matters will keep her occupied," averred she. "But we must also take care to avoid the notice of the servants. They are loyal to her. Laura will likely keep my confidence, but I am not confident in any of the others. Regardless, I do not wish anyone to know at present."

Though she wondered if she should be offended, Elizabeth was aware of the reason for Miss de Bourgh's sentiments, so she said nothing. When they had spoken for some little more time, Elizabeth excused herself to return to her room, citing the need to retire. The need to think on this newly changed circumstance was equally important in her mind.

As she rose to depart, the sound of Miss de Bourgh's voice caused her to stop and turn to look at the woman.

"I would be happy if we could dispense with formality, at least when we are alone. I would be pleased if you would call me Anne."

The hesitant nervousness in her tone almost broke Elizabeth's heart, and she knew that whatever restrictions they were forced to adopt, she had made the right choice in accepting this woman's friendship.

"Then you must call me Elizabeth or Lizzy."

The expression of heartfelt delight which spread over Miss de Bourgh's—Anne's—face became her and suggested a prettiness which might lurk behind her unflattering dresses, severe hairstyles, and general impression of malaise and ill health. Elizabeth did not think the woman had ever been so happy as she was now, which was truly a pity. In that moment, Elizabeth decided she would do everything in her power to bring a little joy into Anne de Bourgh's life.

Chapter VI

"But I drive my phaeton. Is that not enough?"

"Do you consider *that* good exercise? You do nothing but sit and manipulate the reins. The horses do all the work."

Miss Anne de Bourgh sat back and considered what Elizabeth said. "Is that why you walk often, Miss Bennet? Is it due to the desire for exercise?"

"That is one of the reasons," replied Elizabeth. "The greater purpose is because I love nature and wish to be out among the trees and grasses, to glory in nature and know I am alive, and even to catch a glimpse of wildlife on occasion." Elizabeth smiled at the other woman. "Have you ever seen a deer close by, Anne?"

"I have seen them from my windows at times, and I once caught a glimpse of one from my phaeton, though it quickly fled."

"Yes, they tend to be shy of humans. But to come on one at a much closer distance is another matter altogether, and it is much more likely without all the noise a phaeton makes. They are such majestic creatures, especially the bucks with their large antlers. Now, you do not wish to come too close to them, for they are large and can be dangerous at times. But the sight of them is wonderful."

A frown settled over Miss de Bourgh's face. "I had never

considered it that way before. My mother always tells me that I am too ill to walk—or to do much of anything, really."

"And what do you think?"

"I do not know. Perhaps I would enjoy walking if I had the chance. But it is out of the question. My mother would never allow it, and there would be such a to-do if she discovered that I was disobeying her."

Elizabeth paused for a moment, gathering her thoughts. This was one of those instances she found quite trying—Lady Catherine, for all that she was Anne's mother, should not have enough power over her to direct her in everything. Anne was of age and could do as she wished!

"I am not trying to induce you to disobey Lady Catherine," said Elizabeth, speaking slowly and with care. "But you are of age and may do as you please. You need not be beholden to her every whim."

"No, but the furor and outcry which must proceed from flouting my mother's strictures are not worth the gratification I might receive." Anne paused and then smiled at Elizabeth. "Come, let us ride in the phaeton for a time. Perhaps we might be fortunate enough to see a deer or some other animal."

Agreeing, Elizabeth returned to her room and took a bonnet and spenser to wear, informing Tilly that she and Anne would be out for a time. As she made her way down through the house, she considered the problem that was Anne and Lady Catherine. Elizabeth had quickly learned that she was entirely mistaken about the Anne de Bourgh, though given how she had presented herself, Elizabeth did not think she could be blamed.

In the first place, though she was not robust and did not possess an especially hardy constitution, Anne was also not frail. In fact, more of the frailty she often displayed before company was nothing more than Lady Catherine's coddling. How Lady Catherine could treat her daughter, a woman full grown, in such a manner was beyond Elizabeth's understanding. She had also learned that part of Anne's seeming ill-health was because Anne, herself, presented it that way as a means to keep her mother at bay.

"You must retire for your nap, Anne!" cried Lady Catherine the afternoon after Elizabeth had agreed to become Anne's friend. "You are quite clearly exhausted, no doubt from Miss Bennet's overactive sense of exercise."

"I will own to a little fatigue," said Anne, and when Elizabeth looked on her, she could see that Anne was drooping, her eyes heavy lidded. "I shall take Miss Bennet with me and retire to my room."

"Of course, she must go with you," said Lady Catherine, waving to dismiss them both from the room. "She is your companion, is she not?"

By this time, Elizabeth was inured to Lady Catherine's words and the sneering tone she often used when she spoke to or of Elizabeth, so she did not care about what Lady Catherine said. Anne rose and Elizabeth followed her from the room, but she watched her charge as she climbed the stairs, and Anne did not give the impression of a woman who was asleep on her feet, for she climbed the stairs spritely enough.

"What shall we do with the afternoon, then?" asked she when they had gained the security of her room. "Perhaps we could read together?"

"Are you not fatigued?"

Anne only laughed and shook her head. "I have often found that my mother prefers that I rest often, so I give her ample opportunity to order me from the room."

Even now, a few days after the event, Elizabeth was not certain what to think of Anne's subterfuge. On the one hand, that anyone would desire to be out of Lady Catherine's company was not a surprise—Elizabeth rarely wished to be *in* her company! On the other, however, such behavior only encouraged Lady Catherine to continue to treat Anne as if she was a girl of seven, rather than a woman of more than twenty.

Elizabeth truly was not attempting to foment discord in the house, nor was she trying to teach Anne defiance. But she was an adult; should she not be allowed—encouraged even—to make her own decisions? In this house, and with such a passive disposition, Elizabeth could not help but suppose that Anne would never be able to choose for herself, and furthermore, if her mother suddenly passed on, what would Anne do then? It was imperative, in Elizabeth's mind, that the Anne develop a hint of independence.

Another discovery Elizabeth had made was that Anne was quite intelligent. They spoke together on an equal level, and though Anne was not quick with a reply like Elizabeth, her intelligence was sufficient for her to hold her own in a discussion of differing opinions. What she lacked was the courage to disagree with her mother—or rather to state that disagreement openly.

"I do not wish for an argument," replied Anne one evening when they had been discussing some piece of literature Elizabeth had introduced to her.

Intrigued, Elizabeth asked her what she meant. "It is simply that . .

. Well, I do not think I agree with you, so if I say my opinion, then I risk an argument."

"Not all discussions end in argument, Anne. Some of the most interesting discussions in which I have ever engaged were contrary in nature, with differently held opinions. But debates are healthy, for they encourage critical thinking and learning."

Anne paused and considered this. "But these debates of yours—did they not end in hard feelings between you?"

"The trick is to respect the other person for their opinions, even if you disagree with them. Just because you and I read the same passage and interpret it differently, for example, should not be cause for us to hate each other. As we are different people with different experiences, it is not a surprise that we think in a different manner too."

"My mother would never agree. Her opinion is paramount, and she does not tolerate disagreement."

"With all due respect to Lady Catherine," replied Elizabeth, "she is not perfect, and as such, she cannot have a perfect understanding. There is only one perfect person in the history of the world, and I can assure you that your mother is not that person."

Anne giggled, and then she directed a mock glare at Elizabeth. "Do not allow mother to hear you say that. I am certain she has never considered the possibility she might be wrong about *anything*."

"Of course," replied Elizabeth. "I would never argue with her. But you will allow me to disagree in the confines of my own thoughts, I hope."

Though Anne was intelligent, Elizabeth soon learned that she was not well educated at all. Lady Catherine, it seemed, was more interested in informing Anne of what *she* thought Anne needed to know and avoid all those pesky consequences which would result in her daughter's having any opinion which that contradict with her own. Anne had read relatively little literature, she had not been to London to partake in anything of culture, and she showed a shocking lack of knowledge of anything which was happening in the world at the time, whether it was the war with the French or the situation between England and its former colonies.

When Elizabeth reached the bottom of the stairs, she made her way toward the stables where the phaeton was being made ready by the stable hands. Anne was already there, and she watched the activity with an almost child-like excitement. It was one of the only things that she was allowed able to do by herself and without Lady Catherine looming over her—Lady Catherine herself rode in a carriage wherever she went. From this, Elizabeth had determined that Anne longed to be free, but she, unfortunately, lacked the ability to even contemplate removing herself from her mother's domination.

This was where Elizabeth came in and had found her place in Anne's life. Though she knew she would be required to depart for her father's home, she hoped that she would be successful in imparting some of her skills to Anne. Perhaps Anne could assert her independence in small measures over time, giving her mother an opportunity to become accustomed to each step and the new reality of her daughter's life. But for Anne to be successful, Elizabeth knew she would need the tools, so Elizabeth spent as much time as she could educating Anne of the world beyond her mother's estate.

"You are to go out in your phaeton?"

Elizabeth turned at the sound of Lady Catherine's voice, and she noted the lady walking toward them, her appearance neither pleased nor displeased.

"Yes, Mother," replied Anne. Elizabeth had noted that she never referred to her mother as "mama" or any other more familiar term.

Lady Catherine nodded. "Do not stay out longer than an hour—you remember how strict I am about such things."

"Of course."

"And Baines will ride along behind you."

"Yes," replied Anne, gesturing toward where a towering footman was inspecting the saddle of a gelding. This footman accompanied Anne whenever she drove out.

"Very well, then." Lady Catherine turned to Elizabeth. "Remember to leave your bonnet on, Miss Bennet. I will not stand for anyone of my household becoming excessively brown."

Lady Catherine had forgotten that Elizabeth was to depart for her father's house before too many weeks had passed and seemed to consider her the same as she would one of her employees. Elizabeth had known this was likely, and she had decided there was no reason to contradict the lady. She only assented to Lady Catherine's instructions and watched as the woman retreated.

"It seems you are becoming proficient already, Elizabeth. It is much better to simply agree with her, then she will only nod and take her leave."

Though she agreed with her companion, the brief exchange brought another thought to Elizabeth's mind. Anne was, she decided, far more rebellious against Lady Catherine than Elizabeth—or Anne herself—had ever thought. But her rebellion against her mother was of a more passive variety. Anne would not contradict Lady Catherine, nor would she disobey her when given a direct order—unless she managed to wriggle free when the woman was not looking. It was these traits, this ability to recognize that she did not always wish to do exactly as she was told, which gave Elizabeth hope that Anne would one day succeed in asserting her independence.

"Let us go," said Anne, breaking through Elizabeth's reverie. She climbed up onto the front seat beside Anne and watched as the other woman flicked the reins, the pony in front of her beginning to move forward.

They rode on in silence for some time, Elizabeth enjoying the feeling of the wind in her face and the warmth of the sun shining down upon them. It was still late March, and the wind still carried a bit of a bite, but, overall, Elizabeth was pleased by the weather which had been laid out for them. Anne handled the reins with an expertise borne of much practice, her subtle motions guiding the ponies with no hesitation. But whereas Elizabeth was enjoying the weather and the scents of the season, Anne seemed to enjoy the movement of the phaeton, of being in control, and the ability to escape Rosings.

"It is a lovely day, is it not?" said Elizabeth when they had been traveling some time.

"Yes," replied Anne. "I do not like it when it rains, as I am denied this pleasure."

Elizabeth looked at the woman with sympathy. The phaeton was truly her only pleasure, and it must be hard, indeed, to be denied it.

"Where did you receive your instruction?" asked Elizabeth.

"We used to gather with my extended family every year. My uncle, who is the Earl of Matlock and my mother's brother, as well as my aunt, who was my mother's sister, and their families. Before my aunt's husband passed away, he insisted on alternating the location of our gatherings, so we would travel to Derbyshire, as their estates are quite close. It was on those occasions when I first learned to drive, though I was young enough that I was not allowed to do it myself.

"Of course, my mother has often given me instruction as well, though her words have always been more commands. It is even more curious as I have never seen my mother drive, and I am not sure if she has ever learned."

Elizabeth was forced to stifle a laugh, for she knew exactly to what Anne was referring. But then Anne surprised her by confirming Elizabeth's opinion and speaking of the matter out loud.

"In fact, I have come to the conclusion that my mother, though she claims superior knowledge about any subject, actually knows very little."

This time Elizabeth could not hold in her laughter, and she said: "Yes, but if she had ever learned, she would be a true proficient."

Anne joined her in laughter. "I see you have been listening when my mother mumbles her officious nothings."

"Indeed, I have," replied Elizabeth, wondering at her companion's sudden critical comments of her mother. Apparently, Anne saw her expression.

"I have always recognized these things about my mother, Elizabeth. But I have no desire for confrontation with her."

Elizabeth nodded, still not quite understanding. "Then of what shall we speak? We are in a position where we cannot be overheard. It would be wise of us to take advantage of that fact."

And speak they did. They discussed one of Shakespeare's sonnets which they had read that morning, and Elizabeth was heartened to hear Anne espousing an interpretation different from that which Elizabeth had stated. They spoke of the war in France, Anne informing Elizabeth that her cousin, the second son of her uncle the earl, was a colonel in the army and had seen battle in Spain against the tyrant's forces. They spoke of some of the art Lady Catherine had displayed in the house at Rosings—Elizabeth had learned that art was an interest Anne possessed, though she had never visited any art galleries in London and had only the pieces her mother possessed for reference.

Through these discussions, Elizabeth attempted to tutor her charge, encouraging her to state her opinions with confidence, but also to be open to the opinions of others. Of the supposed engagement between herself and Mr. Darcy, nothing was spoken, and Elizabeth did not expect her to share such private matters. But she was quickly coming to the opinion that Anne deserved better than to be tied for life to such a stern, unfeeling man as Mr. Darcy.

"I am astounded at your having such well-formed opinions," said Anne as she was guiding the ponies back toward Rosings, which loomed in the distance. "My mother would consider much of what we discuss to be unladylike."

"Perhaps she would," replied Elizabeth. "But I do not think that women should be ignorant of what happens in the world around us. Though there are certain separations of what the sexes can properly do, we should still be aware."

"How did you become so educated? Did you attend school?"

"No, I had not that pleasure, though I would have appreciated the opportunity. My father is an intelligent man. He allowed his daughters to direct their own education, to concentrate on those subjects for which we had an interest, and he assisted us when we identified those subjects which bring us pleasure."

"Your father educated you?" asked Anne, her tone incredulous. "My mother always says that daughters are not of much consequence to a father."

"But my father has no sons," replied Elizabeth. "I was always my father's favorite, for I am most like him in temperament. But it is not completely accurate to say that he educated me—rather, I educated myself, with his assistance."

"Is that what you are attempting with me?"

Elizabeth blushed and demurred. "I am not educating you, Anne."

"Because I am educating myself. You need not spare my feelings, Elizabeth. It has become clear to me that I have not learned the things that I should have. I am quite indebted to you for taking me under your wing."

There was nothing to say to that. Elizabeth only smiled at her companion and indicated that she was happy to be her friend. Anne, who had likely never had a friend in her life, beamed, as she always did when Elizabeth spoke of friendship, and guided the ponies to a stop outside the stable. The animals and the conveyance were left to the care of the stable hands, and the two women returned to the house. It was clear almost immediately that there was some uproar.

"I suppose we should attend my mother at once," said Anne. The reluctance in her tone matched Elizabeth's feelings, for she had learned that Lady Catherine was unpleasant when vexed. "If we do not, she will seek us out later."

They approached the sitting-room, from whence the commotion was emanating, and when they stepped in, it was to the sight of Lady Catherine with a piece of paper clenched in one fist, her heightened color suggesting that she had been in this state for some time.

"What is the matter, Mother?" asked Anne, approaching the virago with more confidence than Elizabeth.

"What is the matter?" echoed Lady Catherine. "Your cousin has written to inform me that he will not visit Rosings this year! He claims some matter of business which prevents his being away from town. What business could possibly be more important than attending you, his future bride?"

"I know not, Mother, for I have not read his letter."

It was clear that Lady Catherine had hardly even noted Anne's response. "No, no, no, this cannot be allowed to stand. Darcy will do his duty and attend to us as usual. I shall write him a letter, informing him of his duty."

"But his matter of business," said Anne. "Surely he would not have cancelled his visit if it were not imperative."

"It matters not!" snapped Lady Catherine. "He must come. I know you have your heart set on marrying him, and I was counting on his proposing this year. If he proposes, you will no longer need a companion, and Miss Bennet may return to her home."

"Then I will leave you to your letter writing."

The reminder that she was to write a letter provoked Lady Catherine to action, and she turned, without acknowledging them, and hurried to the escritoire. Within moments, the scratching of her pen testified to her imperious demands to her nephew, and Elizabeth wondered that she had not torn holes in the paper.

Without a word, the two ladies departed, leaving Lady Catherine to her anger and her furiously written letter, and they made their way back toward Anne's room. Elizabeth could not help but be curious.

"Are you set on marrying Mr. Darcy?"

Anne's eyes found Elizabeth and her brow furrowed. "Are you acquainted with my cousin?"

"I am," replied Elizabeth, now wishing she had kept her own counsel. "Mr. Darcy stayed for some months in Hertfordshire last autumn at the leased estate of his friend, Mr. Bingley."

"I did not know that," replied Anne. "In response to your question, I believe it is *my mother* who is set upon the marriage. "I esteem my cousin, but I do not think I wish to marry him. He is far too austere for my tastes."

It was an opinion with which Elizabeth could agree. "It does, indeed, seem like your mother is set upon it."

Anne shrugged. "I believe I have no fear. When he comes, Darcy pays me no more than civility, I am certain due to my mother's propensity to assume anything more is an indication of an imminent proposal. I have never known Darcy to do anything he does not wish, so I am certain I am safe."

"No," replied Elizabeth. "Mr. Darcy strikes me as a man who likes to have his own way."

"And he has the means to have it," replied Anne. "My mother, however, speaks of nothing else when he is here. I am confident that he has decided against visiting in order to avoid my mother's diatribes on the subject. As I am quite content, I shall not blame him."

"Then why does your mother expect it?" asked Elizabeth. She had heard from Mr. Wickham about this supposed engagement, but he had never been explicit about it. Elizabeth suspected it was mostly because he did not know himself.

"My mother insists it was an agreement she made with Lady Anne, Darcy's mother," said Anne with a shrug. "Darcy and I have never spoken of it, so I do not know what he thinks, or if there was ever such an agreement."

"But he does not appear willing to oblige your mother, so it seems he does not see it as valid."

"That much is certain. If Darcy was aware that his mother had made such an agreement, I am certain he would consider himself honor bound. He is most attentive to all those things and would never renege if his mother wished for it."

Elizabeth thought it curious, indeed, for she was aware that Mr. Darcy did not seem to care about breaking his *father's* word with respect to the bequest left to one George Wickham. Would he consider his mother's commitments to be any more binding than his father's? It was beyond comprehension.

Upon arriving at the top of the stairs, Elizabeth first returned to her room to refresh herself and stow her bonnet, but once that was accomplished, she returned to Anne's room. There, she found her friend, and she noted that Anne was in a contemplative, almost bemused, mood.

"I have never considered actually marrying my cousin," said Anne, "though at times I have wondered why not. It is not as if he is ill-favored. Do you not agree?"

Elizabeth was uncomfortable at Anne's question—she had other feelings which rendered objectivity questionable when it came to Mr. Darcy. But she could do nothing other than answer.

"Yes, he is. As handsome a man as I have ever seen."

"I wonder what it would be like." Elizabeth could sense that Anne was not talking to her, perhaps did not even remember she was there. "Being married to him could not be a trial, though he is tall and intimidating. A woman could do much worse than to be the focus of such a man's attentions."

"Perhaps," said Elizabeth. "I know that much of society looks for a marriage partner with qualities other than attraction and compatibility, but I would not wish for such a marriage."

"You prefer to have a marriage of affection?"

"My elder sister, Jane, and I have always maintained we would only marry for the deepest of love. To be tied to someone whom you disdained—could there be anything more objectionable?"

The look Anne gave her was positively mischievous. "I suppose that is why you rejected your cousin's offer?"

Starting with surprise, Elizabeth blurted: "You know of that?"

"Mr. Collins is eager to share *everything* with my mother. When he returned to Hunsford after becoming engaged to your friend, one of his first actions was to visit my mother, and one of the first words out of his mouth was how he had returned engaged, in accordance with her instructions. It was not soon after when he informed her of how you had refused, terminating his obligation to his family."

"I suppose I should have known," muttered Elizabeth.

"Yes, I dare say you should have." Anne giggled. "Though I had never met you, I was immediately impressed with your sagacity in refusing him."

Elizabeth shuddered. "No, I could never be happy with such a man for a husband. I wish for a true meeting of the minds with my future husband and will not settle for anything less."

"I can see how that would be desirable."

Though Anne fell silent, Elizabeth could see that she was considering the matter at further length, and though she did not say anything, Elizabeth wondered at her conclusions. She did not see how anyone could be happy in such a marriage, but she would never wish Anne to live by her principles if she did not share them. She had made that mistake with Charlotte.

"I would need to know Darcy better if I was to ever accept an offer," said Anne a little later.

"You said he would not offer," replied Elizabeth.

"And I still believe that. But if he *were* to offer for me, I would wish to know more of him. Of course, with my mother in attendance, I would never receive the opportunity, for she would interfere constantly."

"Perhaps you should go to London, then. You could attend events of society and culture with him and learn more of him. I have found that conversation while dancing often reveals more of a man than he would wish a lady to know. He must put some of his concentration into the steps, after all, and that lack of concentration on his words will often cause him to reveal more than he wants."

"But I have never danced!"

Elizabeth stared at Anne as if she had suddenly sprouted a second head. "You have never danced?"

It appeared like Anne was amused at Elizabeth's surprise. "You *do* remember who my mother is, do you not? Anything she deems unnecessary to my education—or more importantly, does not forward her design to see me married to Darcy—is ignored. Why should I be taught how to dance? I am to marry Darcy, so the normal rules of courtship do not apply. Besides, if I were to dance with other men, I might take a fancy to one of them, and that would never do."

Though Anne spoke in a matter of fact tone, Elizabeth could hear the bitterness inherent in it. Even more distressing, Elizabeth thought that Anne was hardly aware of it herself. It was simply another facet of her life, one which was, and could not, be changed. But underneath Anne's seeming complacency, Elizabeth wondered if there was not a burning sea of resentment, one which might flow out at any time.

"No, that will not do, indeed!" exclaimed Elizabeth, shooting to her feet. "And it is something we must remedy immediately. Please stand, if you will."

Anne was confused, but she readily rose and looked at Elizabeth askance. "Dancing is a skill every woman should learn, and I will not have you remain ignorant."

"You propose to teach me how to dance?" gasped Anne.

"I do." Elizabeth gave her a mischievous grin. "My sisters and I have often stood up with each other when there are not enough gentlemen, so while I am not an expert at the steps a man would use, I am at least competent."

"But we have no music," said Anne. Though she continued to protest, Elizabeth thought she was not averse to it—in fact, the light of interest shone in Anne's eyes, a curiosity which had often been absent, but now appeared with greater frequency.

"I have a voice, and it is tolerable for singing," replied Elizabeth.

She began to hum the tunes of a well-known and beloved dance, and she began to move in the steps. It was quite obviously a bit of a mishmash, but Anne laughed and quickly began to move with Elizabeth, her feet executing the steps where Elizabeth directed. In this pleasant way, they passed the rest of the afternoon.

Chapter VII

The next days were pleasant, and Elizabeth was certain it was largely because of Lady Catherine's absence from their lives. The lady was in high dudgeon those days, ranting about her nephew's lack of consideration and less than pleasing attention to his duty whenever they were in her company. But the initial days of her displeasure were nothing compared to the fury she displayed when Mr. Darcy returned her letter, reiterating his inability to present himself at Rosings and confirming the cancellation of his visit. The younger ladies happened to be present when it arrived, and Elizabeth thought Lady Catherine might suffer apoplexy, for her face was as red as a beet, and she stood and stormed about the room, flinging her hands wildly in the air and ranting.

Elizabeth and Anne quickly excused themselves from the room, eager to be out of her company and removing themselves as possible targets for her ire. They did not see much of Lady Catherine for the next several days, even to the extent that she sent for a tray in her rooms rather than coming to dinner. Elizabeth found she could endure the loss of Lady Catherine's society quite cheerfully.

"It has always been thus," said Anne once they had reached the safety of her room. "My mother, as you have seen, does not take well to being denied. She will brood for a few days before she regains her prior composure, and then she will act as if nothing happened."

"Such sudden rage cannot be good for her health," ventured Elizabeth.

With a sigh, Anne shook her head. "No, I suppose it is not. It is fortunate they happen infrequently, for rarely does anyone defy her to this extent. But I have worried for her."

They fell into silence and stayed that way until Anne perked up and decided she wished to dance again. Dancing was one of their most diverting amusements in those days, and Anne took every opportunity to indulge. She was not light on her feet, and Elizabeth thought that to be due to a lack of exercise, for she was not heavyset or ponderous. But as they practiced, it was clear she was a quick study, for she quickly became, if not proficient, at least competent, though Elizabeth could not know how she would do in a ballroom with music playing.

Another activity they discovered was music. Elizabeth, though she could never consider herself extraordinarily talented, could play with sufficient skill, and one day when they were talking on the subject, Anne expressed an interest.

"I assume your mother has never given you leave to learn?"

"My health does not allow for it." By now, Elizabeth was used to these matter of fact statements from Anne. But recently they had been colored by a hint of exasperation, and more than a hint of resentment.

"I do not know how much health is required to simply sit on a bench at the pianoforte," replied Elizabeth. "Is there one in the house we could use without exciting your mother's suspicion?"

Anne considered it. "There is one in Mrs. Jenkinson's old room. We would have to be careful, as there will be servants in that part of the house."

"If we close the door and the servants become accustomed to me playing, word should not get back to your mother."

"Exactly."

Thus, they began to visit Mrs. Jenkinson's room. The first few times, Elizabeth played for Anne, who enjoyed hearing her, but when they thought the servants were becoming accustomed to hearing the sounds echoing through the halls, Elizabeth began to give Anne tutelage, showing her some simple exercises which she could use to increase the dexterity and strength of her fingers. The progress was necessarily slow—one did not learn to play overnight, and Elizabeth did not consider herself an excellent teacher. Of course, it would have been foolhardy to assume word of their frequent presence in Mrs. Jenkinson's room would not reach Lady Catherine's ears.

"I understand you have been using the pianoforte below stairs," observed Lady Catherine one day. She had finally emerged from her self-imposed exile exactly as Anne said she would. Even an oblique reference to her nephew would bring a scowl, so they avoided that subject at all costs.

"Yes, Mother," replied Anne. "Elizabeth plays for me—I do so enjoy it, for she plays very well, indeed."

Lady Catherine grunted. "She could do with more practice, for one can never become proficient without the benefit of frequent practice."

"Then Elizabeth is taking your advice seriously."

The look with which Lady Catherine pierced her daughter suggested suspicion. "You now refer to her by her Christian name?"

"Of course," replied Anne, never batting an eyelash. "She is near to my own age, unlike Mrs. Jenkinson. It is simpler to refer to her informally."

"And does she refer to you in a similar manner?"

"We maintain formality for the benefit of the servants, Mother."

It was clear Lady Catherine wished to rebuke them further, but instead she changed the subject again. "Why do you not play in the music room then, Miss Bennet?"

"We thought it would be better to play below stairs, so we did not disturb you. Miss de Bourgh and I both understand the extensive work you do for Rosings and the surrounding community."

There was no better way to gain Lady Catherine's approval than to flatter her vanity. The lady's expression softened at Elizabeth's words, and she nodded with evident approval.

"Very well. But I would appreciate some music in the main rooms of the house as well."

"Of course," replied Elizabeth. "I would be happy to play for you in the evenings."

The two young ladies were soon dismissed, and they returned to Anne's room, neither able to stifle their giggles as they walked. "You have become adept at deflecting my mother," whispered Anne as they entered her room.

"It is not difficult," replied Elizabeth. "In some ways, redirecting her is similar to how I would do the same with Mr. Collins, or even my own mother."

"Lizzy!" gasped Anne. "Did you just compare my mother to her sycophantic parson?"

"Perhaps I did," replied Elizabeth, and they both collapsed with laughter. "You have to own the likeness!"

"I suppose it is true, though I will say my mother is more intelligent than Mr. Collins."

"That is not difficult, Mr. Collins being what he is."

Anne laughed again, but then in an imperious imitation of her mother, she rose and held out her hand. "Come, it is time for my dance lesson."

They had only been engaged in the activity for some few moments before Anne's maid entered the room from her dressing room. Anne halted her steps and regarded Laura with wide eyes. They had taken great care to avoid notice of any of the servants, but they had both simply forgotten to check her rooms before they began.

"Laura!" exclaimed Anne. "We did not know you were here."

"Yes, mum," said the girl. "I was inspecting your dresses to ensure there are none which require washing."

Anne's eyes darted nervously at Elizabeth before returning to the maid. "I hope word of this . . . incident will not make it back to my mother."

The maid hesitated, and Elizabeth could see in her eyes something that she had not expected—sympathy for Anne.

"You understand I would lose my position if Lady Catherine were to learn that I knew of this and did not report it."

"I do understand," replied Anne. "But she will not. I do not intend for her to find out, and even if she does, I will ensure you are not involved."

It was clear to Elizabeth that the maid had no confidence in Anne's ability to resist her mother. But she nodded her head and agreed, prompting a smile of thanks from Anne.

"But you should be aware that none of the other servants will keep your secret. Should any of them become aware of this, Lady Catherine will know of it instantly."

"I believe we have apprehended that fact," replied Anne. "We will take care."

The incident highlighted Anne's continuing hesitance to assert herself, frustrating Elizabeth in the process. She did not wish for there to be argument and disharmony at Rosings, but she was coming to the opinion that if they continued in this manner, it was approaching all the same.

As Elizabeth was coming to know Anne better, she was finding that she liked her very much, indeed. Anne was an estimable sort of girl, and even though her ability to interact with others was at times rudimentary, and she often betrayed an imperiousness about her which could only be attributed to her mother, she was also kind, thoughtful, and displayed an eagerness to please, which itself was quite pleasing. Elizabeth only wished she could be more assertive, could direct her life in a manner which *she* saw fit, without constantly bowing to her mother's demands. But Anne was not yet willing to draw Lady Catherine's attention or risk her ire. Given what Elizabeth was teaching her, she thought it would be better to weather the explosion sooner, rather than later. In the end, she could only practice patience and attempt to coax her toward more independence.

The other problem Elizabeth was facing was that the time for her departure was quickly approaching, and though she could not have fathomed it when she first came to Rosings, she was loath to leave. Or perhaps it was more truthful to say she did not wish to leave Anne — to Rosings she had no particular attachment. When she mentioned this concern to Anne, she was confronted with such a look of dejection, she was quick to offer to stay.

"I can, perhaps, stay a few weeks longer. But there will come a time when my father will require my return. He has already written of it."

"I would be grateful if you could stay," said Anne. "I have come to rely on your company."

So, it was settled. Elizabeth wrote to her uncle, requesting that he allow her to stay two more weeks, and he responded, agreeing with her request, but noting that her father might call her home at any time.

The subject of Anne's continued timidity continued to prey on Elizabeth's mind, and it was not long before she wished for another opinion. Speaking to Anne of it was, of course, of little use, but there was one in the neighborhood on whom Elizabeth could rely to keep her confidence. Thus, on a day when Anne decided to nap in the afternoon — such occurrences had been rare in recent days — Elizabeth left Rosings and made her way to the parsonage to confer with her friend.

Charlotte greeted and welcomed her, pleasure evident in her voice and posture, and even Maria seemed happy to see her. It was the work of a few moments to convince the younger girl that Elizabeth had confidences to share with her sister, and she withdrew with cheerful willingness, retiring to the back lawn to walk in the gardens.

"I have heard you have extended your stay," said Charlotte when her sister had gone. "Considering how you dreaded going to Rosings in the first place, I find it to be rather surprising. I had thought you would be impatient to be gone."

"You would have been correct," replied Elizabeth. "But I have learned certain things which render my presence at Rosings desirable. In fact, I have come seeking your advice on a matter which has been troubling me."

"Oh?" asked Charlotte, one eyebrow raised in surprise.

So, Elizabeth told her friend what had been happening these past weeks, informing her of her new understanding of Anne's character. She left all mention of Mr. Darcy's failure to attend them out as it was irrelevant, but she was careful to inform Charlotte of all her observations about Miss de Bourgh, her worries for her, and her desire that Anne become more independent.

When she finished, Charlotte sat quietly for some moments, contemplating what Elizabeth had told her. There was little Charlotte could do—Elizabeth understood this. She simply hoped that Charlotte might have an insight that Elizabeth had not considered.

"I am not surprised," replied Charlotte at length. "I have always thought there was some greater depth to Miss de Bourgh that could not be seen on the surface." Then she turned a mischievous eye on Elizabeth. "I am less surprised that you believe it your duty to rescue her from her glass prison. Is she not like the pathetic animals you always wished to help when you were a child?"

"Charlotte!" exclaimed Elizabeth, but her friend only laughed.

"You must own there is a similarity, Lizzy. Your romantic nature has always led you to champion the cause of the less fortunate. It is what has made you such a wonderful gentleman's daughter, as evidenced by your care of Longbourn's tenants. It is part of what will make you an excellent gentleman's wife."

Elizabeth had never been certain she would ever marry, but she shook the thought off as irrelevant. She was not concerned with marrying, at present—the subject at hand was what to do about Anne's situation.

"I am not certain what you *can* do, Lizzy," replied Charlotte when pressed. "It is up to Anne. While I agree with you that it would be desirable for her to learn independence, if she does not wish it, you cannot force her. The only actions you may take are to continue to encourage her." Charlotte smiled. "If I know anything of your determination, you will be successful in goading her toward freedom."

"Goading her?" exclaimed Elizabeth.

Charlotte laughed. "Is that not what it is? Lizzy Bennet does not take no for an answer. I believe, in the end, Miss de Bourgh will have little choice."

"I am grateful that your opinion of me is so transcendent," replied Elizabeth, feeling cross with her friend.

"You know I have the highest opinion of you, Lizzy. I cannot become involved, of course, for my husband would not appreciate any position in opposition to Lady Catherine. But I am happy to host you and Miss de Bourgh whenever convenient, so that you may work your magic away from Rosings."

"I knew you would not be able to act yourself, Charlotte," replied Elizabeth. "I just wished for a sympathetic ear and, perhaps, a little advice."

"Then my advice is to continue to be her friend and show her what life can be without her domineering mother standing over her. There is nothing you can do for her which would be of greater value, I am sure."

With those words, Elizabeth was forced to be content, for at that moment Mr. Collins walked into the room.

"Ah, Cousin Elizabeth," said he as he entered, a great beaming smile fixed on her, one such as she had never thought to see, considering her refusal of his suit. "I can see you have come to visit my dear wife. How are you today?"

"Very well, indeed, Mr. Collins," said Elizabeth.

"Excellent!" exclaimed the man. "And the fair Miss de Bourgh? I hope she is well and enjoying your company?"

"I believe so," replied Elizabeth. "Miss de Bourgh is napping at present, and since I was free of obligations, I had thought to visit with Charlotte. It is unfortunate my stay at your house was interrupted, but Miss de Bourgh is amiable, and I am happy to be in her presence."

Clearly, nothing she could have said would have been greeted with greater approval. "Yes, she is! And I am happy that you have taken so well to her company. I visit with Lady Catherine frequently, as I am certain you understand, and though the lady does not say much of how you are performing your duties, I have seen you on occasion with Miss de Bourgh, especially when you ride in her phaeton, and I can see you are getting on famously.

"I am particularly grateful for this, as Miss de Bourgh has wanted for companionship her own age, and has benefited from your offered camaraderie. I thank you, Cousin, for being what she needs in such a trying time."

Though she was surprised that Mr. Collins had recognized Anne's need for friendship, Elizabeth could only smile and acknowledge his thanks. "I am quite happy to do it, Mr. Collins. She is a wonderful girl, and I find myself quite happy to be in her presence."

"My dear Charlotte has also informed me that you have lengthened your stay to be of use to Miss de Bourgh."

"I have," said Elizabeth.

"That is kind of you, for I know you must long to return to your family."

"I do," replied Elizabeth. "But I was happy to do it when she asked. The only part of the situation I repine is that I have not been able to visit with Charlotte nearly so much as I would have liked."

Mr. Collins nodded with sage agreement. "It is a pity, to be certain. But allow me to inform you now that we would be happy to extend the invitation again next year, or at any time of your choosing. We have been quite happy to have you, and I cannot but think that Miss de Bourgh will be eager to renew your friendship at that time."

The visit continued for some few more moments, and Elizabeth was treated to all the surreal astonishment of being the recipient of Mr. Collins's approval. It was clear that her refusal of his suit had been forgotten, replaced with his gratitude at her ability to befriend Anne without upsetting Lady Catherine. That it made his life easier was not a fact to which Elizabeth was insensible, but though it did make her think a little better of him, she still found his society tiresome. It was not many more minutes before she excused herself to return to Rosings. In a final bit of civility, Mr. Collins offered to produce his gig and drive her back, but she was allowed to leave when she assured him she would appreciate the short walk.

When Elizabeth returned to Rosings, she was confronted by Lady Catherine, and if Mr. Collins had witnessed it, he might not have been so confident of her favor with the great lady. She was standing by the front entrance to the estate, and Elizabeth could feel the heat of her gaze upon her as she climbed the stairs. The lady's gaze raked over her, measured and deliberate, and when the lady's eyes found hers, Elizabeth could see the exasperation in them.

"I see you have been out walking again. Might I assume you have spent the whole of the afternoon wandering dirty lanes, your hair becoming disheveled in all this wind?"

In reality, Elizabeth's hair had not become ruffled at all, for there was only a hint of a wind. Of course, Lady Catherine would not appreciate being contradicted in such a manner.

"I have just come from Hunsford where I visited with Charlotte and Mr. Collins. If you recall, that *is* the reason I came to Kent in the first place."

The lady sniffed with barely concealed disdain. "I suppose it is. And how are the Collinses?"

"Very well," replied Elizabeth. "Mr. Collins invited me to return again next year, as I have not had much time with Charlotte."

If possible, Lady Catherine's gaze became even more pointed. "You are not leaving yet."

"Actually, my original departure date was set for next week," replied Elizabeth, noting the lady's increasing displeasure. "But Anne requested that I put off my departure, and I have obliged her. I shall stay for another two weeks complete."

At first, Lady Catherine appeared as if she would reply to Elizabeth's suggestion that she would not stay indefinitely, but she decided not to at the last moment. "Thank you for your civility."

It was, as thanks go, rather lukewarm in nature, but it was the best Lady Catherine could muster, so Elizabeth voiced her pleasure in obliging her.

"It seems clear that Anne enjoys your presence."

There was a probing quality in Lady Catherine's statement which concerned Elizabeth. But her courage in the face of intimidation would not be suppressed, and she was able to reply:

"I believe she does. I, in turn, have come to appreciate Miss de Bourgh very much, indeed. You should be proud, Lady Catherine, for she is a wonderful woman."

"Of course, she is," snapped Lady Catherine. "With her lineage and upbringing, she could not be anything else."

There was nothing to say to that, so Elizabeth only nodded.

"Very well, Miss Bennet. I only ask you refrain from scampering about the country at all hours, more likely than not returning with some impurity clinging to you. Anne is, as you must know, of very delicate health, and I will not have it compromised by your wild ways."

Then the lady turned and strode away, leaving Elizabeth all bemused, watching her as she departed. There was no purpose in even considering a response to Lady Catherine's ridiculous words about Elizabeth's habits, so she shunted them to the side. Of greater importance, it seemed like Lady Catherine was still unaware of the true state of her daughter's friendship with Elizabeth, and for that she could only be relieved. She would not wish to consider how the lady might act, for surely she would consider Elizabeth's actions improper, reaching for a sphere to which she had no right.

Chapter VIII

As the time of her residence at Rosings Park wore on, Elizabeth became aware of another problem which had begun to manifest itself. The signs of Anne's resentment for her mother that she had noted previously were now making a more frequent appearance, and Elizabeth wondered if it might not boil over before long.

Elizabeth could not see any way to navigate the shoals of this coming confrontation, and extricating themselves from Rosings did not seem to be an option. When she had come to Rosings and begun her campaign to see Anne become more independent, she had not considered the possibility of a falling out between mother and daughter. Rather, she had thought that if Anne showed her new confidence by degrees over time, Lady Catherine would become accustomed to it, and though she might not like it, she would accept it.

But Anne remained stubbornly unwilling to contradict her mother, and the two ladies behaved the same way around each other as they ever had. However, Elizabeth was privy to more caustic comments the young woman made about her mother and noted annoyance simmering in her eyes when Lady Catherine made her pronouncements, particularly those that concerned Anne. It was like waiting for a volcano to erupt—the smoke was visible on the horizon, and the earth rumbled and groaned with the weight of the pressure built within. One could not be certain when the explosion would come but knew it would be spectacular when it did.

On an evening when the three ladies retired to the sitting-room after dinner, Elizabeth began to notice the first hint of overt discord between mother and daughter. Lady Catherine had been in a foul mood that day, and though Elizabeth could not be sure, a letter clutched in her hand seemed to be the reason, leading her to wonder if Lady Catherine had once again written to Mr. Darcy and been rebuffed. Whatever the reason, there was little that could satisfy her — dinner had been overcooked and bland, the room was too cool for her comfort, and a host of other complaints issued forth from her mouth. Anne and Elizabeth attempted to ignore her by conversing between themselves quietly, but it was impossible to disregard the woman, as she demanded their attention.

"When you are speaking in my sitting-room," said the lady, eyeing them with displeasure, "you will speak for all the company to hear. I will not have you whispering like a pair of schoolgirls."

It was fortunate, indeed, that Lady Catherine could not see her daughter rolling her eyes. As it was, Lady Catherine did not allow them to respond just yet.

"It shows a remarkable lack of manners, Miss Bennet. I am certain your mother would have taught you better. Of what have you been speaking? You must allow me my share of the conversation."

"I only mentioned the letter I received from my sister, Lady Catherine," replied Elizabeth. She attempted to tamp down the annoyance by reminding herself that she certainly had not whispered to Anne when she had mentioned her sister's letter and the lack of cheer inherent in it.

"That is not appropriate sitting-room conversation. Why, Anne does not even know your sister, and I cannot imagine a situation in which she would ever be introduced. Do not bore her with accounts of people she cannot possibly know."

"On the contrary, Mother," replied Anne, "I am interested to hear about Elizabeth's sisters. Jane Bennet sounds like an estimable lady, and one I would consider it a pleasure to gain an introduction."

It was the first time Elizabeth had ever heard Anne contradict something her mother said, and she almost cringed because of it. Lady Catherine's eyes bulged at so hearing her daughter speak, and for a moment she seemed at a loss for how to respond.

"Of course, it is not a topic of conversation of which we can speak at length," continued Miss de Bourgh in a more conciliatory tone. "I do not know the lady, after all. Of what would you prefer to speak, Mother?"

Lady Catherine's gaze was fixed on Anne, and Elizabeth could see the suspicion raining down on her. When she looked at Elizabeth herself, the expression became harder.

"Perhaps conversation is not needed. Miss Bennet, you will oblige us by opening the pianoforte and playing until we retire."

Grateful the explosion had been averted for the present, Elizabeth acquiesced and sat at the instrument. She began a song with which she was familiar, and while she played she noted that Lady Catherine was speaking, and though Anne murmured a few replies here and there, for the most part she was silent. Elizabeth was uncertain Lady Catherine noted anything in her behavior, but to Elizabeth it was obvious Anne wished to be anywhere but where she was.

At length, the pianoforte was closed, and the ladies retired. "It is time for you to go to bed, Anne," said she in her most imperious tone. "You know you require your rest."

"Of course, Mother," replied Anne.

Lady Catherine was satisfied with that, for she led them upstairs toward their bedchambers, but as they were walking up the stairs, Anne caught Elizabeth's eye and motioned toward her room with her head, a clear invitation for Elizabeth to join her. It was an act of furtive defiance, and one Elizabeth could not have imagined Anne perpetrating when she had come to Rosings, and for a moment Elizabeth thought to shake her head in the negative. But she was here for Anne's benefit, not Lady Catherine's, and Elizabeth decided to attend her friend, nodding her agreement.

Once in her room, Elizabeth accepted Tilly's assistance to ready herself for bed, and then dismissed the girl. She waited some few moments for her to be gone, and then went to the door, opened it a crack, and looked out into the hall. There was no one in evidence—the candles had been extinguished, and the hallway was silent, shadows running its length from the window at the far end. Taking care to remain silent, Elizabeth slipped from the room, closing the door behind her, and made her way the short distance to Anne's door, letting herself in. Then she made her way through the sitting-room to the door of Anne's bedchamber.

"Elizabeth!" exclaimed Anne, though Elizabeth was grateful the girl had thought to moderate the volume of her voice. "I thought you would never come!" Anne was dressed in a nightgown and robe, the same as Elizabeth, and Laura was not in evidence.

"I had to dress for the night and send Tilly away," replied Elizabeth, joining Anne and sitting on the bed. "I did not wish to encounter a servant and be forced to explain why I was wandering the halls."

Anne nodded. "Yes, we would not wish to be discovered by my mother. She has been in high dudgeon today; anything contrary to her designs would no doubt be looked on with extreme disapproval."

The exasperation and discontent were evident in Anne's tone, and her voice was pitched higher than Elizabeth wished, especially if they meant to remain undetected.

"Your mother will not hear us?" asked Elizabeth. "Will the light not be visible from the window?"

"There have been times when I have kept a candle on at night," replied Anne. She ducked her head in embarrassment. "When I was young, I was terrified of the dark, and often kept a candle burning. Mother did not mind if I kept it away from the curtains and where it would not start a fire. Though I do not do it much anymore, there are times when the flame comforts me.

"Besides," said Anne with a giggle, "I believe my mother sleeps very soundly. Do you know that her bedchamber is on the other side of this wall?" She brushed her knuckles against the wall behind the head of her bed. "At times, I have heard her snoring."

The image of a high-born lady such as Lady Catherine snoring loudly in her sleep struck Elizabeth as amusing, and the two girls descended into giggles. Of course, that was the exact moment when a snort—which must have been deafening on the other side of the wall—reached their ears and set them to laughing once again.

"It appears you are correct," said Elizabeth, trying to stifle her laughter.

"Perhaps she heard us and was voicing her displeasure concerning such a notion," said Anne.

"Please, do not even suggest such a thing!" replied Elizabeth.

They indulged in their mirth for some few more moments before Anne once again spoke.

"Mother had another letter from Darcy today. He has refused to oblige her by coming here, and I do not blame him. Mother is considering going to London in order to put me in his path again."

"Oh," said Elizabeth. "She is determined, though I suppose I should not be surprised."

"I dissuaded her by pointing out the house in town is likely uninhabitable." Anne gave Elizabeth a wan smile. "We have not visited it in many years, and Mother will not hear of leasing it out to anyone. I believe there is a small staff there who looks after the place and keeps it clean, but I cannot imagine the condition it is in. Of course, my mother only turned it around and said we may just stay at Darcy's house."

Anne sighed and sank back against her pillows. "I wish she would let go of this doomed fantasy of hers. Darcy does not wish to marry me, and I have no wish to marry him. But it is clear that only his marriage to another will induce her to desist."

There was nothing to say in response, so Elizabeth allowed Anne to simply continue to speak, to be a bearer of the woman's burdens along with her. Elizabeth could well understand Anne's reluctance to marry the proud and disagreeable Mr. Darcy. It was something she would never consider herself.

Something in her expression must have alerted Anne to her thoughts, for she fixed her gaze on Elizabeth's face, a slight frown creasing her forehead.

"Elizabeth," said she, "I have often had the impression that you are not fond of my cousin. Has he done something to offend you?"

Surprised, Elizabeth said: "I have not been in Mr. Darcy's company for above four months, Anne. I am sure I feel nothing for him, for he is naught but an acquaintance."

"Your reaction whenever he is mentioned gives the lie to your assertion," replied Anne. When Elizabeth made to protest, Anne shook her head. "I do not wish to force a confidence, but it seemed to me you were subjected to some foul scent when I mentioned him just now. I have been raised by a woman who loves the sound of her own voice, and because my opinion is not often solicited, I have made it a practice to study those about me. I am not a great observer of others, but I can often tell by their reactions what they are thinking, and I have noticed your distaste for Darcy several times. Shall you not share your experiences with me?"

Elizabeth was hesitant to sink Mr. Darcy's character to his cousin, but Anne asked in so sincere a manner that she felt she could not demur. As a result, Elizabeth soon found herself relating their first meeting, including Mr. Darcy's slight against her.

"Not handsome enough to tempt me, he said." Elizabeth attempted to make light of it, using a playful tone to imitate Mr. Darcy's stern and unyielding one. "I was slighted by other men, and he would not give me any notice because of it. I have never been subject to such incivility in my life!"

"I dare say you have not." Anne directed a strange look at Elizabeth. "I can imagine that as first impressions go, it was not a good one. Darcy was very wrong to say it. But I wonder why it affected you so."

"Should it not?" demanded Elizabeth. "What woman would like to hear such things said about herself in so public a forum as a dance hall?"

"No one, of course. But Elizabeth, you are a beautiful girl—why would such sentiments affect you? If Darcy cannot see your beauty, why should you concern yourself?"

The words caught Elizabeth off guard, and her cheeks bloomed as she gaped, wondering of what Anne was speaking. "I am not beautiful, Anne. I am naught but a country girl, and though I believe I am pleasantly featured, I do not lay claim to any beauty. My sister Jane is the beauty in the Bennet family."

Though Anne did not respond directly to Elizabeth's denial, the look she returned was mysterious in nature, and it made Elizabeth feel quite cross.

"Elizabeth," said she in a tone of exaggerated patience, "though I was not there, of course, it seems to me that my cousin's words were spoken in ill humor. I cannot think that he truly meant to disparage you. It is possible he was simply attempting to induce his friend to leave him alone. It seems to me that you have taken this much more to heart than you ought."

"You know your cousin well enough to divine his intentions?" asked Elizabeth, challenging her friend's perception. "This was not his only affront, Anne. He was rude to all my friends and neighbors and gave the impression that he felt himself to be above the company."

"Was he not? I do not defend him, Elizabeth, but he *is* the grandson of an earl and the nephew of one. I do not know the extent of his fortune, but I know that Pemberley is a vast estate, and he has other wealth besides. Should he not feel a little superiority?"

"Perhaps he does. But should it be displayed for all the company? Should he set himself up as a paragon, looking down on all those beneath him with contempt and ridicule?"

Anne only shook her head, though mischief gleamed in her eyes. "My mother would find nothing amiss with his behavior."

When Elizabeth rolled her eyes, Anne laughed, forcing Elizabeth to join her.

"As you know, I am not close to my cousin," continued Anne. "Though I have known him all my life, I do not *know* him well, for reasons of which you are aware. But for all this, I have never known Darcy to be anything other than scrupulously proper. My other cousin, Anthony Fitzwilliam, who is my uncle's son, has often lamented that Darcy is far too rigid for a young man of his situation. It was wrong of him, indeed, to slight you and to behave in such a way. But it is quite different from what I understand of his character.

"Consider this: one of his avowed closest friends is Mr. Bingley, is it not?" Elizabeth was forced to concede Anne's point. "Then I hardly think that he would consider your friends, who are gently born, even if they are not wealthy, to be inferior to his friend, who is, after all, the son of a tradesman. Does it not strike you as odd if he does?"

"That is part of what frustrates me when I try to take Mr. Darcy's likeness. His actions and words are contradictory, and the accounts I have heard of him do not make sense."

Anne's interest was piqued at Elizabeth's statement, for she asked: "Accounts of Darcy? My understanding was that you only met him for a brief time last year, and his only friends with whom you are acquainted are Mr. Bingley and his sisters." Anne shook her head. "And since Mr. Bingley is, by all accounts, an amiable, friendly sort of man, and one who looks up to Darcy, and his sisters are grasping social climbers, I doubt any of them would criticize him. Have you met someone else who is acquainted with Darcy?"

"Yes, I have, Anne." Elizabeth paused, wishing she had held her tongue. She tried to deflect Anne by stating: "But I am reluctant to speak of matters which may sink your estimation of your cousin."

"But now you have engaged my interest. You cannot refuse to elucidate."

Though Elizabeth remained reluctant, she could see no way to refuse to oblige her companion, and she wished she had not opened her mouth. What cared she if Anne thought her dislike for Mr. Darcy was due to naught but vanity? Surely it could not affect her.

"Very well," said Elizabeth when Anne pressed her again. "I *have* met another who is acquainted with Mr. Darcy, and his story renders your cousin in an entirely different light."

Anne appeared quite intrigued and motioned for Elizabeth to continue.

"Not long after Mr. Darcy had come to Hertfordshire, a young man by the name of Mr. Wickham joined the regiment of militia which was quartered there for the winter. Mr. Wickham, I discovered, is the son of old Mr. Darcy's steward. He is an amiable man, one who is friendly to all and esteemed by many. Mr. Wickham has also been wronged grievously by your cousin."

"Tell me," prompted Anne.

Elizabeth did so with a will, the old feeling of offense on Mr. Wickham's behalf welling up within her. "It seems that Mr. Darcy's father wished to provide for Mr. Wickham, and he left a valuable family living in his will. But when the living fell vacant, Mr. Darcy refused to present Mr. Wickham with the living, reneging on his father's promise."

"And had Mr. Wickham taken orders? And for that matter, how was Darcy able to flout his father's instructions, which were backed by the legal authority of a will?"

Taken aback, Elizabeth could only stammer: "I have no idea if Mr. Wickham took orders. I imagine he did not, given how Mr. Darcy refused to present him with the living. As for the will, I was told that there was enough informality in the bequest to give him no hope from an appeal to the law. A man who was dedicated to his father's memory and intent upon abiding by his wishes could not have doubted, but Mr. Darcy chose to doubt."

It was not long before Anne's scrutiny began to make Elizabeth uncomfortable, for though she did not speak, she regarded Elizabeth for a long moment. Unwilling to allow her friend to intimidate her, Elizabeth returned it with a raised eyebrow, daring her to contradict. Thus, Elizabeth was surprised by Anne's laugh.

"Do not be offended by the observation, Elizabeth, but you almost reminded me of my mother. She, too, does not appreciate it when someone challenges her." Elizabeth was, indeed, offended, but Anne continued to speak. "I will confess that I know nothing of this situation. I do not know Mr. Wickham personally, nor do I know what was contained in my uncle's will. But there are a few things I would like to point out that do not quite make sense to me."

Elizabeth gave her a curt nod, at which Anne laughed again.

"The first is that I am confident of Darcy's character and his knowledge of his duty. Darcy and his father were very close. If his father wished to provide for Mr. Wickham, he would have informed his son, and I do not doubt that Darcy would have felt honor bound to follow his father's wishes.

"The second thing I would like to mention is that there is something that does not quite add up in Mr. Wickham's story. I do not quite know what it is, but it disturbs me all the same. What possible reason could Darcy have for denying his friend his support? I cannot fathom it. But I also cannot but wonder why Mr. Wickham would have shared such a personal matter with you. I have the impression that he did not know you long before he shared it?"

"No, he did not," replied Elizabeth, feeling much subdued. "In fact, he informed me on my second meeting with him. The subject came up because I had noticed both men's reactions upon seeing the other and could immediately discern that theirs was not a cordial relationship."

"Then it was doubly improper for him to have spoken of such a subject. I have not much experience with meeting new acquaintances, but I could never have imagined of speaking of some of the confidences we have shared recently when we were first introduced."

Elizabeth was forced to concede that Anne was correct.

"Finally, though I will stress again that I do not know Mr. Wickham myself, I *have* heard something of him. My cousin—Anthony Fitzwilliam—who is a colonel in the regulars, visits Rosings with Darcy every spring. I have heard them speak of Wickham, and when I asked, Fitzwilliam informed me that he was not a subject for polite company."

"Does he know Mr. Wickham himself?" asked Elizabeth. "Or has he just had his account from Mr. Darcy?"

"I believe he does. Mr. Wickham and Darcy were raised together as boys, and Fitzwilliam was one of Darcy's most treasured companions. And Fitzwilliam did not speak of Mr. Wickham as if he had heard of him through another. I believe they are quite well acquainted, indeed."

"I hardly know what to think," said Elizabeth. It felt like her eyes were being forced open, and though she still could not consider Mr. Darcy an agreeable man, what Anne had suggested of Mr. Wickham made too much sense. In fact, Elizabeth wondered why she had never considered it herself.

"Darcy is not a bad man, Elizabeth," said Anne quietly. "Yes, I have observed a rigid formality of his manners, and I understand that he can be haughty and aloof, but I have heard he is esteemed by his friends and considered by all to be a good, liberal man." Anne paused and directed a wan smile at Elizabeth. "And do not allow my mother to hear you speaking of Darcy in such a manner. She would not appreciate it."

Elizabeth attempted a smile in return, but it felt rather sickly. Anne seemed to notice this, for she patted Elizabeth's shoulder. "Do not concern yourself, Elizabeth. Fitzwilliam claims that Darcy is adept at displaying himself to his worst advantage. I am certain you are not the only one to have a poor opinion of him.

"Now, if you do not mind, I believe it is time to retire."

"Of course, Anne."

Elizabeth returned to her room and made herself ready for her bed, but when she lay down on it, her thoughts continued to be full of the conversation she had just had with Anne. A part of her longed to disregard Anne's assertions—after all, Anne had confessed that she did not know her cousin well. Might she not be incorrect about Mr. Wickham?

But Elizabeth was nothing if not truthful with herself, and she knew it would be a mistake to disregard what they had discussed. There were many facets of the situation, and though she did not wish to think of it now, she knew it was likely these thoughts would keep her awake much of the night. As the time of her residence at Rosings Park wore on, Elizabeth became aware of another problem which had begun to manifest itself. The signs of Anne's resentment for her mother that she had noted previously were now making a more frequent appearance, and Elizabeth wondered if it might not boil over before long.

Elizabeth could not see any way to navigate the shoals of this coming confrontation, and extricating themselves from Rosings did not seem to be an option. When she had come to Rosings and begun her campaign to see Anne become more independent, she had not considered the possibility of a falling out between mother and daughter. Rather, she had thought that if Anne showed her new confidence by degrees over time, Lady Catherine would become accustomed to it, and though she might not like it, she would accept it.

But Anne remained stubbornly unwilling to contradict her mother, and the two ladies behaved the same way around each other as they ever had. However, Elizabeth was privy to more caustic comments the young woman made about her mother and noted annoyance simmering in her eyes when Lady Catherine made her pronouncements, particularly those that concerned Anne. It was like waiting for a volcano to erupt—the smoke was visible on the horizon, and the earth rumbled and groaned with the weight of the pressure built within. One could not be certain when the explosion would come but knew it would be spectacular when it did.

On an evening when the three ladies retired to the sitting-room after dinner, Elizabeth began to notice the first hint of overt discord between mother and daughter. Lady Catherine had been in a foul mood that day, and though Elizabeth could not be sure, a letter clutched in her hand seemed to be the reason, leading her to wonder if Lady Catherine had once again written to Mr. Darcy and been rebuffed. Whatever the reason, there was little that could satisfy her—

dinner had been overcooked and bland, the room was too cool for her comfort, and a host of other complaints issued forth from her mouth. Anne and Elizabeth attempted to ignore her by conversing between themselves quietly, but it was impossible to disregard the woman, as she demanded their attention.

"When you are speaking in my sitting-room," said the lady, eyeing them with displeasure, "you will speak for all the company to hear. I will not have you whispering like a pair of schoolgirls."

It was fortunate, indeed, that Lady Catherine could not see her daughter rolling her eyes. As it was, Lady Catherine did not allow them to respond just yet.

"It shows a remarkable lack of manners, Miss Bennet. I am certain your mother would have taught you better. Of what have you been speaking? You must allow me my share of the conversation."

"I only mentioned the letter I received from my sister, Lady Catherine," replied Elizabeth. She attempted to tamp down the annoyance by reminding herself that she certainly had not whispered to Anne when she had mentioned her sister's letter and the lack of cheer inherent in it.

"That is not appropriate sitting-room conversation. Why, Anne does not even know your sister, and I cannot imagine a situation in which she would ever be introduced. Do not bore her with accounts of people she cannot possibly know."

"On the contrary, Mother," replied Anne, "I am interested to hear about Elizabeth's sisters. Jane Bennet sounds like an estimable lady, and one I would consider it a pleasure to gain an introduction."

It was the first time Elizabeth had ever heard Anne contradict something her mother said, and she almost cringed because of it. Lady Catherine's eyes bulged at so hearing her daughter speak, and for a moment she seemed at a loss for how to respond.

"Of course, it is not a topic of conversation of which we can speak at length," continued Miss de Bourgh in a more conciliatory tone. "I do not know the lady, after all. Of what would you prefer to speak, Mother?"

Lady Catherine's gaze was fixed on Anne, and Elizabeth could see the suspicion raining down on her. When she looked at Elizabeth herself, the expression became harder.

"Perhaps conversation is not needed. Miss Bennet, you will oblige us by opening the pianoforte and playing until we retire."

Grateful the explosion had been averted for the present, Elizabeth acquiesced and sat at the instrument. She began a song with which she was familiar, and while she played she noted that Lady Catherine was speaking, and though Anne murmured a few replies here and there, for the most part she was silent. Elizabeth was uncertain Lady Catherine noted anything in her behavior, but to Elizabeth it was obvious Anne wished to be anywhere but where she was.

At length, the pianoforte was closed, and the ladies retired. "It is time for you to go to bed, Anne," said she in her most imperious tone. "You know you require your rest."

"Of course, Mother," replied Anne.

Lady Catherine was satisfied with that, for she led them upstairs toward their bedchambers, but as they were walking up the stairs, Anne caught Elizabeth's eye and motioned toward her room with her head, a clear invitation for Elizabeth to join her. It was an act of furtive defiance, and one Elizabeth could not have imagined Anne perpetrating when she had come to Rosings, and for a moment Elizabeth thought to shake her head in the negative. But she was here for Anne's benefit, not Lady Catherine's, and Elizabeth decided to attend her friend, nodding her agreement.

Once in her room, Elizabeth accepted Tilly's assistance to ready herself for bed, and then dismissed the girl. She waited some few moments for her to be gone, and then went to the door, opened it a crack, and looked out into the hall. There was no one in evidence—the candles had been extinguished, and the hallway was silent, shadows running its length from the window at the far end. Taking care to remain silent, Elizabeth slipped from the room, closing the door behind her, and made her way the short distance to Anne's door, letting herself in. Then she made her way through the sitting-room to the door of Anne's bedchamber.

"Elizabeth!" exclaimed Anne, though Elizabeth was grateful the girl had thought to moderate the volume of her voice. "I thought you would never come!" Anne was dressed in a nightgown and robe, the same as Elizabeth, and Laura was not in evidence.

"I had to dress for the night and send Tilly away," replied Elizabeth, joining Anne and sitting on the bed. "I did not wish to encounter a servant and be forced to explain why I was wandering the halls."

Anne nodded. "Yes, we would not wish to be discovered by my mother. She has been in high dudgeon today; anything contrary to her designs would no doubt be looked on with extreme disapproval."

The exasperation and discontent were evident in Anne's tone, and her voice was pitched higher than Elizabeth wished, especially if they meant to remain undetected.

"Your mother will not hear us?" asked Elizabeth. "Will the light not be visible from the window?"

"There have been times when I have kept a candle on at night," replied Anne. She ducked her head in embarrassment. "When I was young, I was terrified of the dark, and often kept a candle burning. Mother did not mind if I kept it away from the curtains and where it would not start a fire. Though I do not do it much anymore, there are times when the flame comforts me.

"Besides," said Anne with a giggle, "I believe my mother sleeps very soundly. Do you know that her bedchamber is on the other side of this wall?" She brushed her knuckles against the wall behind the head of her bed. "At times, I have heard her snoring."

The image of a high-born lady such as Lady Catherine snoring loudly in her sleep struck Elizabeth as amusing, and the two girls descended into giggles. Of course, that was the exact moment when a snort—which must have been deafening on the other side of the wall—reached their ears and set them to laughing once again.

"It appears you are correct," said Elizabeth, trying to stifle her laughter.

"Perhaps she heard us and was voicing her displeasure concerning such a notion," said Anne.

"Please, do not even suggest such a thing!" replied Elizabeth.

They indulged in their mirth for some few more moments before Anne once again spoke.

"Mother had another letter from Darcy today. He has refused to oblige her by coming here, and I do not blame him. Mother is considering going to London in order to put me in his path again."

"Oh," said Elizabeth. "She is determined, though I suppose I should not be surprised."

"I dissuaded her by pointing out the house in town is likely uninhabitable." Anne gave Elizabeth a wan smile. "We have not visited it in many years, and Mother will not hear of leasing it out to anyone. I believe there is a small staff there who looks after the place and keeps it clean, but I cannot imagine the condition it is in. Of course, my mother only turned it around and said we may just stay at Darcy's house."

Anne sighed and sank back against her pillows. "I wish she would let go of this doomed fantasy of hers. Darcy does not wish to marry me, and I have no wish to marry him. But it is clear that only his marriage to another will induce her to desist."

There was nothing to say in response, so Elizabeth allowed Anne to simply continue to speak, to be a bearer of the woman's burdens along with her. Elizabeth could well understand Anne's reluctance to marry the proud and disagreeable Mr. Darcy. It was something she would never consider herself.

Something in her expression must have alerted Anne to her thoughts, for she fixed her gaze on Elizabeth's face, a slight frown creasing her forehead.

"Elizabeth," said she, "I have often had the impression that you are not fond of my cousin. Has he done something to offend you?"

Surprised, Elizabeth said: "I have not been in Mr. Darcy's company for above four months, Anne. I am sure I feel nothing for him, for he is naught but an acquaintance."

"Your reaction whenever he is mentioned gives the lie to your assertion," replied Anne. When Elizabeth made to protest, Anne shook her head. "I do not wish to force a confidence, but it seemed to me you were subjected to some foul scent when I mentioned him just now. I have been raised by a woman who loves the sound of her own voice, and because my opinion is not often solicited, I have made it a practice to study those about me. I am not a great observer of others, but I can often tell by their reactions what they are thinking, and I have noticed your distaste for Darcy several times. Shall you not share your experiences with me?"

Elizabeth was hesitant to sink Mr. Darcy's character to his cousin, but Anne asked in so sincere a manner that she felt she could not demur. As a result, Elizabeth soon found herself relating their first meeting, including Mr. Darcy's slight against her.

"Not handsome enough to tempt me, he said." Elizabeth attempted to make light of it, using a playful tone to imitate Mr. Darcy's stern and unyielding one. "I was slighted by other men, and he would not give me any notice because of it. I have never been subject to such incivility in my life!"

"I dare say you have not." Anne directed a strange look at Elizabeth. "I can imagine that as first impressions go, it was not a good one. Darcy was very wrong to say it. But I wonder why it affected you so."

"Should it not?" demanded Elizabeth. "What woman would like to hear such things said about herself in so public a forum as a dance hall?"

"No one, of course. But Elizabeth, you are a beautiful girl—why would such sentiments affect you? If Darcy cannot see your beauty, why should you concern yourself?"

The words caught Elizabeth off guard, and her cheeks bloomed as she gaped, wondering of what Anne was speaking. "I am not beautiful, Anne. I am naught but a country girl, and though I believe I am pleasantly featured, I do not lay claim to any beauty. My sister Jane is the beauty in the Bennet family."

Though Anne did not respond directly to Elizabeth's denial, the look she returned was mysterious in nature, and it made Elizabeth feel quite cross.

"Elizabeth," said she in a tone of exaggerated patience, "though I was not there, of course, it seems to me that my cousin's words were spoken in ill humor. I cannot think that he truly meant to disparage you. It is possible he was simply attempting to induce his friend to leave him alone. It seems to me that you have taken this much more to heart than you ought."

"You know your cousin well enough to divine his intentions?" asked Elizabeth, challenging her friend's perception. "This was not his only affront, Anne. He was rude to all my friends and neighbors and gave the impression that he felt himself to be above the company."

"Was he not? I do not defend him, Elizabeth, but he *is* the grandson of an earl and the nephew of one. I do not know the extent of his fortune, but I know that Pemberley is a vast estate, and he has other wealth besides. Should he not feel a little superiority?"

"Perhaps he does. But should it be displayed for all the company? Should he set himself up as a paragon, looking down on all those beneath him with contempt and ridicule?"

Anne only shook her head, though mischief gleamed in her eyes. "My mother would find nothing amiss with his behavior."

When Elizabeth rolled her eyes, Anne laughed, forcing Elizabeth to join her.

"As you know, I am not close to my cousin," continued Anne. "Though I have known him all my life, I do not *know* him well, for reasons of which you are aware. But for all this, I have never known Darcy to be anything other than scrupulously proper. My other cousin, Anthony Fitzwilliam, who is my uncle's son, has often lamented that Darcy is far too rigid for a young man of his situation. It was wrong of him, indeed, to slight you and to behave in such a way. But it is quite different from what I understand of his character.

"Consider this: one of his avowed closest friends is Mr. Bingley, is it not?" Elizabeth was forced to concede Anne's point. "Then I hardly think that he would consider your friends, who are gently born, even if they are not wealthy, to be inferior to his friend, who is, after all, the son of a tradesman. Does it not strike you as odd if he does?"

"That is part of what frustrates me when I try to take Mr. Darcy's likeness. His actions and words are contradictory, and the accounts I have heard of him do not make sense."

Anne's interest was piqued at Elizabeth's statement, for she asked: "Accounts of Darcy? My understanding was that you only met him for a brief time last year, and his only friends with whom you are acquainted are Mr. Bingley and his sisters." Anne shook her head. "And since Mr. Bingley is, by all accounts, an amiable, friendly sort of man, and one who looks up to Darcy, and his sisters are grasping social climbers, I doubt any of them would criticize him. Have you met someone else who is acquainted with Darcy?"

"Yes, I have, Anne." Elizabeth paused, wishing she had held her tongue. She tried to deflect Anne by stating: "But I am reluctant to speak of matters which may sink your estimation of your cousin."

"But now you have engaged my interest. You cannot refuse to elucidate."

Though Elizabeth remained reluctant, she could see no way to refuse to oblige her companion, and she wished she had not opened her mouth. What cared she if Anne thought her dislike for Mr. Darcy was due to naught but vanity? Surely it could not affect her.

"Very well," said Elizabeth when Anne pressed her again. "I *have* met another who is acquainted with Mr. Darcy, and his story renders your cousin in an entirely different light."

Anne appeared quite intrigued and motioned for Elizabeth to continue.

"Not long after Mr. Darcy had come to Hertfordshire, a young man by the name of Mr. Wickham joined the regiment of militia which was quartered there for the winter. Mr. Wickham, I discovered, is the son of old Mr. Darcy's steward. He is an amiable man, one who is friendly to all and esteemed by many. Mr. Wickham has also been wronged grievously by your cousin."

"Tell me," prompted Anne.

Elizabeth did so with a will, the old feeling of offense on Mr. Wickham's behalf welling up within her. "It seems that Mr. Darcy's father wished to provide for Mr. Wickham, and he left a valuable family living in his will. But when the living fell vacant, Mr. Darcy refused to present Mr. Wickham with the living, reneging on his father's promise."

"And had Mr. Wickham taken orders? And for that matter, how was Darcy able to flout his father's instructions, which were backed by the legal authority of a will?"

Taken aback, Elizabeth could only stammer: "I have no idea if Mr. Wickham took orders. I imagine he did not, given how Mr. Darcy refused to present him with the living. As for the will, I was told that there was enough informality in the bequest to give him no hope from an appeal to the law. A man who was dedicated to his father's memory and intent upon abiding by his wishes could not have doubted, but Mr. Darcy chose to doubt."

It was not long before Anne's scrutiny began to make Elizabeth uncomfortable, for though she did not speak, she regarded Elizabeth for a long moment. Unwilling to allow her friend to intimidate her, Elizabeth returned it with a raised eyebrow, daring her to contradict. Thus, Elizabeth was surprised by Anne's laugh.

"Do not be offended by the observation, Elizabeth, but you almost reminded me of my mother. She, too, does not appreciate it when someone challenges her." Elizabeth was, indeed, offended, but Anne continued to speak. "I will confess that I know nothing of this situation. I do not know Mr. Wickham personally, nor do I know what was contained in my uncle's will. But there are a few things I would like to point out that do not quite make sense to me."

Elizabeth gave her a curt nod, at which Anne laughed again.

"The first is that I am confident of Darcy's character and his knowledge of his duty. Darcy and his father were very close. If his father wished to provide for Mr. Wickham, he would have informed his son, and I do not doubt that Darcy would have felt honor bound to follow his father's wishes.

"The second thing I would like to mention is that there is something that does not quite add up in Mr. Wickham's story. I do not quite know what it is, but it disturbs me all the same. What possible reason could Darcy have for denying his friend his support? I cannot fathom it. But I also cannot but wonder why Mr. Wickham would have shared such a personal matter with you. I have the impression that he did not know you long before he shared it?"

"No, he did not," replied Elizabeth, feeling much subdued. "In fact, he informed me on my second meeting with him. The subject came up because I had noticed both men's reactions upon seeing the other and could immediately discern that theirs was not a cordial relationship."

"Then it was doubly improper for him to have spoken of such a subject. I have not much experience with meeting new acquaintances, but I could never have imagined of speaking of some of the confidences we have shared recently when we were first introduced."

Elizabeth was forced to concede that Anne was correct.

"Finally, though I will stress again that I do not know Mr. Wickham myself, I *have* heard something of him. My cousin—Anthony Fitzwilliam—who is a colonel in the regulars, visits Rosings with Darcy every spring. I have heard them speak of Wickham, and when I asked, Fitzwilliam informed me that he was not a subject for polite company."

"Does he know Mr. Wickham himself?" asked Elizabeth. "Or has he just had his account from Mr. Darcy?"

"I believe he does. Mr. Wickham and Darcy were raised together as boys, and Fitzwilliam was one of Darcy's most treasured companions. And Fitzwilliam did not speak of Mr. Wickham as if he had heard of him through another. I believe they are quite well acquainted, indeed."

"I hardly know what to think," said Elizabeth. It felt like her eyes were being forced open, and though she still could not consider Mr. Darcy an agreeable man, what Anne had suggested of Mr. Wickham made too much sense. In fact, Elizabeth wondered why she had never considered it herself.

"Darcy is not a bad man, Elizabeth," said Anne quietly. "Yes, I have observed a rigid formality of his manners, and I understand that he can be haughty and aloof, but I have heard he is esteemed by his friends and considered by all to be a good, liberal man." Anne paused and directed a wan smile at Elizabeth. "And do not allow my mother to hear you speaking of Darcy in such a manner. She would not appreciate it."

Elizabeth attempted a smile in return, but it felt rather sickly. Anne seemed to notice this, for she patted Elizabeth's shoulder. "Do not concern yourself, Elizabeth. Fitzwilliam claims that Darcy is adept at displaying himself to his worst advantage. I am certain you are not the only one to have a poor opinion of him.

"Now, if you do not mind, I believe it is time to retire."

"Of course, Anne."

Elizabeth returned to her room and made herself ready for her bed, but when she lay down on it, her thoughts continued to be full of the conversation she had just had with Anne. A part of her longed to disregard Anne's assertions—after all, Anne had confessed that she did not know her cousin well. Might she not be incorrect about Mr. Wickham?

But Elizabeth was nothing if not truthful with herself, and she knew it would be a mistake to disregard what they had discussed. There were many facets of the situation, and though she did not wish to think of it now, she knew it was likely these thoughts would keep her awake much of the night.

Chapter IX

As Elizabeth woke the next morning, her mind returned to the discussion of the previous evening, and she was surprised to realize the subject of Mr. Darcy and Mr. Wickham had *not* kept her awake late into the night. Her thoughts drifted back to when she had retired, and though she could not be entirely certain, she thought it entirely likely that she had been asleep only moments after her head had settled onto her pillow.

Of the intelligence she had learned from Anne, the light of day did not grant her any greater clarity of what constituted the truth of the matter. But there were certain facts to which her eyes had been opened, and now they had been pointed out to her, she could not discount them. Mr. Wickham's early dissertation, the eagerness with which he had made the communication, and even the manner in which Mr. Wickham and Mr. Darcy had reacted to the sight of the other—Mr. Darcy with a redness which spoke of anger, contrasting Mr. Wickham's paleness, bespeaking consternation—were in the process of overwhelming Elizabeth's initial assertion that there had been "truth in all Mr. Wickham's looks."

Furthermore, another memory had sprung into Elizabeth's mind unbidden—that of Mr. Wickham declaring that he would never sink

Mr. Darcy's character because of his godfather, which he had thereafter proceeded to do by relating the whole of it to her. He could not have had any confidence in her discretion, having met her only that day. Of course, the fact that the matter was on the tongue of every gossip within days of Mr. Darcy's departure also did not help his cause. Then there was his insistence that he would not be run off by Mr. Darcy, followed by his failure to attend the ball at Netherfield—Elizabeth had thought it evidence of his forbearance at the time, though now she was uncomfortably aware that it was nothing more than cowardice. All of these pieces of the puzzle suggested that Mr. Wickham's motivations in relaying the matter to her were less than altruistic.

She did not know the truth of the matter—she *could not* know the truth of it—but she now knew not to trust Mr. Wickham's account implicitly. He had taken her in with the skill of a master artist, and though she thought there was some extenuating circumstances to explain her gullibility, there was little chance of her ever understanding what of his story had been truth and what had been fantasy.

She did know two things, however: first, that Mr. Wickham was not to be trusted, and the second was that even if Mr. Darcy was acquitted of cruelty to him, his behavior had still been objectionable in other ways. She was, therefore, required to think *better* of Mr. Darcy, but she was not required to think *well* of him.

As it was Sunday, Elizabeth rose from her bed and with Tilly's help prepared herself for church. She met Anne and Lady Catherine—who attended services without fail—and made her way there in the de Bourgh carriage. At the small church in Hunsford, Elizabeth greeted Charlotte with pleasure and sat in the de Bourgh pew with Lady Catherine and Anne, to the left of the pulpit in the front row.

As usual, Mr. Collins's sermon was long, rambling, and often seemed to go over the same material multiple times. Whatever her previous feelings for Mr. Collins had been, or of what they consisted now, there was no denying the man was pompous and possessed a talent for putting half the congregation to sleep. In this number was included one Elizabeth would never have expected.

"It seems not all find the good reverend's sermon to be edifying," whispered Anne as she nudged Elizabeth. She pointed across her body to her mother, and there, seated in the front row for all to see, sat Lady Catherine, her head nodding as she struggled to stay awake.

Elizabeth managed to stifle a snort, but it was a near thing, indeed.

Charlotte, who was sitting across the aisle, caught Elizabeth's gaze and she looked skyward, once again trying Elizabeth's composure. It was fortunate that Mr. Collins drew his sermon to a close soon after. After services, the Collinses were invited to Rosings for dinner, and Elizabeth was able to enjoy the company of her dearest friend, even if the company did include the silly Mr. Collins.

Thus, the final two weeks of Elizabeth's stay in Kent began. Over the next few days, Lady Catherine once again returned to her former self: in other words, she was domineering, meddling, overbearing, and intent upon ruling the lives of those around her. At least she was not, however, vocal about her nephew's intransigence. Elizabeth could not say if the woman had abandoned the notion of going to London, but the matter was never brought up in her presence. Elizabeth and Anne spent most of their time together, and if Lady Catherine sometimes looked on them with an unreadable expression, and at times interrupted, dominated the conversation herself or admonished Elizabeth for some imagined offense, the two managed to ignore her. She was still busy enough with the estate and those in the parish that she was not often in their company.

In those days, the weather was fine. As a result, Anne and Elizabeth were often to be found in her phaeton. Elizabeth was able to see much of the environs of Rosings in that manner, and the mobility allowed by their conveyance meant that there was much more to be seen than might otherwise have been the case.

"Will you not now concede that driving my phaeton is much superior to walking?" asked Anne when Elizabeth made that observation. The ladies had driven out, with the faithful Baines in attendance, and had just pulled into the lane which led away from Rosings.

"I certainly do not concede it," replied Elizabeth in a haughty imitation of Lady Catherine's voice. Anne laughed at her. "After all, the fact still remains that you do not receive much of the benefit of exercise from your phaeton."

"No, I will grant you that. But I do not think you have repined it."

"I have not, especially since I have kept up with my walks, though I have not walked nearly so far as is my custom in recent weeks."

"It is the best of both worlds, then. Your walks allow you your exercise and your delight in close communion with nature while my phaeton allows you the greater variance of views it would take you too long to observe were you on your feet."

"That is true," replied Elizabeth.

"I wish I could walk." Anne's tone was wistful, her mien introspective, even as she flicked the reins and expertly guided the horses. "With all you have told me of your pleasures, I do not doubt I would derive great benefit from it."

"Perhaps a short stroll in the gardens would be beneficial?" asked Elizabeth. In fact, Elizabeth thought a short stroll, just enough to sate her desire for it but not long enough that Lady Catherine could make any conceivable objection to Anne jeopardizing her health, would be an excellent start in asserting her independence. However, it was not to be.

"Oh, I could never do that," replied Anne. "Mother would be furious with me."

She thought to push Anne even further, but Elizabeth grimaced and decided it was best to hold her tongue. They were silent for several moments, Elizabeth thinking on the best way to encourage her friend without infuriating the lady. For her part, Anne's thoughts were unfathomable, though when Elizabeth looked at her friend, she thought she caught a glimpse of anger in her eyes and a hardness in her jaw.

"Mother does not wish for me to do anything of my own free will. I have never had the chance to live like other ladies of my station—I was not allowed to dance, denied society of any kind, other than my mother's ancient friends, denied the pianoforte, denied anything that would bring me pleasure. I have not truly realized it before, but mine has been a truly cheerless existence."

For a moment, Elizabeth was uncertain of what she was hearing. Anne had never stated anything so overtly critical of her mother as the words which had just passed her lips.

"She is excessively concerned for your wellbeing," replied Elizabeth carefully. "While I understand it is irksome, I do not think she does not care."

A noncommittal huff was Anne's response, and when she finally spoke after a few moments, the resentment in her voice was clear.

"She cares not for the opinions of others, least of all mine. She browbeats and intimidates and screams to have her own way."

"She only needs to understand that you are your own person. There is no reason to be fearful of your mother."

"I am not afraid of my mother. It is simply . . ." Anne's eyes were distant, as if she could see to the very edge of the world and beyond. "I have never considered doing anything contrary to her design. She informs me what she wishes and I do it, and there has never been any question about whether I will obey."

"You are of age, Anne." Elizabeth was not even certain her friend had heard her quiet comment, but she continued nonetheless. "I do not advocate rebellion and discord between you, but eventually she must take your wishes into account. You are your own person, intelligent and capable, and you must be treated as such."

Elizabeth's words had no visible effect on Anne, but she thought they were heard all the same. As they continued along the road, Anne was quiet and contemplative, and Elizabeth did not know what to say. When they had ridden on for some minutes, she thought she heard her friend say, "I just wish to live," but she could not be certain.

It was also common for them to stop by the parsonage during their phaeton rides, and they did again that day. Elizabeth appreciated Anne's seeming desire for Charlotte's company, as it allowed Elizabeth more time with her friend.

That day, Charlotte was at home and in her parlor with Maria, and as Mr. Collins was elsewhere, the ladies enjoyed an agreeable few minutes with dear friends. Even Anne, Elizabeth thought, was coming to appreciate Charlotte's solid dependability.

"Miss de Bourgh, Lizzy!" greeted Charlotte with pleasure. "I am happy you have stopped by today. Do come in!"

The ladies were soon seated, Charlotte having ordered a tea service, and they sat and chatted for some time—in reality, Charlotte and Elizabeth carried the conversation, as Anne displayed her usual reticence in company and Maria was much too intimidated by the heiress to say much. The tea was delivered and they sat down to partake of it. After she had served them all, Charlotte turned her attention to Anne.

"I must thank you for this piece of civility, Miss de Bourgh. It seems you and Lizzy have been making use of your phaeton much more of late. I enjoy your calls and appreciate your bringing Lizzy to visit me, for I know she will return to her home before long."

The look Anne returned to Charlotte was unreadable, and for a moment Elizabeth wondered if she was unhappy in some way. "Yes, she will. And it will be a great loss, I am sure, not only as you are her dear friend, but also for the diminution of the party at Rosings. My mother and I have become quite accustomed to her presence. Her absence will be missed, indeed."

Elizabeth blushed at the praise, but Charlotte only turned an expressive gaze on her. "Yes, Lizzy is valued wherever she goes. In Hertfordshire, she is a highly sought-after dance partner and conversationalist, and I can think of many who consider her to be quite the most intelligent lady they have ever met."

"Charlotte!" exclaimed Elizabeth. "I am sure I deserve no such praise."

"And I am certain Mrs. Collins understates the effect you have on others, if anything," said Anne. "I know that Rosings shall be quite desolate when you go, Elizabeth. I find myself wishing you could stay."

The atmosphere had become a little mawkish at Anne's words, and Charlotte attempted to change the subject.

"Surely you will have a new companion when Lizzy departs? Has your mother had any luck in locating a suitable woman?"

"Not that I am aware," replied Anne.

It was a diplomatic way of saying that Lady Catherine had not even made the attempt to find a replacement since Elizabeth's arrival—in fact, Elizabeth was certain the matter had quite vanished from Lady Catherine's mind. She clearly thought it would be no trouble at all to coerce Elizabeth into staying on as long as the lady liked. The truth was that Elizabeth was enjoying herself with Anne, even when considering Lady Catherine's objectionable presence, and she was loath to leave her friend. But it was time for her to return to her home, for she had been absent long enough. And nothing Lady Catherine could say or do would convince Elizabeth to stay.

"I hope she has success soon," said Charlotte, seeming to understand that she had stumbled onto an objectionable subject. "Perhaps you will be able to continue your friendship through correspondence. You have become so close that it would be a shame for your relationship to cease due to distance."

"I believe I would like that very much," said Anne, turning a shy smile to Elizabeth. "If you will oblige me."

"Of course, Anne," replied Elizabeth. "I would be happy to maintain a correspondence with you."

"And Mr. Collins and I would be happy to invite her again next year," said Charlotte. "My husband has already indicated how agreeable he finds Elizabeth's presence, and how he would welcome having her back in our home."

"That would also be welcome," said Anne.

For the rest of the visit, Anne was even quieter than was her wont, for she seemed to be caught in the throes of some great introspection. Elizabeth and Charlotte continued to carry the conversation. However, Charlotte's frequent glances at Miss de Bourgh spoke to her notice of the woman's behavior, and Elizabeth's concern was aroused. She resolved to question Anne when they departed.

It was unfathomable that they would be able to visit Hunsford without an appearance by its master, and as Mr. Collins had realized that they had been frequent visitors at his home of late, he had obviously attempted to be nearby so he could greet the daughter of his patroness. Thus, it was about five minutes before they were to leave that he walked in the door and greeted them in his usually expansive manner.

"Miss de Bourgh, Cousin Elizabeth," said he. "I had a notion you were visiting with my Charlotte today. I hope you are both well."

"Very well, indeed," replied Elizabeth when Anne was slow in responding. "We were just riding in Anne's phaeton when we decided to stop to visit."

"Excellent!" cried Mr. Collins. "I have often seen you driving the lanes of the neighborhood of late. It has obviously been beneficial to you both, for your countenances glow with the healthy light of ones who are often to be found in the sun. As my Charlotte has often commented, it is very beneficial to be out of doors, and I, myself, often walk to my parishioners' places of residence. I also care for my own garden, which, I flatter myself, is industrious and constructive."

"It is, indeed, Mr. Collins," said Anne.

Elizabeth, for her part, stifled a giggle, for she was aware—as Anne obviously was—that the man was stating an opinion in opposition to the one Lady Catherine would espouse—at least when it came to her daughter—and he would be mortified by that fact.

"We were just speaking of how valuable our Elizabeth's removal to Rosings has been for Miss de Bourgh," said Charlotte, directing an amused grin at Elizabeth. "They have become great friends in such a short period of time."

"Yes, indeed they have," agreed Mr. Collins, a beaming smile directed at Elizabeth. "I am sure, Miss de Bourgh, that you must have the highest opinion of my cousin and agree that her presence has been a boon. I have heard she plays for you all day long and that your own happiness has been increased as a result."

Anne and Elizabeth shared an amused glance, knowing that the music often emanating from Mrs. Jenkinson's room—where they still visited frequently—was often Anne playing, rather than Elizabeth.

"I can honestly say that I have been blessed with Elizabeth's presence," said Anne. "More so, in fact, than anyone else in my life."

Mr. Collins fell silent in confusion and concern, and he replied with a tentative: "Other than the presence of your excellent mother."

"Of course," replied Anne, restoring his previous pleasure.

The visit only lasted a few moments longer, and Elizabeth and Anne soon took their leave to return to Rosings. They stepped up onto the seat, and Anne took the reins, and then they were off. Not much was said between them as Anne drove, and Elizabeth regarded her, noting that her introspection had returned. It was not until they drove up before the stable, alighted, and began to walk back toward the entrance that Anne spoke again.

"Elizabeth, I wish to thank you for your presence and encouragement, and the unstinting friendship you have offered me during your stay here. It has not gone unappreciated, I assure you."

"I was happy to offer it, Anne. You are a wonderful person, and I have benefited from knowing you."

The look Anne directed at her showed her heart in her eyes. "I do appreciate that. I am not unaware of what you have had to endure with my mother."

"Lady Catherine is much less able to intimidate me than she believes. I have not been unhappy or felt like I was being attacked."

"That is a credit to you, Elizabeth," murmured Anne. Then she shot Elizabeth a playful look, one at which she had become proficient in the previous weeks. "I shall even forgive you when you return to Hertfordshire, though it will leave me in my mother's sole company. I would be tempted to hate you forever for such a betrayal, but I shall resist the temptation."

Elizabeth laughed. "Thank you for this civility, Anne."

They continued to walk, up the steps, and into the house, and from there to their rooms. Once again Anne had fallen prey to her pensive thoughts, and Elizabeth watched her, wondering if there was anything she could do to comfort her friend. But when Elizabeth asked, Anne only shooed her to her room for a rest.

"I am able to handle myself, Elizabeth. In fact, for the first time in my life, I have confidence in my abilities. It is all your doing, you know."

"The fortitude always existed within you, Anne," replied Elizabeth. "I have merely encouraged you to allow it loose from its chains."

"Perhaps. But without your indomitable courage, I doubt it ever would have been free. When you leave, I shall be well, though I think there is a long overdue discussion I must have with my mother. But in deference to your sensibilities and to avoid the blame falling on you, I will wait until you are gone before I approach her."

"I would be happy to support you," replied Elizabeth, concerned for her friend's almost fatalistic attitude.

"I thank you. But this time I believe I need to fend for myself."

And with that, Anne was gone, leaving Elizabeth with no other option than to return to her room. She was happy that Anne was considering taking control of her own life, but a part of her worried. Lady Catherine would not relent easily, and furthermore, Elizabeth was worried that Anne would let loose the resentment she had seen under the surface. Such a clash could hardly be productive.

Chapter X

The next day the fireworks began.

As it had been some time since Elizabeth had last walked further than the back gardens, she awoke earlier than usual, dressed herself without Tilly's assistance, and took herself from Rosings toward the woods to the south. Finding a footpath which had been one of her favorites when she had been staying at the parsonage she wandered amid the glorious woods for some time, thinking about all that had happened these past weeks. Elizabeth considered Anne at length as she walked, but no conclusions or paths forward presented themselves to her. Thus, Elizabeth resigned herself to the knowledge that she had done as much for her new friend as she possibly could and trusted that Anne could find an accommodation with her mother.

The walk was a balm to Elizabeth's soul, one she realized she had missed. It was, by now, May. The evidence of the new life which had sprouted in the early spring had now reached a maturity of sorts, a splendor and beauty which would last the summer months until autumn arrived, with its rains and winds and cooler days, to render the leaves their brilliant shades, when all would sleep until the spring sun awoke them again next year. There was little to compare with the woods of Rosings, and Elizabeth found herself enjoying them far longer than she usually did.

Upon her return to Rosings, she was greeted by a smiling Anne, and she was reminded of their beautiful new friendship when Anne teased her.

"You have been walking long this morning, Lizzy."

Anne rarely called her by her shortened name, and it was greatly to be treasured when she was feeling playful enough to do so.

"The woods are so beautiful, I could not help myself."

"I am sure you could not. You are fortunate that mother breakfasted earlier than usual and immediately left the house to visit one of our tenants. I had cook keep some of your favorite muffins warm for you. Come."

Elizabeth followed willingly, their conversation characterized by an easy camaraderie. "Has your mother returned?" asked Elizabeth as she began to eat her breakfast.

"Yes, she has. She is now closeted with Mr. Collins, reviewing some matters of the parish." Anne smirked. "As you know, they are both quite long-winded, so I suspect it will be long before we are subjected to their presence."

Though she laughed, Elizabeth was concerned all over again for Anne's caustic comment concerning her mother. She still did not say such things where Lady Catherine could overhear, but it spoke to a growing bitterness.

"Then what do you wish to do this morning?" asked Elizabeth, pushing the concern aside for the moment.

"Shall we not retire to Mrs. Jenkinson's room? I feel like practicing that piece a little more will see me become quite proficient at it."

With a nod, Elizabeth agreed. Anne was overestimating her skill by a great deal, but Elizabeth was pleased with the progress she had made, though she knew it would be many months before Anne began to play with any true skill.

They removed to the aforementioned room soon after, and Elizabeth played for a short time, after which she ceded the bench to Anne. After diligently doing her exercises, she began to play the piece in question. It was a short work by Beethoven, one Elizabeth considered a favorite which was perfect for a beginner to practice. But it was not many more moments before a knock sounded at the door, startling both ladies.

They quickly exchanged places, and Anne called out permission to enter. The door opened, revealing a young footman who bowed to them and said: "Pardon me, Miss de Bourgh, but your mother has requested Miss Bennet's presence in the sitting-room."

"Miss Bennet's presence?" asked Anne. "Whatever for?"

"I cannot say," replied the footman. His eyes, shifting from Elizabeth to Anne and back again, accompanied by his heightened color, gave the lie to his words. Elizabeth, however, understanding that the man was only following his orders, took pity on him.

"Of course, I will come," said she, favoring the man with a smile.

His relief was apparent, and he bowed, shooting her a look of gratitude. "I shall inform Lady Catherine," said he, after which he turned and departed.

"Perhaps she saw you when you were on your walk," said Anne as they rose together.

"Unless she was up at the crack of dawn, I can hardly imagine it," replied Elizabeth. "I was within the confines of the woods soon after and never left them. Of course, it is possible that some servant saw me and reported it."

"That is entirely possible," replied Anne, a hint of tightness in her tone. "They are nothing more than her network of spies."

Elizabeth thought that Anne was completely correct in her statement, but she rather thought it impolitic to state it in so open a manner while they were walking the halls of her mother's house. They continued in silence, and Elizabeth could not help but wonder if she was about to receive a severe tongue lashing, though she supposed it was equally possible that Lady Catherine, knowing she was to depart in less than two weeks, wished to order her to stay. Elizabeth had been expecting that conversation for some time now.

The sitting-room door was ajar, and the footman who had summoned them was standing outside. He bowed to them and opened the door for them. Something in his manner, the way he avoided looking at her, told Elizabeth that this interview was not to be so benign as an appeal to her to remain in Kent.

Had Elizabeth's suspicions not already been aroused, she still would have noted the displeasure in Lady Catherine's gaze, the way her eyes raked over Elizabeth in disdain, not to mention the firm set of her mouth and her stiff back. Elizabeth did not know what had changed in the time since their latest meeting, but she was now certain that Lady Catherine was displeased with her.

By her side sat Mr. Collins, but while Lady Catherine's gaze impaled her, he watched her approach with something akin to trepidation, and he appeared to be quite confused. Had Elizabeth's opinion of the man not improved, she might have thought he had been carrying tales of her to Lady Catherine. As it was, she wondered if he had not made some innocuous comment and been surprised by his patroness's response.

"Yes, your ladyship?" asked Elizabeth, using formality as a shield. "You have summoned me?"

"I did," was the lady's short reply. But rather than say what she wished to Elizabeth, she instead turned her attention to Anne. "Your presence is not required. You may leave."

"If you will pardon my saying so, Mother, as Elizabeth has come to Rosings at my insistence, I believe I have the right to hear whatever you must say to her, and as your demeanor shows you to be displeased, I would know what you have against her."

Clearly the daughter had never spoken to the mother in such a fashion. Lady Catherine's eyes almost bulged out of their sockets at such pointed comments and she did not know what to say. It could not be supposed that the lady would remain bereft of her tongue for long, however, and her ire soon returned with a vengeance.

"This does not concern you! Go to your room!"

"And yet I shall remain. I assume that whatever has offended you is related to Elizabeth's behavior to me. Thus, you cannot say it does not concern me."

"Anne!" barked Lady Catherine. "You will obey me now!"

"I am a woman full grown and may choose for myself. I shall stay."

The wild look Lady Catherine directed at her daughter spoke to her frustration, but in her pique, it was at Elizabeth she lashed out. "I believe I see the defiance of Miss Bennet in your manners, Anne. I installed you in this excellent position, Miss Bennet, to care for my daughter, and this is how you repay my kindness?"

"I am unaware of your charges," replied Elizabeth, though inside she was cringing at how this exchange was proceeding. "Perhaps you would explain to me what, particularly, you find offensive?"

The way Lady Catherine's eyes darted between them, Elizabeth was certain the lady was searching for some way to evict her daughter from the room. Why she thought it necessary, Elizabeth could not be certain—if the lady thought Elizabeth would cower before her more readily without Anne's presence, she was sadly mistaken.

At length, Lady Catherine favored her daughter with an imperious glare, one which promised punishments to come, before she directed her considerable displeasure back on Elizabeth.

"Mr. Collins tells me you have been taxing Anne's strength."

"Pardon me, Lady Catherine—" began Mr. Collins, but he was

silenced by a stern glare. He appeared not to know where to look or what to do, but he directed a wide-eyed appeal at Elizabeth which she would never have expected to see.

"Well, Miss Bennet? I am waiting for your response."

"I am afraid I do not understand your charge," replied Elizabeth. "In what way have I taxed Miss de Bourgh's strength?"

Lady Catherine's eyes bored into Elizabeth. "Do not be coy with me, Miss Bennet. I am not to be trifled with."

"Indeed, I do not," replied Elizabeth. "I am merely asking for clarification. I walk out often, but Anne does not accompany me. Anne retires to her rooms in the afternoon as per your decree, and as far as I am aware, she is not exerting herself any more than she usually does. Might your ladyship explain exactly what you have to accuse me of?"

"The matter of Anne and her phaeton!" cried Lady Catherine. "Not only has it been out every day this week, according to my stable hands, but you have visited Mrs. Collins every day you have been out."

"I thought your ladyship encouraged Anne to drive her phaeton."

"Within reason," snapped Lady Catherine. "Of course, she may drive it, but too much air is detrimental to her health. Besides, she does not need to pay such civility to my parson's wife." The sneer which fell over Lady Catherine's face was truly ugly. "Mr. Collins is not of her sphere, after all, and I would not have Anne tainted by too frequent association with those who are inferior."

"That is patently ludicrous, Mother!" interjected Anne. "You have the Collinses to dinner and tea regularly. Shall I not visit her in return?"

"You may count on me to take up that office. You need not concern yourself for it."

"By your reckoning, am *I* not inferior?" asked Elizabeth. Anger was beginning to build, at Lady Catherine's ridiculous and strident objections. Elizabeth thought that Lady Catherine had been looking for something of which to complain, if she was eager to make a fuss about such a silly subject.

"I knew this was a mistake," replied Lady Catherine, shaking her head. "I knew I should not have acceded to this. I should have gone to London to find a woman experienced and willing to follow my dictates. Instead, I allowed myself to be persuaded to this . . . this . . . farce." Lady Catherine glared at Elizabeth. "You are in no way suited to be my daughter's companion, and I should have trusted my instincts."

"That is enough, Mother!" Lady Catherine fell silent, shocked at the forceful tone of her daughter's command. Mr. Collins, who had shrunk back in apparent terror as the combatants' voices had begun to raise, was startled from his fear by Anne's rejoinder.

"First, Mother," continued Anne, "if you believe we are riding out in my phaeton too much, you may direct your reproofs at *me*, and not Elizabeth. I am the one who decides how often we go out, and as I am the one who drives, the decision to stop at the parsonage is mine alone. Do not berate Elizabeth for something I have done.

"Second, I would have you remember that Elizabeth is *my* friend. You do not pay her—she is not your employee."

"No, but I may rescind my invitation to her at any time."

"And I will reinstate it. Elizabeth stays here at *my* invitation, and I will not have her depart until she is ready to.

"Finally, I do not know what measure you use, but Elizabeth and I are equals in the eyes of society. I might have a more substantial dowry, but she is a gentleman's daughter."

"How can you possibly speak such nonsense?" It was clear Lady Catherine was offended. "You are the granddaughter of an earl. What are *her* connections?"

"Oh, I am sorry," interjected Elizabeth, though she knew it would be better if she remained silent. "I was not aware that there is some other title to which I should refer to you, Anne. Should I be addressing you as Lady Anne de Bourgh?"

Anne shook her head in amusement, even as Lady Catherine shook with fury. "No, indeed, Elizabeth. My father was a baronet, yes, but I am naught but *Miss* de Bourgh."

"That is well. I was worried that I had offended you."

They exchanged glances and could not hold in their laughter. Lady Catherine was affronted all over again.

"Stop this silly giggling!" screeched Lady Catherine. "I will not have it in my sitting-room. What has this hoyden done to you, Anne?"

"She has been my friend, shown me what it is to live, Mother," replied Anne. Her implacable tone was a revelation, for Elizabeth had not truly known if Anne had it in her to openly defy her mother. "She will continue to be my friend. I will not give her up."

"Her wild ways have infected you! Can you not see how you have become rebellious and improper? Are you to be polluted by such indelicacy as she possesses?"

"There is no pollution, Mother," replied Anne, and Elizabeth was impressed by how she had held her temper. "Rather, association with Elizabeth has given me a measure of confidence I would never have expected to gain. You have always treated me like a child, but I am a woman full grown. I do not require you to direct every facet of my life."

"You are sickly and unwell. You require special care. Is this the thanks I receive for giving it to you all of your life?"

"I am not nearly so sickly as you would like to believe, Mother," replied Anne. Her voice was soft, and Elizabeth felt the emotion inherent in it. She was not surprised, however, when Lady Catherine did not.

"Miss Bennet, you may not stay here any longer," said Lady Catherine, turning her attention to Elizabeth. "It is clear I should have thought twice before agreeing to this. I shall write your father and inform him that he must come and retrieve you without delay."

Though the lady might have thought that was the end of the matter, she was shocked by Elizabeth's responding laughter. "You may write to my father all you like, your ladyship. I would be quite surprised if my father would receive it with any seriousness. In fact, I rather suspect he would see it as naught but a joke."

"Is he witless?"

"No, in fact he is very intelligent. But he loves to be amused by follies and inconsistencies, and the charges you have laid at my door are ridiculous, and would, no doubt, prompt naught but his laughter."

"Miss Bennet, I insist on being satisfied. You will pack your trunks and be gone today." Lady Catherine turned to Mr. Collins. "She may return to your house until arrangements may be made to return her to her father's house, or wherever else she wishes to go. You will not invite her again, for I will not have her corrupting my daughter."

"Mother, that is enough!" cried Anne.

By Lady Catherine's side, Mr. Collins was watching with visible terror, and he had started to rise when Lady Catherine delivered her edict, but he sank down again when Anne opposed her mother. For the first time, Elizabeth saw something in the man she had never thought to see—uncertainty when confronted by his patroness's opinion. He had tried to interrupt several times, but was silenced when the combatants had continued to speak.

"Mr. Collins," said Anne, seeming to notice the man's consternation. "This dispute does not concern you, and we do not need to solicit your opinion. Please return to the parsonage."

Had Elizabeth not witnessed it, she might not have believed a man could move so quickly. He was on his feet in an instant, stammering out an apology, and then moving out of the door at a speed which could only be termed as flight. And this all happened before Lady Catherine, who seemed shocked that Anne had dismissed him, could even think of responding.

"Now you dismiss my servants in my stead?" snarled Lady Catherine. The lady rose and bore down on them, fury in her eyes.

"Mr. Collins is *not* your servant, Mother," replied Anne, stopping Lady Catherine short. "He is your parson, and his primary responsibility is the care of the people in the parish. Though you treat him as if he is a servant, and he does whatever you decree, he is a servant of the church and should be respected as such."

"He is an idiot!" snapped Lady Catherine. "Mr. Collins would spend all day deciding which of his feet to insert into his shoes if I did not direct him."

"Perhaps if you gave him a little more autonomy, he would surprise you."

Lady Catherine snorted, but she did not pursue the subject. "That is not the point. I wish for this hoyden to be gone this instant. I will be obeyed."

"I am sorry, Mother," replied Anne. "Elizabeth shall not depart until it is time for her to leave. She is *my* friend, and I have need of her. Now, if you will excuse us, we shall return to my room. Come, Elizabeth."

Anne turned on her heel and left the room. Seeing there was no other alternative—and grateful it had not turned into a physical confrontation—Elizabeth followed her, leaving the lady gaping after them. The footman who had summoned her was standing outside the open door, and he was openly watching Anne with wonder, never having heard her speak so forcefully nor Lady Catherine being so overtly challenged. Elizabeth hurried behind her friend as she marched forward, wondering what had happened to her timid friend.

They gained the safety of Anne's room, and Anne firmly—but kindly—dismissed Laura. When they were alone, she began to pace the room, her face flushed and her movements clipped and forceful.

"The gall of the woman!" exclaimed she. "She has gone too far this time!"

"Anne," said Elizabeth, attempting to calm her with soothing tones, "you should calm yourself. This can do you no good."

But Anne only shook her head. "In fact, I have never felt as alive as I do at present. I will not allow my mother to throw you from the house as if you were nothing but chattel."

"I had thought you would induce your mother to accept the

changes in you if they were brought to her attention in increments," said Elizabeth. "I certainly had no notion of you challenging her in such a manner. I do not think this is productive, Anne. I will depart if that will make it better."

Her pacing stopped, and Anne turned to look at Elizabeth. For a moment, Elizabeth thought she had managed to provoke her friend's ire, but as Anne regarded her, the lines on her forehead smoothed, and she walked toward her, sitting on a chair situated close by where Elizabeth was sitting.

"I appreciate your desire to promote harmony, Elizabeth. But the peace of this home has been rent, if it ever truly existed. I will not return to being dominated by my mother."

"Anne," said Elizabeth, choosing her words carefully, "I do not excuse your mother's behavior, but I would also urge you to see this from her perspective. This is an abrupt change in your relationship. I believe it would be better to ease your way into the changes you wish to make. There is nothing to be gained from alienating your mother."

"I would, Elizabeth," replied Anne, favoring Elizabeth with a fond smile, "but for your presence here. You have taught me what it is to be alive, and I cannot go back now."

Elizabeth had been about to suggest again that she depart, but when Anne made her point, she found that she could not. What would her departure now do but embolden Lady Catherine and make Anne's life more difficult? If she stayed, then at least Anne would not be forced to face the dragon alone.

"Of course, I do not wish to leave you," said Elizabeth. "You have my support, regardless of what comes."

"Thank you, Elizabeth," said Anne. "I have never had a friend like you." Anne laughed. "I have never had a friend, but I cannot imagine a better one. I have no wish to give you up, despite whatever foolishness my mother has gotten into her head."

Elizabeth was pleased, but she soon turned her attention to the problem at hand. "I will stay with you, Anne. But we must take some thought to what we will do. Rosings will become uncomfortable if we stay here with your mother. She will continue to try to force you to obey her."

"She will not have any luck," replied Anne. Her manner was dark and defiant, and though Elizabeth's opinion of her friend had been growing by leaps and bounds, she was not certain that Anne had the ability to defy her mother yet.

"Is there anywhere else you may go?" asked Elizabeth. "Distance may be the best in this instance—your mother cannot attempt to browbeat you if you are not at Rosings."

Anne chewed her lip in thought. "There is the house in town I mentioned. But Rosings is my family's only property."

"What about your relations? Surely they would not wish for you to be ruled in such a manner as this."

"That is a possibility." Anne's eyes darted to Elizabeth's face, and for a moment Elizabeth felt she was being weighed, indeed, judged. But the moment soon ended when Anne sighed. "I will think on this matter further. For now, let us simply enjoy what is left of the afternoon."

"Very well," replied Elizabeth. But in her heart, she could not help but wonder where this would end. Lady Catherine was not a woman to be gainsaid; she would continue to attempt to send Elizabeth home, if she did not simply order her servants to forcibly remove her from the house. It could not end well.

Chapter XI

Open warfare had descended on Rosings Park. Or perhaps it was not quite so open, considered Elizabeth, though it was certainly tense. She had almost expected Lady Catherine to simply order Tilly to pack her belongings and her footmen to deposit them on the lawn like so much trash, but she did not. In fact, they heard nothing further from the lady that evening, a circumstance which prompted much gratitude from both ladies.

Feeling drained because of the events of the afternoon, Elizabeth slept for a short time on Anne's bed, and though she thought Anne herself might succumb to a short nap at the very least, her last sight of her friend before she dropped off was of Anne sitting at her escritoire, brooding. When Elizabeth awoke, Anne was a little more cheerful, but still quite distracted.

That evening, Elizabeth and Anne ordered trays from the kitchen, rather than attend Lady Catherine at the dinner table, an action Elizabeth thought would bring the lady's anger down upon them again. But there was no such response, and they soon learned that Lady Catherine herself had also ordered a tray to her room.

"She has been in her rooms all day?" asked Anne of Laura when the latter made the communication concerning the dinner trays.

"That is what her abigail has informed me," replied Laura. "She went there soon after . . . your argument and has not emerged since."

"Has she given any orders to the housekeeper or butler?"

Laura shook her head. "None of which I am aware." The maid paused, seemingly hesitant, but Anne in a kindly voice, prompted her to speak. "It is simply so very surprising that you would choose to confront your mother in this way. If she decides to order the footmen to remove Miss Bennet from the house, there is nothing you can do to prevent it. The loyalty of the servants is all on Lady Catherine's side, though many have some sympathy for you."

"I know," said Anne. "I shall take steps to prevent that. But I cannot imagine my mother so lost to decency as to descend to such violence. She likes to get her way very much, but she knows what response would come should she do such a thing. Miss Bennet's father would be incensed, and as he's connected to Mr. Collins, she must tread carefully."

"As you say, mum," said the maid. Then she curtseyed and went about her duties again.

Anne turned to Elizabeth with a raised eyebrow. "What say you, Elizabeth?"

In truth, Elizabeth was not quite certain how to account for Lady Catherine's behavior, and her response echoed that uncertainty. "Your mother is not reacting in the way I would have thought. I almost expected her to simply call in her burliest footman and have me deposited on the front steps, barring the door behind."

"That would have been as likely an outcome as any."

For a moment, Elizabeth felt cross—if Anne had expected such a response, it seemed like she was playing a little cavalierly with Elizabeth's safety. But Elizabeth knew that Anne had meant no such thing, and she decided to make no comment about it.

"Though I hesitate to paint your mother with so harsh a brush, it is possible that she is nothing more than a bully, one who oppresses the weak, but cannot stand when faced with someone who will not cower before her."

At first Anne winced at Elizabeth's description, but soon she became contemplative, and she turned a considering eye on Elizabeth. "That is perhaps it, but I cannot imagine it will last for long. She might hesitate to use a footman to evict you from the house, but there is one of whom she could make use."

"And yet, Mr. Collins's behavior was startling," replied Elizabeth. "I would have thought he would bluster and rant, parroting your mother's words and demands. But he simply sat there and watched, and for a time, I thought he might actually contradict her."

"Perhaps we may work on him," said Anne. "What say you to a ride on my phaeton tomorrow, with a stop at the parsonage? It is possible we could ensure his neutrality on the matter before my mother makes her demands."

"I am certainly willing," replied Elizabeth, thinking it would be a relief to escape the house for a time.

But it was not to be. When they went to the front door the next morning, they were met by the footman who normally accompanied them, and though Anne requested he open the door, he stood in sullen silence, looking at them.

"I am sorry, Miss de Bourgh," replied Baines, and Elizabeth thought the man truly was apologetic. "I have been given strict orders that you are not to leave the house, and your phaeton is off limits. Furthermore, if Miss Bennet . . ." His eye darted to Elizabeth and he paused. "Should Miss Bennet leave the house, she is not to be admitted again."

Anne regarded him, causing the man to squirm. "You are aware there are many doors to Rosings. My mother cannot guard them all."

A nod was his response, but he looked at Anne, swallowed hard, and said: "The stable hands have received orders concerning your phaeton. No one will risk their positions by preparing it for you. I apologize, Miss de Bourgh, but I am afraid that your desire to drive today will not be gratified."

Though reluctant, it appeared Anne was not insensible to the futility of railing against Baines, a man who was likely in fear of losing his own position. "Very well. Thank you for informing us of this, Baines. I understand the difficult position in which this places you and all the staff."

A sense of relief fell over him, but he again spoke. "The staff is . . . We are all beholden to your mother for our positions, and she pays us well for our loyalty. But do not think that we are insensible to your plight."

Anne nodded, and the two girls turned from the door, where they were witness to the insolent sneer given them by one Lady Catherine de Bourgh, who stood at the top of the main stairway watching them. Elizabeth expected sparks to once again fly between them, but Anne merely sniffed and glided away, Elizabeth following behind. She thought she heard an irritated huff from the great lady but could not be certain.

It was to the music room that Anne led them, and when they had entered, Anne requested some music. Elizabeth was only too happy to oblige, and for a while, she lost herself in the playing and forget the troubles present in the house. For a time, Anne was introspective, as if attempting to determine what was to be done. Elizabeth only continued to play.

After a time, Anne rose and approached Elizabeth, a smile lighting her face. "Thank you for serenading me, Elizabeth, with your wonderful playing. If you do not mind, I believe I would now like to take a turn at it."

Uncertain, Elizabeth regarded her friend. "Do you think that is a good idea? Your mother may walk in through the door at any time."

"And what better way for her to learn that she will not control me than by seeing me play? She cannot complain that I am exerting myself too much, nor can she claim that it is beyond my strength, as I will already be seated at the instrument."

Though Elizabeth still did not agree with Anne's intention, she ceded the seat and allowed Anne to sit. She began by running through some of the exercises that Elizabeth had taught her, and Elizabeth acknowledged that Anne was beginning to become quite adept at them. It might be time to introduce her to some more advanced techniques.

When Anne began to play, Elizabeth fretted for a few moments, wondering if Lady Catherine would come walking through the door. She did not have long to wait.

It could not be supposed the great Lady Catherine de Bourgh would enter a room by opening the door herself, and Elizabeth heard a muffled but imperious command, and soon after, the door opened. Anne kept playing, her fingers searching for the correct keys, and Elizabeth could not detect even a hint of hesitation. Taking her cue from Anne, Elizabeth kept her eyes on the hands of the performer, intent upon not appearing to dare the lady's response. For a moment, Lady Catherine stood just inside the room, watching them.

"Is there no depth to which you will not descend, Miss Bennet?"

Elizabeth turned at the sound of the lady's voice, which had been accusatory, but not so loud as Lady Catherine's normal annoyance would be. "I am sorry, Lady Catherine I do not take your meaning."

"You know exactly to what I refer. I am aware of your attempts to ingratiate yourself with Anne, to improve your own situation at the expense of my relationship with her."

"Oh, do be silent, Mother," said Anne, never hesitating as she continued through the piece, now for the second time.

"You will not speak to me in such a way!"

"It seems I must, as you will not hear sense if I do not. Elizabeth has been the best of friends to me. It seems as if you merely wish to control me, to make me do your bidding regardless of my opinion."

Lady Catherine's visage darkened, but Anne was not finished. "Are you upset that I am playing?"

"You know it is beyond your strength."

Anne laughed. "It seems like it is not. Else I would not be sitting here." Anne finished the piece and turned to Lady Catherine. "You may leave us, Mother. I would appreciate your absence, so that I may practice without interference."

Her nostrils flaring, Lady Catherine glared at Anne, and Elizabeth was certain she was about to make some caustic reply when she turned on her heel and marched from the room. It was perhaps fortunate that Lady Catherine was not one to open and close doors herself, for Elizabeth was certain the door would have slammed behind her otherwise.

They were watched closely for the rest of the day, and though it often appeared as if they were alone, in truth Elizabeth was certain Lady Catherine was rarely far from them. They continued their usual activities, sometimes reading or talking in Anne's room. Anne even insisted that they walk the halls of Rosings in order to make up for Elizabeth's lack of exercise that morning.

"Come, Elizabeth," said Anne, laughing at Elizabeth's consternation, "you were not able to walk this morning. Since my mother has decreed that you are not to be allowed back in should you depart, do you not feel the need to stretch your legs and gain whatever benefit you can?"

"I much prefer it if I am able to walk outside," groused Elizabeth.

"Though the scenery in the house is not nearly so pleasant, I am certain it shall be enough today."

Reluctant though she was, Elizabeth allowed herself to be persuaded, and soon they had begun to walk, beginning from the far end of the wing in which the family apartments were situated, and through the halls toward the guest wing. Elizabeth walked, Anne holding her arm as if she was a gentleman walking his sweetheart, and for a moment they were silent, Elizabeth chewing her lip in thought.

"This cannot continue for long, Anne," said Elizabeth.

"Being confined to the house?" asked Anne.

"Yes. I do not mean that I cannot give up my walks for a few days, but this standoff between ourselves and your mother will eventually escalate, and someone will do or say something unforgiveable. We cannot continue this way forever."

"I know," replied Anne simply. "Do not concern yourself—the matter will be resolved before long. Perhaps even this afternoon."

Utterly confused, Elizabeth turned and looked at the other woman, but Anne only smiled knowingly at her. "Just wait, Elizabeth. All will be well."

Elizabeth sensed that Anne would not share the reason for her confidence, and she was a little cross with her friend. There was little choice, however, so she allowed her protests to remain unspoken.

They made their way down the stairs and through the lower halls of Rosings and walked the length of the halls several times. Knowing Anne had rarely walked, Elizabeth was concerned for her, even though their pace was slow. But her worries were proven groundless—Anne was as cheerful as ever, and she did not suffer any visible ill effects from their half hour walk. Elizabeth did notice Lady Catherine watching them a time or two, but the lady said nothing. Elizabeth might have thought the lady introspective, had she not known that she was completely incapable of that state.

Of course, the short comments, snapped commands, or little insults did not stop. At times Lady Catherine barked at Anne, admonishing her to refrain from exceeding her strength or remember her capabilities. Anne either ignored her or returned her comments with calm rejoinders, which often consisted of nothing more than a statement that her interference was not welcome. More often, however, the target of Lady Catherine's ire was Elizabeth, and her comments were not nearly so benign, nor so politely stated.

They made it through until dinner that evening, and though Elizabeth was inclined to once again eat above stairs, Anne insisted upon their joining Lady Catherine in the dining room. "You have said you wished for my mother to accustom herself to the changes in my life. I will not hide from her, and neither shall you. She must learn that I will not be treated like a child any longer."

"It will be nice once we have our home to ourselves again," said Lady Catherine to Anne. They had sat at the table, Anne ensuring Elizabeth was to her side, thus placing herself between them, and Lady Catherine had spoken when she had given the order for dinner to be served.

"To ourselves?" asked Anne, as she took a sip of her water. "I am certain I do not know to what you refer, Mother."

"Why, when Miss Bennet finally leaves our home, of course." The steel in Lady Catherine's eyes might have impaled Elizabeth, had she been able to fashion it into the right implement. "Then you and I may return to our previous comfortable ways."

Anne snorted, but she did not respond, drawing her mother's pointed look. When it did not have any effect, Lady Catherine decided to ignore it.

"I have placed ads in all the newspapers to find your new companion," continued Lady Catherine in a conversational tone. "They will be required to travel here to be interviewed, of course, but for such a prestigious position, I cannot think it will be an inconvenience." The lady paused. "It is unfortunate that I have already settled Miss Pope in with Lady Metcalf's daughter—she would have been perfect for the position."

"I am happy to hear it, Mother," said Anne, ignoring the bit about Miss Pope. Lady Catherine smiled in response, obviously thinking she was starting to persuade her daughter to her way of thinking. "However, please recall that I will not accept any woman as my companion whom I have not approved myself. Also, please remember that *I* will be her mistress—not you."

The smile ran away from Lady Catherine's face. "What are you saying, Anne? Of course, I will be her mistress. I will be paying her wages."

"Perhaps you will, but I will not relent. I have no desire to see you hire another Mrs. Jenkinson, a woman who has no care for my comfort beyond obeying your every whim."

"Anne!" barked Lady Catherine. "You will not speak to me in such a way! I am your nearest relation, and I have naught but your interests in mind."

For the first time since they had begun speaking, Anne turned to Lady Catherine, and whatever was in her eyes must have been unexpected, for Lady Catherine started at the sight.

"No, Mother," said Anne. "You have naught but *your* interests in mind. I am five and twenty, and for my entire life, I have been forced to live at your whim, to live at your pleasure. I will not do it any longer!"

"Lady Catherine," said Elizabeth, feeling it incumbent upon her to try to play peacemaker between mother and daughter, "I am certain you wish for the best for Anne. As a woman herself, should you not consider what makes her happy? She is five years my elder, and yet you treat her as if she were a child."

"Miss Bennet," said Lady Catherine, her jaw working in her anger, "you will be silent and not speak another word. You are the cause of these difficulties, and I will not have you blowing the conflagration hotter. Gentleman's daughter or not, I will have you carried kicking and screaming from this house if you say one more word."

"Clearly, I was correct, Elizabeth," said Anne, rising from the table and fixing a pointed glare on her mother. "It is pointless to attempt to reason with her, for she is far too set in her ways. Come, let us return to my room. I shall have the housekeeper bring us our dinner."

"You will go to bed hungry if you step out that door!" screeched Lady Catherine.

"Then so be it." Anne turned a pitiless glare on Lady Catherine. "I cannot begin to tell me how much you disgust me, Mother. You are far worse a tyrant than Bonaparte ever could be!"

And the two ladies departed, leaving Lady Catherine sitting alone at the table. Elizabeth managed to obtain one more glance at her, and what she saw nearly set her to shivering. This could not continue much longer, for if it did, she would be worried for Anne's safety, not to mention her own.

It was the next day when the situation finally came to a head. Elizabeth and Anne had managed to break their fast the next morning by arriving for breakfast long before the lady usually descended. Later they walked the halls again until Lady Catherine made her appearance and retreated to Anne's room when the lady was once again present.

When they were once again within Anne's room, they amused themselves for a time, reading to each other from a book of sonnets Elizabeth had brought with her from home. Unfortunately, it was not long before Anne became bored with the activity, and, closing the book, she rose and began to pace the room.

"Perhaps we should simply go to the stables, saddle two horses, and make for London."

"I hardly think we could do that, Anne," replied Elizabeth. "I can ride, but I am not practiced, and you have never been atop a horse. Besides, I had understood you did not wish to go to London."

"I think these past days have changed my mind," muttered Anne. Then she gestured imperiously for Elizabeth to rise. "Come, Elizabeth, we have not danced for some days. I would like to continue my lessons."

Uncertain, Elizabeth rose to her feet. "Are you certain that is wise?"

"I am not certain anything is wise, but if I do not have something else on which to think, I shall go mad."

Sighing, Elizabeth stepped forward. At this point, it was unlikely the situation could be made worse. They stepped together and Elizabeth began humming music which she had often heard used in the Boulanger, and the girls stepped together. And for a time, Elizabeth forgot the strain the past days and simply enjoy times when they had been more carefree.

Then disaster struck, of course. Lady Catherine walked into the room.

"What is the meaning of this?" demanded the lady. "What other subversive things have you been teaching my daughter? Do you not remember me telling you that she was incapable of such exertions?"

"Stop it, Mother!" cried Anne. "I *am* doing it. How can you possibly say that I cannot, when I have been these past weeks?"

Lady Catherine turned an unattractive shade of puce. "This cannot stand! Laura!"

The maid peeked into the room, her fright obvious for them all to see. Elizabeth felt sorry for the girl, wondering if she was about to be dismissed.

"Go downstairs and send a footman on a fast horse to the parsonage. If Mr. Collins is not within my sitting-room within ten minutes, he may find himself another parish."

The girl squeaked and took flight, but Elizabeth did not miss her expression, like a man condemned to the hangman's noose being granted a reprieve. Elizabeth was not allowed to consider the matter for long, for Lady Catherine turned back to them and pointed one talon at Elizabeth.

"You will pack your bags this instant, Miss Bennet, for you will be departing at once!"

Then the lady turned and stalked from the room, and this time the door did impact against the frame with a loud crash.

"I am only surprised it took her this long to come to this conclusion," said Anne, her voice dispassionate.

"I do not think this is a time for jests, Anne," replied Elizabeth. "I suppose I shall have my effects prepared for departure."

"Very well," replied Anne. "But you may yet be surprised."

Elizabeth could not determine of what Anne spoke, but she repaired to her room, instructing a wide-eyed Tilly to have her things packed, and then met Anne back in the hallway.

"I saw Mr. Collins hurrying toward the Rosings out the window of my room," said Anne when they came together. "The silly man appears to be taking my mother's threat seriously."

"She cannot take the living away, of course," replied Elizabeth. "But she has the power to make my cousin's life quite difficult, if she chooses."

Anne nodded but did not reply. They descended the stairs and made their way to the sitting-room, to be greeted by the sight of Lady Catherine pacing the room. She spared them not a glance as they stepped in, and as Anne motioned to a nearby pair of chairs, Elizabeth nodded and accompanied her there, sitting beside her friend. Elizabeth had been surprised at Anne's determination these past days, but the way Anne's hand found hers and grasped it with a grip which seemed to say she never intended to let go reminded Elizabeth that she was still insecure and required assistance. No matter what happened, Elizabeth vowed to stay by her friend and give her the support she required.

The sound of Mr. Collins's coming preceded him in the sharp tapping of his feet on the hallway tiles, and when he entered, it was clear he had run the entire distance from the parsonage, for he heaved like a horse that had just run the breadth of England. Perspiration flowed down his face, and his ever-present handkerchief rose to mop it up. Moreover, his eyes were wild, and he looked on Lady Catherine with trepidation, and Anne and Elizabeth with a mute plea.

"Mr. Collins!" Lady Catherine's voice snapped like a whip.

"Y-yes your lady . . . ship," replied Mr. Collins. His eyes reminded Elizabeth of a terrified dog she had once seen, its eyes rolling in its fright.

"How dare you bring this . . . this . . . improper chit into my house? Do you not know what she has done to my daughter?"

"Well . . . That is to say . . ." Lady Catherine's glare bore down on Mr. Collins with the heat of a thousand suns, and he could only squeal: "Miss de Bourgh has been so much happier in my cousin's company!"

"Happier? How can she be? Have you not heard me say from our earliest acquaintance that Anne's delicate constitution required constant care and rigid control? And now Miss Bennet has her dancing and walking, driving her phaeton at all hours of the day and night, sitting at the pianoforte which will cause her to injure her delicate back. But the greatest betrayal of all is how she has imparted her rebellious attitude to Anne. My daughter has never spoken to me in such a way as she has these past days.

"Now, Mr. Collins, you will remove your cousin from this house and you will do it immediately. She will be put on the first coach returning to her father's house, and not only will you never invite her here again, but you will break off all contact with her family. When her father dies, we may discuss then how you shall act, but considering her betrayal, I am inclined to advise you that they be put out at the first opportunity."

It was clear that Mr. Collins was befuddled, for he peered at her, wondering if he had ever seen her before. His confusion, however, was nothing to what it became when Anne's harsh laughter sounded, drawing Lady Catherine's attention to them, the fury of murder alight in the dark depths of her eyes.

"This is admirable, Mother. You must truly think you are our lord himself, if you think you can order Mr. Collins in such a manner as this. His family relationships are none of your concern. Was it not you who demanded he restore his family ties with the Bennets?"

"I was mistaken," snapped Lady Catherine.

"It is not the only matter of which have been mistaken, Mother." Anne faced Lady Catherine, and had Elizabeth's hands not been caught in her steely grip, she might have thought her confidence to be supreme.

"I will save you the trouble of evicting Elizabeth, Mother," continued Anne. "We shall both be departing. I will not live in this house another instant."

"You will go nowhere! I am your mother!"

"And I am of age! I will call on the aid of my uncle — he will support me in this."

"How do you intend to gain his attention?" Lady Catherine sneered. "If you walk out the door, you shall walk to London."

"So be it!"

Anne stood, drawing Elizabeth with her. "You disgust me, Mother. I cannot begin to tell you how much contempt I have for you. Good bye, for I shall never see you again."

"Baines!" shrieked Lady Catherine. "Come here this instant!" She turned her glare on Mr. Collins. "Remove your cousin from this house! I care not where she goes!"

"It would be best if you did not obey that order, Mr. Collins."

Starting at the sound of a deep voice, Elizabeth turned to the door, spying two tall men standing there.

"Mr. Darcy!" exclaimed Mr. Collins, summing up Elizabeth's feelings perfectly.

Chapter XII

Darcy could hardly believe his eyes. It had been a typical dull day, full of correspondence which required attention, business to conduct, and all the other trappings which went with being a landowner. The season was in full swing now, the invitations to balls, dinners, and parties seemed like a huge wave roaring over the deck of a ship. He rejected most of them, as there were few men and even fewer ladies whose society he could tolerate with any degree of equanimity. His cousin laughed at him, calling him dour and unsociable, but when Darcy called him on it, noted how he had little more taste for society himself, Fitzwilliam only laughed, claiming that at least he was able to hide his revulsion better.

But everything had been turned upside down at the express letter waiting for him when he had returned that evening. Darcy had accepted an invitation to a dinner with a close friend and had managed to spend an agreeable evening in company. His butler had handed him the express upon his return, and its contents had shocked Darcy.

"Is my cousin here at present?"

"He returned not fifteen minutes gone, sir."

"Please inform him I have need of his attendance at once."

When the man turned to follow his instruction, Darcy made his way to his study and began to pace, throwing the offending letter on the desk and muttering as his shoes clattered against the tiles beneath his feet. The information contained in the letter was vague and unclear, but it seemed the woman had finally taken leave of her senses. And what was *she* doing in Kent, and staying at Rosings, no less? Darcy could not begin to fathom what had been taking place at his aunt's estate this past month.

When Fitzwilliam walked in, he eyed Darcy with his usual insolent manners. He had changed from his regimentals into a typical gentleman's suit, an indication his own evening had been spent in the company of society, rather than soldiers. And when he spoke, Darcy could hear the usual lack of gravity in his voice.

"I say, Darcy, I have rarely seen you this riled. Has that Bingley woman stormed the house? Or maybe she attempted to compromise you at whatever gathering you attended this evening, and her spineless brother did nothing to stop it."

Darcy only scowled at his cousin and gestured at the letter still sitting on the desk, continuing his pacing without hesitation. Fitzwilliam, taken by surprise at his reply, turned and picked up the letter, scanning its contents with open curiosity. It was not long before he frowned, and he read aloud:

> *My mother is an unreasonable despot, and I will not endure her interference in my life any longer. I fear for my safety, Cousin, and that of Miss Bennet, and I abjure you, in the strongest language possible, to make haste to Rosings and remove us from this situation immediately. Please do not think this is a ploy of my mother's — we are at your mercy!*

"Darcy, what the blazes is this?"

"A letter from Anne. Can you not see the signature?"

"And when did it arrive?"

"I received it only a few moments ago. It was sent by express."

Fitzwilliam inspected the letter again. "Darcy, this is dated yesterday. It is not so far distant from Rosings that a letter could not arrive here within four hours."

"I am aware of that," was Darcy's testy reply. "According to my butler, the express rider apologized profusely. It seems his horse pulled up lame, and he was forced to walk several hours to Bromley."

"Even that does not account for the delay," growled Fitzwilliam.

"I have no more explanation than that. We must make haste to

Rosings. I do not know what the devil has being happening there, but it seems Anne has finally decided to make a bid for her independence."

"The day is too late for a departure now. We shall be forced to depart in the morning."

"At first light, Fitzwilliam. Will you be able to obtain leave?"

Fitzwilliam scratched his chin. "It should not be a problem. I have leave accumulated and am between assignments at present. I will send a note to the general at once. I should have a reply by the morning."

"Very well. I will order the carriage for the morning. I believe I shall retire, though I am certain it will be a long night."

In the end, however, Darcy surprised himself by managing to sleep at least a few hours, though the night had begun as inauspiciously as he had expected. The first thoughts to pass through his mind were concerning his aunt, her autocratic ways and insistence upon his attendance to them at Rosings. Though Darcy had spent a long month fending off her entreaties, her demands, and at times even her understated threats, he was now to return to the place which had held little pleasure for him, and more than a little aggravation. If there was ever a relation for whom to blush, it was Lady Catherine.

Then, of course, his thoughts had turned to Anne, and he had wondered at this apparent change in her. Was she openly defying her mother? The very thought was incomprehensible. And for her to suggest that she was in danger from her mother . . . How could such a thing be? Surely Lady Catherine could not be so far gone from decency to threaten her only daughter with harm.

And then there was Miss Bennet, and if anything, she was the most confusing part of the whole mess. How did she factor into this? How did she even know Anne? The stirrings of the infatuation which had driven him from Hertfordshire, had led him to convince his friend that he could not consider her sister for a wife, now hit him with the full force of a speeding carriage. It was as if he had not been parted from her these past months, so strong was the inclination to see her again, as he knew he would on the morrow.

Thus it was that though Darcy managed to sleep, his thoughts returned to these subjects upon awakening, leaving him feeling a little out of sorts the following day. When he entered the carriage before eight o'clock the following morning, he attempted to hide his unsettled feelings from his cousin, though Fitzwilliam, always astute and knowing Darcy better than any other, likely saw through it. For once, the severity of their errand seemed to divert his cousin from his usual flippancy, and the talk surrounded the situation they were likely to find at Rosings.

"Have you had any word from Rosings these past months?"

"Only what I have told you of our aunt's continued insistence that I attend her. The woman has grown more strident over time, so much so that I have ceased to answer her letters."

Fitzwilliam nodded—Darcy's complaints on the subject were not new to him. "What of Anne? Has she not written?"

"Only the express we saw yesterday." Darcy grimaced. "Anne usually does not write to me. We both know what will happen if Lady Catherine discovers any letters passing between us."

"She would begin ordering Anne's trousseau," replied Fitzwilliam. The men exchanged a rueful glance. "To be honest, Cousin, I have wondered why she has not fixated on *me* as a mate for her daughter. *You* already own an estate, after all—and more than one."

"You own an estate yourself," pointed out Darcy.

"I do, but it is nothing to Pemberley. If anyone needs to be provided for, it is me, for you have the Darcy wealth, and James is heir to all my father has."

"She wishes to combine Rosings and Pemberley," replied Darcy with a shrug. "Though I do not know if she truly thinks she can rule them both, I know she wishes to consolidate the family wealth. Perhaps she even thinks a title can be obtained, if I possessed so much wealth."

Fitzwilliam barked laughter. "Then she does not know you well."

"I did not say the woman was sensible. That is only what I suspect and what I have discussed with your father."

"It seems as likely as anything else," replied Fitzwilliam with a grunt. "What I cannot understand is what this Miss Bennet has to do with the matter. I assume she is the woman Lady Catherine hired to replace Mrs. Jenkinson?"

Though he was loath to speak of Miss Bennet, Darcy felt incumbent upon himself to reply: "Miss Bennet is not unknown to me."

"Oh?" was Fitzwilliam's lazy reply, the light of interest shining in his eyes.

"At least, I assume it is she to whom Anne refers." It was clear that Fitzwilliam was not about to let the matter rest, so Darcy was forced to further explain. "Miss Bennet is from Hertfordshire. Her family lives near the estate Bingley leased last autumn."

Fitzwilliam frowned. "Then what the blazes is she doing in Kent, of all places?"

"Her cousin is the rector of Lady Catherine's parish, so there is a connection. When I met the man, he was yet unmarried, but it is possible that he did marry and that she is visiting."

"If he is the rector of Hunsford, then he cannot be at all sensible," said Fitzwilliam with a snort. "Which makes me wonder if *she* is sensible either."

"Quite the contrary, in fact," replied Darcy, though quietly. "Miss Bennet impressed me as an intelligent woman, indeed."

The interest in Fitzwilliam's gaze made Darcy uncomfortable. "If this Miss Bennet is visiting, it would make more sense for her to be visiting the parsonage. Anne's note implies that she is at Rosings."

"I cannot explain it," replied Darcy, holding his hand up. "I could not have imagined she would be in Kent."

Fitzwilliam directed a level look at him. "Georgiana mentioned something about a woman you referenced in your letters, and I seem to remember the name Bennet. Is this the same woman?"

"Yes, but I only mentioned her in passing. She had a talent for confounding Miss Bingley, and I knew that Georgiana would find her antics amusing."

"Then I suppose I must approve of her!" Fitzwilliam guffawed. "Any woman who can confound the odious Miss Bingley will forever have my approbation." Darcy could do naught but chuckle with his cousin—Miss Bingley *was* odious, and there was little argument on the matter.

"Was Hertfordshire not the place where you recently saved Bingley from a most imprudent attachment?"

The reminder brought to Darcy's mind the discomfort he had felt the previous evening, for though he had never thought Jane Bennet cared for Bingley, he understood he had directed Bingley away from her as much for *his* benefit as Bingley's.

"Yes, it was. But since we are to be in company with Miss Bennet, I would ask for your circumspection. The young lady in question was Miss Bennet's sister."

"And how many sisters does she have?"

"There are five, all told. Miss Jane Bennet—Bingley's angel—is the eldest, while Miss Elizabeth Bennet, to whom you will shortly be introduced, is the second. The younger sisters are, in varying degrees, silly and improper."

The long look Fitzwilliam directed at Darcy soon made him uncomfortable yet again. But it was nothing to what he felt when Fitzwilliam finally spoke.

"I do not believe Anne mentioned the lady's Christian name in her letter—how do you know it is Miss Elizabeth Bennet who is at Rosings?"

Darcy gaped at his cousin and opened his mouth to speak, but he quickly closed it with a frown. "You are correct, I suppose. It could just as easily be the eldest Miss Bennet, though I doubt it would be one of the younger girls, who are still full young to travel alone."

"And why would you assume it to be Miss Elizabeth then?"

"Probably because it is she with whom I am most acquainted," replied Darcy. He affected a disinterest in the subject, but he was aware of Fitzwilliam's skepticism. It was fortunate, then, that his cousin chose not to press him any further, though Darcy thought it a near thing.

They spoke further, strategizing what they would do when they arrived at Rosings, but there was little they could plan, given they did not know the truth of the situation. After some time, they fell silent, and Fitzwilliam, as was his habit, fell asleep in the carriage, leaving Darcy to his brooding thoughts. Doubt had settled over him, and he knew that his cousin was correct. It might not be Miss Elizabeth at all who was present at Kent, and the thought brought him a measure of relief, though an equal sense of loss.

When the roof of Rosings rose in the distance, Darcy shook his cousin awake, gesturing toward the approaching house. The carriage pulled to a stop in front of the house, the dust billowing out from their passage to be carried away on the stiff breeze which blew that day. The footman opened the door and they both stepped out, mounting the steps in a hurry. The butler, a cadaverous man by the name of Smith, was already waiting for them. But before they could even greet the man, the sound of voices raised in anger reached their ears.

"No need to announce us, Smith," said Darcy over his shoulder as he hurried into the house. "We know the way."

When they reached the parlor, they found a footman stationed outside, obviously distressed. He noted their approach and turned to open the door, his sudden actions not hiding the relief which appeared on his countenance. Darcy and Fitzwilliam entered the room to see an argument in progress, and though Lady Catherine's heightened color and shrill voice were no surprise, Anne—standing with Miss *Elizabeth Bennet's* hand in a tight grip—was a revelation.

"You disgust me, Mother," said Anne, her voice louder and more powerful than Darcy had ever heard. "I cannot begin to tell you how much contempt I have for you. Good bye, for I shall never see you again."

"Baines!" shrieked Lady Catherine. "Come here this instant!" She turned her glare on Mr. Collins. "Remove your cousin from this house! I care not where she goes!"

"It would be best if you did not obey that order, Mr. Collins," said Darcy.

Four sets of eyes turned and found Darcy and Fitzwilliam where they stood, and their reactions could not be any more different. Mr. Collins, Darcy thought, appeared almost ready to pass out with relief, while Miss Bennet watched him, surprised at his coming, but otherwise unreadable. Anne, though she had spoken most forcefully only a moment before, looked like a flower wilting beneath a fiery sun. As for Lady Catherine, she looked on his coming with savage glee.

"Darcy! You have finally come. Now everything may be restored to order."

"It does, indeed, appear as if order is lacking in your home, Lady Catherine," replied Darcy. "What is the meaning of this argument? I would have thought I was approaching a fish market when I entered the house."

"It is all that *girl's* fault!" screeched Lady Catherine, a long, bony finger pointing at Miss Bennet. "She has brought this upon us, pushed my daughter to this mutiny! I demand you remove her from this house immediately!"

"Anne?" asked Darcy, turning his attention to his cousin. "You called us here. Shall you not explain what has happened?"

"Anne called you here?" demanded Lady Catherine.

"By means of an express I received last night." Darcy turned to Anne. "I apologize, Cousin, but there were delays in receiving your letter, and it came when I was away from the house yesterday evening. We came as soon as we could."

An imperious wave was Anne's first response, an action he might have thought to see from Lady Catherine. "It is of no matter, Cousin. You are here now. I will ask you to return us with you to London, so that I may seek my uncle and beg for his protection."

"You will go nowhere!" shrieked Lady Catherine. "I will not allow it."

Had Darcy not seen it, he would never have believed the frigid expression which came over his cousin's countenance. Lady Catherine, too, appeared shocked, and for the first time in living memory, she was rendered speechless. Unless Darcy missed his guess, she was a little fearful at what she was seeing. Anne approached Lady Catherine, walking slowly, and though Miss Bennet walked behind her, she seemed to sense that Anne needed to act for herself, for she only looked on as Anne spoke.

"Let me tell you this for the last time, Mother. I am of age and may do what I please, and you can do nothing about it. All my life you have kept me locked in this house, restricted me from anything which brought me pleasure, forced me to live this sterile existence which has sapped my strength, left me wishing the pain of this life would simply end."

"No! Anne, what are you saying?"

"That you have been nothing more than my jailor. That you have ruled over me and kept me in a cage—a gilded cage, yes, but still a prison. I have never had any joy, never been able to indulge in those activities which other ladies of my station take for granted, and poisoned me with your continuous nonsense about an engagement with Darcy. I have grown to be five and twenty, never knowing what it is like to live, and now that I have begun to assert a little independence, and have gained a friend as wonderful as Elizabeth, you attempt to take her away from me, to lock me back into my room, feed me tonics, and insist that I am too ill for life yet again.

"I will not return to that cage." Anne's voice, though low, was filled with pain and heartache, and Darcy felt his heart breaking along with hers. "You may do what you wish, but I will leave with Darcy and Fitzwilliam today. I mean to live."

"If you walk out of the doors of Rosings, you will be disowned!" said Lady Catherine, one final, desperate—and obvious—attempt to keep her daughter under her thumb.

"So be it," replied Anne, her tone pitiless. "It is better to live my life as a penniless spinster than to return to your oppression. I despise you, Mother!"

And then Anne whirled and buried herself in Miss Bennet's embrace, sobbing as if her heart was broken. And silence descended on the room, other than the sound of Anne's continued tears.

Though it was difficult to fathom the emotions which were passing between mother and daughter, and Elizabeth felt a measure of sorrow at such a break playing out in front of her very eyes, she could not be prouder of Anne. Yes, she would have wished for the scene to have been avoided, but Elizabeth knew Anne was correct. She had lived an oppressed, cheerless existence which Elizabeth would not have wished on her worst enemy.

Lady Catherine stood, facing Anne and Elizabeth, her countenance stricken and devoid of all color. Their eyes met, and for a moment

Elizabeth thought the lady might continue to berate her. Instead, a wordless understanding seemed to pass between them, and the lady staggered back and sat heavily in a chair situated not far behind. All the fight had departed from her.

It was surprising, but Mr. Collins was the first to move. It seemed he was unable to witness the distress of his patroness, for he approached her and took a knee near her chair and began to speak to her in a low voice.

"Perhaps it is best that Miss de Bourgh go with these fine gentlemen, Lady Catherine. Though I would never give credit to any notion that you do not know best, perhaps in this instance it is better to allow her to direct her own life. I am certain you wish her to be happy."

"Be gone, Mr. Collins," was Lady Catherine's reply, but its imperious note was but a shadow of its usual strength. "I have no need of your platitudes."

Uncertain, Mr. Collins arose, and he directed a stricken look at Mr. Darcy. For his part, Mr. Darcy shook his head. He then turned his attention to the other man standing at his side, and an understanding seemed to pass between them. The second man nodded once and moved to approach Lady Catherine, while Mr. Darcy came to Elizabeth and Anne, who was still crying on Elizabeth's shoulder.

"I believe it is best to remove Anne to London, Miss Bennet. It appears she is most comfortable with you—shall we take her to her room so that she may recover for our departure?"

It was a tone Elizabeth had never heard from Mr. Darcy, one which was soft and gentle and which spoke to affection and warmth, but was not demanding, like those which he usually used in her experience. Elizabeth could do nothing but nod, and she began to guide Anne from the room, Mr. Collins following behind, appearing like a lost puppy.

The time until their departure was a flurry of activity. Elizabeth saw Anne to her bedchamber and coaxed her to lie down upon her bed. Instructions were given to Laura for her mistress's clothing to be made ready. Elizabeth herself spent her time between her own room and Anne's, ensuring everything was proceeding apace. The surprise of Mr. Darcy, however, was one which did not depart, for he was solicitous and concerned for her wellbeing.

"How is Anne?" asked he when Elizabeth emerged from Anne's room for the first time.

"I believe she is recovering. She has been so strong these past days . . . I can hardly imagine what it cost her to stand up to Lady Catherine the way she did."

"Anne was strong?" asked Mr. Darcy. He seemed hardly able to imagine it, and Elizabeth could understand, though her ire was raised slightly in defense of her friend.

"She was," replied Elizabeth simply, eager to avoid one of their infamous arguments.

"And how did you come to be in the middle of this mess?" asked Mr. Darcy, turning his attention once again to Elizabeth. "Why are you even in Kent?"

"I do not have time for lengthy explanations, sir," replied Elizabeth. "My cousin married my dearest friend, Charlotte Lucas, and I was invited to visit them. After Mrs. Jenkinson passed, Anne convinced her mother to ask me to live here as her companion until I return home, and I agreed."

Mr. Darcy seemed still uncertain, but he did not question her any further. "More detailed explanations may wait until we are in the carriage. For now, I must thank you for all you have done for my cousin. It seems, from her reliance on you, that you have become close in a short period."

"She is a wonderful woman," replied Elizabeth. "I am quite fond of her. But, yes, if you will excuse me, I will make certain all is prepared for our departure." Elizabeth paused, and then addressed him, a matter of concern having entered her mind. "What is to be done with our maids? Tilly was not aware of my friendship with Anne, but Laura helped us. I am afraid they will both be targets for Lady Catherine's displeasure once we are gone."

"They will accompany us, of course," replied Mr. Darcy. "You will both need your maids in London. I will see that one of Lady Catherine's servants' carriages is prepared, so they may travel behind us."

Then Mr. Darcy bowed and moved away, leaving Elizabeth bemused behind. She soon shook off her thoughts of the man in favor of the urgency of the situation, and she returned to her room, instructing Tilly to also prepare herself for a removal to London.

"If you do not wish to go, you are not required to, of course," said Elizabeth, when the girl appeared doubtful. "I have managed without a maid, and I may do so again. I am only concerned that your mistress might find fault with you, considering the events of the past days."

"Oh no!" exclaimed Tilly. "She would never do so. But I do not have any objection to accompanying you to London. It is only I am not certain what is to become of my employment . . . ."

"I am certain Mr. Darcy understands you will require your pay," said Elizabeth, certain she was correct, though they had not spoken of it. "I know not how he will handle it, but I should think you would find employment in his house."

"And will you stay for long?"

Elizabeth shook her head. "I do not doubt that I will remove to my uncle's house when we arrive in London. I hope to keep up my acquaintance with Miss de Bourgh, but it is time I returned home."

"Very well, mistress. I will ensure we are ready to leave within the hour."

With that task completed, Elizabeth returned to Anne's room to have a similar conversation with Laura, and although Anne's maid did not say so much, Elizabeth thought she was as uncertain as Tilly had been. Elizabeth did what she could to put the girl's mind at ease, and in this instance, she felt more confident in what she was saying. Anne would likely be staying with either Mr. Darcy or her uncle for some time, and Laura, as her maid, would be added to the staff wherever she stayed.

When Elizabeth returned to Anne's bedchamber, she noted that Anne was sitting up on her bed, though her posture was folded over, her arms held tightly around herself. Elizabeth approached her and knelt by Anne's side, noting the tears staining her cheeks.

"How you must think me to be nothing more than a weakling," said Anne, her voice almost inaudible.

"I think no such thing." Elizabeth reached out and grasped Anne's hand, pulling it to her and holding it between both of her own. "You have grown so much these past weeks, Anne. It is no less than astonishing."

"I should not have spoken to my mother in that way."

"While it is true I would have wished for a more amicable resolution with your mother, what is done is done. It took much strength to oppose her as you did, and I do not blame you for it. I cannot say why your mother has treated you as she has, but it is clear she should have taken your feelings into account and allowed you to live your life. There is no shame in standing up for yourself."

A slight smile came over Anne's face. "How could I not, with such an excellent example before me. My heart hurts at this break with my mother, though I am unsure she deserves my regret. But I cannot be happier that you have become my friend. I hope you will agree to remain my friend, Elizabeth, no matter what comes."

"Of course, I shall," replied Elizabeth. "There is nothing I wish more. And you never know—your mother may see the truth of what you told her. You may be reconciled to her someday."

"Only if she agrees to change and treat me as an adult," replied Anne. Some of her former spark was returning, and Elizabeth smiled at her resilience.

The two ladies sat for some time, though not many words were exchanged between them. Within fifteen minutes, Laura informed them that the carriages were ready, and they could depart. As one, the two ladies rose, and they left the room. Elizabeth was struck by how Anne held her head high and departed, never looking back at the room which had been her domain for all her life.

Chapter XIII

Lady Catherine de Bourgh was not on hand to witness the departure of her only daughter. Given the lengths to which the woman had gone to ensure Anne remained under her control, Elizabeth might have thought they would not be able to leave without her interference. But their leaving was accomplished without any hint of the lady's presence, and though Anne looked around once or twice, likely expecting her mother to suddenly appear and clap her in chains, she never came. The man who came to Rosings with Mr. Darcy was able to give them a little intelligence.

"I escorted her to her bedchamber, and that is where I suspect she is now. I have never seen your mother in such a state, Anne. She was pale, her movements jerky and uncoordinated, and I almost thought her guilty of introspection."

"Fitzwilliam," said Anne, shaking her head at her cousin, who displayed more than a hint of amusement. "We truly have had a devil of a time. I do not wish to make sport with my mother, but I am determined we shall never meet again if she does not change her ways toward me."

The man sobered immediately. "I cannot imagine what it has been like, Anne. I only wish we could have been of use to you before."

"It would not have done any good." Anne clutched Elizabeth's arm. "If it were not for Elizabeth, I would still be in mother's thrall. I am grateful to her for her assistance—more than I can ever say."

Elizabeth blushed and turned away, and though Fitzwilliam appeared as if he wished to tease—she had done it so many times in the past, she was intimately familiar with what it looked like—he held his tongue. Anne continued to speak with him, but Elizabeth's eyes were caught by the sight of an uneasy Mr. Collins, standing and watching them.

A pang of regret coursed through Elizabeth. With the events of the morning, she had quite forgotten Charlotte, and she now knew she would not be able to take her leave of her friend before they departed. Elizabeth disengaged her arm from her friend's grasp and approached Mr. Collins, and the man appeared relieved at the opportunity to speak with her.

"My dear Cousin," said he, bowing in his usually expansive manner. "I wished to thank you for your kindness in coming to Kent to visit my dear wife, and moreover, for the friendship you have selflessly offered to Miss de Bourgh. It is clear to me that she has benefitted greatly from knowing you . . . ."

Mr. Collins trailed off, and Elizabeth knew he was thinking about his patroness's sentiments, which had been made abundantly clear. Knowing it was best not to allow him to think too deeply on the subject, Elizabeth smiled.

"I thank you for inviting me here, sir. I am only sorry that I was not able to spend more time with Charlotte."

"It is, indeed, a shame, but I believe you have been called by some higher purpose. Miss de Bourgh clearly required an advocate, and in you she has found one I do not think could be matched in many others."

"I am happy to be called her friend," replied Elizabeth.

"Yes, she is a good woman, much like her . . ." Mr. Collins paused and dismay seemed to fall over him. He swallowed once and looked on her, pleading her to understand. "My patroness truly does possess the best of nobility, intelligence, munificence, and a deeply held understanding of true Christian values, Cousin. I do not know what I would do in the parish without her boundless wisdom, for there is never a problem for which she is without a solution. I would have you understand this, for I do not speak merely to gratify her vanity."

When Elizabeth murmured that she understood—it cost her nothing to agree with him, even if she could not credit such assertions—Mr. Collins seemed to relax a little, and then he became troubled again.

"I do not know what has afflicted her regarding her daughter, and I cannot understand how she cannot see how you have assisted Miss de Bourgh and made her life better. She seemed so sad and lost when you left the room—so . . . *alone*. I am not certain what to do."

"I would recommend you simply provide her with whatever support you can," said Elizabeth. "Lady Catherine has received a shock, not only because of the changes in Anne, but also because of what Anne said."

Mr. Collins darted a glance at Anne, saying: "Loath though I am to censure her, speaking to her mother in such a fashion was not well done. Children are to honor their parents, not to denigrate them."

"I agree, Mr. Collins," replied Elizabeth. "But Lady Catherine sought to oppress and control her daughter, and that is not any better than a child who does not respect their parents."

"You are correct," replied Mr. Collins simply. "I have difficulty thinking of my patroness in such a fashion, but it is clear she has not acted as she should."

"Mr. Collins, I believe Lady Catherine will need someone who is willing to listen, but at the same time inform her of those truths she needs to hear, but may not wish to. As the spiritual guide of this parish, I believe this task will fall to you. I would suggest you listen and commiserate with her, allowing her to spill her innermost feelings, and not judging her when you find them contrary to the church's teachings.

"However, it is also your responsibility to correct where there must be correction, to help sinners see where they have erred, and to assist them in taking the proper actions to improve." Elizabeth smiled at her cousin, who was looking on her with wonder. "It is a difficult task, but one I believe you are qualified to perform. Trust the holy book, Mr. Collins, but also trust in inspiration to guide you."

"My dear cousin!" exclaimed Mr. Collins. He reached for her hands and grasped one, bowing over it several times. "I am, indeed, happy that you have come, and I cannot be more grateful to you. You have spoken the exact words I needed to hear, and I cannot thank you enough. Please convey my regards to your excellent mother and father. And do not concern yourself for Lady Catherine, for I shall do everything in my power to assist her."

Then, excusing himself, Mr. Collins made his way to where Anne was still speaking with her cousin, and he paid his respects to her.

Elizabeth watched, amused at the astonishment with which Anne regarded the man. Mr. Collins, it seemed, did not do anything half-heartedly—anything to which he put his mind consumed all his energy.

"That was well done, Miss Bennet."

The voice came from behind her and startled Elizabeth, but when she turned, it was to see Mr. Darcy watching her, intensity in his gaze. Dark thoughts began forming in Elizabeth's mind, but then she remembered what he had said, and it seemed incongruous with his level look, which she had always assumed to be critical of her.

"I think that Mr. Collins is essentially a good man, though I am not well acquainted with him," continued Mr. Darcy, his expression light and his tone conversational. "He seems to want direction, and as my aunt readily provides that, he accepts it. Unfortunately, he does not stop to think about the nature of the guidance he receives, rather he simply accepts it. As he is still a young man, I do not doubt his gratitude to Lady Catherine for providing him with a living long before he might have expected to obtain one also colors his opinion."

"All this you recognized without being acquainted with him?" asked Elizabeth, her familiar archness evident in her tone. She was surprised by Mr. Darcy's words, for he was essentially correct.

Mr. Darcy allowed a soft chuckle, surprising Elizabeth again. "I do not think his is an intricate character, Miss Bennet. As you once said about my friend Bingley, the fact that it is not complex does not make it any less estimable.

"But returning to what I said before, Mr. Collins required direction. And you gave it to him in language he could understand, while giving him a purpose he may have struggled to find. It was very sagacious advice, indeed."

"Thank you, sir," replied Elizabeth, not knowing what to say. She was not accustomed to being the recipient of Mr. Darcy's approbation.

"Darcy," said Fitzwilliam, drawing Elizabeth's attention to who she assumed was another of Anne's cousins. "The carriage is loaded; we should depart."

A nod was Mr. Darcy's response, but he hesitated for a moment, glancing from Elizabeth to Mr. Collins. "You will pardon me, Miss Bennet, but I overheard your words concerning your friend. If you wish, we may take Mr. Collins back to the parsonage, and there you can farewell your friend."

Astonished at this bit of unexpected civility, Elizabeth indicated her eagerness. Mr. Darcy soon proposed the solution to Mr. Collins and was treated to the man's appreciation for his condescension in the verbose manner to which Mr. Collins was accustomed. Soon, the five had entered the carriage and it was rumbling down the drive of Rosings. Though it was only a short journey to the parsonage, Elizabeth found she had much on which to think. It was not surprising that much of her thoughts were centered upon the man in whose carriage she was currently sitting.

Could this truly be the same man? He was calm and pleasant, and he spoke to her gently and made his approval for her actions plain to see. This contrasted with the haughty and displeased man she had met in Hertfordshire, the man who had refused to stand up with her and had deemed the neighborhood to be beneath his magnificence. There was the matter of Mr. Wickham to consider, though Elizabeth could not be certain about that any longer and, of course, whatever role he had played in Mr. Bingley's removal from Jane.

Then Elizabeth thought of a comment Mr. Bingley had made at Netherfield in November, a suggestion that Mr. Darcy could be agreeable, indeed, if he was in the company of those he esteemed. Even Mr. Wickham had allowed that he was able to please when he felt it worth his while. Perhaps he now felt that. Either way, Elizabeth thought more study was required before she could hope to understand a man who was suddenly becoming much more complex.

Darcy could hardly believe he was in Miss Bennet's presence again. His memories of the woman could not match the reality of her presence, a charisma which he found as intoxicating as he had in Hertfordshire. This woman had invaded his dreams, and even the passage of the months had not dimmed her presence in them. And now she was once again before him.

There was not a time when he had not been cognizant of her true worth, or if there had been, Darcy could not now remember it. She was intelligent and compassionate, empathetic and energetic, happy and contented. A few moments earlier, Darcy had listened to her as she had spoken to Mr. Collins, marveled about how she seemed to understand exactly what the parson needed to hear. The way Mr. Collins chattered the entire way, his thanks to Miss Bennet for attending them at his house, his wishes for her speedy and safe return to her home, his desire that she visit them again in the future, spoke to his appreciation for her assistance.

And what an alteration the woman had managed in his sickly and cross cousin. Though Anne did not say much, her attention on Mr.

Collins, her sharp focus, in contrast with what he had always thought to be a fog of illness and indifference, proclaimed her to be a different person from the last time he had seen her. Darcy still did not know how it had all come about, but he meant to have answers, and he was certain those answers would revolve around Miss Bennet. She was the most exquisite creature he had ever beheld.

The carriage stopped for a brief time to allow Mr. Collins to disembark and the ladies to share an emotional farewell. Between Mrs. Collins and Miss Bennet the most tears were shed, but it also seemed like Anne and Mrs. Collins had become fond of each other. They all promised to stay in touch and to be in one another's company again as soon as may be. Only one complicating factor was raised, though it was resolved quickly.

"What of Maria?" asked Miss Bennet, gesturing to another young woman, who Darcy realized, given her resemblance to Mrs. Collins, must be her younger sister. He vaguely remembered seeing her when he was in Hertfordshire, though he was not sure he remembered her being introduced to him.

"Do not concern yourself for my sister," said Mr. Collins, interjecting into the conversation. "I will make certain she is returned to her father's home when the time comes."

"And I have asked her to stay with me for a few more weeks," added Mrs. Collins. "Since I am to be losing my dearest friend, I appreciate the company of a dear sister."

That resolved, the travelers made ready to depart yet again. The ladies were handed into the carriage, the gentlemen followed, and soon they were off. The farewells followed them as they drove out of Hunsford's grounds and onto the main road leading toward Bromley.

Once they were on the road, Fitzwilliam spoke up, his impatience a match for Darcy's own. "Now, Anne, I would appreciate an explanation. I have never been so surprised as when I read your express last night. What in the blazes have you been doing at Rosings these past weeks?"

"Where are your manners, Fitzwilliam?" asked Anne, her tartness shocking to more than just Darcy, given Fitzwilliam's reaction. "Should I not introduce you to my friend and savior?"

Fitzwilliam's eyes swung to Miss Bennet, who blushed a little at his scrutiny. "Of course, Anne, I would never wish to slight your friend. Perhaps you would do me the honor of introducing us?"

The introductions were completed quickly, the appropriate words exchanged, and then Fitzwilliam turned his attention back to Anne.

"Now propriety has been satisfied, I would hear your story. I am certain it will be fascinating."

"Of course, Cousin," said Anne. "I would not dream of keeping you in suspense."

The astonishment Darcy had felt at Anne's behavior was nothing compared to what he was feeling when she began to relate what had happened at Rosings. Starting with the death of the unfortunate Mrs. Jenkinson, Anne related the entire story of how Miss Bennet had come to Rosings, her part in making certain Lady Catherine offered the position to her, their weeks in company with each other, and how they had managed to forge a friendship which had not only led Miss Bennet to delay her departure, but had also resulted in Anne gaining a sense of self and had led them to defend each other so vigorously. Lady Catherine's behavior was not surprising—he had often thought on how she would react upon being thwarted—it was one of the reasons he had never seen fit to take a firm stance regarding her ridiculous insistence that he marry Anne.

"That is an amazing story, Anne," said Fitzwilliam when the tale had run its course. "I am quite shocked at it. But I must thank your intrepid companion for all she has done." He chuckled. "I have often thought you possessed a streak of independence that only needed the correct encouragement to bring it out. It seems that Miss Bennet was exactly what you required."

The blush which spread over Miss Bennet's countenance spoke to her discomfort, and she attempted to demur. "I have not done anything noteworthy. All I did was provide friendship to Anne, and I was very happy to do that much."

"But many would not have done that much," said Darcy. "And many would have simply fallen in with what my aunt wished."

"Aye," added Fitzwilliam. "For that alone we must be grateful. It seems my cousin was fortunate to have secured such an exceptional friend, Miss Bennet. The thanks of our family can never be enough, but I offer them unreservedly, regardless."

"Thank you," replied Miss Bennet, seemingly eager to leave the present topic of conversation behind."

They turned to other matters then, a brief discussion on the journey, how long it would take them to reach Bromley and then London itself, as well as Darcy's stated intention that they would break at Bromley and perhaps seek luncheon from the post inn there. He did not think that the ladies had had a chance to partake of any sustenance before their hurried departure, and he thought they would be hungry. The plan was agreed to by all.

But other than that one comment, Darcy did not say much at all, for he was much more agreeably engaged watching Miss Bennet, listening to her as she shared her opinions, watching the expressions on her face, listening to her laugh. This was what he had feared—to once again be in her company and to be helpless before the sheer force of her allure. He had left Hertfordshire—had fled Hertfordshire, to be more accurate—knowing that his attraction to her was overwhelming his sensibilities. Now that he was in her company again, had tasted the sweet nectar of her honeyed call, he did not know how he would ever resist her again.

As the carriage proceeded toward London, Anne began to be suspicious. It was nothing overt, for her cousin was one of the most inscrutable men she had ever known. Elizabeth had made her opinion of Darcy quite clear, and she had mentioned something of his scrutiny of her, how he watched her to judge and disapprove. As Anne did not truly know her cousin well, it was nothing she could have ever refuted, and she had accepted Elizabeth's words as fact.

But Darcy's behavior did not fit with Elizabeth's assertions. In fact, as Anne watched him, she began to wonder if Darcy's steady look consisted of disapproval at all. There was nothing in his facial expression which suggested censure, and furthermore, Anne thought she sensed a warmth in his eyes which spoke to anything *but* distaste.

When they reached Bromley, they did, indeed, stop at the post inn and ordered a light luncheon there. Anne had been so caught up in the events of the morning that she had not realized that she was famished, and if Elizabeth's eagerness to partake of the meal was of any indication, her friend was in the same state.

"Excuse me, Miss Bennet," said Darcy after they had been sitting there for some little time, "but I am sorry for my incivility. Your family—are they all well?"

"I thank you for asking, yes," replied Elizabeth. Then a hint of mischief seemed to come over her and she asked: "My sister Jane has actually been in town these past months. I wonder if you have ever had a chance to meet her."

"No, I have not had that fortune," replied Darcy.

"I suppose it is not to be wondered at," said Elizabeth, turning her attention back to her food. "I must assume you move in very different circles from my aunt and uncle."

"Perhaps," replied Darcy.

"Is that what you call it?" asked Fitzwilliam, directing a lazy grin at Darcy. "For your information, Miss Bennet, Darcy hardly moves in *any* society unless he absolutely must."

Elizabeth laughed. "I can easily believe it, Colonel Fitzwilliam." She turned a saucy look on Darcy. "Mr. Darcy strikes me as a fastidious man, one who chooses his friends carefully, and given his performance in Hertfordshire, I suspect he does not enjoy much society."

"That is an understatement," replied Fitzwilliam.

For his part, Darcy only smiled. "It depends on the society, Miss Bennet. You are correct that I often do not enjoy it, and that is especially true when I am not well acquainted with them. I do, however, appreciate the society of good friends and relations, those who understand and support me, and whom I understand and support in turn."

Elizabeth's eyes once again lit up with her usual playfulness and she said: "Then your behavior in Meryton is no longer to be wondered at, for you did not know us well at all. With Mr. Bingley, I thought you were completely open."

"He *is* a good friend of longstanding."

"One could not say so of Bingley's sister," interjected Fitzwilliam.

"On the contrary, Colonel, I thought Mr. Darcy to be an intimate of Miss Bingley's. Several times, I saw them with their heads quite close together, indeed."

Fitzwilliam did his best to hold back a hearty guffaw, and he turned his questioning gaze to Darcy. Anne did not know the woman, other than a few comments Elizabeth had made in her presence, but even so, the distaste for Miss Bingley was easily visible in her cousin's eyes.

"I am not Miss Bingley's particular friend, Miss Bennet. Though she seems to wish . . ."

Darcy trailed off and Fitzwilliam was quick to fill the void. "She wishes to be mistress of your estate, Darcy—there is no doubt about it."

"Perhaps she does at that," replied Darcy, his manner completely unaffected. "But there is little chance of her ever obtaining her desire."

"That is a great pity, indeed," murmured Elizabeth.

Anne watched the interaction before her and attempted to puzzle it out. Though Elizabeth was perfectly polite and unassuming, her comments to Darcy carried more than a hint of bite, not surprising, given what Anne knew of her feelings for her cousin. But as before, Darcy was the more difficult one to determine. He watched Elizabeth a great deal, and he seemed to derive great pleasure from hearing her speak. And furthermore, he seemed unable to understand her caustic undertones, as even a hint of her teasing drew him back like a moth to the flame.

There was something more happening here, something Anne could not quite make out. It was as if Darcy admired Elizabeth, though she was not certain of that interpretation.

A movement caught her eye, and Anne looked across the table, noting that Fitzwilliam was watching her with mirth in his eyes. He looked at her expressively, and then looked at Darcy and Elizabeth in turn, then returned his gaze to Anne and arched his brow. Anne was determined to ask him about it.

When they finished their meal, they separated for a time to prepare for their departure and the final hours to London, and Anne maneuvered herself into close proximity to Fitzwilliam.

"What was the meaning of your actions in the inn?" asked she without preamble.

Fitzwilliam grinned. "You mean you have not understood our dear cousin?"

"You must recall that you know Darcy much better than I," replied Anne, feeling more than a little put out at his teasing. "Darcy and I have rarely spoken more than two words together since his father's passing. You are aware of the reasons why."

"Yes, I am afraid I am. Let us simply say that I have seen Darcy in society for several years now, and I do not think I have ever seen him so much as give any woman a second glance. Miss Bennet was right—he is terribly fastidious. But when it comes to *her*, it seems like his particular nature has found something of which to approve."

Anne gasped. "Darcy admires Elizabeth?"

Laughing and shaking his head, Fitzwilliam only patted Anne on the back. "Just watch him, Annie. He can hardly keep his eyes off her, and when she speaks, his attention is fixed on her. I do not know if he will ever act on whatever admiration he feels, but it is there all the same, though I would wager that it is not returned."

"No, it is not," replied Anne, distracted by what her cousin had told her. "She thinks him arrogant, conceited, condescending, and above his company, and by that I mean her and those from her home in particular."

Fitzwilliam chortled. "How very accurate a picture she has of him!"

"He is a good man in essentials," said Anne, glaring at her cousin. "I do not know him well, and even I know that."

"Yes, he is. He never sets out to offend, but somehow he manages it nonetheless. I know not what is in their past, but it is clear she does not see him in quite the same light in which he sees her." Fitzwilliam laughed and shook his head. "Ah, well, I suppose it does not truly signify. It is not as if she possesses the necessary allurements to knock him from his high horse. I have no doubt it shall all come to naught."

As the carriage was almost ready, Fitzwilliam moved away to speak to the coachman, and Darcy soon joined them. Shortly after, Elizabeth exited the inn and joined Anne while they waited. Anne eyed her friend, wondering at the intelligence she had just gained. Elizabeth did not favor Darcy it was true, but Anne wondered how much of that disapprobation was grounded in misunderstanding.

"Are you well, Anne?" asked Elizabeth after they had stood there for a few moments.

"I am very well, Elizabeth," replied Anne. "I am anticipating this new facet of my life keenly. I do not doubt we shall be happy in London."

"I am sure you will be," replied Elizabeth, and Anne did not miss Elizabeth's use of the word "you."

As they entered the carriage and it departed, Anne turned her head to the problem. It was clear Elizabeth meant to return to her uncle's house when they arrived in London, and from there it was no leap to assume she would leave for her father's house soon after. Anne had become quite accustomed to her new friend's close association and society, and she was loath to lose Elizabeth now.

Furthermore, given what she had learned of Darcy's feelings for Elizabeth, Anne wondered if Elizabeth could be softened toward him. Perhaps it was a hopeless cause, but Anne wished for the best for her friend, and from what she knew of Elizabeth's situation, what could be better than a marriage to a wealthy man who adored her? The benefit of having Darcy removed from consideration as *Anne's* future husband did not escape her either—if that happened, perhaps Anne could finally come to an accommodation with her mother.

There must be some way to keep Elizabeth with her, and Anne decided to do whatever she could to bring it about. She would not descend to any blatant matchmaking, but if the opportunity existed to improve Elizabeth's understanding of Darcy, she would not allow it to pass by.

Chapter XIV

As the bustle of the city began to make itself known beyond the confines of the carriage, Elizabeth allowed herself to feel a sigh of relief. She had truly treasured her time in Kent and specifically in Anne's company, but it was time for her to begin thinking about returning to her home.

The carriage clattered on, unheeding of Elizabeth's introspection, and as they began to pass through the outer reaches of London, she began to see evidence of the city. The avenue through which they traveled was broad and busy. Other carriages both plainer and more opulent than Mr. Darcy's shared the road with horses and carts, as well as the constant traffic of those individuals swiftly walking on errands, or the trudge of laborers, indifferent to their surroundings. On one street corner, a young boy cried out the headlines of the day's paper, brandishing one as if it were a weapon. On another corner, she saw two matrons speaking earnestly to each other, their frequent darting glances toward a nearby alley suggesting they were sharing some sort of gossip.

The streets grew ever cleaner and soon trees lined the sides, swaying in the spring breeze, their summer buds providing the greenery of which Elizabeth was so fond in the middle of the barren city. All at once, Elizabeth realized they were likely heading toward Mr. Darcy's home, for she had never seen such buildings as they were now passing. Furthermore, Mr. Darcy had not asked her for the directions to her uncle's house, and though she was not certain why the matter had not been raised, she felt it time to do so.

"My uncle's house is near Cheapside, as you may remember," said Elizabeth, looking at Mr. Darcy and unable to keep the hint of challenge from her voice. "They are not expecting me today, but I am certain it will be no trouble for them to receive me."

"Yes, I do remember," said Mr. Darcy without a hint of an adverse reaction visible to Elizabeth's eyes. "But I would be pleased if you would accept my hospitality, Miss Bennet. You have done so much for Anne—unless I am very much mistaken, I believe she is loath to part from you."

"Oh, please do, Elizabeth," added Anne, turning her beseeching eyes on Elizabeth. "You have my apologies for not considering the matter before, but I would be pleased if you would continue to stay with me for a time." Anne flashed Elizabeth a grin. "You were still not to return to your uncle's house for some time yet, as I recall."

"It is another week before he expects me," replied Elizabeth, "but I also believe it must be time for me to return. Do you not wish to be among family at this time?"

"I hope my cousins will take no offense," said Anne, "but I believe I will appreciate your company as much as theirs."

"And my sister is in town at present, Miss Bennet," said Mr. Darcy. "I believe she will be pleased to make your acquaintance."

"Georgiana is a sweet and gentle girl, and I am certain you will like her very much," added Anne. "Please, do say you will stay with us."

Elizabeth was having a hard time following their conversation, and it appeared as if they had previously planned to ambush her with their entreaties to stay, much though she knew it was a silly notion. The idea of staying with Anne was appealing, as was the thought of meeting the infamous Georgiana Darcy. Unfortunately, staying with Mr. Darcy was not quite so inviting, though Elizabeth chastised herself with the thought—Mr. Darcy was not so bad as she had originally thought, and she was still required to remind herself of the fact on numerous occasions.

"Will you not consider it, Miss Bennet?" asked Mr. Darcy. "We would be very happy to have you."

"I would not wish to be an imposition," said Elizabeth, thinking of her stay with Jane the previous autumn at Netherfield. "My sister Jane is staying with my uncle as well, and I wish to be reunited with her. I am certain I may see you frequently, even if I am not staying in the same house."

"I assure you, Miss Bennet, that it is no imposition," said Mr. Darcy. "We might just as easily say that you may see your sister frequently if you stay with us, though I do not suppose we are nearly as dear to you as your sister."

Mr. Darcy's words were spoken in earnest, and Elizabeth almost believed him, had it not been for his instantaneous look of discomfort when Elizabeth mentioned Jane. As it was, she wondered at it, wondered how involved he had been with Mr. Bingley's abandonment of Jane. He had said he had not seen Jane in town since her coming in January, but had he known of it nonetheless?

"Please, Elizabeth," said Anne, giving her no time to ruminate on the subject of Mr. Darcy, Jane, and Mr. Bingley. "If only for a few days, I would appreciate your presence to help me settle into Darcy's house. We would all be grateful to have you."

"I suppose I might be persuaded," replied Elizabeth, though slowly. "But I should write to my uncle and request his permission. Even if he is not expecting me back yet, he still believes me to be in Kent."

"Then it is settled," said Mr. Darcy. "If you will write your letter upon our arrival, I will dispatch a footman with your letter and instruct him to await a response."

"Thank you, Mr. Darcy," said Elizabeth.

Anne squealed and embraced her. "We shall have so much fun, Elizabeth! And Georgiana will no doubt be happy to make your acquaintance, and I would like to meet your sister and your family too. I am anticipating your continued society very much!"

As Anne continued to extol the benefits of Elizabeth's continued companionship, Elizabeth happened to notice Colonel Fitzwilliam looking at her with evident fondness. When he noticed Elizabeth's scrutiny, the colonel smiled and nodded in thanks, and Elizabeth returned it. She had not done anything so especially praiseworthy, Elizabeth thought—she had been given the opportunity to provide friendship to Anne, and she had done it without hesitation. Anyone might have done the same.

The house before which the carriage halted was large and impressive, three stories rising from the street, with a drive and a massive façade which spoke to the affluence of its owner. The carriage was immediately attended to by several footmen, who began the tasks of securing the conveyance for its removal to the stables and the unloading of Elizabeth and Anne's trunks. Assisted by the gentlemen, Anne and Elizabeth stepped down and were led into the house.

On the inside, it was not any less impressive. The entrance hall was spacious, the décor was elegant but not especially formal, and there were two long halls leading in opposite directions to the separate wings of the house, as well as a large stairway to the second floor. They were introduced to the housekeeper and butler, both solid and dependable sorts of people, who immediately set about making certain Elizabeth and Anne were welcome.

"Miss Darcy is engaged in her lessons at present, Mr. Darcy," said Mrs. Mayson, the housekeeper. "Shall I have her summoned?"

"No, that is not necessary. Let us get the ladies settled and perhaps rested, and then I will introduce Georgiana to Miss Bennet's acquaintance."

"Very good, sir." Mrs. Mayson turned to Elizabeth and Anne. "If you ladies will follow me, I will show you to your rooms."

They climbed the stairs following the housekeeper, while Mr. Darcy stayed behind to speak with the butler. Of the colonel, Elizabeth could see no immediate sign. As they walked, the housekeeper spoke, ostensibly to inform them of their new situation, but Elizabeth thought it was mostly to put them at their ease.

"I have given you the room next to Miss Darcy's, Miss de Bourgh, and Miss Bennet has been placed on your other side. I understand that you and the lady are friends, so I am sure you will be comfortable with the other close at hand."

"I am certain we will, thank you," said Anne. For her part, Elizabeth wondered if her placement in what was obviously the family wing would be completely acceptable to Mr. Darcy. But his housekeeper would surely not put her there if she thought the master would disapprove, so she decided it was unlikely he would object.

"I will ensure your maids are directed to your rooms as soon as they enter the house," continued Mrs. Mayson. "There is wash water for your use, and the beds have been turned over, in case you would like to nap before you rejoin the family."

"Might I ask for some paper to write to my uncle?" asked Elizabeth. "Mr. Darcy mentioned sending a footman to his address, for I need to ensure my uncle is aware of my change of plans."

"Of course, Miss Bennet. There is paper on the desk in the room. Feel free to make use of it and simply summon a servant to convey it to me—I will ensure it is sent to your uncle at once."

"Thank you," replied Elizabeth.

She was led to a set of rooms which consisted of a sitting-room, a bedchamber, and a large dressing room, the likes of which Elizabeth was certain would hold all her clothes, as well as every article each of her sisters possessed in their own wardrobes. The rooms were decorated in a mixture of soft pastels and darker blues, and Elizabeth thought either a man or a woman would be comfortable in it. The bed was large — as large as the one in which she had slept at Rosings — but the furniture, though still fine, was not nearly so gaudy as that she had seen at Rosings. Clearly either Mr. Darcy or his parents possessed different taste in furnishings from Lady Catherine's preferences.

She took her leave from Anne, noting her friend already looking at the bed in her room with evident intent, and she realized that as much as her own day had been trying, it had been so much more emotional for Anne. She would sleep for a time, and no doubt it would do her good.

For herself, Elizabeth washed quickly and, when Tilly appeared with her trunks, welcomed a change of clothes. Then she sat down and composed a short letter to her uncle and arranged for its disposition. When those tasks were complete, Elizabeth turned to her own bed, realizing how weary she felt. She was soon resting on the counterpane, and though she might have thought her mind would be full of all that had happened, she soon fell into a restful slumber.

It was perhaps two hours later when Elizabeth awoke, and for a moment she was disoriented, wondering where she was. Her memory soon flooded back, and the sound of a carriage moving past her window spoke to her new location in London. She rose from the bed and stepped to the window. Looking out, she noted that her room was situated at the front of the house, from whence she could see the street on which Mr. Darcy's house sat. There was little traffic, naught but a carriage or two, and the avenues, as she had noted before, were wide and well-maintained. In the distance down the street, she noticed an area which teemed with the growth of tall trees and lush grasses and, given Mr. Darcy's wealth and the path they had taken through the city, she wondered if it was the famed Hyde Park. The beauty of that bit of nature in the middle of a city called to Elizabeth, and she longed to sample the delights which awaited her.

Tamping down on her eagerness, Elizabeth turned to the dressing room and, noting that Tilly was not there, stepped to a low vanity and tied her hair in a simple knot. Then, satisfied with her appearance and noting that her dress had not received an abundance of wrinkles because of her nap, she stepped from the room and made her way to Anne's.

Her friend was just waking from her nap when Elizabeth stepped in, and they exchanged happy greetings. Elizabeth rang for Laura, and Anne's appearance was soon repaired from her short nap; she proved eager to descend and greet her young cousin, whom, she informed Elizabeth, she had not seen in some time.

"You will like Georgiana very well, indeed," said Anne as they left the room and made their way toward the stairs. "She is quite shy, but once you become her friend, she will talk your ears off."

"And you have firsthand knowledge of this?" asked Elizabeth playfully. She was thinking of Mr. Wickham's description of the girl and wondering if it would prove to be a true likeness.

"I have not been in her company often, but when I have, we have been friends." Anne made a face. "Of course, we were forced to be circumspect when in my mother's company—Georgiana is quite terrified of her, and I suppose you will apprehend that if I became too friendly with her, my mother would press Darcy even further."

Elizabeth laughed. "I can well imagine it. You have given her quite the recommendation. I cannot wait to make her acquaintance."

They descended the stairs where they were met by Mrs. Mayson. "The master and Miss Darcy are in the sitting-room, waiting for your attendance. And Miss Bennet, a reply has come from your uncle."

Mrs. Mayson produced a letter from a pocket in her gown and passed it to Elizabeth, who received it gratefully. She then turned and led them down the hall and Elizabeth, eager to hear from Mr. Gardiner, opened it as they walked, reading his short missive and nodding to herself with satisfaction.

"Your uncle has given his permission?" asked Anne quietly as they walked.

All Elizabeth could manage was a nod, for they were soon led into the sitting-room. Mr. Darcy was there, as the housekeeper had told them, and seated by his side were two ladies. The first was young, about sixteen years of age, tall and willowy, and she was possessed of a handsome face which bore some resemblance to Mr. Darcy. The other lady was some years older than Mr. Darcy and sat by Miss Darcy with an air of watchfulness. Elizabeth thought she must be the girl's companion.

Though Elizabeth had not allowed herself to think of Georgiana Darcy much, if she had examined her feelings she would have felt herself rather ambivalent about the prospect of being introduced to her, notwithstanding Anne's recommendation. Part of this was undoubtedly due to Mr. Wickham's words which, though she was not certain could be trusted, had given her an initial poor opinion of the girl, supported by her poor opinion of Mr. Darcy. However, even more than this, Elizabeth realized that Miss Bingley had set Miss Darcy up as a rival to Jane. Considering Jane's heartbreak over Mr. Bingley's defection, Elizabeth's approval was hardly guaranteed.

But as she and Anne entered the room to Mr. Darcy's welcome, and the two ladies rose to greet them, Elizabeth noted the look of trepidation and the way the girl's eyes stayed on the floor, and the encouragement offered by the other lady. The introductions were completed and those newly acquainted made their curtseys to each other, but in all that time Miss Darcy did not look up at Elizabeth's face even once. Within two minutes, Elizabeth was convinced that Mr. Wickham had misrepresented the girl at best—or lied at worst—and that Miss Darcy was only exceedingly shy. As for the other matter of Jane and Mr. Bingley, Elizabeth decided not to hold it against Miss Darcy—if the girl was fond of Mr. Bingley, Elizabeth could hardly blame her for her feelings.

They sat down to visit and become acquainted, which turned out to be a difficult prospect. Miss Darcy rarely spoke two words together, most of her responses tending toward monosyllables. Mr. Darcy attempted to coax her to speak, and Anne spoke with her in a friendly manner which prompted a response, but with Elizabeth, she could not be induced to be anything other than reserved.

"I see you have a letter, Miss Bennet," said Mr. Darcy after they had sat for some moments. "Might we assume that permission has been granted for your stay?"

"It must have been," added Anne, turning to Elizabeth with a playful glint in her eye. "Otherwise, I do not have doubted Elizabeth would have demanded a carriage to return her to her uncle's home."

"You are not being fair to Miss Bennet." The company turned as one to see Colonel Fitzwilliam walking toward them. He bowed to the ladies and greeted Miss Darcy with affection and then addressed Anne again. "I am certain our Miss Bennet would be more likely to insist that she could just as easily return home in a hack, as to demand a carriage."

Anne laughed and pressed a fond hand to Elizabeth's arm. "That is a very close likeness to my dear friend. You *would* do that, would you not?"

"I believe I will refuse to answer, Anne," replied Elizabeth. "If I confirm your supposition, I appear to be demanding, while the colonel's suggestion makes me seem a little silly. If I leave you all guessing, it adds a bit of mystery, do you not think?"

They all laughed at her reply, and even Miss Darcy, who seemed startled at their playful manners and looked at Elizabeth with wonder, was seen to have an almost unwilling smile on her face.

"Oh, do let us stop this teasing," said Anne. "What did your uncle say?"

"He has granted his permission," replied Elizabeth. "But he said he would like to see me to hear for himself what has happened to necessitate this change in plans."

Anne's face fell a little. "Likely as not he will not wish you to stay here when he hears of my mother's behavior."

"I hardly think that likely," said Elizabeth, squeezing her friend's hand in support. "Mr. Gardiner is intelligent and fair. He would understand that you were not to blame."

"You must have him come here whenever convenient," said Anne, throwing off her earlier dismay. "Then he may learn for himself what has happened and be reassured that you have not fallen in with those of questionable character."

It was Elizabeth's inclination to laugh at Anne's jest, but she happened to catch sight of Mr. Darcy when Anne suggested Mr. Gardiner visit Mr. Darcy's house, and his look of distaste. All the ill feelings she had ever felt for Mr. Darcy flooded back in that instant, and she was offended on Mr. Gardiner's behalf.

"Oh, that is not required, Anne," said Elizabeth, deliberately avoiding the sight of Mr. Darcy to avoid castigating him. "I am certain I can hail a hack to take me to my uncle's home. I would not presume to impose my relations on you when I may go there just as easily."

In light of Anne's earlier jest, Elizabeth did not expect anything other than a laughing response from her friend. "You do have the strangest sense of humor at times, Elizabeth. Of course, your uncle may come here."

"Indeed, I second my cousin's sentiments."

Elizabeth turned a bland expression on Mr. Darcy. It seemed, little though Elizabeth could credit it, that Mr. Darcy was abashed, as if he was aware that she had seen his reaction. And well he should be, thought she, for it did not speak well of a man to think poorly of another because of his profession and without actually meeting him.

"In fact," said Mr. Darcy, "Mr. Gardiner will no doubt wish to see your situation here for himself, as he is your de facto guardian while you are in London. I will write another note to him and inform him that he is welcome to visit at any time convenient. I will be happy to receive him and answer any questions he might have."

Elizabeth returned his look, wondering if he simply meant to mollify her or if he was serious in his desire to show respect to her uncle. In the end, Elizabeth decided it did not signify.

"I appreciate your civility, sir," replied Elizabeth. "His attendance will be predicated on his availability, but I imagine he would come within the next day or so."

"Then we will await his coming. If you will excuse me, I shall write to him immediately." Mr. Darcy then rose and went to a small desk situated between two windows on the outer wall and wrote a quick note, which was quickly delivered to the housekeeper. Then Mr. Darcy rejoined the rest of the group.

"Miss Bennet," said he, "can you tell me anything of your uncle's business?"

For a moment Elizabeth thought to throw Mr. Darcy's belated interest—which stank of attempting to appease her—back in his face. Her mind was changed, however, by the interest he seemed to radiate, and the fact that she could not, in good conscience, behave with anything other than perfect civility to anyone, regardless of how objectionable she found him.

"He is an importer, Mr. Darcy," replied Elizabeth.

"That is interesting," said Colonel Fitzwilliam. "Darcy, did you not say that Bingley's father was an importer?"

"His uncle still runs the family business," replied Mr. Darcy, though he appeared a little uncomfortable at the mention of Mr. Bingley. "Bingley is following his father's wish of purchasing an estate and joining the ranks of the landed gentry, but his uncle is quite content to remain in trade."

"That is interesting, Mr. Darcy," replied Elizabeth, "for by my account, Mr. Bingley has neglected his estate sadly. Does this mean that he has no intention of purchasing Netherfield? If so, it would be better for him to give up the place so that another family could move into the neighborhood."

This time Mr. Darcy's discomfort was more apparent, though he quickly moved past it. "I have not seen Bingley in some months, Miss Bennet, for he has gone to the north to visit his family. It is quite possible he shall visit there rarely in the future, and it would not surprise me at all if he was to give the place up entirely. But that will be for him to decide when he returns."

"And when do you expect him back?"

Mr. Darcy smiled. "Given Miss Bingley's affinity for society, I would expect their return at any time. However, Bingley himself can be somewhat unpredictable, as he confirmed himself last year. I do expect them to return before the season ends."

"Enough talk of Mr. Bingley and his dynastic ambitions!" exclaimed Anne. "I am much more interested in this news of Mr. Gardiner's import business." Anne turned to Elizabeth. "What does your uncle import? Is there anything of interest to young ladies?"

"Many things," replied Elizabeth, amused at her friend and suspicious she had interrupted their conversation due to its tense undertones. "He imports primarily from the orient, though he also has contacts in the continent. I have often found lovely fabrics in his stores and have had gowns made from them."

"Excellent!" said Anne. "I think we should pay a visit to Mr. Gardiner's warehouse."

Anne turned an expressive glance at Elizabeth and they fell to giggling together, and even Georgiana, who still appeared unsure of Elizabeth, joined in their conversation. The gentlemen looked on indulgently, and Elizabeth was forced to acknowledge that though Mr. Darcy was often as objectionable as any man she had ever met, he looked on his sister with the devotion of a beloved brother. She could not fault him for that.

Chapter XV

The presence of Miss Bennet in Darcy's home was like a fine wine—something to be served chilled and savored on the tip of the tongue. Darcy had often imagined her in his home in town and at Pemberley, had envisaged the joy and delight he would receive from nothing more than her mere presence, being witness to her wit and liveliness, debating and discussing items of common interest, living with her as his wife and lover.

And that was, of course, the dilemma. Darcy had left Netherfield almost a half a year earlier intending to remove himself from the temptation of her incandescence, and though he had never forgotten her and had, at times, indulged in reflection of what his life might be like with her in it, he thought the distance had been achieved successfully. Her objectionable situation had not changed in the intervening months, regardless of her kindness in befriending Anne and enduring his Aunt Catherine.

Now that she was in his home—and, indeed, had been there only a few short hours—the temptation had returned tenfold, and Darcy knew not how he would ever resist her call. How could a man possibly escape her? It was unfathomable that he would not be drawn to her, that he would remain unaffected by her, a woman he was becoming more and more convinced was the perfect mate for him. If only she possessed *some* connections to those for whom he would not be required to blush!

But the invitation had been issued—though Darcy realized he never should have offered it—and since Anne depended on her, there was nothing to be done. For a moment during that long afternoon when she took great pains to become acquainted with his sister, Darcy thought it might be best if he invented some excuse to repair to Pemberley, to remove himself once again from her presence. That would not do either; Fitzwilliam, and perhaps even Anne, would soon see through his subterfuge, even if Miss Bennet did not. And see through it he thought she would. She might understand and even applaud his decision, for she was an intelligent woman. But he would not behave in such a way.

The evening passed amicably for all involved, and they sat in company until the ladies decided that the excitement of the day necessitated an early night. They retired amid whispered plans concerning what they intended to do the following day. Left at loose ends, Fitzwilliam challenged Darcy to a game of billiards. It seemed, unfortunately, that Fitzwilliam had something other than a simple game in mind when he made his challenge.

"You do understand that Miss Bennet noted your reaction when Anne suggested her uncle come here, do you not?"

Darcy, who had just broken, shook his head and concentrated on sinking his next shot. He had not lost control of his reactions in some time, but the presence of Miss Bennet was enough to leave him feeling disquieted and uncertain.

"I see you do," continued Fitzwilliam. "Might I ask what prompted it? Is Mr. Gardiner so objectionable that the thought of his visit is enough inducement to offend a young lady who is a guest in your home?"

"I have never met the man," said Darcy, the loud clack of the cue ball striking another accompanying his words and feeling a proper outlet for his current unsettled feelings.

Fitzwilliam's eyebrows rose at his confession. "Then what prompted you to behave in such a way?"

His next shot presenting itself, Darcy lined up his cue and struck the ball. Unfortunately, his pique led him to strike the ball too firmly, and the shot went awry. A grin appeared on Fitzwilliam's face, and he took Darcy's place, his questioning glance displayed as he went.

"Mrs. Bennet—Miss Bennet's mother—is perhaps the most

uncouth woman I have ever met. She is loud and obnoxious, openly schemes in a mercenary manner, and proclaims the incomes of every single gentleman in the county with avaricious precision. Mr. Gardiner is her brother; I have little hope he will prove to be any better than his sister."

Fitzwilliam struck another ball, which went neatly into the corner pocket. He stopped to survey the table and when he had done so, he moved to his next position and sighted down the length of his cue, measuring the long shot. "I cannot believe you would be so close minded. Consider this: are my father and Lady Catherine the same people? Are they so alike as to be indistinguishable from each other?"

"You know they are not," replied Darcy. He watched Fitzwilliam as he carefully aimed, the uncomfortable inference of Fitzwilliam's words convincing Darcy that he had not considered the matter properly.

"Then you should not judge Mr. Gardiner until you have met him." With a loud clack, Fitzwilliam sent the cue racing toward another, striking it neatly and inserting it into the side pocket. "By all accounts, he is successful, and a man does not have success in business by being a fool. Furthermore, Miss Bennet obviously esteems and respects him, and as she is an intelligent woman, I believe you must allow her the benefit of understanding what constitutes good behavior."

As Fitzwilliam moved from shot to shot, Darcy watched him and thought of his words. It was clear he had not considered the matter in any detail, and to his discomfort, he knew it was because of Mrs. Bennet and her obviously improper behavior. Fitzwilliam was correct — it would not do to prejudge the man before he had even made his acquaintance.

"Thank you, Fitzwilliam," said Darcy quietly. "You are correct, of course."

"Well, the man will be here within the next day or two, so you will be able to judge for yourself." Fitzwilliam sunk another ball and then laughed. "*If* he is objectionable, your house will withstand the pollution it will receive in the short amount of time he is here."

Annoyed, Darcy frowned at him. "Do you take me for Lady Catherine?"

"No, my dear cousin. Sometimes you only resemble her. It must be the family connection."

In this instance, the barb was uncomfortably near the mark, and Darcy decided it was best to remain silent. Darcy knew himself to be demanding, and at times it led him to be critical of those who were not his circle, little though he cared for many of *them*. But he was not all pride and haughtiness, as his friendship with Bingley showed. This Mr. Gardiner was at the same level Bingley's father had been—he could meet the man without reservation and proceed based on how he behaved.

"Besides," said Fitzwilliam as he strode to another part of the table, "if you mean to impress Miss Bennet, insulting her dear relations is not the best way to guarantee your success."

"Impress Miss Bennet?" asked Darcy. "Of what are you speaking?"

Fitzwilliam only shook his head and took his shot—a carefully and slowly struck ball which impacted against the black ball, sending it rolling toward the corner pocket, where it disappeared into the depths. With a satisfied nod, Fitzwilliam took his cue and placed it into the stand, then turned to face Darcy.

"Thank you for an excellent game, Cousin. I believe I shall now retire."

"And what of your comment about Miss Bennet?"

"Exactly what I said." As he passed by Darcy, heading out of the room, he clapped him on the shoulder. "You were quite transparent with your admiration, old boy. I am certain even Anne noticed, though perhaps Miss Bennet did not."

And then he was gone, leaving Darcy to his thoughts.

The next day the ladies decided to stay close to the house, and though Elizabeth would have liked to walk to the park she had seen through the window, she resisted its beckoning call in favor of staying with Anne and coming to know Miss Darcy better. Mr. Darcy was not much in evidence that day, as he had informed them he would be away from the house on a matter of business. Elizabeth wondered if he intended to absent himself to avoid her uncle's coming, until he drew her aside before departing to inform her of the truth of the matter.

"I received another note from your uncle this morning," said he. "It seems he will be unable to visit today because of some matter which has arisen. He instead proposes to come tomorrow morning, to which I have agreed."

Elizabeth nodded, considering how it had not been required for Mr. Darcy to explain this to her. "He is often quite busy—some days my aunt quite despairs of him."

"The life of a man of business," replied Mr. Darcy with a nod. "I remember Bingley's father was much the same."

"It is much the same as managing an estate, is it not?" asked

Elizabeth, curious to hear what he would say.

The smile Mr. Darcy directed at her contained a wry quality. "At times, I feel it is, especially in the early spring and the autumn harvest seasons when I am much engaged at Pemberley. But a man of business is often obliged to deal with such matters on an ongoing basis, whereas the life of a gentleman leaves much more time for leisure. In the winter, particularly, there is little to be done on an estate, and though I busy myself with other projects and have other business interests to manage, I would never say that your Mr. Gardiner is not busier than I."

Elizabeth absorbed this and nodded, knowing that he was correct. A gentleman could be as involved or distant from his estate as he pleased, even on a large estate, as long as those he employed were trustworthy and knowledgeable. Her father, even though he had no steward, certainly held the estate at arm's length, though he did do what was necessary to keep his family clothed and fed. Mr. Darcy, it seemed, was much more involved.

"I am happy to receive Mr. Gardiner tomorrow," continued Mr. Darcy, "and have structured my schedule accordingly. I shall complete my tasks today so that any work I must do tomorrow may be done from my study. Thus, he may call at any time."

"Thank you, sir," replied Elizabeth, not quite knowing what to say.

"It is no trouble, Miss Bennet. Now, if you will excuse me, I must be about my business."

With a bow, Mr. Darcy said his farewells to his sister and cousin, and he left the room, Elizabeth staring after him as he went. She was uncertain what to make of him. Even her own observations—to say nothing of what others had told her about the man—were contradictory and confusing, and she felt herself wondering who Mr. Darcy truly was.

"Now, what shall we do today?" said Anne, interrupting Elizabeth's thoughts. "My cousin has been given the day to herself, so we will necessarily be required to amuse her." Anne turned a mischievous grin on Miss Darcy, who blushed and looked down. "To be honest, I suspect that Mrs. Annesley has done it only to have some time away from a most difficult charge."

"Anne!" exclaimed Miss Darcy, forgetting her shyness.

But Anne only laughed, and soon the younger cousin was forced to join her, though her embarrassment lingered.

"I know much about difficult charges," said Elizabeth, winking at Miss Darcy. "After all, I spent more than a month acting as Anne's companion."

"Elizabeth!" This time it was Anne's turn to protest, though Miss Darcy giggled, as Elizabeth had intended.

"I have heard that you are very accomplished in music, Miss Darcy," said Elizabeth, turning away from Anne very deliberately. "Perhaps we should retire to the music room, so you may dazzle us with your skills."

Once again the girl ducked her head. "You should not believe everything William tells you, Miss Bennet." It took Elizabeth a moment to realize she was speaking of her brother. "He is a most attentive and encouraging brother, but I believe he is too kind when he praises me."

"Your brother did acknowledge your talent," said Elizabeth, "but it is not he who extoled it."

Taken by surprised, Miss Darcy looked up, a question written on her brow.

"It was actually Miss Bingley, whom I met in Hertfordshire last autumn, who informed me of your abilities. She claims she has rarely heard something so exquisite."

"But Miss Bingley has heard me play only once or twice," protested Miss Darcy. "I hardly know her."

Her suspicions confirmed, Elizabeth only smiled. "Then apparently you made a great impression on her those few times you played in her company."

"Yes, let us do so," added Anne. "Elizabeth has been teaching me, but her skill is so much greater than mine. If you are as skilled as this Miss Bingley claims, I would very much like to hear you."

It was clear that Miss Darcy was less than eager to display her talents, but she assented and led them to the music room. Like all the other rooms Elizabeth had seen, it was decorated in colors and pieces of furniture which suggested graceful restraint, but in truth Elizabeth hardly noticed the room itself. Her attention was immediately caught by the large pianoforte which dominated the room, its fine lines and superior workmanship proclaiming it to be a truly beautiful piece.

"What a lovely pianoforte!" exclaimed Elizabeth. "I have rarely seen its like."

"Even better than my mother's at Rosings?" asked Anne.

Elizabeth shot her an amused glance. "Even better than that. The one at Rosings is smaller and not nearly so fine."

"It is an instrument my father purchased for my mother," said Miss Darcy, her pleasure for the subject seeming to overcome her reticence.

"William has promised to purchase a new pianoforte for our music room at Pemberley, as the one we have is old and difficult to keep in tune, but this one is still in good condition, and we will not part with it for sentimental reasons."

"I can understand why," replied Elizabeth.

Feeling a great deal of reverence, Elizabeth touched a few of the keys, noting the exquisite tone of the notes it produced. The keys were weighted perfectly, and the instrument gleamed as if every servant in the house had polished it all morning. For the first time—even more than the sight of the house and its rooms—Elizabeth realized just what it meant to be wealthy. If she had such a superior instrument on which to practice every day, she might even be induced to practice as much as she ought!

"Shall you play first, Georgiana?" asked Anne, fixing her cousin with a playful grin.

"Oh, no!" exclaimed Elizabeth. "For if Miss Darcy is as skilled as I believe, she will outshine my poor efforts. Thus, I believe I must go first so that I may be given some degree of credit."

The three ladies all laughed, even Miss Darcy allowing a short giggle. "I am sure your playing is lovely, Miss Bennet," said she. "But if you wish to go first, I will happily cede the instrument to you."

The three spent a lovely morning in the music room, alternating turns at the pianoforte, laughing and talking, and though Miss Darcy remained reticent, she became livelier as the morning progressed. It was interesting, Elizabeth decided, that the siblings were so different. Mr. Darcy was as confident a man as she had ever met, self-possessed and determined, while Miss Darcy was shy and retiring, and though she had begun to become more open with them, she was still quiet and spoke in soft tones.

"It is truly a beautiful instrument," said Elizabeth, caressing the keys lovingly when she had finished playing a short Mozart piece. "If the one your brother is purchasing is anything compared to this, I can understand why you would be excited."

"I believe it will be," said Miss Darcy. "It is to be delivered this summer, and I cannot wait." Miss Darcy turned to Anne. "You have been playing only a few weeks?"

"Yes," said Anne, rolling her eyes. "My mother did not see fit to have me instructed. Elizabeth has been helping me."

"I think in time Anne will become skilled," said Elizabeth. "But I believe she requires the assistance of a master to realize her potential, as I am not much of a teacher."

"But Miss Bennet," said Miss Darcy, her earnestness evident in her gaze, "you play beautifully."

"Not very beautifully at all!" exclaimed Elizabeth. "I have not had the patience to practice as much as I ought."

"I could not hear much of a deficiency."

"Elizabeth does play well," said Anne, "but it is clear which of you is more diligent in your practice."

"Exactly!" said Elizabeth. "Miss Darcy plays with much more crispness and confidence than I do. You must own to that, Miss Darcy."

"Perhaps," said Miss Darcy, her tone noncommittal.

They left the pianoforte and sat on some nearby sofas, speaking of nothing of consequence. Miss Darcy spoke of her brother and how he was often out engaged in his business concerns, and of her cousin and his position in the regulars. In return, Elizabeth spoke of her family, and particularly what it was like growing up with four sisters.

"I cannot imagine it!" said Miss Darcy as Elizabeth related some anecdote. "I have always wished for a sister, but it is only William and me."

"I, on the other hand, have always wished for a brother," replied Elizabeth. "For you see, I have no one to tease me or to scare away potential suitors."

"And of these you have many?" asked Anne.

"No, not a one," replied Elizabeth, winking at Miss Darcy who giggled. She decided not to consider Mr. Collins a suitor, so objectionable and silly had been his attentions.

"You should both be grateful for what you have," said Anne, eyeing them both, a mock severity in her tone and look. "I have no siblings. I believe I would have liked to have at least one."

"Then we shall simply have to behave as if we are sisters," said Elizabeth. "I would never wish for you to go without."

The three laughed and moved to other topics. As Miss Darcy became more at ease, she became more open, though she was certainly not as lively as Lydia. Elizabeth participated in the conversation, but she also studied Miss Darcy, wondering at the differences in her beyond what she had been told. This business of Mr. Wickham was puzzling, as his own account was so different from Anne's caution, and Miss Darcy was nothing like what he had told her.

And then a notion struck Elizabeth: here was an opportunity to understand a little more of the man. Though Mr. Wickham was Mr. Darcy's age and had been, in his own words, a friend of his patron's son, Elizabeth remembered Mr. Wickham's tales of playing with Miss Darcy as a child. The possibility existed that Mr. Darcy had poisoned his sister against his former friend, but Elizabeth thought the man considered Mr. Wickham to be beneath his notice, and thus, would not take the trouble to sink his character in his sister's eyes.

"Actually, Miss Darcy," said Elizabeth during a lull in the conversation, "it has just entered my remembrance that I am acquainted with another who is known to you."

Miss Darcy turned a quizzical look at Elizabeth. "Truly?"

"Yes. For you see, last autumn another man came to Meryton to join the regiment of militia there, and he was not only known to Mr. Darcy, but he claimed an acquaintance with you. Do you know Mr. Wickham?"

Whatever Elizabeth might have expected from her mention of Mr. Wickham, it was not what she was seeing. Miss Darcy's eyes widened until the whites were easily visible and her face paled as translucent as a sheet. And when she spoke it was in a voice barely above a whisper.

"You know Mr. Wickham?"

"I do," said Elizabeth, now uncertain as to the wisdom of mentioning the man's name. "He is a member of the militia near my home, though I believe there is some talk of them decamping for the summer."

"I . . . I . . ." stammered Miss Darcy and her eyes darted back between Elizabeth and Anne. Then she burst into tears and fled the room.

Shocked, Elizabeth watched her go, unable to make her limbs move in response to Miss Darcy's sudden distress and flight. By her side, Anne was in similar straits, though she recovered more quickly.

"Why did you speak of Mr. Wickham, Elizabeth?" hissed Anne. "I informed you I did not think he was a good man."

"I thought only to mention a common acquaintance," protested Elizabeth. "I thought she would at least have been acquainted with him—there is no way I could have predicted a response such as this."

Anne shook her head, only a little mollified. She rose and gestured for Elizabeth to follow her in a motion which reminded Elizabeth of Lady Catherine. "Let us see to my cousin. I apologize, Elizabeth—no, you could not have known how she would react. I hope, however, that you do not still consider this Mr. Wickham's word to be gospel."

"No, indeed," replied Elizabeth, much subdued. "Much of what he told me seems suspect, and I no longer know what to think of him."

"That is good," said Anne, her voice harsh. "For we are likely to learn of something neither of us is aware, and I would ask you not to protest if Georgiana does share her knowledge of the man."

"I would not dream of it," replied Elizabeth.

They hurried up the stairs in silence and made their way to the door to Miss Darcy's room. When they determined she was not in the sitting-room, Anne led Elizabeth through it to the door to her bedchamber, and Elizabeth was relieved to find it open. There on the bed, sobbing in despair, was Miss Darcy.

"Georgiana, dear, what is wrong?" asked Anne.

The girl only sobbed harder. They approached the bed, and Anne touched Miss Darcy, coaxing her to rise off the mattress and put her head against Anne's shoulder, while Elizabeth moved her hand in soothing circles on the girl's back. For some few moments they were silent, the friends recognizing her need to exhaust her tears before she could speak clearly. When she at last quieted, they continued to allow her to regain her composure before they began to press her for an explanation.

"Now, Georgiana," said Anne, "shall you not explain why the mere mention of that man's name has caused this storm of weeping?"

"You must both think me a silly girl."

The words were spoken quietly, and Elizabeth, given how Miss Darcy was facing Anne, had to strain to hear her.

"We will only think you silly if you do not explain yourself."

Miss Darcy heaved a great sigh. "I was hoping Miss Bennet would become a friend, but it is clear she *knows*. How can she be a friend to such a failure as I?"

"I assure you that I know nothing, Miss Darcy," said Elizabeth. The girl dared a peek at her when Elizabeth moved around to face her. She pulled a chair close so that she was facing both Anne and Miss Darcy and continued in a gentle tone: "Anne mentioned that she thought Mr. Wickham was not a man to be trusted, but I did not listen to her, as I thought you must at least know him. I must have been mistaken, given your response."

"He has told you of me?" asked Miss Darcy, her voice containing a desperate quality.

"Only that you were haughty and proud," replied Elizabeth. "Given such blatant falsehoods, it must be nothing more than lies, as I can see you are naught but a sweet, shy girl."

"Please tell us what he has done to you," said Anne.

Another sigh was Miss Darcy's reply, and she brooded for a moment before speaking. "I am . . . loath to speak of this, for I do not wish you to think ill of me."

"If Mr. Wickham has offended you, then *he* is the one at fault," said Elizabeth, speaking firmly to instill confidence in the girl. "We will not judge."

Her words of encouragement seemed to affect Miss Darcy, and she nodded, though she was still hesitant. "Mr. Wickham is my brother's childhood friend and the son of my father's steward. He and William were close friends as children, but as they grew older, they grew apart. I was not aware of it, but Mr. Wickham developed some habits which my brother found distasteful, and after my father's death, he broke all contact between them after Mr. Wickham received his inheritance from my father."

Though Elizabeth was of mind to interrupt her, to see if Miss Darcy knew anything of the living Mr. Wickham claimed was denied him, she decided to keep her peace. It was obviously costing the girl much to make this communication, and Elizabeth would not make it any harder for her.

"Last summer, Mr. Wickham . . . became known to me again when he happened across my companion and me when we were visiting Ramsgate for a time. Knowing nothing of his character, I was happy to see him and gratified when he returned the sentiments.

"Mr. Wickham was charming and declared himself happy to see me, and soon I was seeing him every day. Then one day he claimed to love me and entreated me to accompany him to Gretna Green where we would be married."

Elizabeth's gasp was echoed by Anne. Miss Darcy only smiled, though it was a particularly mirthless expression.

"At first, I refused to even consider such a thing, and he continued to press me. My companion—a Mrs. Younge—at first required Mr. Wickham to leave, informing him it was not proper for him to propose in such a way to a girl who was underage and not attended by her guardian. But Mr. Wickham persisted, and Mrs. Younge was eventually persuaded to relent, to agree that his attentions were sincere. She said that though it was not usually done, if my love for Mr. Wickham was equally sincere, that I should follow my heart."

"How dare she!" exclaimed Anne. "It is not for a companion to make such a determination. Her responsibility is to protect her charge. She should have written to your brother immediately."

Miss Darcy nodded, a particularly desolate light in her eyes. "We discovered that there had been a previous connection between Mrs. Younge and Mr. Wickham and that his coming had been by design.

Their object, you see, was my dowry. To my eternal shame, I was persuaded to agree, and we planned our departure for the following day."

"But you did not," said Elizabeth. "Given you are here and Mr. Wickham is a lieutenant in the militia, you must have thought better of it."

The way she shook her head, the dejection in every line of her body broke Elizabeth's heart. "You give me too much credit, Miss Bennet. In fact, not thirty minutes after we had made our plans, my brother arrived at the house. By chance he had decided to visit us, and in doing so, he saved me from ignominy and disgrace.

"Mrs. Younge was investigated, her references determined to be forgeries, and she was dismissed from her post. Mr. Wickham, though I am certain my brother wished to call him out, was warned never to speak of what had happened and escorted from the premises."

"Oh, Miss Darcy," said Elizabeth, her heart going out to this shy young girl. "How you must have suffered."

But Miss Darcy only shook her head. "It is all of my own doing and quite deserved. I understand if you do not wish to be friendly with a . . . a . . . fallen woman such as I."

She hid her face again in Anne's shoulder, but Elizabeth was not about to allow her to hide.

"Of course not!" Miss Darcy looked up, startled by the vehemence in Elizabeth's voice. "First, I must apologize for mentioning the man's name. I should never have done so—I knew better, and I did so anyway, and for that I apologize."

"It is nothing," said Miss Darcy.

"It *is* something," interjected Anne. "It is true Elizabeth should not have mentioned the man's name, but it is also clear you must become accustomed to it, Georgiana. You cannot burst into tears every time Mr. Wickham's name is mentioned."

Though she appeared a little shamefaced, Miss Darcy readily agreed. Elizabeth nodded to Anne in gratitude.

"Of more importance," continued Elizabeth, "is a man of Mr. Wickham's years pursuing a young girl not out in society for nothing more than her dowry. That is reprehensible, Miss Darcy. I cannot tell you how disgusted I am with Mr. Wickham's behavior."

Georgiana started and looked at Elizabeth with astonishment. "You do not blame me for it?"

"The greater part of the blame lies with Mr. Wickham and none other," replied Elizabeth. "It is true that you should never have agreed to an elopement, but with this charming man and your faithless companion conspiring against you, it is not surprising that eventually you capitulated to their insistence.

"My advice is to use this as an opportunity to learn, but do not let it affect your life." Elizabeth smiled. "You are a wonderful girl, one who was taken advantage of by a determined scoundrel. Do not let him affect your life. You have so much to live for—he does not deserve your tears."

A heart felt expression of relief came over Miss Darcy, and when she opened her arms, Elizabeth willingly joined her in an embrace. "Thank you, Miss Bennet," said Miss Darcy quietly. "I am thankful for your friendship."

They sat there for some time giving support to Miss Darcy, until she decided she wished to rest before luncheon. Elizabeth and Anne willingly agreed, but before they left, Miss Darcy fixed Elizabeth with a hopeful grin.

"I hope . . . That is to say, I consider you a friend now, Miss Bennet. Might we not . . . dispense with the formalities?"

Delighted, Elizabeth agreed. "I would be very happy to, Georgiana. I am as happy to be your friend as I am to be Anne's."

Georgiana nodded her gratitude, and Elizabeth and Anne stepped from the room, making their way back down below stairs. It had been an eye-opening morning, and though Elizabeth was still not certain of just what Mr. Wickham was, she was now convinced that he had misrepresented himself grievously. The question was, what to do about it.

"It seems you have a talent for comforting young ladies of my family," said Anne when they had returned to the sitting-room. "Perhaps we should employ you on a permanent basis."

"I do not think it shows any great talent to simply listen to a young girl's story and provide advice."

"Perhaps," said Anne. Her mien was introspective and her manner troubled, and when Elizabeth asked her what was the matter, she sighed.

"Elizabeth, do you not remember that my mother interviewed a lady by the name of Miss Younge? I was simply wondering if it was the same woman."

"It is possible," replied Elizabeth. "I seem to remember Mr. Collins telling me that your mother sent her away because she did not like the look of her."

"Then it is possible she is still scheming with Mr. Wickham."

It was possible, but Elizabeth did not know what she could do about it. Of her actions with respect to Georgiana, Elizabeth could now only be ashamed. She knew she should have held her tongue, but given what she had learned, she was relieved she had spoken. It would put her on her guard with respect to the man she now knew was no gentleman.

Chapter XVI

A distracted Elizabeth thought about what she had learned about Mr. Wickham, and she was not quite certain how to act. The man had gone from amiable and unfortunate to contemptible and mercenary, a change so stunning that had she not heard from Georgiana's mouth exactly what had happened, she might not have believed it. What this did to her opinion of Mr. Darcy, Elizabeth preferred not to think—she knew a large part of her disdain for Mr. Darcy had been based on his supposed treatment of Mr. Wickham—if that foundation was removed, then her opinion of Mr. Darcy must necessarily change.

But Elizabeth decided that she could not dwell on Mr. Darcy at this point—she was polite to him, as she must necessarily be at all times now that she resided in his house, but she did not go to any trouble to learn more of him at present. She was more concerned about what to do about Mr. Wickham.

At present, Elizabeth had no notion of any of Mr. Wickham's other sins. She knew he had attempted to elope with a girl of fifteen years and had lied about his knowledge of another man, though whether that was in revenge for the foiling of his plans or for some other reason, she did not know. The things that she had learned did not speak well to his character. But were they the extent of his sins? Was there some danger to those in Meryton? And most importantly, were her sisters in danger? Mr. Wickham was a regular visitor to Longbourn, his tales accepted as truth, his position in the community and regiment, secured.

"Why do you not simply ask Darcy?" asked Anne early the next morning. She had noticed Elizabeth's distraction and asked about it, and though Elizabeth had been reluctant to say much, her friend had wheedled the truth from her.

"I hardly think Mr. Darcy wishes to speak of his past with Mr. Wickham, especially to one such as I."

The look Anne bestowed upon her was not amused. "Are you still caught up in this unreasoning animosity you have for my cousin?"

"I hardly think any animosity between Mr. Darcy and myself is unreasoning," replied Elizabeth. "But no, it has nothing to do with that. It is clear Mr. Darcy and his sister have been hurt by Mr. Wickham, and I would not dredge up unpleasant memories. Besides which, he truly has no reason to tell me anything he does not wish."

Anne regarded Elizabeth for a moment before she spoke. "I would not wish to bring the subject to Georgiana's attention again—at least not so soon after yesterday's events—but Darcy is made of much sterner stuff, and he has known Mr. Wickham all his life. Furthermore, I would think he would agree to speak when he understands your fears, especially if Mr. Wickham is as poor of character as I suspect. You say Darcy does not have a care for anyone in your neighborhood, and you may be correct—but do those of good character not have a duty to inform others of those who mean to harm them?"

"Then why did he not speak with the gentlemen about Mr. Wickham?" challenged Elizabeth.

"I do not know," replied Anne. "Perhaps it was in an effort to protect Georgiana, or perhaps the man is not so morally deficient as we think. Or perhaps he is, as you obviously think, proud and unwilling to concern himself with those he considers beneath him." Anne impaled Elizabeth with a look. "I do not see this measure of proudness in him, but I was not at Meryton when you first met. But I doubt he could simply brush off an appeal to him if he knows this Mr. Wickham is not to be trusted."

Elizabeth chewed on her lower lip in thought. "You may be correct. I shall have to think on it."

The look Anne returned informed Elizabeth that she had best think quickly and come to a resolution. While Elizabeth attempted to focus on the problem of Mr. Wickham, her earlier resolution of not considering Mr. Darcy was frayed, and there were times her mind wandered to the complicated man. And the item which came to her mind most often was that if Mr. Wickham was not a good man, then perhaps Mr. Darcy was not quite the villain she had thought him to be.

When Mr. Gardiner arrived at the house, Darcy was in his study reading some letters of business. Fitzwilliam had been there for a time, but he had departed for his barracks, stating that he would prefer to keep his leave if there was no real requirement for him to use it.

Darcy had received a letter that morning from Bingley. In it, though it was sometimes difficult to decipher the man's writing, Darcy learned that Bingley would be returning to London with his family shortly. It presented a dilemma—Darcy did not think his friend had recovered from his fascination with Miss Bennet, yet the woman's sister was staying at Darcy's house at present. Their meeting would lead to questions about Miss Bennet, and Bingley would no doubt discover her presence in London. It was unfortunate, but Darcy had no notion of how to avoid it—Miss Elizabeth was quite ensconced here, and Anne—and Georgiana, he suspected—did not wish her to leave. Perhaps he could arrange to meet Bingley at their club. Darcy snorted—he might even have an unknowing ally in Miss Bingley, for he knew she would visit here the moment she returned to town, and when she discovered Miss Elizabeth staying here, her interest in keeping her brother away would be aroused.

Of Miss Bennet herself, Darcy decided not to think too much. The knowledge that he had purposely aided Miss Bingley in keeping her presence in London from Bingley was troublesome—as always, any such deceptions made him uncomfortable. It was unfortunate she was ambivalent about Bingley, for Darcy would have had no true objections to their union otherwise, and now that Miss Elizabeth was once again in his life, Darcy secondary motive was not a consideration.

The knock on his door provided a distraction away from his thoughts, and when the door opened, his butler announced Mr. Gardiner, Darcy rose to greet him.

"Mr. Gardiner, welcome," said Darcy simply, extending his hand to shake the other man's.

"Mr. Darcy." Mr. Gardiner was shorter, a little portly, appearing about ten years Darcy's senior, or perhaps a little more. He was dressed fashionably, though in practical clothing, devoid of any of the fluff tradesmen often chose to adorn themselves to make it appear they were higher in society. His features were pleasant and good-humored, and in his eyes shone the light of intelligence. It appeared Fitzwilliam had been correct in his assertions.

"Thank you for receiving me, Mr. Darcy," said Mr. Gardiner, sitting when Darcy invited him to do so. "I understand that many men of your stature would consider my coming an imposition, and I appreciate your forbearance on the matter."

"Not at all," Darcy was quick to reply. "Your niece is staying with me, and I understand you wish to ensure her living conditions are appropriate."

Mr. Gardiner laughed. "I hardly think that staying with the Darcys of Pemberley could be deemed inappropriate, sir."

"You are familiar with my family?" asked Darcy, trying not to frown.

"Only by reputation, sir. I have heard something of you, and none of what I have heard is negative in any way. My wife is also familiar with your family name. I hope you are able to meet her some time, as I believe you would know some of the same people and locations."

Though intrigued by this statement, Darcy decided not to ask. He was still not certain if Mr. Gardiner wished to use this circumstance to claim an acquaintance with him, or worse. Something in his expression must have shown, for Mr. Gardiner chuckled and shook his head.

"You need not fear, Mr. Darcy. I have no interest in making our acquaintance to be more than it is. You are hosting my dearest niece, and I wish to see her and hear of these mysterious circumstances which have led to her residence in your home. It was only a few days ago that she asked my permission to extend her stay in Kent."

"I would never have expected a beloved relation to Miss Elizabeth to behave in such a manner," said Darcy, attempting to cover his slip.

"Mr. Darcy," said Mr. Gardiner, leaning forward and placing his arms on the edge of Darcy's desk, "you do not need to dissemble with me. You have met my sisters, have you not?"

Feeling a little ashamed, Darcy owned that he had. "I am acquainted with Mrs. Bennet, though I have only made your other sister's acquaintance in passing."

"Then you are familiar with her character. As an intelligent man, I hardly think you could have missed it." Mr. Gardiner paused. "My sisters are not the most intelligent creatures, but they are, at heart, good women. Mrs. Bennet is ruled by her fears of the entail, but she *does* wish the best for her daughters. Lizzy, however, would tell you that her idea of the best does not always coincide with her daughters' opinions."

Darcy shook his head and laughed. "There is many a society mother who is exactly the same, sir."

"Then you understand my meaning. I am quite used to being an object of curiosity to those who have met my sisters and taken their measure. Now that I have proven myself to be of *some* intelligence, I hope you will acquit me of their brand of foolishness."

"I never would have expected it, sir," replied Darcy, thinking of Fitzwilliam's opinion. "And whatever her mother's faults, it is clear Miss Elizabeth does not suffer from similar deficiencies."

"I see you have met Lizzy," replied Mr. Gardiner with a hearty laugh. "No, Lizzy is more her father's daughter than her mother's. Given her outspoken nature, I almost wonder if this difficulty in Kent was in some way exacerbated by that frankness."

"I would not have you think so," replied Darcy. "She has been of great assistance to my cousin, and Anne, it seems, cannot do without her. As for the particulars, I shall leave them to Miss Bennet to relate."

"Then shall we join them?" asked Mr. Gardiner. "I find that I am impatient to hear her tale."

Agreeing with his guest, Darcy rose and led Mr. Gardiner from the room. As they walked, they chatted about inconsequential subjects. Darcy's mind was taken back to his conversation with Fitzwilliam again, and he was reminded of his previously meager opinion of Mr. Gardiner and how unjustified it had been.

It was a lesson to be learned, he decided. To think meanly of the world, particularly of those who, by society's standards, were not of his own level, was a serious mistake. Had he not befriended Bingley to the scorn of many of his acquaintances? Bingley's relative wealth in no way made him more acceptable to most of society, and still Darcy had not cared. Given what he had seen of Mr. Gardiner, Darcy doubted the man's wealth was appreciably less than Bingley's. Darcy steeled himself to ensure he did not make the same mistake again.

"Uncle!" said Elizabeth when the gentlemen entered the sitting-room where Elizabeth had been conversing with Georgiana, Anne, and Mrs. Annesley.

Throwing all caution to the wind, Elizabeth rose and threw herself into her uncle's arms. "I did not know you had come."

"You appear well, Lizzy," said Mr. Gardiner. He held her at arms' length as if to inspect her. "I hope you have not been giving these fine people too much difficulty."

"Oh, Uncle!" exclaimed Elizabeth. "At times, you are as bad as Papa."

Mr. Gardiner only grinned. "*Someone* must tease you when your father is not present."

"Will you please introduce us?" asked Anne, turning Elizabeth's attention back to her friend. "I believe your uncle will be an effective check on your behavior. I know I have not had much luck calming your exuberance."

"You may all laugh at my expense if it pleases you," said Elizabeth when they did just that. She glared about the room. "But I warn you to beware of my uncle. His wit is not quite so satirical as my father's, but it is not benign either!"

"I have missed you, Lizzy," said Mr. Gardiner with a fondness which could not be hidden. "Please, introduce me to your friends."

Elizabeth readily obliged, and the company sat down to visit. "In fact, I spent a few moments with Mr. Darcy in his study after he had received me in his house. I understand there are a few events of which I should be informed concerning your removal to London. Should I look to you for this explanation, or would one of your companions be better suited to give me a full understanding of what has happened?"

Though Elizabeth was not quite certain what to make of Mr. Darcy's seeming amity with her uncle, she declined to think on it at that moment. Her attention was instead directed toward Mr. Gardiner's query. She was not quite certain how to answer him, however, as she did not wish to offend those with whom she was currently staying.

"You do not need to hesitate, Elizabeth," said Anne, and all at once Elizabeth realized her silence was of such a length that it had been noted. "My mother's behavior to you was reprehensible. There is no need to attempt to paint it in rosy colors."

"You must have affected her to a great degree, Miss de Bourgh," said her uncle, winking at Anne. "I have never known Elizabeth to be anything other than forthright."

"You would lead them all to believe I possess no tact!" exclaimed Elizabeth.

"Tact you have aplenty," replied Mr. Gardiner. "But your sense of outrage often overwhelms your discretion."

It was clear they would continue to tease her until she related what had happened, so Elizabeth began speaking in an attempt to avoid their wit. Mr. Gardiner listened intently, interjecting a question or requesting clarification at times, but for the most part he simply listened. Though Georgiana and Mr. Darcy were largely silent, Anne also inserted comments in numerous places, her observations usually caustic and humorous, and at times Elizabeth almost grew cross with her friend, as her interruptions lengthened the tale and made it more difficult to relate.

When all had finally been shared, Mr. Gardiner shook his head and gazed at her fondly. "Only you, Elizabeth, could cause such havoc in a place you only visited for a short time."

Elizabeth made to protest, but Mr. Gardiner only held up his hand. "I do not speak to censure, my dear. You have been of great assistance to Miss de Bourgh when she stood in need of it."

"That is exactly it," said Anne, her steady gaze embarrassing Elizabeth all that much more.

"You have always done what you thought was right, regardless of the consequences," continued Mr. Gardiner. "I am not surprised that you have followed that same principle in this instance."

"I am glad she did," said Anne. "My association with your niece has changed my life for the better, sir. I would not wish to give up her society."

Mr. Gardiner sighed. "Unfortunately, that will not be for me to decide." Mr. Gardiner turned to Elizabeth. "I assume you are already aware of your father's desire for your return."

"I received a letter from him not long before I left Kent," confirmed Elizabeth.

"He may be persuaded to relent. But you know he has always been most comfortable when you are home." Mr. Gardiner turned to the rest of the company, and his expression showed him to still be feeling a little mischievous. "Elizabeth has always been his intellectual partner, and as my sister and her younger daughters tend a little toward silliness, he feels Elizabeth's absence keenly."

"I can well understand that," replied Anne.

Mr. Gardiner smiled and turned back to Elizabeth. "I believe we may put him off. How long did you mean to stay?"

"Miss Bennet is welcome to stay as long as she likes," said Mr. Darcy. "She and Anne are great friends, and my sister has also become fond of her."

The shy nod Georgiana gave was acknowledged by Mr. Gardiner. "A month or two should be acceptable. I will write to him and inform him of the situation and your current circumstances. I do not doubt he will be agreeable, at least in the short term.

"Now, I am certain you must be aware that Jane wishes to see you."

Mr. Gardiner chuckled. "In fact, it was difficult convincing her that I should come alone this morning."

"And I long to see Jane." Elizabeth turned to Anne. "I should like to introduce you to my sister. In many ways, she is much like Georgiana."

"I am quite happy to be introduced to your sister," agreed Anne. "I am certain we could commandeer my cousin's carriage to go to your uncle's home, and perhaps she could visit us here, when convenient. Your wife would also be welcome, of course."

"Why do you not come to dinner with your family, Mr. Gardiner?" asked Mr. Darcy. "We would be happy to have you. My cousin, Colonel Fitzwilliam, is also living at my house, and I believe he would appreciate an introduction as well."

To say Elizabeth was shocked was an understatement. Mr. Darcy's distaste at receiving a tradesman at his home had been evident only a few days before. Surely the desire to be agreeable would not induce him to such measures of civility!

"We would be happy to attend," said Mr. Gardiner, apparently thinking nothing of the invitation. "I must consult my wife concerning our schedule, but I do not foresee any difficulty."

They spoke on the matter for a few more moments, deciding to gather for dinner three days hence, and after it was agreed, Mr. Gardiner soon took his leave, Elizabeth walking him to the front door. They walked in silence for the most part, only speaking when they had reached her uncle's carriage.

"It seems you have fallen in with excellent people, Lizzy. I will attempt to convey this when I write to your father to inform him of your circumstances." Mr. Gardiner paused and grinned. "I might put a word or two in for your mother too, for I suspect that if she discovers where you are staying, she will have no desire for your return."

Elizabeth shook her head. "I doubt that very much, Uncle. She did not have a high opinion of Mr. Darcy when he was in Hertfordshire."

"Perhaps not. But as wealthy and well-connected as he is, I expect she will realize the possibility of your moving in higher circles and the possibility of snaring a husband from those circles. And the friendship of Miss Anne de Bourgh is also a boon, as I am certain you understand."

"I do," replied Elizabeth simply. "I am unsure how Mama will take it. As for Papa, he might desire my return anyway."

"He might at that. I will do whatever I can to hold him off."

And with that, Mr. Gardiner stepped into his carriage, which drove out of sight. Elizabeth watched him go and was forced to think of her own desires in the matter. She enjoyed Anne's company and had come to understand that Georgiana was a sweet girl. But some part of her wished to simply return to her home and her less complicated existence. In Meryton, she could keep a watchful eye on Mr. Wickham and ensure her sisters were not an object of prey for the man.

But she would not disappoint her new friends, so she would stay for the present. Nevertheless, she still needed to decide what to do about Mr. Wickham and whether she should approach Mr. Darcy on the matter. She was beginning to think that Anne's suggestion was not so inadvisable as she had first thought.

Chapter XVII

Being, as it was, the middle of April, it was also the height of the season in London. Having never attended any events herself, the thought that Mr. Darcy might receive invitations had never crossed Elizabeth's mind. But that matter was brought to her mind in the days following her arrival at his house.

"I would not wish you to decline invitations on my account, Cousin," said Anne, overhearing a comment from Colonel Fitzwilliam. "You may attend any functions that you like. But I believe Elizabeth and I are not ready yet to accompany you and will stay at home."

This last was said with a raised eyebrow in Elizabeth's direction. For herself, Elizabeth was not opposed to being in company — she had always felt at home in any social function and thought she would acquit herself well should she be thrust into a similar position here, even if Mr. Darcy associated with a higher level than that to which she was usually accustomed. But there were other considerations.

"I am willing to be guided by you in this matter, Anne. Though I will own to some curiosity and have no objection to society, I can do without it just as easily."

"What, Miss Bennet?" asked Colonel Fitzwilliam, staring wide-eyed at her with mock astonishment. "You do not wish to be in company with the people with whom we usually associate? As an intelligent and unpretentious woman, you surprise me. I would have expected you to be anticipating the ridiculous behavior which permeates the first circles."

Elizabeth laughed. "I believe a little of such behavior goes a long way, Colonel."

"It is likely for the best," said the colonel, grinning widely. "Darcy here would not be your best guide in society—not when he does whatever he can to avoid it himself."

"Is that so?" asked Elizabeth, turning an arch look on Mr. Darcy. "I should never have guessed, given how splendidly Mr. Darcy acquitted himself in Meryton."

"Darcy acquitted himself?" Colonel Fitzwilliam shot an amused glance at Mr. Darcy. "I would never have guessed. Do tell how he accomplished this?"

By this time both Georgiana and Anne were giggling, and Mr. Darcy appeared uncomfortable at his cousin's teasing. It seemed he decided, however, that nonchalance was his best option, and Elizabeth, already having taken the colonel's measure, could only agree.

"I do well enough in company when there is sufficient inducement," said Mr. Darcy, though shortly. He turned to Anne and favored her with a smile. "I know you are but newly arrived, and I suspect you would appreciate a little time to adjust before attending any events."

"Given how I have never attended any events at all," replied Anne, "I am quite happy to forgo them at present. I have no desire to be an object of curiosity to society."

"Or prey," said Colonel Fitzwilliam, his joviality replaced by seriousness. "There will be many who will wish to win your dowry, Anne, which, as you know, consists of Rosings. You must be vigilant."

"We will be there to support you, of course," added Mr. Darcy. "Few men will try anything underhanded with Fitzwilliam's threat nearby to deter them."

"Perhaps I should resign my commission," muttered Colonel Fitzwilliam. "I suspect safeguarding Anne will be an arduous task."

"I am not without intelligence," said Anne primly. "And I shall have Elizabeth with me. I shall be well."

It seemed to Elizabeth that her hosts conveniently neglected to consider that she was not a permanent resident with them, but she decided there was little reason to revisit the matter.

"Perhaps we should visit the dressmaker and assure we are attired properly," said Anne. "I would not wish to embarrass the family by being unfashionable."

Colonel Fitzwilliam guffawed, and Mr. Darcy allowed a smile at her quip. "I believe Georgiana would be more than willing to introduce you to her modiste."

"What fun!" exclaimed Anne. She turned to Elizabeth. "Let us go on the morrow, then. We shall make certain we are all presentable."

"Anne," said Elizabeth, feeling a little uncomfortable, "I have no need of new clothes, and I have not sufficient funds for such purchases."

"I absolutely insist, Elizabeth," replied Anne. It was not the first time Elizabeth had heard the steel in her friend's voice. "I believe the style of dress you will find in London will be quite different from what it is in your home, or even in Kent. I would not wish for you to be made uncomfortable by it."

"Anne is correct," added Mr. Darcy.

"I did not realize you were so conversant with women's fashions," said Elizabeth.

Mr. Darcy colored a little and his cousin laughed, but he soon recovered. "I must be to a certain extent, as I am guardian to my sister. I do not know the particulars, but I think those who attend events in our circles use costly materials and more elaborate styles."

"And you need not concern yourself for the expense, Elizabeth," added Anne. "Given your unstinting friendship and unwavering support, I will be happy to do this for you. Please allow me."

There was little Elizabeth could say to her friend's plea, so she allowed herself only a smile and a nod, after which Anne turned an arch look on Mr. Darcy.

"Of course, since I am currently estranged from my mother and have no access to the de Bourgh funds, I will rely on my cousin's kindness until I am able to repay him."

Once again Colonel Fitzwilliam laughed at his cousin, but Mr. Darcy only smiled. "I am quite happy to do it, Anne, and no repayment is necessary. Georgiana, if you will write a note to Madam Fournier, I am certain she will be able to find time for you."

And so, the letter was dispatched and the appointment, confirmed. Thereby, Elizabeth was to be treated to the styles and fabrics that only the very wealthy could afford. She continued to protest, as she was certain the expense was quite significant, but Anne was firm.

"You are my friend, Elizabeth," said she, "and I am grateful you have agreed to stand with me in the face of my mother's actions. Please allow me to do this for you as my dearest friend."

When Anne spoke in this manner, Elizabeth felt she had no means of persuading her otherwise. Consequently, as Anne's manner toward her was so earnest, she allowed her to have her way. They looked at Georgiana's wardrobe for ideas of different fashions. Although most of the girl's dresses were those of a young girl still not out in society, her clothing was finely made, and the fabrics were obviously costly. But Elizabeth herself was not entirely without experience with respect to fine fabrics.

"My uncle's warehouses contain fabrics of this sort," replied Elizabeth when Anne asked her about it. "Though we do not, of course, presume to help ourselves to all his stock, he often allows us to cut a length off the bolts that we like to have dresses made."

Anne and Georgiana shared a look. "Then I think our previous determination to visit your uncle's warehouses should become a priority. I would very much like to sample what he has in his stock."

Clearly agreeing with her cousin, Georgiana nodded vigorously, and Elizabeth could only laugh. "Then I shall ask him the next time I see him. I am certain he will be happy to allow us to browse, as long as we promise not to pauper him in the process."

"I am not certain we can promise that," was Anne's arch reply, "but we shall do our best."

The day was spent in happy companionship with her two friends, and Elizabeth soon began to esteem Georgiana as much as she did Anne. The girl was quiet, and she tended to allow the more talkative Elizabeth and Anne to carry the burden of conversation, but she was sweet and gentle and reminded Elizabeth of Jane very much. Her sorrow the day before when Elizabeth had mentioned Mr. Wickham's name had all but dissipated, as Anne and Elizabeth did their best to distract her from those thoughts. Furthermore, Elizabeth had an additional piece of advice for the girl and shared it as soon as the opportunity presented itself.

"Think of the past only as it brings you pleasure," said Elizabeth when she noticed Georgiana had descended to introspection. "If you allow Mr. Wickham power over your life, then he has won. Do not give him the satisfaction."

"But should I not remember my mistakes and learn from them?" asked the girl, deep in thought.

"Of course, we should all learn from our mistakes," replied Elizabeth. "But you would do better to remember the good times, rather than dwelling on the bad. Do you think Mr. Wickham remembers you with anything other than anger at not being able to obtain your fortune?"

Georgiana's countenance darkened. "I imagine not."

"Then remember the lessons you learned because of his improprieties, but forget about the man. Think of the good times you have had with your cousins or anything else which brings you pleasure. Let Mr. Wickham reside in the past where he belongs."

A grateful smile was Georgiana's reply, and the subject was dropped.

When Elizabeth had come to stay at Mr. Darcy's house, she could never have imagined she might have come into contact with a member of high society. Of course, she was aware that Mr. Darcy *was* a member of that society, but considering how she had known him for some time and in Meryton, of all places, his stature had never seemed real. And Anne, though her own mother was the daughter of an earl, she had never required Elizabeth to acknowledge her own standing in society, though that standing had been affected by the de Bourghs' absence from society for many years. But that day, in the late afternoon, Darcy house was visited by a man who could only be termed as high on society's ladder.

Hugh Fitzwilliam, the earl of Matlock and Colonel Fitzwilliam's father, was a tall man of about five and fifty, and within moments of his entrance, Elizabeth could see the resemblance between father and son. Not only was there a definite physical similarity, but it seemed like the colonel had his irreverent and playful manners from his father. Lord Matlock greeted them with expansive delight and sat among them, and Elizabeth could detect no hint of superiority in his manner.

"Anne, my dear," said he, catching his niece into a quick embrace, "I am so happy to see you here in London."

"I am happy to be here," was Anne's simple reply.

"You have waited long enough for it. In fact, I cannot help but wonder if your family has failed you." The earl shook his head. "I should have intervened long ago, I am afraid."

"Do not castigate yourself, Uncle," replied Anne. "In all truth, I did not even know myself that I wished to escape until Elizabeth showed me what it was to live."

Elizabeth could not help but blush at the praise, which was made worse when the earl turned his attention to her. "Ah, yes, the intrepid young lady who had the fortitude to stand up to my sister. I thank you very much for your assistance, Miss Bennet. You have done more for

Anne than her family has, and for that I can only be grateful."

"I am certain it was nothing," said Elizabeth. "I only provided friendship—Anne did the rest herself."

"Is that not what anyone truly worthy of their heroism claims?" asked the earl. He favored her with an outrageous wink, prompting both Anne and Georgiana to burst out into laughter.

"Regardless, I believe it was *not* nothing," continued the earl. "And whether you believe you deserve it, I still give you the family's thanks." The speculation with which the earl regarded Elizabeth quickly made her uncomfortable. "Anthony was correct about you, Miss Bennet. I do not know how long you mean to stay with Darcy, but I believe you will bring much to our family party. I suspect there are those who do not wish you to depart at all."

The earl turned a significant look on all the room, and then turned back to Anne. "You need not fear your mother's interference, Anne. Tomorrow I shall journey to Rosings, and I will inform her she is not welcome to join us here until she has mended her ways. She is most difficult to control, but I have always found that informing her of my wishes in such a way as to leave no room for debate is the likeliest road to success."

"Thank you, Uncle. I wish . . ." Anne paused and she turned away in embarrassment. Elizabeth thought the earl did not miss the way she grasped Elizabeth's hand tightly. "I do not want to remain at odds with my mother for the rest of my life, but she must accept that I am an adult and may do as I please."

"Of course, you are," said the earl. "I will ensure she understands this before I leave her."

The subject was then changed, and they enjoyed a pleasant visit. When the earl rose to depart, he did so with affection for his family, and for Elizabeth, he displayed his unreserved approval by bowing over her hand. Elizabeth was certain her mother's heart would stop if she knew that an earl had greeted her with such affability.

"I believe my wife will wish to know you as well, Miss Bennet," said he as he was preparing to leave. "I hope you will agree to be introduced to her when she returns to town."

"Aunt Susan is not in town at present?" asked Anne.

"She is currently at Snowlock," replied the earl. Then for Elizabeth's benefit he added: "Snowlock is the family estate in Derbyshire, not far from Darcy's estate. She will be returning to London within the next few weeks, at which time I will bring her by."

"Of course, sir," said Elizabeth, amazed that an earl was asking her for permission to introduce his wife. "I would be happy to make her acquaintance."

"Excellent!" The earl then favored her with a mischievous wink. "If you will excuse me, I must return to my home. As you are aware, facing my sister requires fortitude, so I had best retire early tonight to shore up my strength."

The earl took his leave and was shown out by Mr. Darcy, leaving Elizabeth all bemused at his attention and words to her. Perhaps her uncle was correct—if her mother learned that Elizabeth had met an earl, she would give her father no rest until he agreed to allow her to stay as long as she wished. Perhaps that was the key to allow her to stay for some time in the company of her friends.

There was another left preoccupied by the earl's visit, but his reasons were entirely different. The longer Miss Bennet had been in his home, the more Darcy began thinking thoughts which should be forbidden. Perhaps it was their prohibited nature which drew them to his mind; perhaps it was the allure of the woman herself; perhaps it was nothing more than the woman's clear superiority over every other woman he had ever known. Darcy was not certain, but the distance he had achieved by leaving Hertfordshire, the welcome—though tenuous—peace of mind occasioned by being out of her company, was now completely undone, and his defenses seemed to have disappeared.

It was evident that the earl approved of Miss Bennet as his performance that day had shown. But Darcy knew that for all his joviality and ease, his uncle was a jealous guardian of his family's respectability, one of the foremost reasons for his journey to Rosings on the morrow. Accepting Miss Bennet as a woman who had assisted one of his nieces escape from her domineering mother was one thing—Darcy thought his approval would quickly vanish should Darcy do the unthinkable and propose to her.

And what of Georgiana? Marrying Miss Bennet would materially damage her own prospects for marriage, as there were many who would not even consider her if her connections included the Bennets. It was a quandary he knew, but he was not certain how he could pull himself from the abyss. Miss Bennet was a siren, a veritable succubus sent to torment him, and he did not know how he could possibly resist her.

That evening they gathered for dinner, much as they had done every night since their return from Kent, and Darcy watched, being the only man in attendance—Fitzwilliam was eating at his barracks that night due to some duties which required his attention. Darcy watched as the three ladies chatted and laughed, noting that not only was Anne's behavior nothing like he had ever seen, but Georgiana had become close to her in only a few short days. It was nothing short of amazing that she had charmed the entire family, holding them all in the palm of her hands like some benevolent goddess. Or it was not only his family, for he had often seen her charm those about her with little more than her wit and vivacity.

When they retired to the music room after dinner, they were treated to Georgiana and Miss Bennet's talents on the pianoforte. With a laugh and a shooing motion, Anne rejected their entreaties to join them. "I do not play nearly so well as you two. I am quite comfortable being admitted to the pleasure of hearing *you* both play."

Darcy was of a mind with Anne, though he said nothing, and soon Miss Bennet had begun to play with Georgiana attending her close by. She played through a song, then ceded the pianoforte to Georgiana who played, and then they exchanged places once again. There appeared to be much merriment between the two girls, further evidence of their new intimacy.

As Miss Bennet seated herself and began to play again, Anne leaned to Darcy, laughter in her gaze. "It is a delightful scene, is it not?"

"It is, indeed," replied Darcy. His attention was firmly fixed on his sister and her guest. That was why he did not see the impish glint in his cousin's eye.

"Did you have prior knowledge of our uncle's intention to visit us today?"

"Fitzwilliam did mention that he had spoken to his father. I did know he wished to see you, but not that he would visit today."

There was a moment of silence, and Darcy fixed his attention on the countenance of the fair performer.

"You know, I believe it was our uncle's way of approving of Elizabeth."

His attention captured, Darcy looked over at his cousin. "He was quite clear that he appreciated her efforts on your behalf."

"That is all?" asked Anne. When Darcy returned her look blankly, Anne rolled her eyes at him. "Can you not see anything else in his behavior today which suggests more than a simple appreciation for her friendship?"

Darcy shook his head. "I know not of what you speak, Anne. It was clear exactly what the earl's sentiments were."

"Yes, they were clear, and yet you appear to have missed the most pertinent part." Anne glanced skyward when he did not respond. "You have been quite transparent, Cousin. Your admiration for Elizabeth is obvious, though she continues to deny its existence.

"Did you not see his interaction with her, how he welcomed and thanked her? What of his cryptic statement to the effect that 'some members of the party' would not wish to see her depart? His comments concerning her heroism? He approves of Miss Bennet, Darcy, and I suspect he was trying to subtly tell you that he approved of her for *your* sake."

Though Darcy wished to refute Anne's assertions, he could not find it within him to do so. Thus, Darcy attempted obfuscation by a more oblique means.

"He was only in company with us for a very few moments. How could he possibly have seen through me?"

"Ah, but you forget, Darcy," replied Anne, and Darcy found her smugness grinding away at his composure. "Fitzwilliam knows you as well as you know yourself. He has seen your admiration for Elizabeth. I am certain he informed his father of it."

That was not only possible, but highly probable as well, Darcy noted with rueful annoyance. It would be just like his cousin, and the father was no better when it came to making sport with Darcy.

"You may, thus, proceed without fear of the family's disapprobation." Anne stopped and grinned. "At least you may be assured of the lack of censure from any member of the family who is *not* my mother."

Shocked, Darcy could only blurt: "I am surprised you would say such a thing, Anne."

Anne tilted her head to the side and regarded him. "Why should you be surprised?"

As he gazed at Anne, Darcy recalled the fact that he had never known what Anne wanted, as he had never allowed himself to become close enough to her to discover it. But when he made this observation to her, Anne only shook her head.

"I know why you felt you could not engage me, Cousin." Anne stopped and smirked. "If you ever had, you might have found yourself engaged *to* me."

"Perhaps it might have been better to find some way," replied Darcy. "Though we are cousins, I feel we hardly know each other. I apologize for it, Anne—it was unconscionable."

"If it was unconscionable, I do not think you were the only one caught up in it," replied Anne. "I do not hold it against you. Now that we have the opportunity, perhaps it would be best to attempt to come to some understanding. We have time, it appears, since our uncle will forbid my mother from coming here."

Darcy allowed himself a slow nod. "Then the first subject to canvass is your opinion of your mother's wishes regarding us."

"I never wished to marry you, even before I began to assert my independence." Anne fell silent for a moment, apparently deep in thought. "Whether this was simply because I did not wish to bow to mother's desires or due to a latent desire to find my own way I cannot say. But I was reasonably certain I would not be forced into it by your own behavior, Cousin. I assume you have always been of like mind."

"I have no desire to marry you," replied Darcy with a slow nod, his eyes darting to where Miss Bennet and Georgiana were seated at the pianoforte, laughing and chatting while they attempted to play a duet together. "This cradle betrothal your mother pushes was never mentioned to me by my mother, and my father openly derided it. I am not willing to be bound to something so wholly without foundation."

"Then we are agreed!" exclaimed Anne. "We shall both live our lives in a manner which *we* find pleasing."

It was as if a weight had suddenly been lifted from Darcy's shoulders. He favored Anne with the first true smile he had ever given her, and she returned it in like fashion.

"I believe I might have something to hold against Lady Catherine," said Darcy, and though he attempted to inject a hint of a playful quality into his voice, his words were true. "I believe we might have been good friends had your mother not interfered. That is unfortunate, as I do not have so many friends that I will not repine the loss of one."

"And I have almost none," agreed Anne. "But from this day forward, we may forward that friendship, for now that we are both determined, regardless of what Mother says, I believe we have nothing more to fear."

They spent the rest of their time that evening speaking, and Darcy began to get a sense of his cousin as a person. But in the back of his mind, he kept thinking of his own situation, having Miss Bennet in his house and the pleasure and pain it afforded him. And the more he thought of it—in the music room while in the company of the three women, and later in his own room—he began to wonder if pursuing Miss Bennet would be such a detriment to his family. Georgiana and Anne loved her, Fitzwilliam esteemed her, and even the earl had given her his approval. What more did he require?

It was not until late in the evening that he was struck by an epiphany which changed his whole outlook. Though he had determined for years to avoid being forced into marriage with his cousin, Darcy only now realized how that had affected him. The specter of this so-called engagement and the knowledge of Lady Catherine's ire should she become aware of his attentions to another had played a large part in his avoidance of any young lady of society, beyond his reticence and unwillingness to marry a woman who did not stimulate him intellectually.

Furthermore, the feeling of freedom he had experienced when he and Anne had determined their mutual lack of interest in the other told Darcy that in some way, he had felt guilty for ignoring her all these years. Exactly how much that had affected him with other young ladies, he was not certain. But he thought it had exerted some effect, possibly preventing him from truly looking at another young woman or considering her for a wife.

It had taken Miss Bennet, her magnetic allure, and *joie de vivre* to work their way past his barriers and prick his interest. And now it had grown from a mild amusement, to an admiration of her fine eyes, to a knowledge of her radiant character, to an all-consuming desire to be the man to whom she gave her love. And he knew what he had to do. There was no impediment against his interest in her. And he would allow nothing to get in his way.

Chapter XVIII

The first opportunity Darcy obtained to put his newfound resolve into action arrived the following morning. It had been clear to all present in his house that Miss Bennet had longed to visit Hyde Park and indulge in the beauty of nature, and though she had exercised laudable restraint, she declared her resolve to go the day before her relations were to come to dinner.

"I am only surprised you have managed to hold yourself in check this long," said Anne when Miss Bennet made her intentions known. "I thought we might lose you yesterday."

Georgiana giggled along with Anne's assessment, but Miss Bennet only smiled. "Well you know my habits, Anne."

"I do, indeed. But I am sure we can spare you for a time. I would only ask that you take a footman along for your protection. London is not Rosings, after all."

"Of course, I will," replied Miss Bennet.

"If I might impose, Miss Bennet," said Darcy, "I believe a little exercise would do me some good as well. Perhaps I could accompany you in the footman's stead."

That Miss Bennet was surprised by his application, Darcy could easily see. She turned to look at him, and for a moment, Darcy thought she might refuse his company. To his relief, however, she voiced her acceptance, though quietly. Anne shot him a smirk, which Darcy returned as blandly as he could, and they soon quit the room and left the house.

The streets which led to the park were clear and relatively free of other walkers, the fashionable hour for walking being later in the afternoon. Darcy had always known he was fortunate to live in such a locale where the avenues were broad and pretty and the problems of crime were distant. The park itself was a welcome boon, as it was a retreat from the bustle of the city, though he tended to avoid it during fashionable hours.

"Have you ever walked in Hyde Park, Miss Bennet?" asked he when they had arrived.

"No, Mr. Darcy." Miss Bennet turned what he thought was a shy smile on him. "There is a park near to my uncle's house in which I have often walked, but I have no experience in so grand a place as this."

"Then you are in for a treat," replied Darcy, feeling remarkably at ease with this young woman. "You could come to Hyde Park every day for a month and not explore every path it has to offer. There are many different types of trees and bushes, and the flowers are quite beautiful. And then, should you become more adventurous, you could enter Kensington Gardens and explore all they have to offer, including Round Pond and the various formal gardens."

"You are intimately acquainted with all these sights?" asked Miss Bennet, a hint of teasing in her manner.

"I do live nearby for at least part of the year. Georgiana and I often come here to walk or ride in a curricle, though on occasion we have ridden our horses together. When I come myself, it is usually on horseback."

Miss Bennet regarded him with amusement. "You come to see and be seen, do you?"

"Come now, Miss Bennet," replied Darcy, diverted by her teasing, "you do not think *I*, of all people, come to be in company with others, do you? And Georgiana, who is not out and is shy of those she does not know—would you think she would be interested in being paraded in front of society for all to see?"

With a shaken head, Miss Bennet said: "No, I would not have thought it of either of you. Then you avoid society by walking here in the mornings?"

"Terribly unfashionable of us—is it not?"

"Perhaps," replied Miss Bennet. "But I cannot imagine I would behave any differently. Too many people would interrupt my enjoyment of nature."

"Then you would enjoy seeing my home at Pemberley." Darcy looked out over the grounds of the park, but in reality, he was seeing the vistas of his home, imagining *her* there, as they walked along the lake or strolled the paths of the gardens. "Hyde Park is a marvelous creation, and it is a beautiful retreat when in town, but in truth, it pales in comparison with my home."

Darcy walked on for a few moments, lost in his own thoughts, but after some time he remembered that he was not alone. He turned a rueful glance on his companion, and he noted her watching him with something akin to wonder.

"I apologize, Miss Bennet," said Darcy. "At times, when I have been away from my home, I find my thoughts returning there. I prefer it to the city, you see."

"That is something I can well understand, Mr. Darcy," replied Miss Bennet. "I hope someday to be afforded the opportunity to see it, for you have made your love of it clear."

"Have you ever traveled anywhere else?" asked Darcy as a means of avoiding a long silence and in the hope of coming to know her better.

"Alas, no," replied Miss Bennet. "I have been to Kent, as you know, but other than my aunt and uncle's house, I have not been anywhere else. My father, you see, is not fond of traveling, and even the short journey to London is a trial on his nerves, especially when he must travel with six ladies."

Darcy laughed and shook his head. "I can well imagine."

"But I have never truly missed this lack, though I do hope to travel more in the future," said Miss Bennet. "I love the scenes of my home and have walked them extensively."

They spent some pleasant moments discussing Miss Bennet's knowledge of Hertfordshire, and Darcy listened with rapt attention. He had agreed with Bingley's assessment the previous year of his leased estate's beauty, but though he had ridden the hills and woods of Hertfordshire extensively, he had not truly stopped to consider it to any great extent. Miss Bennet's memories made the area feel more alive than it had been when he had been in residence. It made him wonder if he had passed his time in Hertfordshire fast asleep.

Their wanderings through the park eventually brought them to the shores of the Serpentine, and Darcy produced a bag he had procured from the kitchens for the purpose, sharing a few pieces of bread with Miss Bennet. They occupied themselves for several moments, breaking off small chunks and feeding them to the ducks which almost always frequented the shores of the lake.

"That fellow in particular seems to take great enjoyment in our benevolence," said Darcy, pointing at one large male, who was, at that very moment, eying them closely, eager for the next treat to be provided.

"And he is quite aggressive too," said Miss Bennet.

She broke off another piece and, quite deliberately, threw it at another mass of waterfowl, and though the large specimen they were discussing made a valiant attempt at it, one of the nearby birds scooped it up first. The baleful glare the duck directed at Miss Bennet prompted their shared laughter.

"I believe you have offended him, Miss Bennet," exclaimed Darcy between his chortles.

"It serves him right!" exclaimed she. "He should not be such a glutton."

Darcy shook his head with amusement. "I suppose his mother did not teach him to share."

"You may laugh, Mr. Darcy," said Miss Bennet, affecting affront. "But I shall not encourage bad behavior. I think our voracious friend has had enough from my hand."

Then, of course, it became a game. Miss Bennet would deliberately throw her bread away from the large duck, and it would squawk in protest at her treachery. Then he learned to watch her as she threw, moving as her arm was in motion, even managing to scoop up the prize once, prompting Elizabeth to protest again.

"Come, Mr. Darcy," said Miss Bennet when the bird was watching her, its manner faintly triumphant. "You must assist me." She tore off another piece, feigned throwing it in one direction, then reversing and throwing it to a different part of the lake, again drawing the bird's ire. "Together we can ensure some of those other poor creatures receive some of our bounty."

Darcy chuckled, but he did not disagree. They took turns throwing the bread, but even though Miss Bennet's subterfuge did not always work, as the duck—and several others who caught on—would often watch as she affected a throw and then follow her second one, much to her annoyance. But when they worked as a team, Darcy throwing after Elizabeth pretended to throw, sometimes alternating, and sometimes making several motions in succession without divesting themselves of their treats, the clever birds had no solution for them. Finally, their friend squawked and flew off to sulk on another part of the lake, prompting Miss Bennet's delighted peals of laughter.

"It looks like he has tired of the game," said Darcy. "And none too soon—I have run out of bread to feed them."

Miss Bennet tossed her last few pieces into the pond, and they turned and made their way to another part of the lake. "I am sorry, Mr. Darcy," said she, affecting primness, "but I simply cannot abide gluttony."

"I can see that, Miss Bennet. Unfortunately, our friend does not appear to agree with your assessment of his greed."

When they had gone some distance up the lake, Darcy searched around for several moments. Finding several smooth rocks, he skipped stones on the surface, watching with satisfaction when they skipped four, five, or even six times. But he found that he was not the only one with the talent. After Miss Bennet had made a particularly fine toss, Darcy turned to her with interest.

"I was not aware you could skip stones, Miss Bennet."

"Is it not an unladylike practice, sir?" asked she, favoring him with an arch of her brow.

Darcy laughed. "Not completely unladylike. Georgiana and I have often engaged in this same activity at Pemberley, though her skill is not so great as yours. Where did you learn?"

"You forget that my father has five daughters and no sons, sir. I am his favorite and the most like him in temperament, and I was always the most adventurous of my sisters. He showed me how to do it when I was naught but five years of age. My skill, you see, is the result of many years of constant study and practice."

"I dare say you have used your time well, then," replied Darcy, laughing again.

They spent some few more moments looking out over the lake. Miss Bennet asked him about it, specifically how deep, and Darcy shared what he knew of its construction and pointed out the bridge in the distance, where the rest of the waterway became the Long Water, and beyond it, Kensington Gardens. Miss Bennet then indicated a desire to see more of it some other time.

"I would be happy to accompany you, Miss Bennet." She shot a glance at him and Darcy wondered if he was being a little too open too soon, and he added: "Perhaps we could make a party of it. Georgiana enjoys the gardens, and I think Anne would enjoy them too."

"I would be happy to go with you then, sir."

They turned and began to walk back along the banks of the lake, and from thence they struck a path which would take them east toward Mayfair and his house. For a first attempt at coming to know her better, Darcy thought it had been remarkably successful. He reveled in the comfortable silence which had fallen between them as they strode back toward his home and hoped there would be many such events in the future, for he fully intended to make her his wife.

So intent was he on his own reflections that he almost did not notice when she stopped and faced him, and he noted for the first time the seriousness of her countenance. His heart fell a little.

"I am sorry, Mr. Darcy, but though I am reluctant to end our tête-à-tête with so objectionable a subject, I feel compelled—not only because of what I have learned, but also due to certain worries I possess of the situation in Hertfordshire—to approach you concerning what I am certain is a delicate subject."

"Of course, I am at your disposal, Miss Bennet," said Darcy, taken aback by her behavior.

"Thank you, sir. I should like to ask you concerning Mr. Wickham, who I am aware is known to you. Can you tell me what kind of man he is?"

And with those words, the good feelings, the wonder of the morning, the closeness he had felt in her company, all vanished.

Though Elizabeth could not know exactly of what Mr. Darcy's thoughts consisted, it was clear to see that his good mood had disappeared. She was not certain of the wisdom of bringing this matter to his attention, but Elizabeth's reflections the previous days had produced a heightened sense of worry for her sisters and the people of her home. She had concluded that she did not know the man, and the more she thought of it, the more she feared that the defects in his character of which she was aware likely meant greater vices. Kitty and Lydia, silly and stupid as they were, would be a target for an unscrupulous man interested in naught but his own pleasure. It was imperative that Elizabeth learn as much as she could as quickly as possible, so her father could be warned.

"Mr. Wickham?" echoed Mr. Darcy, the smile running away from his face.

"Yes, Mr. Darcy," replied Elizabeth, gathering the cloak of her courage about her.

"I believe we spoke of Mr. Wickham once before Miss Bennet. Did you not take heed of my words?"

Elizabeth was made uncomfortable by the intensity with which Mr. Darcy regarded her, but she gazed back defiantly, determined not to be intimidated. "I am sorry, Mr. Darcy, but if you recall, that conversation was adversarial in nature, and at the time we were not on congenial terms."

"I know not of what you speak, Miss Bennet. By my account, we have always been friendly."

"We have?" asked Elizabeth, eying him with skepticism. "What of our frequent disagreements, both at Netherfield when I stayed there and during our dance? What of the necessary traits of an accomplished woman, and the fact that I was made to feel like I could not be counted as one myself?"

"That was put forward by Miss Bingley, if you recall."

"I suppose it was, though it seems to me your agreement with her position was assured. If not those instances, what about the phrase 'not handsome enough to tempt me'?"

Mr. Darcy frowned, as if attempting to recall, but Elizabeth decided they had argued for long enough.

"I did not mean to bring up disagreeable memories, Mr. Darcy. Let us agree to leave those in the past. What interests me is your understanding of Mr. Wickham's character, his habits, etc. I wish to know how he has come to this point in his life."

"Then you still take an eager interest in the gentleman."

Elizabeth was startled by the resentment in Mr. Darcy's voice, and she wondered why he should be so affected by this subject. A gentleman would wish for those of his acquaintance to be protected from the predations of another, would he not? The old specter of Elizabeth's distrust for Mr. Darcy was aroused, and she once again wondered if she had been misled as to his character.

But then sanity reasserted itself. Whatever Mr. Darcy was, it was obvious that Mr. Wickham had grievously misrepresented himself—Georgiana's tears had not been feigned. Elizabeth again drew in the shards of her courage and faced Mr. Darcy, and this time her annoyance rose along with it.

"Yes, Mr. Darcy, I take an eager interest in Mr. Wickham. Would you like to know why?"

It appeared that Mr. Darcy was aware of how he had offended her, for the look he returned was more than a little wary. "I am not certain, Miss Bennet. Mr. Wickham possesses the ability to please where he likes. I would not wish for you to be drawn in by his tales."

"Then I would ask you to answer me, Mr. Darcy. He has accused you of blasting his prospects, of betraying your father's memory for nothing more than petty jealousy. I will own that when I first heard his tale, I *was* taken in by it. How could I not be? You were above your company and treated us all with barely concealed contempt."

"Treating others with contempt—if that is what you call it—does not necessarily suggest unchristian behavior."

"No, it does not," replied Elizabeth, deciding to ignore his assertion. "But I knew no good of you, though I will confess that I knew no good of *him* either.

"But let me say that I have heard other accounts of Mr. Wickham in recent days which put his character in an entirely different light. This has caused me to re-examine what I know of him and my interactions with him, and it has led me to much disquiet. It is for this reason I am asking you for your account of him. I care nothing for Mr. Wickham — I care for the security of the neighborhood and of my sisters who will have no defense against him if he is what I have come to suspect."

Having made her impassioned plea, Elizabeth fell silent, hoping it was enough to induce him to be explicit. Mr. Darcy regarded her for several moments with apparent dispassion, though she could not be certain, given his inscrutability. At least the anger of the previous moments seemed to have dissipated.

"If you recall, Miss Bennet," said he, "I informed you that Mr. Wickham was not a man to be trusted."

"Yes, you did. But you must see that your warning was given in a most ambiguous manner. Would you have me indict a man based on nothing more than the assertion that he is unable to retain friends?"

"It seems you convicted me on similar grounds."

It was a challenge, and one Elizabeth knew was deserved. "I have already confessed to my culpability in the matter, Mr. Darcy. I was wrong to put such faith in his words. But I abjure you, sir — if there is some danger to my family or friends, I ask you to inform me, so that I may share your information with my father."

Mr. Darcy turned away and looked back down the path toward the Serpentine from whence they had come. For the first time since she had asked him the question, Elizabeth looked about. There was no one nearby, for which she was grateful, though it could not be said that they were alone on the path. In the future, she decided that she must take care, for it would not do to be found in a compromising situation with a man who found her only tolerable.

At length Mr. Darcy sighed, and he turned back to her. "There may be some danger from Wickham, though it may not be what you fear. Since he has mentioned the living, can I also assume you know of the connection between us?"

"Only what he was willing to tell me, sir," replied Elizabeth, her sense of relief at his willingness to speak of Mr. Wickham settling the nerves which had made themselves known in the past few days. "He said he was the son of your steward, that he was known to you from a young age. The only other thing he spoke of in depth was the living which he said was denied by you."

Mr. Darcy huffed, his irritation plain to see. "That is one of the reasons why he is dangerous, Miss Bennet. He injects just enough of the truth into his tales to make the rest of it sound reasonable. His connection with my family is true enough, as is the bequest in my father's will. However, the connection was dissolved five years ago after my father's passing, though he still returned from time to time to beg for more money because 'he was my father's favorite' and I have not 'discharged my duties' with respect to his future."

Mr. Darcy's snort told Elizabeth everything she needed to know of his feelings for Mr. Wickham's assertions. "Unfortunately, Mr. Wickham leaves out the damning aspects of the story. My father did ask me to advance him in his chosen career as much as I could, and if he should choose to take orders—which my father and his hoped he would—that a valuable family living be given to him for his support.

"But you must understand, Miss Bennet, that Mr. Wickham is in no way suited to be a parson, as his character will not allow it. Yes, I thought highly of him when we were young, but the older we grew, the more I realized he was of a depraved character, dissipative and grasping. His faults included, amongst other things, a fondness for gaming, a penchant for petty theft, though always cleverly executed, and a like fondness for the company of young ladies of . . . questionable morals. If it was only houses of ill repute he visited, it would be better, but he has no respect for any woman and will seduce any who catch his fancy, whether servant or gentlewoman. To the best of my knowledge he has never had the opportunity to seduce one of higher standing, though it is not for want of trying."

As her worst fears seemed to be confirmed, Elizabeth made to interrupt, but Mr. Darcy held up a hand to silence her. "I understand you will have questions, Miss Bennet, but if you will, it would be much simpler if you allow me to tell you all. I will then answer any questions you might have remaining."

"Of course, sir," replied Elizabeth softly.

Mr. Darcy paused for a moment and then took up his tale again. "As I mentioned, my father *did* recommend Mr. Wickham in his will to be put forward to receive a family living if he took orders, and my father, furthermore, instructed me to assist in his support in obtaining the skills to undertake the profession of his choosing, if he did not choose the church. I have discharged this obligation, though he maintains I have not. Either way, he is no longer entitled to the living by his own agreement.

"Not long after my father's death, Mr. Wickham came to me to receive his inheritance." Mr. Darcy snorted. "He was to be disappointed, as I am certain he thought my father would bestow upon him one of the secondary estates we own. Instead, my father left him an immediate bequest of one thousand pounds."

"That is a healthy bequest for a servant's son," said Elizabeth.

"It is, indeed, though it was not what he had expected. He attempted to claim that my father's affection for him made it unlikely that he was left so little. That is when I told him of the living." Mr. Darcy's smile was particularly mirthless. "He was less happy after I informed him of that.

"He left Pemberley, and I did not see him for some months after. He already was in possession of his bequest, and I am certain he had already managed to begin depleting the funds. That was when he hit upon another scheme to obtain money from me. He returned, informing me that he had decided against taking orders and asserting his intention of studying the law, noting that he was more suited to such work. As such, he was certain I must agree that he could not support himself on the interest of one thousand pounds while thus engaged.

"Mindful of my father's wishes, I agreed and informed him I would be willing to compensate him for not taking the living with a more immediate pecuniary gift, to which he agreed with alacrity. I knew he ought not to be a clergyman, so I was eager to pay him off and induce him to leave, so long as he resigned—in writing—all claim to the living and any future obligations from the Darcy family. Seeing only the money he was to immediately obtain, he agreed. Of course, he wanted more for the living than I would ever give him, but such is his greed. He requested ten thousand pounds."

"Ten thousand pounds?" asked Elizabeth, incredulous of the man's audacity. "Surely a living, no matter how valuable, could not be worth a quarter that much."

"You are correct, of course." Mr. Darcy sighed. "I gave him too much, I suppose. Though I certainly would not allow him to extort that much money from me, I was eager to see him gone, and I did not bargain hard enough because of it. In the end, we settled at three thousand pounds. I wrote him a bank draft, arranged for him to receive his money, and he departed, but not until after I told him never to return to Pemberley."

Elizabeth frowned. "Three thousand pounds, in addition to the one thousand he already had, is a healthy sum for anyone. A man could live for many years on such a sum, as long as he was prudent."

"Prudence has never been one of Mr. Wickham's virtues, Miss Bennet," replied Mr. Darcy. "I have kept track of him over the years, employing investigators to inform me of his movements. The money I gave to him slipped like water through his fingers. Of his particular habits I will not speak openly, for it is not a subject to be discussed with gentle ladies. I believe you can guess for yourself how he comported himself.

"After about three years had passed, he returned, demanding the living. The study of the law he found quite unprofitable, and he was now determined to take orders. He was certain I had no one else for whom I needed to provide, and as the living had recently fallen vacant, if I would only put him forward, he would take orders immediately."

"So you *did* refuse to give him the living."

"I did. But only after he had received compensation and had signed the document renouncing all claim of it. I had him escorted from Pemberley and informed him that he would not be given admittance again. Given his level of audacity, I doubt you will be surprised to know that he abused my name to everyone with whom he came in contact. I suspect he burned with a need for vengeance."

"There is no need to continue any further," said Elizabeth, reaching out and laying a soft hand on his arm. "I have heard enough. It is clear he is a danger to my sisters, and I must inform my father."

"He is also a danger to Meryton," replied Mr. Darcy. "He leaves debts wherever he goes. I have purchased enough of them to ensure he will spend the rest of his life in debtors' prison, should I ever decide to prosecute. But there is one other matter of which you should be aware. Though I myself would wish to forget it, Mr. Wickham's actions are clearly shown to be mercenary, as well as the depths to which he will go to obtain revenge."

"You need not speak of it, sir, for I am already aware of it."

Mr. Darcy gazed at her, surprise flowing from his very being. "You know?"

"I do." Elizabeth paused, ashamed of the distress she had caused Georgiana. "I happened to mention Mr. Wickham's name in Georgiana's hearing. Her distress was such that she recited to us what she had endured at his hands."

"Georgiana," groaned Mr. Darcy and he turned and made to start back to his house.

"You need not concern yourself, sir," said Elizabeth, hurrying to catch him. "She is well and happy and, I think, relieved to have unburdened herself. Surely you have seen her demeanor these past few days?"

"But—" protested Mr. Darcy as he hesitated.

"She is well. And you may rest assured that her secret is safe with Anne and me. We shall never breathe a word of it."

Though he appeared uncertain still, Mr. Darcy stopped and regarded her. "Then I thank you for providing comfort to her. I have no doubt of your secrecy, for I was just about to tell you of her experience myself."

"I should not have mentioned that man's name," insisted Elizabeth. "Anne told me she suspected that Mr. Wickham was not a good man, but I did not listen to her. He has been such an enigma that I simply wished to know what Georgiana thought of him, never suspecting she would respond in such a vehement way."

"I hope some good comes of it," replied Mr. Darcy. "It has taken many months for her to recover from his actions. The event happened less than two months before I joined Bingley in Hertfordshire."

"Then that would explain your mood." Elizabeth swallowed heavily, cursing herself for a fool. "Your sister was still your primary concern, and yet you had already agreed to assist your friend."

"Actually, that agreement came after." Mr. Darcy shook his head. "Fitzwilliam's family was acquainted with the details of these events, and I was told it would be best to absent myself from my sister for a time, for our individual distress was feeding the other's, making it more difficult for us both. It was with the greatest reluctance that I left her behind."

Elizabeth heaved a sigh and looked at Mr. Darcy, knowing that she owed this man her regrets. Though she was uncomfortable, she would not shirk.

"You have my hearty apologies, Mr. Darcy." Her companion's expression softened ever so slightly, which Elizabeth took as encouragement. "It is clear I have been vain and gullible in this matter. I should never have credited Mr. Wickham's tales, and I should never even have listened to them, given how eager he was to share them. I am ashamed of myself."

"I do not blame you, Miss Bennet. I know how persuasive and charismatic Mr. Wickham can be." Mr. Darcy turned away. "In fact, your account has told me that perhaps I have been mistaken too. I never should have allowed him to spread his lies in Meryton. I should have acted to keep him in check."

"Would you expose Georgiana to gossip, sir? Would Mr. Wickham not have retaliated?"

Mr. Darcy shrugged. "I know not what he would have done. He is not as eager to tell stories of Georgiana, for he knows that Fitzwilliam would take a dim view of any gossip of her."

"Colonel Fitzwilliam?" asked Elizabeth.

"You do not know my cousin, Miss Bennet," said Mr. Darcy, a sudden amusement coming over him. "Fitzwilliam is amiable to all, but he is an implacable enemy when aroused. Fitzwilliam found Wickham after I had chased him from Ramsgate, and though he will not inform me of the contents of the discussion, Wickham, from all accounts, left the meeting shaken. I doubt he will tell tales any time soon—at least not about Georgiana."

Elizabeth nodded and turned to start walking back toward the house, noting that Mr. Darcy had fallen into step beside her. For some time, they walked in silence, Elizabeth considering what she had learned. It was only as they approached the house that she spoke up to break the silence.

"I have one more question, Mr. Darcy. I understand your sister's faithless companion was a Mrs. Younge. Do you know if she is still about causing mischief?"

Mr. Darcy appeared nonplused at her question, but by now he knew she would not ask without a reason. "She owns a boarding house in a seedy part of town. Might I wonder why you ask?"

"When Lady Catherine advertised for a new companion for Anne, it was answered by a woman called Miss Younge. I was wondering if she was the same person."

A frown settled over his face. "Part of the conditions of allowing her to be dismissed only was that she would not attempt to pass herself off as a gentlewoman again. It is possible she is still working with Wickham, but I must own that I do not know. But perhaps it is best to investigate further."

Elizabeth agreed that it was. Then she said: "Thank you for answering my questions, Mr. Darcy. I fully understand what you have told me and will inform my father accordingly." Elizabeth paused and smiled. "I will, of course, leave out any mention of Georgiana and her history with Mr. Wickham."

Mr. Darcy thanked her, but she could see that his manner was still distracted. It was not until they were only a few houses down from his that he turned and regarded her, bringing her to a stop.

"You mentioned the phrase 'not handsome enough to tempt me.' Though I cannot remember my words in particular—which should tell you what importance I attached to them—are you perhaps referring to the evening of our first meeting at the assembly?"

Elizabeth blushed. "I was, sir, but I ask you to disregard what I said. It was my vanity which allowed me to be offended."

"Would not anyone be thus affected? I will not offer any justification for my words. I would only ask that we start afresh. That gentleman you met that night is not the gentleman I aspire to be."

"Of course," replied Elizabeth. "I believe neither of us can make the claim of exemplary behavior."

Though Elizabeth could not quite determine if she had heard him properly, she thought he said: "Thank you."

Chapter XIX

Since her family was to come to Darcy house for dinner the very next night, Elizabeth did not have much time to think about her conversation with Mr. Darcy. Georgiana, though she was Mr. Darcy's sister, had never hosted a dinner for anyone, and she was understandably nervous for the coming evening. Anne, of course, had never been allowed to have anything to do with any entertaining her mother had done—which was not much—and Elizabeth, though she had observed her mother over the years, was not experienced herself. Still, with much laughter and support of each other, the three girls managed to make the preparations in a creditable manner.

Her letter to her father was quickly written and dispatched, and though Elizabeth thought the danger posed to her youngest sisters was clear and unequivocal, she could not be certain that her father would not treat it with his typical detachment. Elizabeth considered writing her mother concerning Mr. Wickham—her mother could not resist a piece of juicy gossip and would no doubt have it spread throughout the town within hours. Two facts, however, held her back. The first was the uncertainty about whether Mr. Wickham—who knew she had visited Rosings and might know that she was now in London staying with the Darcys—would retaliate by letting loose his resentment and blackening Georgiana's name, regardless of Mr. Darcy's assurances. The other was that she could not be certain her mother would not embellish whatever she was told, making it all that much worse.

Mr. Darcy was quiet for the rest of the day of their discussion, and even that evening when they gathered together after dinner, he was silent and distracted. His behavior, even more than his usual reticence, drew the attention of his family.

"You are preoccupied, Cousin," said Anne, her tone more than a little teasing. "Could something momentous have occurred on your walk?"

"Of course, there was," said Elizabeth, speaking up to spare Mr. Darcy the mortification of Anne's teasing.

"Oh?" asked Anne, her eyes sparkling with delight.

"Yes. We had a perilous confrontation with several rabid ducks and were fortunate to escape with our lives!"

Anne gaped at Elizabeth for a moment, while the Darcy siblings burst out laughing. Her friend's gaze then became slightly accusing. "At times, Elizabeth, I do not know whether to take you seriously."

"I am deadly serious, Anne," said Elizabeth, injecting a solemnity in her manner which appeared to impress Anne not at all. "Let me relate our experience to you."

And so, Elizabeth began to weave her tale, and though what she told them was nominally the truth, it also contained so many embellishments—a swift retreat from hordes of angry ducks among other hazardous encounters—that it could only be termed a tall tale. In the end, Mr. Darcy was laughing as was Georgiana, and though Anne grinned in delight, Elizabeth could see the hard glint in her eyes which told Elizabeth her friend realized she had been diverted from teasing her cousin.

"Perhaps you should not walk Hyde Park again, Elizabeth," said Anne when their merriment had run its course. "If such things happen, it would be best, for your own safety, if you remained close to the house."

"On the contrary," replied Elizabeth, "I found it most invigorating, and I mean to do it again." She turned a look on Mr. Darcy. "Might I assume you will accompany me to turn back the dangers I might encounter?"

It appeared Mr. Darcy recognized her words for the peace offering they were, for he replied with alacrity. "Of course, Miss Bennet. It was perhaps the most diverting hour I have ever spent."

Anne eyed them suspiciously, but she made no further comment.

Soon after they retired for the night, and as Elizabeth was walking from the room, she felt Mr. Darcy step close behind her. "Thank you, Miss Bennet."

"It was my pleasure, Mr. Darcy," replied Elizabeth with a beaming smile. It was an exchange which seemed to her to carry some deeper meaning, though Elizabeth decided against trying to decipher it further.

When her family arrived for dinner the following evening, Elizabeth was waiting with barely restrained impatience. She had not seen Jane since early March, and though she thought she had seen a marked improvement in Jane's spirits in her most recent letters, she wished to judge for herself the state of her mind.

The Gardiners were welcomed into the room when they arrived, and at the first sight of her dearest sister, Elizabeth let out a little cry and skipped to her sister's side, throwing her arms about Jane's neck and whispering into her ear.

"Oh, Jane! How happy I am to see you."

"I am happy too!" whispered Jane in response. "You must tell me all about your time in Kent." Jane directed an imperious glare at her, though its effect was diluted by the fact that Jane did not have it in her to act as Lady Catherine would. "I suspect your letters have left out some pertinent pieces, no doubt in an attempt to keep me from worrying."

"You shall have it, of course," replied Elizabeth. "I would not dream of keeping anything from you."

"Do you have another room we could use for our visiting, Mr. Darcy?" Elizabeth turned and noticed her uncle regarding them with equal parts amusement and indulgence. "I have never seen two sisters as close as the eldest Bennets. Their reunion may take some time."

"It seems you are correct, sir. Perhaps a retreat to the music room might be advisable? We could have them summoned from here when dinner is ready to be served."

"Assuming we could draw them away, of course."

"Oh, Uncle!" scolded Elizabeth. "At times, you are too much like my father! Jane and I have not seen each other for two months."

"A veritable lifetime to young ladies, I am sure. Perhaps your aunt would appreciate a reunion too? Mayhap we could leave the three of you here."

"I am happy to see my aunt too," said Elizabeth, greeting her aunt with the same happiness with which she had greeted Jane. "But I suppose I should mind my manners and introduce you to everyone."

"I would appreciate that, Lizzy," replied Mrs. Gardiner.

Elizabeth pulled away from Jane and made the introductions in a tolerably composed manner, and they sat down to visit, Elizabeth staying close to her sister. Anne, who had possessed nearly all of Elizabeth's attention in recent weeks, was welcoming to Elizabeth's dearest sister, and soon they were conversing with ease, Georgiana sitting close by and, if not speaking with equal felicity, at least with composure.

They were called in to dinner soon after, and Elizabeth was treated to all the happiness of seeing those she considered most dear being accepted by the family who was, after all, much higher in society than they. Her uncle, as the only other man present, spoke with Mr. Darcy with animation, and the ladies enjoyed one another's company. The table was small enough that they could all talk amongst themselves without having to speak up to be heard.

"I am curious, Mr. Darcy," said Elizabeth after they had seated themselves and the first course of dinner was served. "Colonel Fitzwilliam is not in attendance tonight. Has he some duties which prevent his attendance?"

"The colonel was obliged to attend to a matter of business which, though peripherally connected to the army, was somewhat more personal in nature." Mr. Darcy paused, and Elizabeth thought his manner was slightly mysterious. "He is gone to the north, but I expect him to return by the morrow."

Mr. Darcy turned to his guests. "I apologize for his absence. He was anticipating meeting you all. I am certain there will be many opportunities in the future to make your acquaintance."

"I can well understand the demands of business," was her uncle's jovial reply. "We would to be happy be introduced to him when the occasion presents itself."

Her uncle and Mr. Darcy continued to speak, and Elizabeth watched them. She liked to think that she was well enough acquainted with Mr. Darcy to know when he was obfuscating, and at that moment she was certain she was not being told the whole story. As they were conversing, Mr. Darcy caught her eye, and he smiled and nodded, but there was a hint of smugness in his manner, like he knew something of which Elizabeth was ignorant. But as he turned back to her uncle, and querying him would have been impertinent, she endeavored to put it from her mind.

After dinner, the ladies retired to the music room, leaving the gentlemen behind to their port. Though she might have thought with only the two gentlemen present they would not be eager for the separation, Mr. Darcy appeared quite willing to stay with Mr. Gardiner and speak of some matters of business. It was another facet to the gentleman Elizabeth would not have considered previously—though she had known of Mr. Darcy's friendship with Mr. Bingley, a man whose fortune had been made in trade, she had not considered the possibility that he might become friendly with her uncle, a man who was actively engaged in that detestable profession. But he had surprised her again.

When they had attained the music room, Anne, who had been trying to induce Jane to speak, turned and addressed her again. "Miss Bennet, I understand you and your sister have been from home for quite some time."

"Yes, we have," replied Jane. "Lizzy, as you know, was in London for only a day before she went to Kent, but I came to London with the Gardiners after Christmas."

"That is quite a long time to be separated from your family." Anne smiled in a self-deprecating manner. "Of course, I have rarely been separated from my mother for more than a few days. At present, however, I find that I am quite enjoying the freedom my cousin's house provides."

Elizabeth had not shared anything of Anne and Lady Catherine's situation with Jane, so she appeared a little perplexed at Anne's assertions. But in true Jane fashion, she appeared to take the most agreeable interpretation on Anne's words and said:

"It is very good of your mother to agree to do without you for a time, so that you may visit your family. "I hope someday to make her acquaintance, for our cousin, Mr. Collins, has told us much of her."

It seemed that Anne's question had a definite purpose, for she smiled at Jane—which changed to a smirk when her eyes darted to Elizabeth. "I would be happy to introduce you. My mother loves to be of use to all—I cannot think she would be anything but pleased with the acquaintance."

No doubt she would be horrified at Anne being known to *another* of the impertinent Bennet sisters, thought Elizabeth, but she held her tongue; the chances of that ever happening were rather small in Elizabeth's estimation.

"And what of your parents?" asked Anne, trying to coax Jane to speak. "I assume it must be hard to have their two eldest daughters absent at the same time. Does your mother wish for your return?"

It was evident Jane was not quite certain how to answer Anne's question—from her own letters from her mother, Elizabeth knew that Mrs. Bennet considered it more likely that Jane would catch a husband in London, rather than Hertfordshire, so her demands for Jane to return home would likely only happen should Mr. Bingley—or any other man Mrs. Bennet considered it likely her daughter would attract—return to the neighborhood.

"My mother misses us, of course," interjected Elizabeth when Jane did not immediately respond. "It is more likely that my father will ask for our return. He does not share as many interests with my younger sisters, so he will likely long for our presence before our mother does."

"It is well that you have a loving relationship with your father," replied Anne. "My father died when I was very young, and I do not have any memory of him. It is something I have missed in my life, I think."

The conversation was at risk of turning mawkish, so Mrs. Gardiner spoke up. "Elizabeth especially shares a truly close relationship with her father, though my brother loves all his girls." Mr. Gardiner turned to Georgiana. "I remember *your* mother quite well, Miss Darcy, for I was privileged to know her when I was young."

"You knew my mother?" asked Georgiana, wide-eyed at Mrs. Gardiner's assertion.

"Yes, I did. For you see, I grew up in Lambton, a village with which I am assured you are well acquainted."

"Of course, I am!" cried Georgiana. "My brother's estate is not five miles from Lambton."

"Indeed, it is. When I was young I toured it on occasion. The rector at Lambton parish at the time was my father, and as his daughter, I was much involved in charities in the vicinity, in which your mother was invested herself. Though I did not know her well, she was always kind and attentive, and she always had lovely things to say to me.

"You remind me of her very well, Miss Darcy. You have the same blond hair and blue eyes, and you possess her kindness, though I suspect your shyness—a trait which she also possessed—is in excess of hers."

"She passed when I was very young," replied Georgiana, her ducked head giving evidence of Mrs. Gardiner's assertions. "But there are paintings of her at Pemberley, and my brother has always said that I remind him of our mother very much, especially these past years as I have grown older."

"I believe she would have been proud of you, Miss Darcy. I knew her before you were born, and though she was not one to speak with great energy or to confide in those she did not know well, she always told my mother that she was fortunate to have three daughters, and that she had always wished to have one herself."

"Oh!" exclaimed Georgiana. "I had never considered it in that way."

Mrs. Gardiner bestowed a benevolent smile on Georgiana. "I am certain you have heard much of your mother, Miss Darcy, and I suspect you are aware of her love, though you have never known her yourself. But I would wish you to know that you were always wanted—she pined to have another child and had so many disappointments after your brother's birth. You were very much loved."

The pleasure which shone forth from Georgiana's countenance attested to her gratitude in hearing Mrs. Gardiner speak in such a manner. "Thank you, Mrs. Gardiner. My brother is wonderful, of course, but his memories of my mother are those of a child, since she died when he was still quite young himself, and he does not care for the things a young lady does. Would you . . . If you know any other stories of my mother, would you be willing to share them?"

"I would be happy to, Miss Darcy," replied Mrs. Gardiner. "She was one of the best ladies of my acquaintance, and though I was little more than a child myself when I left Lambton, my memories of her are quite vivid."

The ladies began speaking of this new subject, and Elizabeth was quite happy to hear her aunt tell of her experiences with Georgiana's mother. Though she had been taken from them many years ago, it was evident that the lives of both Darcys had been affected to a great degree by Lady Anne Darcy. Hearing a little more of her seemed to tell her more of both Georgiana and Mr. Darcy, and in a strange way, she felt closer to them both and like she understood them better than she ever had before. In an odd way, it was like becoming their closer friends by proxy.

While Georgiana was engaged in hearing stories of her mother, Anne watched all, especially Jane Bennet, who intrigued her. Consistent with Elizabeth's assertions, Jane was much like Georgiana in essentials, though her quietude was more the product of simply not wishing to betray her feelings, rather than Georgiana's shyness. But there was also something about Jane which seemed to suggest that she was not nearly as content as the façade she showed the world.

As the attention of her companions was riveted on Mrs. Gardiner, and Jane Bennet, though she listened politely, did not seem nearly so invested in the conversation, Anne spoke in a soft voice to Miss Bennet, hoping to understand her better.

"Have you enjoyed your time in London, Miss Bennet?" asked Anne.

There was the slightest pause before Miss Bennet spoke, and a hint of a shadow seemed to pass over her face. "I have. My aunt and uncle are welcoming, and I enjoy staying with them."

"You stay often?"

"Usually at least once every year," replied Miss Bennet. "Lizzy usually stays with them for some time too, though we are not often in London together."

"They seem like they are very fashionable people," said Anne, turning to regard Mrs. Gardiner. "If I was not already aware of Mr. Gardiner's business, I might have thought him to be a gentleman."

"He was educated at Oxford, and he took note of the manners of those gentlemen with whom he attended school. My uncle is also very intelligent and was able to make many friendships which, I believe, have survived to this day."

"And your aunt? By her account she was the daughter of a parson."

"Yes," replied Miss Bennet. "Aunt Gardiner's father was the third son of a gentleman himself. I believe they are close to their relations and are often in company with their friends. As for Uncle, he is descended from a gentleman as well, though his connections are much further distant. I believe there are some Gardiners who are landowners, but my aunt and uncle have no real connection with them."

"Then that explains it." Anne paused, pondering what she could say to further draw Miss Bennet out. "Have you had an opportunity to partake of any of the events of the season, or any of the cultural attractions, London has to offer?"

"Yes, we have. I appreciate the theater, and we have gone since I have been in London. Aunt and uncle also have many friends, and we are often in company with them." Miss Bennet snuck a sidelong glance at her aunt. "They do not move in the same circles as Mr. Darcy, so we have never met him here, but my relations' circle of friends is quite agreeable."

"And do you have any beaux?" asked Anne. "I assume a woman with your natural beauty must have the interest of many gentlemen."

It seemed like Anne had hit upon the problem, for Miss Bennet turned ever so slightly red, though she quickly regained her composure. "I have no admirer, Miss de Bourgh, though there are some younger gentlemen of my aunt and uncle's acquaintance to whom I am known."

There was no further need to press, so Anne directed her comments to another subject and enjoyed a sensible discussion with Miss Bennet. In the other woman, she was pleased to discover intelligence, but reticence—Jane Bennet did not possess her sister's fire or cutting wit, but she was just as Elizabeth had described. Anne thought the most pertinent word which could be used to describe her was "angelic."

But behind that angelic demeanor existed a woman whose feelings had been wounded, and given some of her understated responses, Anne thought it likely that it was at the hands of a man. The matter was truly none of her concern—Anne was well aware of it. But she also remembered Elizabeth mentioning something of Mr. Bingley and her eldest sister, which led her to believe Mr. Bingley was the man in question, and as Mr. Bingley and Darcy were the closest of friends and had been together in Hertfordshire where they had met Miss Bennet, Anne did not doubt that Darcy was involved.

Regardless, she meant to obtain some answers, and she knew Miss Bennet would not be induced to be explicit. Elizabeth, on the other hand, possessed a healthy sense of righteous indignation when the situation demanded it. Anne, therefore, had no doubt her friend would possess an opinion concerning her sister's heartbreak. Thus, it was Elizabeth to whom she would apply for more information.

While the ladies were ensconced in the music room, Darcy leaned back and sipped his port in the company of Mr. Gardiner. Although the man's conversation was engaging and covered such topics as Darcy found interesting, he became aware his mind was wandering.

Mr. Gardiner's realization of Darcy's reluctance to meet him and the reasons why had, quite honestly, shamed Darcy. He had been taught by his parents to judge his fellow man by the content of their characters—in fact, it was those teachings which had largely been responsible for Darcy's acceptance of Bingley's close friendship.

And though Darcy had been averse to meeting Mr. Gardiner in part for his profession, the greater part of it had been because of his knowledge that the man was Mrs. Bennet's sister. By that reasoning, the earl should be a meddling, insufferable snob like Lady Catherine! It was humbling to realize that he had been wrong. And if he had been wrong about that, how wrong was he that he was above Miss Bennet? Could such things matter when it came down to concerns of the heart?

Clearly, they could not, and Darcy was ashamed of himself, while at the same time being hopeful for the future. If he had gone much longer in this attitude, he might have irrevocably lost any chance of obtaining the love of a good woman. He would not make that mistake again.

"It seems to me that you have something else on your mind, Mr. Darcy."

Embarrassed to be caught out by a man he was hoping to impress, Darcy stammered and searched for a reply. Mr. Gardiner only chuckled.

"Do not concern yourself, sir. It seems to me like there is some particular reason why you are less than attentive to my conversation. Is it perhaps another member of my family who has drawn your attention?"

If Darcy had thought he was embarrassed before, it was nothing compared to this. "It seems that I have been far more transparent than I had ever thought I would be."

"You forget, Mr. Darcy," replied Mr. Gardiner, his manner easy, "I have also been a man in love."

There was nothing Darcy could do to refute Mr. Gardiner's words, and he did not even attempt to do so.

"The question I have is concerning Elizabeth. Are you aware of Elizabeth's feelings for you?"

"I understand her opinion was not positive," replied Darcy slowly. "I believe that it has undergone a material improvement since we have become reacquainted."

"It seems to me you have," replied Mr. Gardiner. "If you would like, I will share a little advice about my niece which I believe you have not yet understood."

When Darcy indicated he was happy to have any advice Mr. Gardiner saw fit to dispense, the man continued. "I believe you would benefit by a little more openness, sir. You are, I understand, of a reserved disposition, and that, in itself, is certainly not an evil, as I suspect that Elizabeth is more than lively enough for you both.

"But though Elizabeth would never expect you to suddenly change your character for her sake, I believe she will need to have some assurance of your regard for her, and that will require you to be a little more demonstrative than you might find comfortable."

"Proof of my regard?" asked Darcy, seeking to understand what Mr. Gardiner was telling him.

"Exactly. My niece, Mr. Darcy, wishes for love in a marriage, and she wishes to be respected for being the intelligent woman she is. Showing her that you care for her, speaking to her of things which display your confidence in her insight by discussing subjects a man might not usually discuss with his wife would go a long way toward informing her of your regard."

"Might I ask if you have personal experience in this, Mr. Gardiner?" asked Darcy.

The other man nodded and raised his glass. "I, too, have an intelligent wife, Mr. Darcy, a woman whom I respect as my equal. Though she has not the business experience and knowledge that I possess, I have often found it useful to discuss problems with her. She may not have the answers, but sometimes simply speaking of it to her, knowing she can understand the problem, is enough to lead me to a solution. At other times, her insights have positively astounded me. Lizzy is as intelligent as her aunt, and though I would never presume to tell you how much of your business you should share with her, I would also not suggest you ignore such a useful resource.

"Of course," said Mr. Gardiner after he had drained his glass, "I would not suggest you have such conversations now when you are not even engaged, let alone married. But speaking to her as an equal will show her that such confidences are possible should you succeed in your suit, and that can only help your cause."

Mr. Gardiner stood. "Now, shall we rejoin the ladies?"

"Of course, sir," replied Darcy. "I believe I shall take your advice in the manner it was intended, and I thank you."

"Excellent!" said Mr. Gardiner.

They left the room and made their way to the music room. Darcy soon joined Miss Bennet where she was sitting close to his sister and Mrs. Gardiner, and for the rest of the evening, he had little attention for any other. That a man such as Mr. Gardiner was willing to give him advice concerning what was an obviously favored niece was something for which Darcy could only give thanks. He intended to use what he had heard to the fullest.

Chapter XX

Elizabeth's reunion with her family had been everything she had hoped it would be, leaving her happy and contented the next day. Jane and her aunt had got on famously with Anne and Georgiana, her aunt sharing anecdotes of the young girl's late mother. Mr. Darcy had seemed to esteem Uncle Gardiner, directing a great deal of his attention thither for most of the evening. There was nothing more for which she could have asked.

The following day, they were once again caught up in their pursuits, and Elizabeth found herself lighter than she had been in some time. They were to visit the Gardiner townhouse on the morrow—Aunt Gardiner had been adamant that her children wished to see Elizabeth, who was a favorite, as soon as possible, and as they were dear children, Elizabeth was quite happy to oblige.

But whatever Elizabeth had expected, she had never thought her friend would take such an interest in her dearest sister. As the morning wore on, Elizabeth noted that Anne was watching her, and unless she missed her guess, she thought Anne had some subject of which she wished to speak. After Georgiana was gathered by Mrs. Annesley to attend to her studies, Elizabeth expected Anne to speak almost as soon as her cousin had left the room. She was not mistaken.

"Now, Elizabeth," said Anne, in a forthright manner which was eerily reminiscent of her mother, "I wished to speak to you about last night, for I noted something quite strange."

"Oh?" asked Elizabeth, careful to keep her tone noncommittal.

"Your sister seemed ill at ease. It seemed to me like there was something troubling her."

"I am quite surprised to hear you say that, Anne. You only met her last night!"

"That is true," said Anne, brushing off Elizabeth's protestation. "But I am certain I am correct. Your sister is one who does not display her feelings for all to see, but when one converses with her, if one is observant, it is clear her equilibrium has been disrupted. In fact, were I to guess, I would say it is because of a man."

"Anne, I do not know that we should be speaking of this subject."

"Elizabeth," replied Anne, and she directed a serious look at Elizabeth which made Elizabeth feel like a small child being told to mind her manners, "I do not mean to pry or insert my opinion into matters which are not my concern. I only mean to help."

With a sigh, Elizabeth smiled at her friend—there was no reason *not* to tell Anne of what had happened between Jane and Mr. Bingley. Anne was not the kind of person to refer to the matter in company and further disturb Jane's feelings.

"Unfortunately," said Elizabeth, "I do not think there is anything that can be done to assist." Elizabeth sighed. "It is as you surmise—Jane has suffered a disappointment. I had hoped that she would be much improved by the time we returned from Kent, but she is still affected, which shows how attached to him she was."

"Then this is not a recent disappointment?"

"No. It stems from autumn of last year."

Anne frowned, and Elizabeth wondered at the ferocity of it. "Was that not when Darcy visited Hertfordshire? Surely you do not suggest that Jane developed a tender regard for my cousin."

Her words were spoken in such an incredulous tone that Elizabeth could not help but laugh, though she supposed there truly was nothing humorous in the situation. "No, Anne, Jane does not love Mr. Darcy, and for that I suppose we can all be grateful."

They laughed together, though Anne directed a cross look at Elizabeth. In the end, however, she seemed to push aside whatever thought was on her mind in favor of the subject at hand.

"If it is not some sort of grand secret, can you share it with me?"

"I suppose it would do no harm," replied Elizabeth with a sigh.

"You see, though Jane does not love Mr. Darcy, her attachment was formed when your cousin and his friends—the Bingleys—were staying in Hertfordshire last autumn."

"Tell me."

"It is Mr. Bingley to whom Jane is attached. When he came to Hertfordshire, his regard for her was clear for all to see—everyone in the neighborhood thought an engagement would be forthcoming. He danced twice with her at the assembly, whenever they were in company he was no more than five feet from her side, and I personally know of several instances at the ball he and his sister hosted where he could be accused of incivility because his attention was so fixed on Jane." Elizabeth laughed. "Is not incivility a veritable hallmark of love?"

The grin Anne directed at her seemed lukewarm at best. "I cannot claim to have any firsthand knowledge of the matter, but I agree you must be correct. But if his attentions were so marked, what happened?"

"His . . . his sisters were what happened," said Elizabeth. She had been about to include Mr. Darcy in her accusation, but she decided at the last moment to avoid mention of him. It would do no good, after all, to attempt to blacken his name to his cousin, and Elizabeth did not wish to engage in such behavior anyway. She suspected that he had some culpability in the matter, but given what she learned of him, she wondered if he had had some other reason for involving himself, if he had, in fact, been involved.

"His sisters?" asked Anne, her speculative look demanding answers.

"The day after his ball, Mr. Bingley was obliged to come to town on a matter of business. Before he left, he assured Jane of his swift return, his manner suggesting that it was *she* who prompted such an eager desire to be in Meryton. But the day after he left, Miss Bingley and her sister closed Netherfield and returned to London, and I have no doubt their primary motivation was to persuade their brother against returning to my sister.

"Before they left, Miss Bingley sent Jane a letter all but destroying her hopes. She *informed* Jane that they were bound for London and unlikely to return, and that her brother had no wish to return to Hertfordshire." Elizabeth paused before continuing, uncertain whether she should share the next bit of Miss Bingley's scheming, but when she saw Anne's steady regard, a look which demanded answers, she capitulated. "In her letter, Miss Bingley insinuated that her brother had a *particular* regard for Georgiana, and that he was eager to be in her company. She also specifically said that she had hopes that Georgiana would eventually be *her* sister."

"Oh?" asked Anne, the dangerous flashing in her eyes suggesting she was not amused. "And what did you think of these assertions?"

"I have already told you what I thought of her departure." Elizabeth's jaw tightened at the memory of Jane's distress. "The way she did it the day after Mr. Bingley's departure, the tone of her letter, her obvious disdain for the company and annoyance with her brother's attentions to my sister told me that it was nothing more than a blatant attempt to persuade him away from her."

"And Georgiana? Surely you were not drawn in by her claims in that quarter."

"No," replied Elizabeth, shaking her head. "That claim always reeked of desperation. You see, it is clear to anyone with eyes that Miss Bingley harbors hope with respect to your cousin. I dare say she believes that achieving *one* marriage between their two families will make it easier to achieve a *second*."

Anne's huff of disdain clearly elucidated her feelings on that score. "Then she would be incorrect. You know Darcy and I have never been close, but one thing I know of him is that he would never be drawn in by such scheming. I believe he wishes for affection in marriage, and I doubt he has any affection for this woman."

A laugh escaped Elizabeth's lips. "You are correct. I myself witnessed his evident distaste for her on several occasions. I never thought he would align himself with her. I also never gave any credence to Miss Bingley's assertions of an attachment between Georgiana and her brother, and I give them even less now that I have met her.

"But you must understand that Jane is not only a modest soul, but she possesses not a cynical bone in her body. She is adept at ascribing the best possible motives to everyone she meets, and she has done so in this instance. She feels that Miss Bingley was attempting, most kindly, to put her on her guard and inform her of her brother's indifference, and when I gave her another opinion on the matter, she insisted that she could only hope that Miss Bingley had deceived herself. She has been far from her cheerful self these past months."

For a few moments, Anne was silent, seemingly contemplating everything Elizabeth had told her. For her part, Elizabeth was feeling oddly drained by her recitation and fell silent along with her. The truth was that she had attempted to push Jane's heartache to the back of her mind, especially since she had gone to live at Rosings. Speaking of it again was not, in any way, agreeable.

"You do realize this does not speak well of Mr. Bingley," said Anne after a moment. "There is a decided want of resolution displayed by a man who allows his sister to convince him in such a way."

Elizabeth sighed. "I will own the thought has occurred to me. I have always known that Mr. Bingley was modest, but I had hoped that he would be firm in his admiration of my sister, though his own will not approve."

"And yet you wish her to make a match with him?" asked Anne.

"I only wish for Jane to be happy. I know not what means his sisters used to persuade him against her, but I suspect it was underhanded. I believe that if he was presented to the sight of Jane before him again, he would forget all about his sisters' objections."

Anne's expression only became ever more severe. "From all you have told me of Mr. Bingley and his sister, are you not worried about Mr. Bingley being ruled by his sister and making *your* sister's life miserable?"

"I can only hope that he would be roused to her protection," said Elizabeth. "But in the end, I trust Jane to understand what she wishes. As I have said, I only want her to be happy."

"Then what do you mean to do about it?"

Taken aback, Elizabeth gazed at her friend, wondering if she had heard Anne correctly. "What do I mean to do?"

"Elizabeth," said Anne, her tone gentle yet firm, "Do you not see that you have been given a singular opportunity? You are staying at Darcy's house, and at present there is no limit to the length of your stay. Jane is in town and, if Mr. Bingley is not yet in town, I believe he soon will be. If you wish to end your sister's suffering, your path seems clear."

"Are you suggesting we arrange for them to be together again?"

"Of course," replied Anne. "Darcy has already accepted your aunt and uncle, and I expect they will be in company with us on several occasions. I do not know where Mr. Bingley is or what he is doing, but as Darcy is his good friend, he will naturally wish to be in company with Mr. Bingley."

"And if Mr. Bingley sees me staying here, his thoughts will naturally turn to Jane."

"Exactly. It should not be difficult to get them into each other's company again, and if their feelings are as you suspect, they will do the rest themselves. At the very least, we will have given them the chance to come to their own conclusions while lessening the interference of Mr. Bingley's sisters."

It was tempting. Though it suggested a hint of matchmaking, in reality, Elizabeth had no other thought in mind than to give Mr. Bingley a chance to once again see Jane and render whatever argument his sister had used as irrelevant. However, there was a potential for disaster too. If Mr. Bingley decided against Jane again, her already wounded heart would be further damaged because of it. Elizabeth did not know what to do.

"I think you do your sister a disservice," said Anne when Elizabeth made this observation. "She has been affected by Mr. Bingley's defection—it is true. But I think she has become wiser as a result, and should he appear any different from his previous attentions, I believe she will notice it. It might even help her to overcome her melancholy, rather than draw her down into the depths of despair."

"It is possible," said Elizabeth, though her level of skepticism was high. Jane did have a tender heart, and Elizabeth had seen nothing more from her sister than distress at the abandonment of Mr. Bingley. She was, indeed, too apt to look for the good in others rather than seeing them as they were, but Elizabeth could not help but suppose that in this instance, such traits would serve her ill.

"Perhaps we could see how mention of Mr. Bingley affects her. It may also be possible to see Mr. Bingley, to observe whether his own regard has survived their separation."

"Perhaps," agreed Elizabeth. "I am not opposed at present, Anne, but I would not wish to rush into something and make the situation worse."

"Of course," replied Anne.

Their discussion was interrupted at that moment by the entry of Mr. Darcy, followed by Colonel Fitzwilliam. Though there was no time to continue to discuss the matter, Anne threw Elizabeth a significant look which promised further debate later, and they both turned their attention to the two gentlemen. Mr. Darcy appeared as serious as ever, but the colonel was his usual ebullient self, and his manner carried a hint of smugness. Elizabeth was intrigued.

"Anne, Miss Bennet," said the colonel, and when he looked at her, Elizabeth got a greater sense of his mischievous self-satisfaction. "I hope the day finds you both well?"

"It does, indeed, Cousin," replied Anne. "Now, shall you inform us both of what has you preening like a peacock?"

Elizabeth laughed, as much from the colonel's injured response as from the fact that Anne had seen the same thing in his behavior as Elizabeth had herself.

"I am most certainly *not* a peacock, Cousin," replied the colonel with a superior sniff. "In fact, I am the furthest thing from it. I am a professional soldier, and as such, I am always serious and grave."

Mr. Darcy snorted, even as Anne let loose a derisive laugh. "If you are the model of gravity and restraint, I fear for us against the French. Napoleon might sail across the channel and subjugate us all while you preen in front of a mirror."

"That is not kind, Anne," said Darcy, though his grin told them all how diverted he was by her teasing. "In fact, Fitzwilliam has done us all a service, and I believe we should be thankful for his efforts."

"A service?" asked Anne. Her eyes swung to her cousin, and she seemed to be assessing him. "Then please, share it with us. What have you done which deserves such praise?"

"I doubt it means much to you, Anne," replied Colonel Fitzwilliam. He brushed his nails against his coat and inspected them. Elizabeth was not fooled by his performance in the slightest. "I believe it is of much more interest to Miss Bennet."

"To me?" asked Elizabeth, nonplussed. "I heard you had business in the north. I cannot imagine what it would have to do with me, though I will own I am surprised you are back so quickly."

"Is that what you told her?" asked Colonel Fitzwilliam, swinging his eyes to his cousin.

"It was the truth," protested Mr. Darcy. "I simply did not specify *where* in the north you were or what your business entailed."

"I believe I will become quite cross if you do not stop this teasing!" exclaimed Elizabeth. "What have you done that is so praiseworthy?"

"Nothing of consequence, I suppose," replied Colonel Fitzwilliam. "I *may* have gone to speak with Colonel Forster, who is, as you know, the commanding officer of the militia company stationed in Meryton. During our conversation, we *might* have discussed the habits of one of his officers and what has likely been happening since he joined the regiment. Then, I *may* have ensured that Wickham is no longer any threat to anyone."

Eyes wide, Elizabeth stared at the colonel. He could not possibly be saying what she thought he was saying. Could he?

"I believe you have struck our Elizabeth speechless, Cousin," said Anne in a wry tone. "It may be best if you explain yourself."

"I would be happy to," replied Colonel Fitzwilliam, grinning at Elizabeth. "You are likely not aware of this, but Colonel Forster is known to me. While I would not call us friends, we, at the least, shared a cordial, though brief, acquaintance some years in the past. Knowing what sort of man Wickham is, and having heard of his antics in Hertfordshire from Darcy, we determined that it was time to do something about the reprobate once and for all.

"Consequently, I journeyed to Hertfordshire to speak with Forster, and I laid out everything I knew of the man. Knowing of Wickham's propensity to run at the first sign of trouble, I brought a pair of trustworthy men from my own regiment to take our dear Wickham into custody and prevent his escape."

Colonel Fitzwilliam shook his head, and he chuckled. "I must hand it to you, Miss Bennet, your manners are everything that is elegant and proper, but you have a pair of sisters . . ."

Elizabeth gasped. "You met Kitty and Lydia?"

"They were speaking with Wickham on the street in Meryton when I arrived. It provided the perfect opportunity to clap Wickham in chains without any fuss. Unfortunately, Miss Lydia did not appreciate our treatment of her favorite, and Miss Kitty was little better." The colonel paused and put a finger in his ear, wiggling it about. "I fear I may have suffered permanent hearing damage from their screeching and caterwauling."

Though it was not at all amusing—her sisters were, as she had always lamented, only inches from ruining them all forever—Elizabeth had no choice but to laugh. "Had I any concern you might be misrepresenting yourself, it has been laid to rest. You have taken their measure quite thoroughly."

"Indeed, I have," replied Colonel Fitzwilliam. Then his gaze turned positively roguish. "But they were both quickly diverted from the unfortunate Wickham. I *am* a colonel, after all, and not one bound to the militia. Once they realized this fact, your youngest sisters were rather impressed."

Elizabeth shook her head and buried her face in her hands. How would she ever hold her head up high in the face of such ridiculous and improper sisters?"

"Do not be cast down, Miss Bennet. I immediately set things to rights and sent them home. Your sisters are not so bad—they are young and immature, and their behavior is nothing a little maturity and a firm hand will not correct."

There was no reason to inform the colonel that a firm hand was something it was unlikely they would ever receive.

"Regardless, my conversation thereafter with Colonel Forster was completed quickly, and a little investigation proved that Wickham has once again gathered credit which exceeds his means. His commission was forfeit to settle part of his debts, and his remaining obligations were purchased to provide further leverage over him." Colonel Fitzwilliam grinned at Elizabeth. "Thus, you may be certain that I have *not* rid the world of the stain of one George Wickham, though I was sorely tempted.

"I had him brought in, and he was given two choices: he could either face prosecution from Darcy for all the debts—new and old—Darcy holds, or he could be given one hundred pounds and a ticket on a ship bound for the New world."

Elizabeth gasped. "Mr. Wickham is to depart England?"

"He has already departed," replied the colonel. "Before I left London, we purchased a ticket for him, knowing he would not have a choice, and I escorted him to his ship this morning. Given what I know of his propensities and his over-inflated opinion of his skill at the gaming tables, I doubt he will ever possess the means to return. In fact, I doubt the money he was given will survive the crossing, and I suspect there is some question of him ever reaching the shores of the New World."

It was too much for Elizabeth to understand, and she only stared at the colonel for some moments. Colonel Fitzwilliam, for his part, seemed amused at her reaction, for he watched her, saying nothing, displaying an unrepentant smile for her benefit.

"Then I believe the community and my family, in particular, owes you much, Colonel Fitzwilliam," said Elizabeth at length. "But why did you take it upon yourself to do this much?"

"If you believe it was at my instigation, you are mistaken," replied the colonel, confusing Elizabeth even more. "My cousin, after your conversation about Wickham, determined to do something about him. He was set on going himself, but I argued that I was better positioned to do it by virtue of my position in the army. Besides," added the colonel, the menacing cast to his countenance suggesting Mr. Darcy was entirely correct about his cousin, "I felt that Wickham was owed something more from our family than my cousin would likely give him. Wickham has been a bounder and a millstone around Darcy's neck since he was a boy, and I wished him to understand that he had best not be seen on these shores again."

"Oh, Cousin," said Anne, shaking her head. "Did you explain matters to him in a *pointed* fashion?"

"No, though that was tempting. All I did was allow him to attempt to take his frustrations out on me." The colonel's expression was unreadable. "Wickham's level of fitness is shocking, though he has been in the militia for more than a six-month. It is likely because of his fondness for the bottle and his tendency to spend all his waking moments when he is not on duty—and likely when he *is*—gambling with his fellow officers. It did not take much persuasion to convince him that it was not in his interests to try to best me."

"I am surprised he had the courage to try," said Mr. Darcy. "Wickham has always been deathly afraid of you."

"I may have given him some encouragement. He might fear me, but he has always had a short temper."

"Then he is gone," said Elizabeth with a sigh. "I do not wish him back, though I wonder at the wisdom of unleashing him on the unsuspecting people of the former colonies."

"You have little to worry in that quarter, Miss Bennet," replied Colonel Fitzwilliam, his bared teeth a testament of his disgust for Mr. Wickham. "*If* Wickham survives the crossing—which, given his habits, is not certain—he will find that his fine gentlemanly manners will do him little good. The Americans are far less refined than we are. He might find himself missing some teeth if he is not careful."

Though she supposed she should not find it amusing, Elizabeth laughed anyway. Vindictiveness was not usually a part of her character, but the idea of Mr. Wickham receiving his just desserts for the way he had used her was appealing.

"Then I can only say good riddance to Mr. Wickham," said Elizabeth when she had managed to control her laughter. "I am sorry that his life has been wasted so, but happy he cannot harm those in my neighborhood any longer."

"I am happy to have been of service, Miss Bennet," replied Colonel Fitzwilliam. He favored her with an extravagant bow, winking at her as he rose.

"Do you have any information concerning Mrs. Younge?" asked Elizabeth.

The colonel made a face, but it was Mr. Darcy who responded. "Unfortunately, nothing. She claims she has not attempted to become a companion again, and short of applying to Lady Catherine to confirm if Mrs. Younge is, indeed, Miss Younge, there is little we can do. Since her confederate is now bound for the New World, I decided to leave well enough alone."

Mrs. Younge on her own could not be much of a threat, so Elizabeth allowed herself to be content.

"Now, if you ladies will excuse me," said Colonel Fitzwilliam, "I believe I shall go wash off the dust of the road."

So saying, the colonel exited from the room, leaving a bemused Elizabeth behind. She watched him go, wondering at what she had learned; for Mr. Darcy and Colonel Fitzwilliam especially to have gone to such trouble to protect her family was beyond her comprehension, especially since Mr. Darcy had not seen fit to do anything about Mr. Wickham when he had surfaced in Hertfordshire the previous autumn.

Their little party broke up after Colonel Fitzwilliam left—Anne claimed a desire to rest before luncheon and took herself up to her room, while Mr. Darcy indicated a need to finish some work. But before he could depart, Elizabeth called out to him, unwilling to allow him to absent himself without receiving some well-earned thanks. It was the very least she could do.

"I wished to express my appreciation, Mr. Darcy," said she. Though he had stopped readily enough when she asked him to, Elizabeth felt unequal to the task of speaking with him for perhaps the first time in their acquaintance. "I am aware you did not need to involve yourself again with Mr. Wickham, but I am grateful you did."

"I accept your thanks, Miss Bennet," replied he, his manner grave. "But I will tell you it is not necessary. I should have dealt with Wickham properly the last time—it is because of my inaction that he was allowed to continue to prey on unsuspecting people.

"Besides," continued he, a hint of a smile flitting over his face, "I will note that it was Fitzwilliam who did all the work. I only provided the means to pay Wickham's debts and purchase his ticket for the ship."

"Perhaps, but it was at your instigation that the colonel acted."

"In truth, Fitzwilliam called me a fool for insisting he be given any money at all, and I cannot help but suppose he is correct. He is also correct that Wickham's money is unlikely to last the crossing." Mr. Darcy smiled and gave a helpless shrug. "But Wickham was beloved of my father, and I could not send him off penniless."

"You are a good man, Mr. Darcy," replied Elizabeth with feeling.

She turned away, but she was arrested by the sound of his voice once more. "I will own that protection of your sisters and the people of Meryton was part of my reason for it. But I will also state, Miss Bennet, that in the end, I believe I thought only of you."

And with those final words, the man bowed and departed, leaving Elizabeth staring after him. Had Mr. Darcy declared the sky to be red, she could not have been any more surprised. It seemed like Charlotte's assertions about him were correct, and for the first time, Elizabeth wondered how deep Mr. Darcy's regard for her went.

Chapter XXI

Eager as Elizabeth was to avoid upsetting her sister and seeing her once again brought down to the depths of despair, this plan of Anne's brought her more than a little uncertainty.

"You want the best for your sister, right?" asked Anne when Elizabeth expressed reservation.

"Of course, I do!" In all truth Elizabeth was more than a little annoyed with her friend—though not often, she could see echoes of Lady Catherine in Anne's behavior, and now was one of those times. This was more manipulative than Lady Catherine's imperious commands, but it still struck Elizabeth as controlling. "I am simply not convinced this is in her best interests."

When Anne tried to speak again, Elizabeth interrupted, unwilling to listen to her friend try to convince her. "I have agreed to this, Anne, but please—do not cause Jane any further heartache."

"I assure you, Elizabeth—I have no intention of doing so. I have a high opinion of your sister and only wish her to be happy."

And with that, Elizabeth was forced to be content, though it did not stop her from worrying. This feeling of unease was raised when she and Anne went to Gracechurch Street only a few days after the dinner to visit with Elizabeth's aunt and sister. Georgiana, who had also enjoyed making Jane's acquaintance, stayed behind at her brother's house, her companion indicating that she needed to spend more time on her studies, which had been somewhat neglected of late.

Their journey through the city was unremarkable, and soon they were welcomed into the Gardiners' home. Jane and Aunt Gardiner were present that morning, and though they had already been sent to the nursery and the older to their lessons, the children soon learned that Elizabeth was present and clamored to see her. The Gardiner children consisted of two older girls and two younger boys, and they gathered about her, the younger hopping with excitement while the eldest attempted to give the appearance of maturity and reserve.

Elizabeth introduced them to Anne, and her friend was rewarded with some perfunctory greetings from the younger children—who were, Mrs. Gardiner said with a laugh, far too excited to see Elizabeth to pay attention to any other callers—but with awe and rapt attention from the eldest.

"You are very pretty, Miss de Bourgh," said Amelia—the eldest child—upon being introduced, greeting Anne with a sweet little curtsey. "You are my Cousin Lizzy's friend?"

"I am, Miss Gardiner," was Anne's reply. From the way she smiled at the girl, it was clear that Anne was delighted with her manners. "I met your cousin in Kent, you know."

Amelia darted a glance at Elizabeth before turning her attention back to Anne. "Lizzy stayed here for a night before she went into Kent."

"And I am very glad she did come. You see," Anne lowered her voice and drew the child in as if imparting a secret, "your cousin was of great assistance in Kent, for she slayed a dragon on my behalf."

Eyes wide, Amelia stared back at Anne, her mouth open a little in her surprise. "An actual dragon?"

"Perhaps not *quite* a real dragon, but still terrifying enough. You should not doubt your cousin's bravery, Miss Gardiner. She is a true friend and will do her utmost to protect those she loves."

Amelia nodded, her head a blur of motion. "Yes, she is. She is particularly kind to me, my brothers, and my sister. And she tells the most wonderful stories." She paused to consider and then said shyly: "Do you think my cousin tells stories of her actual exploits rather than making them up? I had always assumed she invents them for our amusement, but if she is able to slay a dragon, I wonder if she has lived her adventures."

Anne's delighted laughter rang throughout the room. By this time,

Jane and her aunt had taken note of the conversation and were listening carefully, taking no trouble to hide their grins. For her part, though Elizabeth was still besieged by the other children, her attention was on Anne. She hardly knew how to feel—she thought she should be vexed with her friend, but since Anne was only speaking with her dear cousin, amusement seemed destined to win the day.

"It is very possible she has actually experienced the stories she relates," replied Anne, with a sort of gravity which gave her words all that much more weight. "I have rarely seen such heroism as when your cousin visited me. You should tell me some of her stories, so that I may help you judge whether they are true or fiction."

"Oh, no!" cried Amelia. "It would be much better if Lizzy tells them, for she is ever so good at it. She even does all the voices and makes the sounds the animals would."

"I shall be happy to," replied Anne. "Perhaps we could persuade her now."

"Unfortunately, I believe it is time for the children to return to the nursery," said Mrs. Gardiner. She affected a sternness to her children, though it was clear she was in danger of breaking out in a wide grin. "You will be able to see Lizzy many times before she returns to your Uncle Bennet's house. Now is the time to allow the adults to speak."

The children protested as they were wont to do, but there was little resistance when they were led away, though each one stopped and embraced Elizabeth before they departed. Little Amelia was the last, and before she could be induced to go up the stairs, she had to say:

"You must tell me if your stories are real, Lizzy. I have never known a heroine before—I should like to know if you are one."

The other three ladies were experiencing difficulty in controlling their laughter, and as she was diverted herself, Elizabeth could not find it in herself to be angry. Instead, she pulled the girl close to her.

"They are just stories, my dear. But I am happy to tell them to you, for they are nothing more than a bit of harmless entertainment."

Amelia looked skeptical at Elizabeth's words, but she allowed herself to be led from the room by the governess. The governess was a woman whom Elizabeth had always considered sensible, if somewhat stern, but it seemed even she could not help but give Elizabeth a smile and a shake of her head, and then she was gone.

"Anne!" cried Elizabeth, fixing her friend with a glare. "You should not lead her on so!"

"Oh, Lizzy!" said Mrs. Gardiner. "It is nothing more than a lark. I found Miss de Bourgh's conversation with my eldest to be quite diverting, indeed."

"As did I," added Jane with her typical diffidence.

Elizabeth attempted to glare at her relations, to show her displeasure for their betrayal, but soon it became too much, and she laughed with them. They had a spirited visit thereafter, and contrary to Elizabeth's fears, Anne did not press forward with her campaign to bring Jane back together with Mr. Bingley. In fact, Anne was solicitous of Jane's feelings, and she was interested to know Jane, as far as Elizabeth could tell. She would not have suspected her friend of duplicity, but Elizabeth could own to having more than a little trepidation regardless.

"I believe you are correct, Elizabeth," said Anne as they departed to return to Darcy house later that morning. "Your sister *does* feel the absence of Mr. Bingley keenly, though her ability to maintain her good humor does her credit."

"It is a surprise to me that you are able to understand her," remarked Elizabeth, not sure what to make of Anne's statement, though she knew it was essentially true. "Jane is reticent, and often it is difficult for even me to understand what she is thinking. You have only met her twice."

A faint smile was Anne's response. "I spent so many years listening to my mother speak that I became adept at watching others. Jane is not so difficult to make out, I think, if you know what to watch for. But had I not already had your account, I might have missed those little signs which now speak louder than words."

"But you noticed them before I ever told you."

Anne shrugged. "Like I said, I am practiced at noticing these things." She smiled, though Elizabeth could not help but wonder if it was a little sad. "That is why I was certain that Darcy would never oblige my mother and offer for me. Besides his avoidance of my company, every little mannerism confirmed he had no intention of marrying me."

"Dearest Anne," said Elizabeth, reaching forward to grasp her friend's hands, holding them in a tight grip. "Do you regret his lack of interest?"

"No, I do not. I never wished for his attentions." Anne paused and turned to look out the window at the passing scenery, her grip flexing rhythmically, though Elizabeth thought her friend had no notion of what she was doing. "I only wish . . . Well, let us say there are times I wish that a man would look on me the way Darcy looks at you."

Elizabeth was not ready to consider Anne's assertion in any detail, so she focused on her friend's despondency. "Then we shall simply have to ensure that someone does just that."

A raised eyebrow and a questioning look were Anne's responses. Elizabeth only laughed.

"We are to engage in society, are we not? We shall dress you in all the finest fabrics and latest styles, find the most flattering ways to do your hair, and present you as a very desirable partner. I am certain we shall have no trouble in making every single man in London *madly* in love with you."

"I am not beautiful, Elizabeth," said Anne, though she positively shone with pleasure. "I think they are more likely to flock to your side, rather than mine."

"I absolutely forbid it," declared Elizabeth. Then she showed Anne a gentle smile. "I think you devalue yourself. The dresses you have ordered will do much to improve your appearance. We shall also improve your hair by curling it—I do not like this style that imitates your mother's, for it seems dowdy and old-fashioned." Elizabeth reached out and touched Anne's hair. "Yes, I think ringlets will do nicely. And as your color is already much better than it was when I first knew you and your cheeks are beginning to fill out, I think you will be far prettier and draw far more attention than you think."

Emotion sparkled in Anne's eyes, and for a moment, Elizabeth thought tears would roll down her cheeks. After a moment, when she seemed able to control herself, she reached out and drew Elizabeth into an embrace.

"Thank you, Elizabeth. You are such a wonderful friend—I do not know what I would do without you.

"Now," said Anne, as she pulled away from Elizabeth, "I believe we are only a short distance from the house. I have a great desire to walk the rest of the way and improve my stamina. Let us alight from this coach."

Though surprised at Anne's declaration, Elizabeth had no objection, so when Anne knocked on the roof, asking the driver to stop, Elizabeth was willing to follow her friend. As they walked back—one of the footmen in tow watching carefully over them—they laughed at the coachman's incredulous expression and the slight shake of his head which seemed to express complete befuddlement in the ways of young gentlewomen. Elizabeth and Anne paid the man no attention—they were far too busy enjoying themselves.

True to their mutual resolve, the ladies spent the next week in each other's company, bringing their plans to fruition. Elizabeth spent many hours in Anne's room with the maid in attendance, attempting to find a style which would most suit Anne's looks. Their results were often diverting, and the girls shared much laughter, but in the end, they found a few, largely those styles which were simple, but elegant, in nature which suited her. Laura soon began using those, rather than the frumpy look her mother had demanded.

Anne also adhered to her intention to build up her strength, and she insisted upon accompanying Elizabeth on her daily walks. She could not walk so far or so fast as Elizabeth—this much was true—but Elizabeth did not mind walking more slowly and taking shorter paths, content as she was with Anne's company and pleased as she was with her friend's progress. Mr. Darcy and Colonel Fitzwilliam often commented on the changes they saw in their cousin, and though she acknowledged them with apparent pleasure, she kept to her course.

The dresses they had commissioned with the modiste were soon completed and delivered, and their appearances improved by the selection of styles and fabrics in which they were now clothed. Though Elizabeth thought Anne was the greater beneficiary of these new looks, Elizabeth did not miss how Mr. Darcy often looked at *her* with greater appreciation. It was becoming more apparent that Mr. Darcy did, indeed, possess some admiration for her. Elizabeth did not miss it, but she remained cautious, preferring to consider the matter herself rather than canvas it openly.

Anne's desire to peruse Mr. Gardiner's selection of fabrics was also not forgotten, much to Elizabeth's amusement and Mr. Gardiner's delight and enthusiasm.

"Of course, I am happy to have you look at my wares," replied he when Elizabeth applied for permission. Then he winked at Anne. "Only take care you do not pauper me, as my wife and nieces often seem intent upon doing."

Elizabeth and Anne only looked at each other and giggled, as Elizabeth had exactly predicted the gentleman's reaction to their request. She was certain that Mr. Gardiner and Mr. Darcy came to some agreement about their access to the fabrics—she spied them shaking hands the day they inspected his wares—but as it was likely beneficial for them both, she held her tongue. They claimed enough fabric from several bolts to be made into dresses for them, and their newfound procurements did not go unnoticed.

"Why, Miss de Bourgh, this fabric is simply delightful," said Madam Fournier when presented with a beautiful bolt of pale pink silk. "Wherever did you find such beautiful cloth?"

"It is from my uncle's warehouse, Madam," replied Elizabeth. "He imports and often has lovely fabrics in his possession."

The lady looked at Elizabeth, some interest in her gaze. Elizabeth had well known that, to Madam Fournier, she had not been the equal of Anne or Georgiana. The lady had treated her with kindness and respect, but most of her attention had been reserved for the other two women. Elizabeth had not begrudged them the attention, but she sensed that it was about to change.

"Miss Bennet," said Madam Fournier, confirming Elizabeth's suppositions, "would you be willing to introduce your uncle to me? If he can obtain fabrics of such quality, I would be happy to purchase them. I cannot imagine any lady in London would not wish to be wrapped in such finery."

"I shall speak to him, madam," replied Elizabeth. "I am certain he would be happy to make your acquaintance. I believe he does supply several dressmakers, but he would be happy to find another buyer."

For a moment Elizabeth thought the lady would protest—she was one of the most fashionable dressmakers in London, after all, and she likely thought an introduction was only her due. In the end, however, she only smiled and claimed her anticipation for making Mr. Gardiner's acquaintance. Mr. Gardiner was, as Elizabeth expected, eager to meet with the modiste, and soon he had agreed to supply her with his fabrics in a mutually beneficial arrangement. Elizabeth was happy, for she knew that her uncle would begin importing more of his fabrics, and his income would increase accordingly.

It was late the next week when Georgiana received a pair of expected, but unwelcome visitors, at least from her perspective. In fact, Elizabeth knew that Anne had been waiting impatiently for these particular ladies to come, for it meant she could unleash the schemes she had been spinning in her mind. Elizabeth's feelings were more ambiguous—she had no love for these particular ladies and knew they viewed her with barely concealed disdain.

When the ladies were led into the room, Elizabeth had gone to the window to look out onto the street, and, consequently, neither saw her when they entered. Thus, she had front row seating from which to witness—and savor—all the ridiculousness of their initial behavior.

"Dearest Georgiana!" exclaimed Miss Bingley as she waltzed into the room as if she was already its mistress. "How wonderful it is to see you! Louisa and I have been quite bereft of your company these past weeks!"

It was clear to Elizabeth that Georgiana's excitement at the sight of the ladies was unequal to Miss Bingley's for her. But she greeted them in a voice which only quivered a little and was almost audible. Unfortunately, Miss Bingley did not allow her to speak further.

"It has been positively an age since we were last in your company — and dear Mr. Darcy's company too! How wonderful it is that you are in town and that we may all once again bask in the enjoyment of our mutual society." She leaned forward, as if to intimidate the girl into acquiescing to her machinations. "My brother, Charles, is quite looking forward to greeting you once again. I declare there was no other subject which could hold his interest during the entirety of our journey from York."

It was a near thing, but Georgiana managed to refrain from grimacing at Miss Bingley's entirely inappropriate speech. Nearby, Anne was also standing, watching the spectacle with open amusement. She did not speak, however, neither to give encouragement nor censure, and Georgiana was forced to deal with the new arrivals herself. For her part, Miss Bingley cast several sidelong looks at Anne, clearly trying to assess who she was. She must have realized from Anne's dress that she was someone of standing, for she did not speak to Anne, instead waiting for Anne to request an introduction.

Finally, Anne turned her head slightly and caught Elizabeth's gaze, and winking at her, she turned to Georgiana and said:

"It seems you have charming friends, with whom, I believe, our guest is also acquainted." Anne turned quite deliberately to Elizabeth. "Elizabeth, would you do the honors, and introduce these ladies to me?"

Mrs. Hurst was the first to follow Anne's gaze, and she gasped upon seeing Elizabeth. Miss Bingley, however, was slower to understand what Anne was saying — rather, she appeared confused, having thought there was no one else in the room. Elizabeth held her laughter at bay and made her way to Anne's side, Mrs. Hurst's eyes following her as she went.

"How do you do, Mrs. Hurst, Miss Bingley?" greeted Elizabeth.

The way Miss Bingley's eyes suddenly found her, Elizabeth thought the woman might pass out from shock. She could only suppose that surprise would soon give way to disgust, for she knew that her presence here could not be agreeable to the proud woman.

"Anne, please allow me to present Mrs. Louisa Hurst and Miss Caroline Bingley to your acquaintance," said Elizabeth, not allowing the woman to recover her composure. "Mrs. Hurst and Miss Bingley are sisters to Mr. Charles Bingley, who leased an estate near my home in Hertfordshire last autumn.

"Mrs. Hurst, Miss Bingley," continued she, turning to the two other ladies, the latter of whom was already recovering, if her disdainful glare was any indication, "please allow me to present Miss Anne de Bourgh of Rosings Park in Kent. Miss de Bourgh is the daughter of Lady Catherine de Bourgh, who is sister to Miss Darcy's late mother, Lady Anne Darcy."

The two ladies retained enough of their grasp on propriety to curtsey to Anne, and the five ladies sat down on the sofas, while Georgiana ordered a tea service. For a few moments no one spoke, and though the silence was uncomfortable, Elizabeth was the only one who seemed to notice it. Anne watched the two ladies, her enjoyment of their surprise all but painted on her face, while Georgiana sat silently, seeming to expect some unpleasantness. For their parts, the Bingley sisters seemed to have been rendered speechless, and while Mrs. Hurst watched with apparent trepidation, Miss Bingley soon regarded Elizabeth with a calculating glance, clearly trying to understand why she was here. Unless Elizabeth missed her guess, the woman was also trying to determine if Jane was present and if not, where she was.

"I see you have returned to town, Mrs. Hurst," said Elizabeth, deciding it would be best to speak and try to avoid the upcoming unpleasantness. She deliberately chose to speak to the elder sister, for she judged her less likely to say something inappropriate.

"Yes, only yesterday," replied Mrs. Hurst, proving, at least, she knew how to behave. "We were visiting relations in the north."

"And how was your journey?" asked Elizabeth, turning herself so that her words could be equally interpreted as being directed to both ladies to include them both in her conversation. "It is quite long and arduous, is it not?"

It was then that the full force of Miss Bingley's disgust was released, for she looked at Elizabeth only a moment before deliberately turning away and directing her reply at Georgiana.

"I *am* surprised, Georgiana, at your having a guest in your home today." Miss Bingley turned and sneered at Elizabeth. "I had not known you were at all acquainted with Miss Eliza Bennet. In fact, I am rather shocked that she actually knew the way here from *Cheapside.*"

Georgiana let out a stifled gasp, and Mrs. Hurst again proved herself to be the more proper of the sisters when she paled and attempted to catch her sister's eye to try to silence her. Whether this was efficacious or Miss Bingley had simply decided to wait for Elizabeth to defend herself, Elizabeth could not know. Anne, however, spoke first, negating the requirement for Elizabeth to speak herself.

"In fact, you are mistaken, Miss Bingley." Anne's manner was all amusement, and she was not making any effort to hide it either. "Elizabeth is here as *my* guest and has been staying here for the past several weeks. Indeed, as she stayed with me at Rosings Park for several weeks before that, Elizabeth and I have been in each other's company for above two months."

Nothing Anne could have said would have wiped the snide smile off Miss Bingley's face more quickly. But Anne was not finished.

"I am, indeed, fortunate to have made her acquaintance. I rely on her company, you see, and would be bereft if she left, for she has become such a dear friend. In this sentiment, I am certain Georgiana joins me, for she has taken to my dear friend with ease. Is that not so, Cousin?"

"It is," replied Georgiana, her chin raised in an attitude which appeared faintly defiant. "I am quite happy with Lizzy's company and acquaintance. I hope she will stay with us for some time yet.

"In fact," said Georgiana, turning to Elizabeth, "it has been on my mind to invite you to Pemberley for the summer. We never stay in town past the middle of June or so. We would be delighted if you would join us there for the rest of the summer."

Miss Bingley and Mrs. Hurst were clearly dumbfounded at this new evidence of intimacy between them, though Miss Bingley attempted to intervene with her usual brand of contempt.

"I know not how this has come about," said she, her glare landing on Elizabeth like a hammer blow, "but I cannot suppose you are aware of Miss Bennet's situation."

"In fact, we are *well* aware of it, Miss Bingley," interjected Anne. This time the steel in Anne's voice was unmistakable. "Furthermore, Darcy approves of her and is willing to host her in his home." Anne's countenance softened a little. "Now, let us have a pleasant visit, for the tea service has arrived."

There was little Miss Bingley could say to such a set down, and perhaps it was to the woman's credit that she did not attempt it. Georgiana poured tea for them all, and they busied themselves with it and some cakes the housekeeper delivered. For the rest of the visit, Miss Bingley was much less loquacious than Elizabeth thought the woman could ever be. But her gaze was fixed on Elizabeth, and there was no friendship in that look. When they went away, Miss Bingley's curtsey to her was almost nonexistent, and she only sniffed when Elizabeth said her farewells. Miss Bingley was not a happy woman. Elizabeth was delighted.

Chapter XXII

To say that Miss Caroline Bingley was unhappy was an understatement. In fact, she was as furious as she had ever been in her entire life. That . . . that . . . *strumpet* was attempting to dig her claws into *Caroline's* Mr. Darcy—she knew it without any hint of doubt. The little tart had been oh so smug about her supposed success, as if Mr. Darcy did not have the wherewithal to see through her poor attempts to render herself acceptable. How dare she!

"It is beyond belief!" exclaimed Caroline after the carriage had traveled some distance. "How could that chit have inveigled her way into Mr. Darcy's house?"

By her side Louisa jumped at her sister's sudden cry, and Caroline was forced to use every ounce of willpower to avoid snapping at her sister. Louisa was compliant and supported Caroline in her machinations and opinions, but Caroline had always wished for a more intelligent, active partner in her schemes. As it was, Caroline only had to point and Louisa would heel. Unfortunately, she was forced to do all the plotting herself, for Louisa had no head for it.

"It does not seem like she beguiled them at all," replied Louisa. There was a tired note in her voice which fanned the flames of Caroline's fury all that much hotter. "In fact, she seemed quite at ease with both Miss De Bourgh *and* Miss Darcy."

"I am unsurprised you were unable to see it, Sister," replied Caroline. She was well aware of the sneering tone in her voice. "But you are often unable to see the motives of others.

"*I* on the other hand, am aware of what Miss Eliza is about. She is a grasping, artful shrew, and I knew from the time we were together in Hertfordshire that she meant to draw Mr. Darcy's attention with her pert opinions and supposedly fine eyes." Caroline made a sound in the back of her throat which she knew was not at all ladylike, but she did not care. "Well, I shall not allow this to stand."

"She is a guest at Mr. Darcy's house," said Louisa, her sniff dismissive, and she turned to look out the window, further angering Caroline. "I know not what you can do about it."

"I shall simply educate Miss de Bourgh on what kind of companion she has allowed into Mr. Darcy's home. It is clear to me that Miss Eliza has managed to pass herself off with some degree of credit, and, in doing so, has completely blinded Miss de Bourgh of her true situation. Once she is aware of the true measure of Miss Eliza's perfidy, I am certain she will not be so eager to continue the acquaintance."

"Oh, Caroline," said Louisa, turning back from her contemplation of the outside scenery. "Do not do anything to bring Mr. Darcy's wrath upon us. Mr. Hurst would never forgive either of us if he was denied Mr. Darcy's society."

"Or more importantly, his wine cellar," replied Caroline, unable to keep the snide note out of her voice. Louisa shot her a look, and Caroline decided this was not the time to argue about her drunkard of a husband.

"How could you possibly assume that Mr. Darcy would be angry if we were to save his cousin from that hoyden?" asked Caroline, focusing on the more important subject at present.

"Miss Bennet's presence in his house states without equivocation that he approves of her. I cannot understand how you can think that he would be in any way moved by what you say. He has known her as long as we have and has been in company with her longer—do you mean to tell him his own judgment is deficient?"

"I will only point out to Miss de Bourgh what she does not know of Miss Eliza," said Caroline, annoyed with Louisa's continued defiance.

Louisa shook her head, but she did not continue to contradict Caroline. "I think you are missing the matter of greater importance. If Miss Elizabeth is staying at Mr. Darcy's house and has gained the friendship and support of his sister and cousin, *where* is Miss Bennet?"

Though loath to confess it, Caroline knew her sister was correct. She had not considered Miss Bennet in this mess.

"That must be Miss Eliza's intention," said she. She tapped her lips in thought, wondering what she could do to safeguard her brother. "Jane must still be staying in Cheapside. We must prevent Charles from learning of Miss Eliza's presence at Mr. Darcy's house."

"I do not know how you mean to do that," replied Louisa. "You know how close they are."

"We shall just have to fill his days," replied Caroline. "There are enough events and we have enough invitations to keep him occupied. It is time he found someone suitable to be his wife anyway." Caroline paused, thinking. "Perhaps we could invite Mr. Darcy to dinner one night."

"Such an invitation must necessarily include *everyone* staying at Mr. Darcy's house."

"Excluding Eliza would send a clear message of our contempt for his little guest," replied Caroline.

"No, Caroline, it is not sound—you know it is not. Whatever Mr. Darcy's feelings for her, you *know* he would never behave in such a way. He is far too proper."

Though grudgingly, Caroline was forced to agree with her sister's assessment. In the end, however, it did not matter. They would keep Charles away from Miss Eliza until Caroline was able to deal with the interloper. And deal with her was exactly what Caroline meant to do—Miss de Bourgh would learn what manner of woman she had accepted as a friend.

After the Bingley sisters left, Elizabeth found herself at loose ends. With Georgiana in her lessons for the morning and Anne having returned to her room, Elizabeth did not know what to do with herself. She returned to her room for a short time, but not being tired, she decided she did not wish to be there, so she left, looking for something to occupy her herself.

Elizabeth's steps soon took her down to the main floor of the house, and though she stopped at the music room and considered the pianoforte for some moments, she decided against playing. Instead, she continued down the hall and eventually found herself outside the library.

Though it might be supposed that Elizabeth, as one who appreciated the written word, could have been found in the library on a regular basis, in fact she had been there little since arriving at Darcy house. This was mostly because she was so often engaged with Anne and Georgiana and had had little time for herself. As she was left to her own devices that morning, she thought it a perfect time to acquaint herself with the delights to be found in Mr. Darcy's collection of books.

It was a large, bright room, with tall windows letting in ample sunlight, rendering it cheery and welcoming. There were two large fireplaces, one on each of the end walls, which together would render it no less welcoming in the winter months when the light would be less plentiful and the house more difficult to heat. There were several large bookcases, ornamental, yet functional, which stood along the spaces in between the windows, and Elizabeth soon discovered the books had been arranged in a thoughtful manner, which made it easy to locate any desired work quickly and easily. And there were so many books on the shelves that Elizabeth, wondered at the man's assertion of a much greater library at his estate. Why, there were more books here than she had ever seen in one place!

For a time, Elizabeth walked along the shelves, perusing the titles, marveling at the eclectic nature of Mr. Darcy's tastes. As she moved, she occasionally took a book out to look at the cover or flip through the pages, the paper crisp and smooth beneath her fingers. The name plates showed the story of the history of this room, and though she found many which bore Mr. Darcy's name, there were far more that bore the names of other Darcys, ones who had once called this place their own and had, in their own ways, loved the written word as much as their descendent obviously did. There was such a treasure of knowledge that Elizabeth did not know where to begin.

A noise startled her from her contemplation of a book she was holding, and she looked up. There, in the frame of a door she had not noticed, stood Mr. Darcy.

"Oh!" said Elizabeth by reflex. "I had not known you were there, sir."

"My apologies for startling you, Miss Bennet," replied Mr. Darcy as he stepped into the room and walked toward her. "I heard someone moving in this room and wondered who was here."

"You heard me, sir?" asked Elizabeth, not understanding his meaning.

"My study is connected to the library through that door. I find it very convenient for when I wish to consult with a book, or even when I wish to remove myself from my office for a time and break from my labors. My study and library at Pemberley are in the same configuration."

Elizabeth nodded but did not respond. Mr. Darcy had approached and now stood quite close to her, and Elizabeth was feeling bashful next to the solid strength and size of his presence.

"You once told me that you could not discuss books in a ballroom, Miss Bennet. Is a library an appropriate place for such a discussion?"

Surprised, Elizabeth darted a look up at him. The man was teasing her!

"I suppose I must answer in the affirmative sir," said Elizabeth, deciding that two could play at that game. "Otherwise you might think me daft."

Mr. Darcy laughed. "I doubt I could ever think such a thing. But you are correct—if you cannot speak of books in a library, where can you speak of them?"

"I am certain I do not know," replied Elizabeth quietly.

With a deliberate sort of look, Mr. Darcy grasped the book Elizabeth held in her hands, causing her to let it go by instinct. He took in the cover of it and smiled. "It seems you have a predilection for works of more thought than a novel." Mr. Darcy paused and showed her a rueful smile. "I wish my sister had your tastes, for it is often a challenge to induce her to read anything else."

"I do enjoy a good novel on occasion, sir," replied Elizabeth. "But I do not confine my reading to such subjections. I am quite fond of thought-provoking works, such as Milton, and though it is not my forte, I am able to read in French and Italian."

"That is impressive, Miss Bennet." He gestured toward a nearby sofa. "Shall we?"

Elizabeth was by no means opposed to speaking with him, and she allowed herself to be led to the sofa. Mr. Darcy was thoughtful enough to go to the door and open it, assuring himself that there was a footman stationed outside for propriety, and they spoke for some time. They debated back and forth some of the finer points of the text now in Mr. Darcy's hands, and though they did not agree on everything, they agreed enough that Elizabeth was surprised and pleased at the approbation of such an intelligent and educated man.

When they had spoken for some time, Mr. Darcy looked up and noted that the morning was almost gone. From the angle of the sun in the windows, Elizabeth thought it was likely almost noon. It would not be long before luncheon was served, and Elizabeth wondered if Anne had descended from her room yet.

She was about to suggest they go looking for the other members of the family when Mr. Darcy once again addressed her. "Miss Bennet," said he, "have you had the opportunity to walk in the gardens at the back of the house?"

"I have not," replied Elizabeth, "though Anne and I did sit on a bench near the door for some time a few days ago."

"In that case, might I persuade you to take a turn? It is a lovely bit of greenery in the middle of the city." Mr. Darcy smiled. "It is not nearly so large or impressive as Hyde Park, but it still boasts a lovely rose garden and some beautiful old trees."

"Would you expect me to refuse such an offer?" asked Elizabeth with a laugh. "I would be happy to see the gardens."

They rose and Mr. Darcy offered his arm, which Elizabeth took with more shyness than she would have thought possible. They made their way through the halls, stepping out through a door on the side, and into a walled garden set against the side of the house. As Mr. Darcy had promised—and as she had noted on her brief sojourn before—it was a small piece of wilderness surrounded by a tall wall on the other three sides. From the door, a small path meandered out into the garden, and the entire area was shaded by tall trees of different varieties, lending it a tranquil, peaceful location Elizabeth thought she could love tolerably well.

They wandered along the path for several moments, Mr. Darcy pointing out various locations of interest—a bench his father had installed at his mother's request; an apple tree he and his parents had planted when he was eight years old; finally, the rose garden his mother had loved, in which she had sat every day the weather was fine enough.

"At Pemberley, you will find a larger, finer garden, one which my mother tended herself." Mr. Darcy was looking in the direction of the flower garden, but Elizabeth could tell that his attention was far away. "I remember accompanying her in the summer. She would teach me about the different variety of flowers, how to care for them and get the most out of them, and often on warm days we would play." Mr. Darcy smiled, still caught within the confines of his memory. "She would chase me about the garden, and when I was young I remember shrieking when she would catch me. And she would always allow me to win when we played hide and seek."

"You were close to your parents."

For the first time since they had stopped walking, Mr. Darcy seemed to realize he was not alone, and his eyes met hers, obviously more than a little embarrassed. Elizabeth only smiled at him, urging him to continue to speak.

"I was. My mother was everything that was beautiful, graceful, loving, and yet she strove to raise me in a creditable manner. My father, though he was sterner, intent on teaching me what I needed to know to become a good master of the estate, was also fair and involved in my life when I was a child. My parents were not like so many others of society, who leave the responsibility for the care of their children with those hired for the purpose. They were my parents and I was their son, and everything I learned about being a member of society was learned at their feet. Until my mother passed away."

Though Elizabeth thought to prompt him again, something told her to hold her peace, so she remained silent. After a moment of searching for the words, Mr. Darcy again spoke in a much subdued manner.

"My mother was never robust. In fact, I have often thought Anne to be much like her. It was one of the reasons why I never had any interest in marrying Anne. Between my birth and Georgiana's, mother had several miscarriages, and each one seemed to take more out of her. I remember when she was with child with Georgiana." Mr. Darcy paused and a spasm of pain passed over his face. "Every precaution was taken, every measure possible to protect her health. But in the end, it was not enough. Georgiana was born and so much strength was lost in the endeavor that she slipped away only days after.

"After my mother passed away, my father was never the same. I believe he grieved her loss until the day he died. Georgiana is so much like her that he often could not bear to be in the room with her, and as a result, her memories of our father are different from mine. I remember him as a loving father and husband, but Georgiana remembers him as a distant man, austere and reticent, and one who did not care to see to her needs or assist in her rearing."

"That is unfortunate, Mr. Darcy," replied Elizabeth. "But it is perhaps not so surprising, since your father loved your mother so dearly."

"He did." Mr. Darcy was silent for a moment. "After her passing, he used to sit in her flower garden at Pemberley for hours at a time. He said it made him feel closer to her. When he passed away himself, I believe he welcomed it. He had lost the will to live and wished to be with her again."

Elizabeth was touched by these memories that Mr. Darcy was sharing with her. In a certain sense, it was difficult for Elizabeth to understand—such closeness as he was describing had never existed between her parents, and though she thought one would miss the other should they be taken, she could not imagine the level of grief as his father had experienced. Despite the obvious disadvantages and the possibility of having a loved one leave her behind, it was what Elizabeth had always wished to have.

It also gave her more insight into Mr. Darcy's character. Though he had spoken of his father's grief of losing his wife, Elizabeth knew that his own sorrow had been profound. The woman who had played with him, raised him to be a good and industrious man, though she had died when he was young, was missed to this day. Elizabeth could not help but feel her heart go out to him.

"I thank you for listening to my remembrances, Miss Bennet," said Mr. Darcy, seeming to recall where he was.

"Not at all, sir," replied Elizabeth. "It is clear you treasured your parents. I am honored that you think enough of me to share such beautiful memories."

Though Mr. Darcy's gaze lingered on her, he did not immediately respond. Instead, he cast around, looking for something in particular. There were several rose bushes nearby, and Mr. Darcy looked long at a few of them. For a moment, Elizabeth thought he would gift her with one of the red or pink roses. She was not certain he knew exactly what they meant and would have been mortified if he would have made such a declaration without realizing what he had done.

But then he shook his head and turned to grasp her hand. "Come, Miss Bennet," said he as he began to walk down the path, pulling her along behind.

Elizabeth went readily, wondering what he was about. They passed swiftly down the path, Mr. Darcy looking this way and that, clearly looking for something as if he could not quite remember exactly where it was to be found. While they walked, he spoke to her softly.

"I have not come back here much of late, and though I remember mother's roses, I do not know where everything can be found."

"For what are you searching, sir?" asked Elizabeth. Her hand felt warm within his. She was amazed at how well his larger one fit around hers and wondered what it would be like if she was always connected with this man in such a way.

Suddenly Mr. Darcy stopped, and a grin shone forth as he regarded several low plants, standing perhaps two feet tall, with low, thin leaves, and large, round flowers. He released her hand and stepped over to the flowers, reaching down and plucking two with long stems and brilliant, beautiful colors. One had petals which were blood red in the center, changing to a lovely pink toward the end of the petal, rimmed with a pale pink, almost white edge. The other was of the same style, though it was the same shade of lovely light pink all the way through the flower. They were carnations.

"Please accept these tokens of my esteem, my lady," said Mr. Darcy, bowing and handing her the two flowers.

Elizabeth accepted them, though she was so shocked, she almost neglected to stretch her hand out to receive them.

"They are lovely, Miss Bennet, but I cannot help but think they pale beside the woman who is holding them."

Though Elizabeth blushed, Mr. Darcy did not stop speaking. "I believe the pink flower matches your dress beautifully. Perhaps if you wore it in your hair?"

It was pure instinct that prompted Elizabeth to reach up with the hand holding the pink flower and insert it in her hair, above her left ear, the blossom situated above her forehead, visible from the corner of her eye. Mr. Darcy's gaze became so tender, that Elizabeth thought the man might lean over and kiss her.

"Exquisite, Miss Bennet. I shall have the gardeners gather up some of these in a variety of colors and have them delivered to your room."

"Thank you, sir," replied Elizabeth. Her head was still spinning as she considered the meaning of these blooms he had given her. Carnations: the flowers of fascination, which spoke to a romantic interest, but one which had not yet blossomed into true love. Could Mr. Darcy possibly be aware of the meaning of the gesture he had just made?

As Elizabeth looked into his eyes, searching, wondering what she would find there, his returning gaze, steady and intent, captured her eyes, holding them in place. And then she knew—Mr. Darcy was *exactly* aware of what he was doing. The meaning of these blossoms was no mystery to him.

And then it became clear. Mr. Darcy *was* fascinated by her, and all his looks when they were in Hertfordshire, and since they had been together in London, became clear. Elizabeth could not understand what she had done to gain his attention in such a way, but it existed regardless. And she knew that to be the focus of his attention was something, indeed!

Though Anne could not be certain, she suspected something significant had passed between Elizabeth and Darcy. On the day of the Bingley sisters' visit, Anne had felt more fatigued than she had in some time and had lain down on her bed, sleeping most of the morning. As a result of her long nap, she had awoken reinvigorated and eager to be in her friend's company again.

There was nothing specific on which Anne could put her finger. To one who was not familiar with them, it seemed like they behaved the same toward each other as they ever had. But they also exchanged little glances and often seemed unnaturally aware of exactly where the other was. If it had just been Darcy, Anne would have shrugged it off, as she had seen similar behavior from him since they had come to London. But not only were *his* glances more frequent than she had ever seen, but the fact that *Elizabeth* was now engaged in the same behavior was even more telling.

Anne thought of pressing her friend for the story of what had changed, but in the end, she decided against it. Elizabeth could be stubborn when she set her mind to it, and while she was open and friendly, she was also private when it came to her own feelings. It was enough for Anne to know they had made good progress, so she sat back and watched them, waiting for the snow to shift enough to produce an avalanche which would take them to love, matrimony, and the rest of their lives.

The last thought almost prompted laughter, which she covered by bringing her hand to her mouth, lest her companions question what she was thinking. Perhaps she had indulged in too much contemplation of such subjects, for it was leading her to think decidedly melodramatic thoughts.

Jane visited and Georgiana joined them for the afternoon in company, having completed her studies for the day. The more time Anne spent with Elizabeth's sister, the more she esteemed the other woman. She might be called naïve, considering her propensity to see the best in people, but Anne soon realized that Jane was not deficient in any way. In fact, she often, with her comments and observations, showed signs of a keen intellect, and one which, much the same as Anne's, was prone to watching others in silence while those of a more open temperament carried the conversation. During Jane's visit, they made plans for some events they would attend, including some exhibits and evenings at the theater and opera, in which Anne had never been able to indulge herself. She found herself anticipating the coming days with impatience.

The next morning, however, they were treated to the return of an unwelcome visitor, but this time, rather than receive a masked level of scorn, Elizabeth was treated to that of a more explicit nature.

"Miss de Bourgh," said Caroline Bingley when she was escorted into the room. "How do you do today?"

"Elizabeth and I are both well, Miss Bingley," said Anne, reminding the woman that her dear friend was in the room.

It was the established protocol for ladies to, at the very least, acknowledge each other when in company, but on this occasion, Miss Bingley did nothing more than sneer at Elizabeth and turn her attention back to Anne.

"I found that I wished to visit you again and come to know you better." The woman oozed insincere flattery, and she continued: "I feel as if we are almost family already, considering my brother's intimate friendship with your cousin."

"That is interesting, Miss Bingley," replied Anne, wondering at the woman's impudence. "I hope that we are *all* able to be friends with one another, and I hope to meet your brother when the opportunity presents itself." Anne smiled, noting that Miss Bingley's countenance had fallen a little. "When will he visit? I am surprised we have not seen him yet, considering his close relationship with my cousin."

"Charles is . . ." began Miss Bingley before she stopped. Anne did not miss the dark look the woman threw at Elizabeth. "In fact, he is much engaged with other matters, now that we have returned to London. I expect he will wish to renew his friendship with Mr. Darcy as soon as may be arranged."

"Excellent! Please inform him he is welcome to come at any time convenient."

Miss Bingley paused, and her gaze darted to Elizabeth again. For her part, Elizabeth was watching them with evident mirth, carefully held in check. Anne looked away from her quickly, afraid she would break out in laughter herself if she did not.

"In fact, I have something of a delicate nature which I wish to discuss with you." Miss Bingley directed a conspiratorial smile at Anne. "Perhaps we could adjourn to another room?"

"I believe this one will do just fine," replied Anne. "Please, you may proceed at any time."

Miss Bingley once again speared Elizabeth with a look, which Elizabeth returned with a false placidity which would have done her sister proud. "My apologies, Miss de Bourgh, but what I have to say is for your ears alone." The sneer made its return when her eyes once again found Elizabeth.

"I would be happy to leave you together," said Elizabeth in response. She rose and smiled brightly at Anne, while Anne glared at her traitorous friend in response. "When your conversation is complete, you may find me in the music room."

With those final words, Elizabeth departed, leaving Anne alone in the company of a vicious shrew. Anne watched her friend as she passed through the door, considering what form of retribution her vengeance might take.

"I thought Eliza would never leave," said Miss Bingley when Elizabeth was gone. She released an exaggerated huff of annoyance and turned back to Anne. "I am not certain if you are aware, but we have spent much time in company with Eliza's family when we lived in Hertfordshire last autumn, and there is little good to be had in any of them. A most unsuitable family."

Anne regarded Miss Bingley, certain she now knew of what the woman wished to speak. "Actually, I know of your connection with the Bennets. Now, Miss Bingley, you have asked for my time and a private conversation, and we are now alone. Of what did you wish to speak?"

Although Miss Bingley seemed surprised at Anne's assertion of knowledge — why she should be shocked Anne was not certain, given her professions of intimacy with Elizabeth — she quickly recovered.

"I wished to speak to you as a friend. I am so happy we have made each other's acquaintance. Might we dispense with the formalities? I would be happy if you would refer to me by my Christian name."

While Miss Bingley's countenance was hopeful, Anne was clearly able to see the haughty arrogance and her assurance that Anne would fall in with her schemes. Thus, it was a pleasure to disabuse her of the notion that she would speak, and Anne would agree with whatever she said.

"I do not believe that would be appropriate, Miss Bingley." The smile ran away from the woman's face, replaced by disbelief. "We have only been acquainted for two days, which is not nearly long enough to truly know each other. Let us allow our friendship to mature before we take such a step."

Miss Bingley did not seem to know what to say, and she stammered for a moment. Anne had not doubted Elizabeth's word on the subject of Miss Bingley, but she began to truly understand exactly how tiresome this woman was.

"Was there something you wished to say?" asked she, attempting to prod the woman along.

"Of course," replied Miss Bingley, as she began to regain her composure. "You have my apologies, Miss de Bourgh. I am happy to take this time to come to know you better." The woman smiled, clearly having come to the best possible interpretation of Anne's words, and feeling certain that they would soon be bosom friends.

"The matter of which I wished to speak is more in the nature of a warning. I understand that Eliza has been staying with you for some time now?"

"*Elizabeth* has, indeed, been with me for more than two months." Miss Bingley started at Anne's firm tone. "She came to Kent to visit her friend, Charlotte Lucas, who is recently married to Elizabeth's cousin, Mr. Collins."

"Oh, her friend married Mr. Collins, did she?" Miss Bingley seemed a little annoyed. "I had thought his . . . affections lay in another direction."

"I am afraid I have no knowledge of that," said Anne, though she knew of what had happened. "Not long after Elizabeth came to Kent, my companion passed away suddenly, and as a friend, Elizabeth agreed to stay with me while she stayed in Kent."

"Eliza agreed to be your companion!" cried Miss Bingley with an odd kind of squealing laughter. "How wonderful! I had not thought her inclined to such a life, but perhaps it suits her, though I cannot imagine she possesses the necessary skills to do it in a creditable manner."

"She is *not* my companion, Miss Bingley," said Anne, injecting a hint of steel in her voice. "Elizabeth is my *friend* and is staying here as my guest. She was not paid to keep me company at Rosings—in fact, she did so because I applied to her as a friend, and as she is both kind and thoughtful, she agreed, even though it meant she would spend much less time with her friend of many years.

"Now, I believe you had something of which you wished to speak. Might I ask you to come to the point?"

As Anne all but reprimanded Miss Bingley for her unkindness, the sardonic smile ran away from her face, and by the end, she was all but gaping. She was not slow of thought, however, and soon recovered, but her look of condescension which replaced the arrogance was nearly as infuriating.

"Miss de Bourgh," said Miss Bingley, "it is clear from all you have told me that you have no notion of the reality of the woman you have accepted as your friend. As I have a greater knowledge of her, I thought to inform you of it, so you may take steps to defend yourself. Your little Eliza, though she is adept at passing herself off with a degree of credit, is not who you think she is."

"That is quite interesting, Miss Bingley. How so?"

"She is the second daughter of five, each one more improper than the last. Mr. Bennet's estate is entailed to Mr. Collins, and now that Mr. Collins has married—and not to Miss Elizabeth—I can only imagine that on the death of their father, the Bennet sisters will be destitute."

It seemed something was offending Miss Bingley, for her voice was rising, taking her color along with it.

"Furthermore, I have it on good authority that they have no greater connections than an uncle in trade and another who is a country solicitor. Mrs. Bennet is perhaps the most avaricious, grasping social climber I have ever had the misfortune to meet. She schemes openly of how her daughters will attach themselves to rich men by whatever means possible, and it was only because of the diligence of myself, with Mr. Darcy's assistance, that my brother was able to avoid being caught in Mrs. Bennet's web. Their father is a slothful man, who does nothing to attempt to teach his family better manners or improve their situation. I have never met such an odious, improper family in all my life."

When Miss Bingley fell silent, she turned her attention back on Anne, apparently expecting her to immediately jump to her feet and insist Elizabeth leave the house. Her brow furrowed when Anne did not do precisely that.

"Those are serious accusations, Miss Bingley," replied Anne at length. "I have never met any of Elizabeth's family in Hertfordshire, so I cannot speak to their characters beyond what Elizabeth has told me."

"I am certain she was eager to portray them in the best possible light," said Miss Bingley.

"Actually, I was amused by her candor." Miss Bingley did not seem to know what to say. "However, I have met Miss Bennet and the Gardiners and have found them to be estimable people."

Miss Bingley paled. "You have met Miss Bennet?"

"I have," replied Anne. "She is perhaps the sweetest woman I have ever met. I cannot imagine how you might have gained any impression of her lack of propriety."

"Miss Bennet *is* a sweet girl," replied Miss Bingley, though her grudging concession was given unwillingly. "But the rest of her family is exactly as I have said."

"And the Gardiners," continued Anne, ignoring the other woman's words, "are everything delightful. Georgiana and I have already benefited from the acquaintance." Anne smoothed her skirts in a deliberate fashion, delighted she had chosen to wear this dress today. "This fabric was obtained from Mr. Gardiner's warehouse. He has many delightful bolts of cloth, and though I know he would not wish for us to use *all* his stock, he was happy to allow us to choose some we found particularly appealing. In fact, Georgiana's modiste, Madam Fournier, has concluded a business arrangement with Mr. Gardiner—he will now be supplying her. Have you used Madam Fournier for your clothing requirements?"

The way Miss Bingley's lip curled, Anne was certain she had not. Madam Fournier was one of the most prominent modistes in the city, and getting an appointment with her was difficult, if not impossible, if one was not a member of a certain level of society, or recommended by one. Miss Bingley, despite her airs, did not meet Madam Fournier's requirements.

"I have not, though I would appreciate an introduction," said Miss Bingley.

Anne was delighted—it seemed Miss Bingley never lost sight of her ambitions, even amid such a stinging denunciation as she was engaged in now.

"But we should return to the subject at hand," replied Anne. "You have made some serious accusations regarding my dear friend, and I must say that your claims are not supported by what I know of my friend's family. As I said, I have never met the family in Hertfordshire, but her sister and her close relations are as estimable as anyone I have ever met."

Miss Bingley appeared to be at a loss, so Anne filled the ensuing silence. "I wonder why you would come here to condemn my friend, Miss Bingley. What would you have me do?"

"Send her back to her family at once!" cried Miss Bingley. "Even if she is not as improper as I have informed you—and I do not believe for a moment she is not—surely a prestigious family as yours should not be associating with those of such a low position in society. Would it not be better for you to choose better friends?"

"Such as you and your family."

Of course, the sardonic tone of Anne's voice was lost on Miss Bingley. "We *have* been Mr. Darcy's particular friends for some time. Mr. Darcy himself decided he would not be known to the Bennets when we left Hertfordshire, and his assistance was instrumental in convincing my brother of the same. Should you not follow his example?"

"Follow his example to eschew knowing those connected to trade," said Anne, to which Miss Bingley nodded vigorously. "By that account, we should not be known to *you* either, Miss Bingley."

The woman paled. "I do not understand you."

"Come, Miss Bingley," said Anne, "I am well aware of your background."

It seemed Miss Bingley recognized the harsh note that Anne had allowed into her voice by the way her face fell—it was time to disabuse this woman of any expectation of intimacy with her, or any expectation she had that Anne would follow her ridiculous designs.

"I thank you for your concern, Miss Bingley, but it is quite unwarranted. For you see, though my mother would be appalled if she knew of my acquaintance with a family in trade—and has, indeed, railed many times against Darcy's friendship with your brother—I am of a much more liberal frame of mind. I do not judge my friends based on their connections, but on the contents of their character."

"That does you credit, of course," interjected Miss Bingley. "But that reason alone is sufficient to disassociate yourself from the Bennets. As I said—"

"I know what you have said," snapped Anne, returning the favor. "There is nothing the matter with Elizabeth or her relations with whom I am acquainted. They are everything lovely and proper.

"Moreover, I consider Elizabeth to be my closest friend and will not give up her society for anything. I thank you for your concern, but in this instance, it is unwarranted. I will thank you to drop the subject and never raise it again."

Miss Bingley's mouth opened to continue her objections, but Anne's glare finally succeeded in quelling them. She subsided, but not with any grace, and her sullen glare reminded Anne of that of a child. Though she preferred not to think ill of her mother, Anne thought she might actually get on with Miss Bingley quite well, indeed. They were the same general characters, looking down on others, intent upon having their own way, and speaking when they should remain silent. The difference was that Lady Catherine possessed the lineage to render her pride understandable to a certain extent. Miss Bingley was nothing more than a pretender.

"Thank you, Miss Bingley, for this illuminating discussion," said Anne, rising to indicate the interview was at an end. "Do bring your brother to visit us whenever convenient—I have heard so much of him that I long to make his acquaintance."

It appeared that Miss Bingley suddenly found Darcy house unappealing, for she could not leave quickly enough. She assured Anne in a most insincere way that she would pass Anne's request on to her brother and then departed with an unseemly haste.

Anne wished to laugh at the woman as she was leaving, but there was too much on which to think. Miss Bingley had revealed certain information during her appeal which shed some light on the situation at present. Now Anne needed to determine what she could share with Elizabeth and what she would need to keep to herself.

Chapter XXIII

"She said what?" asked Elizabeth.

"Yes, you understood me correctly. Miss Bingley advised me that I should send you home because you are connected to trade, of all things."

It was beyond understanding. Elizabeth had known that the woman was a proud and disagreeable sort, she never would have thought her to be so delusional as to forget her own origins.

"Come now, Elizabeth," said Anne. "You are not surprised, are you?"

"I was," replied Elizabeth, "but I suppose I should not be. She has always behaved as if she was above us. But for her to come out and speak of it is beyond astonishing. What a truly odious creature she is!"

"I cannot but agree."

Anne paused and tapped her finger on her lips, and Elizabeth, by now knowing her friend, was certain she had some mischief in mind.

"The problem, as I see it, has several facets, but the solution might be quite simple."

"What do you mean?" asked Elizabeth, dreading the response.

"First," said Anne, ticking each point on her fingers, "we have Miss Bingley, as obnoxious a creature as ever existed and one who is begging us to humble her."

Elizabeth could not help but laugh.

"Second, I suspect you are correct about her brother: he was persuaded to give up your sister against his inclination, and for her to be so intent on keeping them apart, I suspect she is not convinced he is now indifferent. Third, Jane is clearly pining for Mr. Bingley. Fourth, Miss Bingley is not likely to allow her brother to come within a mile of this house, as she does not wish him to accidentally meet you and wonder where Jane is."

Through her continued laughter, Elizabeth said: "I believe you are quite correct, Anne."

"Then we should invite Mr. Bingley and his family for dinner," replied Anne. "The same night, we can invite the Gardiners. I believe, if you are in any way correct, that Jane and Mr. Bingley would take care of the rest of the problem themselves."

"Do you think she would accept? You have so eloquently defended me, and Miss Bingley would know I am still here."

"Ah, but if I insinuate to her that I have reconsidered and seen the light? I am certain I could craft a letter which would *suggest* you will not be present without stating it."

Elizabeth shook her head. "Anne, I believe I have misjudged you. It is clear *you* are far more dangerous than your mother ever could be. Lady Catherine is meddling—you are nothing short of devious!"

"Why thank you, Elizabeth," said Anne. "I am happy you think so highly of me."

They shared a look together before they burst out laughing again.

"If you wish it, then I have no objections," replied Elizabeth. "By all means, let us drive a spike into Miss Bingley's wheel. The woman is overdue for a little humbling."

And so, the two ladies sat down to plan their joke on Miss Bingley. For a time, Elizabeth almost wished her father was here—he would no doubt find great entertainment in their machinations. In fact, Elizabeth was certain her father would get on with Anne famously.

While his cousin and houseguest were engrossed in their scheming, Darcy was at his club, meeting Bingley for the first time since his friend had returned from the north.

"Darcy," said Bingley as he walked up to the table where Darcy had awaited his arrival. "I am glad to see you again, my friend. I trust you are well."

Darcy rose from his chair and shook Bingley's hand, his other hand slapping Bingley on the shoulder. "I am, indeed, Bingley. How was your time in Yorkshire?"

"It was tolerable," replied Bingley. "My family is well, as always, and there were a few items I needed to discuss with my uncle. But Caroline and Louisa do not like Yorkshire, and our time there was a long litany of complaints. While I am happy to visit my family, I am even happier to be back in London where Caroline does not grumble so much."

It was difficult to sympathize with Bingley in this instance. He was her brother, the head of the house, and he controlled her dowry and her living arrangements—it was not beyond Bingley's ability to silence his sister and ensure she behaved better. But Bingley was a kindly soul, one who despised conflict. Unfortunately, his harpy of a sister was aware of this, and she exploited his weakness with a razor-like precision.

"Did you visit your aunt in Kent as you usually do?" asked Bingley.

A waiter came, and they arranged for some lunch to be brought, allowing Darcy the time to think about how he wished to answer the question. While the fact that he had not gone to Kent was something Darcy could discuss with impunity, the fact of Anne's return was a little touchier. In particular, Darcy was not certain if he should mention Miss *Elizabeth* Bennet's presence in his house, and in connection, Miss *Jane* Bennet's presence at the Gardiners' house.

A part of Darcy was made uncomfortable by his complicity in hiding Miss Bennet's presence in town, though it *could* be said that it was not Darcy's responsibility to inform his friend of the fact. Miss Jane Bennet *was*, after all, at least nominally Miss Bingley's friend. Darcy himself would have been unaware of the matter had Miss Bingley not seen fit to crow about how Miss Bennet had visited and how she had taken care in her return visit to ensure the girl understood her intention to sever the acquaintance.

In the end, Darcy decided to avoid the subject, which meant saying nothing of Anne and Miss Elizabeth's presence at his house. Darcy was fully committed to making Miss Elizabeth his wife—if she could be induced to accept him, Bingley would necessarily be in his company again, and since Miss Bennet and Miss Elizabeth were so close, he would encounter her again. If he was still inclined to favor her, he could resume his attentions at that time. Since her younger sister would be married to Darcy, there would be no reason for Miss Bennet to yield to whatever pressure her mother exerted, and thus, if she accepted Bingley, Darcy could be reasonably assured she did so because of inclination and nothing more.

"Actually, this year Fitzwilliam and I decided not to attend my aunt in Kent," replied Darcy. "I had a matter of business which detained me and prevented my going, and as I was not to go, my cousin decided against going without me."

"A matter of business? Or perhaps was it a disinclination for your aunt's company?"

Darcy shook his head ruefully. "No, you are completely correct, and I own it without disguise. I was quite happy to avoid my aunt."

"I knew it!" exclaimed Bingley, rubbing his hands together in delight. "I have heard enough stories of your aunt these past years, my old friend, to know that you are not fond of her company."

"True. It is difficult for anyone in my family to tolerate her society."

"And your cousin too, from what I understand."

Though Bingley laughed at his own jest, Darcy only smiled, though he did not feel at all like laughing. He was still uncomfortable with how the family had treated Anne over the years, and their lack of action in extracting her from an untenable situation. Anne was uncommonly improved since he had seen her last, and Darcy was forced to attribute most of it to Miss Bennet's friendship, though part of it was simply a facet of Anne's character Darcy had never seen. Or had never chosen to see.

"Since I have been in London the entire time you were away," replied Darcy, hoping to steer the conversation away from his cousin, "and I am certain you have no desire to hear of my observations of society, perhaps you should tell me of your journey."

Bingley laughed again. "Did you even participate in society?"

"Only as much as necessary," replied Darcy, knowing his friend would be diverted.

They spoke for some time, eating together when their food arrived. Darcy watched his friend, attempting to discern his feelings, and whether he had recovered from his disappointment with respect to Miss Bennet. And Darcy could not be certain, which was itself something of a surprise. Bingley was not adept at hiding his thoughts from others—in many ways he was an open book. He assiduously avoided any mention of the Bennets or Hertfordshire, and he said nothing of any young ladies to whom he had been introduced, which was again an oddity—Bingley could often be counted on to regale him with tales of his latest angel, even if the acquaintance was slight.

The Bingley of January and February, the man who was depressed and moody, seemed to have disappeared, and the man who spoke and laughed was returned. But there was something missing, and Darcy could not be certain what it was, whether it was a lack of Bingley's irrepressible ebullience or something else entirely.

By the time they went their separate ways, Darcy was thoughtful again. He still thought it was for the best that he had not mentioned Miss Elizabeth or Miss Bennet; he suspected his friend was not yet free of his fascination for Miss Bennet. Should Darcy be successful in his pursuit of Miss Elizabeth, he would do all he could to give Bingley the opportunity to win Miss Bennet's hand. It was the least he could do for his friend.

That evening they were joined by Colonel Fitzwilliam, and as a group of five, they retired to the music room after dinner, Elizabeth and Georgiana obliging the company by playing for some time. Elizabeth truly enjoyed hearing her host's sister play—she was technically proficient and played with a delightful energy, and though her abilities were perhaps not everything Miss Bingley portrayed them to be last autumn in Hertfordshire, the talent was there for the girl to become a true proficient, if she practiced, which was never in doubt. Colonel Fitzwilliam accompanied her to the pianoforte to turn pages for her, while the other three sat on a nearby sofa.

Elizabeth had much to think on. Mr. Darcy's behavior in the garden the previous day had been unmistakable and had forced her to review every interaction she had ever had with him. The insult at the assembly notwithstanding, once she looked back with new insight, she could see that Mr. Darcy had always engaged her, had always done so with more pleasure than she had attributed at the time. He had never been indifferent to her, regardless of the situation.

But whatever the state of their previous interactions, it was clear now that he looked on her with the eyes of a man interested in a woman—there was no other explanation. His message the previous day with the flowers had been more pointed than any she had witnessed before, and likely as much as he would ever do if she did not make her returning interest known. And the flowers themselves had been something of an issue, as Elizabeth had needed to come up with an explanation for their presence in her room.

Earlier that day, sometime after Miss Bingley left, Elizabeth had returned to her room, to be joined by Anne, who wished to speak of her letter of invitation to Miss Bingley. The keen-eyed Anne had entered, and she had not missed the pretty bunch of carnations of all colors displayed in a vase on the table in Elizabeth's sitting-room.

"What is this?" asked Anne, the purpose of her coming forgotten for the moment.

"I adore carnations," said Elizabeth by way of explanation and diversion. "Mr. Darcy allowed me to choose some of my favorite blooms to lighten my room."

"Did he?" asked Anne, her words meaning nothing, and speaking volumes at the same time. "The housekeeper mentioned that you were outside with him for more than an hour yesterday morning."

"Yes," said Elizabeth, wishing her friend would allow the subject to drop. "Mr. Darcy was showing me the gardens, as I had spent little time there."

Anne regarded Elizabeth for several moments, and she began to feel uncomfortable. "She also said that you entered the house with one in your hair."

Though feeling the need to rail at the housekeeper for sharing such a thing, Elizabeth replied with what she thought was tolerable disinterest: "That was just a bit of silliness on my part. Mr. Darcy laughed at me, as I expected he would."

Anne nodded, but she remained thoughtful until Elizabeth asked her about her errand, after which they spoke of Miss Bingley and the tone Anne would use in her letter. In the end, the subject was not raised again, though Elizabeth saw her friend's gaze lingering on the flowers for some time after.

The question was, now that Mr. Darcy had stated his feelings in such an open manner, how was Elizabeth to respond? She could readily imagine being able to fall for his overtures. By this time, she was reasonably certain that in matters of intellect and character, he might be better suited for her than she had ever thought.

But there were many drawbacks. His uncle, the earl, had been welcoming, both when he had first met her and on two subsequent occasions, but she could not imagine him welcoming his nephew's interest in a penniless country girl. And that said nothing of what she imagined Lady Catherine's reaction would be. After taking her daughter away — in her view — the lady would almost certainly fly into a rage if she learned that Elizabeth was about to take her daughter's supposed betrothed as well. Elizabeth thought she was equipped to handle the naysayers of society, but she truly had not had much congress with that world, so she could not be certain how they would act.

The piece Georgiana was playing concluded, and Elizabeth clapped along with the rest of the party. Having played several numbers, Georgiana rose and addressed Elizabeth:

"Will you not play for a time, Miss Bennet?"

Elizabeth smiled. "I would be delighted. But I should have played before you did, so that my efforts would not seem poor by comparison. Then again, I doubt it would have mattered."

"Oh, Elizabeth," cried Georgiana. "You play very well, as you know."

"I will be happy to take my cousin's place and turn the pages for you, Miss Bennet," said Mr. Darcy.

Though of two minds about Mr. Darcy's offer, Elizabeth accepted. Soon she was sitting at the instrument, playing Mozart. She quickly understood, however, that allowing Mr. Darcy to sit beside her was a mistake, for the man's *presence* was like a slowly burning fire situated to her side. Or that is what it felt like, for the heat from his body scorched her as she played. Never had she been so aware of another's presence nor felt so alive in turn. And she was compelled to confess his ardent attentions had, indeed, affected her.

As she watched Darcy and Elizabeth's performance, Anne almost thrummed with excitement. Darcy's interest she had known from the beginning of their time together in London, but Elizabeth's response had been less certain. Her behavior the day before was confirmed in what Anne was seeing before her now, as her friend almost seemed afraid to even brush sleeves with Darcy. Anne was delighted.

When Elizabeth finished playing—Anne noticed that she stopped, having played only two songs—the pair rejoined the rest of the company, sitting nearby. While both were engaged in speaking with the entire group, they seemed to continue their awareness of each other, and before long they had begun to debate some obscure point of literature, leaving the remaining three to speak together. Georgiana, as was her wont, took the opportunity to return to the pianoforte. She played softly and Anne recognized it as a piece she had been practicing lately.

"You appear akin to the cat in the cream, Cousin," said Fitzwilliam after they had been in this attitude for some moments.

"I am simply happy to be in the company of those I love," was Anne's smooth reply.

"Oh, I believe it is something more than that." Fitzwilliam darted a significant glance at Darcy and Elizabeth before he turned back to Anne. "I simply do not know why you favor certain . . . *developments* to such a degree."

Anne returned his gaze, amused that he seemed to be seeing the same thing she had. But she was not about to make it any easier for him to tease, not that he required it.

"Perhaps you should inform me of what you think."

With a shrug, Fitzwilliam looked back at the two who were so engrossed that they did not even notice his scrutiny. "It seems to me there are two possibilities: either you wish for a match between Miss Bennet and Darcy because you have a high regard for them and wish them to be happy, or you hope they will make a match so your mother will quit pestering you about marrying Darcy."

"There is a third option," said Anne, the offhand tone of her voice prompting a raised brow from her cousin. "I may wish to save Darcy from the inevitability of Miss Bingley attempting to compromise him."

Fitzwilliam suppressed the hearty guffaw Anne was certain was about to burst out, and though his reaction did draw Darcy's attention for a moment, it was insufficient to divert him from Elizabeth for long.

"I suppose that is a possibility, though I do not consider it likely," replied Fitzwilliam. "Darcy has been fending Miss Bingley away for some years now, and I believe he would agree that she is far from the worst predatory female he has met in society." Fitzwilliam settled his gaze on her. "Now, my dear Annie, why do you not tell me your purpose in this."

"Do you disapprove?"

Fitzwilliam snorted. "Of course not! He is obviously enamored of her, and I wish for nothing more than my cousin to be happy. It was only after she came to London that Darcy's previous behavior became clear. I had realized that Darcy was altered from last summer, but I did not know why. Now I suspect he was pining after her, though he would not acknowledge to himself that such was the case."

"Oh?" asked Anne, delighted at her cousin's assertions. "How was he different?"

"He was quieter, more thoughtful, and he was often distracted, though only one who truly knows him would notice the difference. And you are changing the subject, Anne."

"Perhaps it is a mix of both," relented Anne. "I *do* love Elizabeth like a sister, and I want her to be happy. If I did not think that happiness could be achieved with Darcy, I would be a most ardent opponent of the match. But I will own that I have considered the . . . relative benefits of Darcy marrying another. Again, if he can make her happy, it would benefit us all."

"She does appear to be softening to him, does she not?" Fitzwilliam paused and chuckled. "I thought her manner was a little cold when we came out of Kent, but it is like someone has started a fire in a hearth—she has warmed considerably."

"You know she had carnations in her room today."

Her cousin looked at her blankly. "Is that supposed to signify something?"

Anne shook her head and looked skyward. "Carnations are the flower that signify attraction and a future romantic attachment."

"Are you suggesting Darcy gave them to her?"

"They *were* out in the gardens for more than an hour yesterday. And when they entered the house, she was wearing one in her hair."

"Well, well," said Fitzwilliam, his smug gaze fixed on Darcy. "I see I must congratulate my cousin for his good taste. She is quite enchanting—I am certain he will be happy with her."

"No, you will not," said Anne, the steel in her voice drawing his eyes back to her. "I do not wish to interfere. They are getting along splendidly themselves without our assistance."

A chuckle and a shake of Fitzwilliam's head was followed by his spoken, "Peace, Anne. I enjoy teasing Darcy as much as anyone, but I will not complicate his courtship. I only hope your mother does not get wind of this little romance. She will be furious if she does."

"I will deal with my mother, if necessary," replied Anne.

Fitzwilliam turned and regarded Anne with a lazy eye. "It seems your association with Miss Bennet has turned you into a bit of a lioness defending her cubs."

"And I would ask you not to forget it, Cousin," replied Anne.

"How could I?" Fitzwilliam paused and noted: "You know, all these years your mother has spoken of a match between you and Darcy, and she would never hear of anything else. I know why she wished to claim him—he is the son of her dear sister and he has Pemberley to recommend him—but I have always wondered why no one thought to attempt to push you and me together."

"What do you mean?"

"Darcy *has* an estate—he possesses several, in fact. But *I* am the penniless soldier in the family, the one who requires a fortune to allow me to keep my style of life. Since Rosings itself is your dowry, we would seem to be well matched."

Anne was uncertain if her cousin was jesting, but she was not about to allow him to embrace such thoughts.

"I am sorry to disappoint you, Cousin, but I do not think we are suited. I love you as a cousin, but I think I am quite content to allow our relationship to stay as it is."

"Ah, cut to the quick!" cried Fitzwilliam, though she noted his disappointment was so acute that he refrained from drawing Darcy's attention by speaking quietly. "To be found wanting in such a fashion—how will I ever recover?"

"Are you incapable of being serious?" asked Anne, shaking her head.

Fitzwilliam grinned. "Oh, I am quite capable of it. I simply do not often choose it. Though the thought has come to me in the past, I have always dismissed it, for I never thought you possessed any more interest in me than I did in you. You are quite safe from me, Cousin. I shall continue to search for that elusive heiress who can give me everything I have ever wanted in life."

"By that you mean a large fortune."

A wink was his reply. "Of course. What else is there?"

"What else, indeed."

They fell silent, but Anne's mind was working, considering the conversation she had just had with her cousin. Since coming out of Kent and gaining her independence from her mother, Anne had not thought of her own future. Her attention was fixed on her friend and her family, watching as Elizabeth and Darcy became closer, and creating a situation whereby Jane could once again be in the company of Mr. Bingley, allowing them to follow their own feelings toward whatever end they desired.

But what of Anne herself? She had been told for so long by her mother that she was destined for Darcy and had hardly been allowed to think of anything else. She had never desired such a union, but she had not considered what it was that *she* wished for.

As she thought and watched Darcy and Elizabeth while they danced around one another in the complex footsteps of courtship, Anne realized that she wanted what it increasingly appeared they had. She wished for a man to look at her as Darcy looked on her dearest friend, wished to esteem a man more than all others. What good was an estate such as the one she would inherit without someone she loved to share it with? Her mother, she thought, had esteemed Sir Lewis, though Anne had been too young to know when he had passed, but she did not think that depth of emotion had been present between them.

It would be in the next generation, Anne decided. She would find someone who adored her and cherished her. She would follow Elizabeth's example.

Chapter XXIV

As the days progressed, the Darcy party began to accept invitations to society events and Elizabeth obtained her first taste of the entertainments of the first circles. At first it was nothing more than a dinner invitation from a friend of Mr. Darcy's, or a card party at another friend's house. The society was not that much different from what Elizabeth had known in Hertfordshire, but when Elizabeth made this observation to Mr. Darcy, she discovered the reason.

"That is because I do not accept invitations from those of questionable character or from whom I am not intimately acquainted." Mr. Darcy smiled at her. "There are many events which I do not deem . . . appropriate, and the few invitations we have accepted are only a small number of those I have received."

"There are times when my brother will receive dozens of invitations in a few days," said Georgiana. The girl shuddered, prompting an indulgent smile from Mr. Darcy. "I am glad I am not yet out, for I would not know what to do with so many at once."

"And you never will," replied Mr. Darcy. "I will never accept an invitation which does not meet your approval. We need not perform before society."

Georgiana beamed and Mr. Darcy turned back to Elizabeth, who could not help but ask: "Are there truly so many objectionable events, sir?"

"Perhaps not," said Mr. Darcy. "There is a certain set of society which indulges in activities I would consider depraved, but the majority are similar to what you have experienced at your home, though much wealthier, connected, and with no lack of pride and arrogance. But as you know, I am much more comfortable in the company of those with whom I am acquainted. While I do attend some of the wider events, I limit the number, as I truly do not enjoy an excess of society. But I am obliged to give some thought to it because of the Darcys' position in society."

Elizabeth regarded him with some curiosity. "Due to your connection to your uncle?"

A faint smile was followed by: "Yes, the Fitzwilliams are our most recent noble connection, but the history of my family is littered with nobility. My ancestors often married noble brides, as prominent as dukes' daughters, and the daughters of the Darcy family have often married into the nobility themselves."

"I had no idea you were so well connected, Mr. Darcy," replied Elizabeth, feeling a little ill at the thought of such high connections. And this man was directing his attentions on *her*?

"It is nothing, Miss Bennet," replied Mr. Darcy. "Though we are connected with the nobility, in truth the Darcys have always been gentlemen farmers and content to remain such. If an offer to be raised to the nobility were to be made to me, I would refuse it, for I have no desire to be placed higher in society."

"I can imagine why," replied Elizabeth.

"When shall we attend a ball?" asked Anne.

"Next week," replied Mr. Darcy. "It is being given by one of my friends from school. He has recently married, and his wife is planning her first ball with her mother-in-law's assistance. As we were close at Cambridge, I am obliged to attend."

And attend they did. It was a far finer affair than that to which Elizabeth had been accustomed in Meryton, including the ball at Netherfield, though it was similar. There were also many more people attending. Although Elizabeth was not acquainted with anyone, there were introductions aplenty, and Elizabeth never wanted for a partner. For that matter, neither did Anne.

"How are you feeling, Anne?" asked Elizabeth later in the evening when they retired to the side of the room for some restorative punch.

Anne had rarely sat down all night, and knowing her friend's still developing stamina, Elizabeth had worried for her.

"I am quite enjoying myself," she responded, favoring Elizabeth with a warm smile, quieting Elizabeth's concerns. "I believe I have you to thank, Elizabeth, for not making a fool of myself. Your lessons have been beneficial, indeed!"

"I am happy to hear it," replied Elizabeth. "Is it everything you thought it might be?"

"That and more, though I will own I do not care for some of the men I have met." Anne shook her head. "I can see that it will be difficult to sort those worthy from those who are not. I smelled the distinct scent of desperation and avarice from several of the young men with whom I danced."

"That is because there are many rakes in society." The two ladies turned to Darcy, who had joined them a moment before. "Your last partner, Lord Trenton, you should take care to avoid. Not only is he a womanizer, but his estate has been failing for some years due to his habits. He would think nothing of compromising you for Rosings, Anne."

Anne favored her cousin with a smile. "Thank you, Darcy. I will be guided by you, for I have no desire to be entrapped into marriage."

Their entrance in society also brought some attention, though not all of it was unwelcome. Lord Trenton, for example, came to Darcy house several times, and it was fortunate that on all but one occasion, they were not present to receive him. The one time he was admitted, his behavior toward Anne was so blatant and familiar that Darcy pulled him from the room and warned him that Anne would not be receiving him again. Though Elizabeth wondered at a member of the nobility being warned away by naught but a gentleman, the earl did not show himself at Darcy house again.

Anne and Elizabeth were also visited by several other gentlemen and no few ladies. Most of these Elizabeth found pleasant, though there were a few who seemed determined to put her in her place, Elizabeth parried their barbs and laughed at their pride. Soon, only those with whom they were friendly visited them and were visited in their turn.

"It seems you were correct about Mr. Bingley," said Elizabeth, one day more than a week after Miss Bingley had first come to Darcy house. "We have attended several events, and yet he has not appeared."

"Did you doubt me?" asked Anne.

"There is no need to be smug!" rejoined Elizabeth with a laugh. "Anyone could have predicted it!"

"But I did," replied Anne. She lifted her nose into the air, her pose a conceited imitation of Miss Bingley. Of course, the friends were unable to stifle their laughter, and they soon allowed it free rein.

"I will own that I am surprised," said Anne a moment later. "I knew she would do everything in her power to avoid us, but she has shown an uncanny ability to predict the events we attend and direct her brother toward others. Do you suppose she has a spy in this house?"

"Perhaps they do not go out. Or perhaps she simply understands Mr. Darcy's preferences from long association and directs her brother elsewhere."

Anne pouted. "I did prefer the notion of a spy. It would suit the woman's character quite well!"

"I dare say it would at that."

Though Anne enjoyed society well enough, she found herself agreeing with her cousin's assessment—too much was not desirable, and once her cousin showed her the dizzying array of invitations he had received, Anne decided that she could dispense with most of them quite cheerfully. Even the three times they had been out that week were plenty for her tastes, and she found herself longing once again for more intimate gatherings with those she most highly regarded.

It was fortunate, then, for her peace of mind that the return engagement to dine at Gracechurch Street was approaching, for Anne was eager to once again be in Jane's company, who had risen high in her esteem. When the evening arrived, they attended the Gardiners at their home, and every expectation was met in the meal and in the company. Anne was forced to own that her mother would not appreciate learning of her daughter dining in such circumstances, but she also thought that should her mother ever be induced to relax her rigid notions of class, she might enjoy the Gardiners' company, as they were estimable people.

One goal Anne had for the evening was to speak to Jane again to delicately probe her feelings and learn if she could prompt her to any reaction concerning Mr. Bingley. Anne's chance came after dinner when Elizabeth became engaged in conversation with her aunt and Georgiana, while the gentlemen were still out of the room indulging in their port.

"I understand you have been in London for some time, Miss Bennet," said Anne by way of opening the conversation.

"I have." Jane paused and then directed a rueful smile at Anne. "My father's letters have been becoming more strident about our return. I suspect Lizzy's letters have been even more pointed, for they are very close."

Anne's gaze slipped to where Elizabeth was speaking with her aunt, and she noted that her dear friend's attention was now split between her current companions and Anne and Jane. Anne only rolled her eyes at her friend and turned back to Jane.

"She has not mentioned it. But she has stayed with us for some time now, and it is approaching the close of the season. It is not surprising your father would wish you both to return."

"And there is also the question of my uncle and aunt's imminent departure. Originally, Elizabeth was to go with them on a tour of the lakes, but I believe that has changed. As Lizzy and I have both been from home for several months, I believe my father is loath to part with us again so soon. As a result, the invitation has been amended to include my middle sister, Mary."

"Ah, Elizabeth has not mentioned that either," replied Anne.

"No, I am not surprised she would not. She would not wish you to feel responsible for missing this tour." Jane paused, regarding her sister for several moments. "I know that Lizzy was anticipating traveling with our aunt and uncle, but matters seem to have changed substantially for her. I wonder if I will be losing my sister before long."

"It is hard, is it not?" said Anne, not attempting to deny the interest Darcy possessed in Elizabeth which Jane had obviously seen.

Jane turned a sad smile on Anne. "It is. She has been my dearest friend for many years. She is my protector and my advocate in all things, and though I have always done what I could to return the favor, I have wondered if I am lacking."

"How so?"

"I am . . ." Jane paused and smiled. "Surely you have seen that Lizzy is outgoing and confident. She takes any slights against me as if they were made to her, and she will protect me to her last breath. The contrast between us is not difficult to see—I am quiet and calm, and my way of dealing with adversity is much different from hers. I do not defend like she does."

"She understands this, Jane," replied Anne. "She would never expect you to step in, claws extended and teeth bared, to protect her. I believe she places great value in your calmness, in your patience, as it provides her with a model of behavior she is able to emulate."

Jane was silent, considering Anne's words. "I have never thought of it that way."

"Do not devalue your worth to Elizabeth," urged Anne. "She defends you because it is in her character to do so—she has extended that same privilege to me, and I feel fortunate because of it. You bring your own strengths to your relationship with her, and she values you accordingly."

It may have been nothing more than fancy, but Anne thought Jane sat up a little straighter at Anne's words, her confidence appearing to have increased apace.

"It is difficult, is it not?" said Anne. Jane's eyes swung to her, a question in their depths. "Having a relation who is larger than life. Your Elizabeth is so irrepressible that it is not difficult to be caught in her shadow. I am familiar with the sensation, for my mother is an unstoppable force, and I have often felt like an adjunct to her.

"What we both must remember is that there is no need for us to be in their shadows. Elizabeth would not wish you to reside there—she loves you as her sister and values you for your strengths."

"And you, Miss de Bourgh?" asked Jane. "From what I understand, your escape from *your* forceful relation was difficult."

"Assisted by your sister," said Anne. "I am free of my mother's shadow at present, and I still have hope that she may be reached and our relationship, restored. But she must understand that the dynamic which existed before has been replaced. I wish for a relationship of equals—it will depend on her willingness to allow it."

In later years, Anne would point to that short conversation as the genesis for a lifelong friendship with Jane Bennet, as the true meeting of minds when they understood each other. But it was not the end of their conversation that day.

"Actually, a thought has just entered my mind which I am not certain if your sister has mentioned. We have recently seen two of your acquaintances and I wondered if they had paid a visit to you."

Jane turned to regard Anne, and her gaze was searching. Though she remained as closed as ever, Anne thought she was well aware of the possibility of Miss Bingley having visited Darcy house. Though, perhaps, she had not been dreading the possibility of hearing of them, she was not exactly sanguine about it either. And Anne had no doubt Jane knew *exactly* of whom she spoke.

"I do not have many acquaintances in London, Miss de Bourgh."

"Please, call me Anne, Jane," replied Anne. She received a nod in reply. "And these are not acquaintances from London, but rather friends you met in Hertfordshire. Mrs. Hurst and Miss Bingley came to Darcy house last week and were introduced to me."

There was just enough in Jane's countenance to suggest she was not indifferent to the mention of the sisters of the man she admired. But Jane, being Jane, managed to respond with a creditable measure of composure.

"How is Miss Bingley?" asked she. "I have not seen her in some months."

"Miss Bingley is well, but I thought her to be a little discontented. Mrs. Hurst is of a much quieter character. I enjoyed her company, but as for Miss Bingley . . . Well, let us say that I do not find her company nearly so agreeable."

"I . . ." Jane paused and turned away, her gaze distant. "When they came to Hertfordshire, I thought her everything that was lovely, but these past months I have been persuaded to your way of thinking." Jane smiled. "And Lizzy's. She never agreed with me about Caroline's merits."

Anne declined to speak. Her poor opinion exceeded that which Jane espoused, and she did not wish to be seen as criticizing, though she knew Miss Bingley deserved it. But to disapprove of Miss Bingley in as oblique a manner as Jane had was the limit of her capabilities, Anne thought, so she decided to allow the subject to rest. Or at least she had until Jane made her next comment.

It was with a decided sense of despondency—the likes of which Anne had never seen from Jane—that she sighed and turned a carefully fixed smile on Anne. "I understand that there is a certain expectation of an eventual marriage between Miss Bingley's brother and your cousin, Miss Darcy." Miss Bennet's eyes flickered to Georgiana, and Anne wondered at the goodness of this woman, to welcome so readily a girl who had been set up as her rival. "I hope they will be happy together."

"Jane, I know not where you have heard such a thing, but it is most patently untrue."

Shocked, Jane's eyes flew to Anne. "But Caroline . . ."

"Ah, I suppose I should have known," said Anne when Jane's voice trailed off. "Jane, though I would not wish to speak ill of a person who is not here to defend herself, in this instance, I must agree wholeheartedly with your sister. Miss Bingley has misled you in this matter."

"She was so certain." Jane's tone was almost pleading. "As his sister, should she not be aware of the contents of his heart?"

"I have never met Mr. Bingley," replied Anne, "but there is no attachment between Mr. Bingley and Georgiana. By all accounts, Mr. Bingley has been in London for almost two weeks, and he has not visited Georgiana once. Does that sound like a man desperately in love with a woman?"

Jane could not respond, so Anne was more than willing to fill the gap. "Furthermore, Georgiana is only sixteen and not ready for entrance into society, let alone marriage. It will be another two years before she is introduced—in fact, it is possible, it will be three seasons, as she has only just turned sixteen. Darcy would never allow any sort of attachment between them. I do not know what gave Miss Bingley this impression, but it is false."

"Perhaps when she is older?"

"That is always possible," conceded Anne. "But for the present, you should put it out of your head."

The glare—or what passed for one from such a sweet woman—rested on Anne, and it felt slightly accusatory. "Lizzy told you of my history with Mr. Bingley."

"I *have* heard something of it," confessed Anne. "But you should not think I am anything other than supportive. I have said that I do not know Mr. Bingley and cannot guess his feelings, but I would not have you labor under the weight of such a blatant falsehood. Do not give it a moment's more thought, Jane, for there is no attachment between Georgiana and Mr. Bingley."

Jane nodded, though she was distracted, and remained that way for the rest of the evening. Though Anne could not be certain, she thought she detected that precious quality in her new friend that evening. Hope.

"You spoke of Mr. Bingley tonight, did you not?"

Elizabeth was aware that her tone was accusatory, but at the moment she did not care. She had not missed Anne's long tête-à-tête with Jane that evening, not to mention Jane's silence after. She was not happy that Anne had once again raised the subject, particularly when Jane's feelings were so delicate. There were times when Anne was too like her mother—meddling and intent upon having her way. Elizabeth did not appreciate this in her friend, and she would not stand for it.

"Actually, we spoke mostly of you," replied Anne.

Not ready for such an unexpected revelation, Elizabeth could not reply. Anne laughed and touched Elizabeth's arm. "In fact, I learned a lot of your relationship with Jane tonight. Do you know she has often felt inadequate when compared with you?"

Elizabeth could hardly believe what she was hearing. "How could *Jane* possibly feel inadequate next to *me*? She is everything good, gentle, kind, beautiful . . . I have none of these things."

"I believe this is a case of you both diminishing your own worth, something I must own I find ironic. Yes, Jane is all the things you mentioned, but you are also many things she is not, including courageous, fierce, and protective, though you are not devoid of your own beauty and kindness. Trust me, Elizabeth—it is natural for her to feel that way in the face of a naturally more vivacious and outgoing sibling. I have experienced some of the same feelings with my mother."

Elizabeth was unequal to the task of responding. The thought that Jane had felt insufficient next to her was beyond her capacity to fathom, regardless of Anne's subsequent words. Jane was, in her opinion, simply the best person of Elizabeth's acquaintance. No one could hope to compare to her, and Elizabeth had never even tried.

"But, yes," said Anne when Elizabeth did not respond, "we did speak of Mr. Bingley. She mentioned Georgiana and offered her felicitations on their future happiness."

"Oh, Jane," said Elizabeth. It was difficult, but she forced the other subject from her mind to be considered later.

"I disabused her of that notion entirely. I could not allow her to continue to suffer under Miss Bingley's delusions."

"And?" asked Elizabeth, almost afraid of the answer.

"She seemed more light-hearted after that. It was the confirmation for which I was searching. It is obvious to me that Jane still admires Mr. Bingley, though I am certain she thinks he does not care, as he has not taken the opportunity to visit her."

Elizabeth rolled her eyes and Anne could only agree. "I did not discuss that with her—I know you believe Miss Bingley has kept Jane's presence in town from her brother, and I am of the same opinion. I believe that putting them into a situation where they can resolve their mutual attraction together to be the right decision."

"I hope so, Anne," replied Elizabeth. "Witnessing Jane so cast down was hard. I would not wish her to be so sad again."

"Then we will have to ensure she has a chance at happiness." Anne threw her arm around Elizabeth shoulder. "I am certain all will turn out well."

Then with another squeeze of her shoulder, Anne left, leaving Elizabeth alone with her thoughts. She hoped Anne was correct, for she was not certain she could endure the Jane of December again.

As for the other matter of which Anne had spoken, Elizabeth did not wish to think of it at all, though she knew her thoughts would go thither without any active assistance. Tilly soon came to help Elizabeth prepare for the night, and she retired. But as she had expected, thoughts of Jane and their relationship stayed with Elizabeth until the wee hours of the morning. There was not much sleep to be had for Elizabeth that night.

Chapter XXV

Elizabeth did her best to remain as she ever was the next day, but she was well aware she had little success in the endeavor. Anne, seeming to understand her distraction, left her to her ruminations, though Elizabeth could not determine if it was to her benefit or not. The other members of the family, however—excepting Colonel Fitzwilliam who was absent because of his duties—did not seem to know what to make of her silence. Georgiana was soon at her lessons, so Elizabeth was not concerned about giving the girl the wrong impression, but Mr. Darcy was another matter.

The knocker had been taken down that day, and Elizabeth was grateful. Anne, who was acting, at least nominally, as Mr. Darcy's hostess, had decided they required a break from society, and Mr. Darcy had supported her. But though they were left to their own devices and it was clear Mr. Darcy wished to be in her company, Elizabeth could not find the heart for such conversation. Instead, knowing she was not fit company for anyone that day, she excused herself and removed to the garden where she could think in peace. She was not to remain undisturbed for long.

The garden was tranquil as it ever was, and Elizabeth chose the bench Mr. Darcy had shown her, the one his father had installed for his mother's use. Whereas Elizabeth had not come to a decision about Mr. Darcy's attentions, in an odd sort of way she felt close to the man's mother, sitting here on this bench which Lady Anne had used so many times. At that moment, she wished she had been able to meet the lady, to know her as intimately and esteem her as deeply as did her son. The life he had described was his as a boy filled her with hope, the future of a family of her own, a doting husband, children to love and receive their love in turn. What she was not yet certain was whether that future could be had with Mr. Darcy.

Not long after she sat, she was alerted to the approach of someone down the path before her, and she raised her eyes to see the man in question approaching. He walked slowly, his eyes betraying his uncertainty of his welcome. Elizabeth did not have it in her to either order him away or welcome his company, so she only watched him as she approached. It did not do anything to boost his confidence.

"You are quite introspective today, Miss Bennet," said he when he stopped a few feet from the bench. "I have never seen the like in your behavior."

Elizabeth laughed in spite of herself. "Are you accusing me of being shallow of character and lacking in the capacity for reflexion, sir?"

"No, indeed," said Mr. Darcy, catching her amused tone. "In fact, I have a healthy respect for the depth of your character, Miss Bennet. It simply seems to me that you are usually so sure of yourself that deep meditation is not required."

"Then it appears that I have managed to occlude myself to a certain extent, Mr. Darcy. I *am* prone to self-examination, much as any other person. However, I am usually able to contain it to those times of solitude when I am unobserved."

Mr. Darcy nodded, but did not reply. They remained in that attitude for some few moments, though Elizabeth was not even consciously aware of how their gazes were locked together. Had the fact been pointed out to her, she would have colored in embarrassment.

"I am happy to lend a listening ear, if you are willing. May I sit?"

Though part of her wished the man away, if only to be free of the confusion his presence brought to her heart, Elizabeth was relieved to be free of her thoughts, if only for a moment. She smiled and indicated the seat to her side, and he accepted the invitation. They sat in further silence for several long minutes. There was a comfort in the silence, though Elizabeth thought perhaps it was because he was not demanding she answer his questions. But it was not to last.

"Will you share what has distressed you, Miss Bennet? I would not pry into your private affairs, but my offer to provide a willing confidant was not an idle one."

"It is not precisely private affairs, Mr. Darcy," replied Elizabeth with a sigh. "It is just . . . I have been made aware of something I had not considered before, and it has unsettled me." Elizabeth paused and laughed. "In truth, I do not know why I am so troubled, for it is nothing which should give me pause."

Mr. Darcy said nothing—instead, he waited with a patience Elizabeth would long have attributed to him, even before she became acquainted with the more estimable aspects of his character.

"Anne and I spoke of my relationship with Jane. Before you returned to the sitting-room last night, she and Jane had a long conversation, and that subject played a prominent role."

A frown settled over Mr. Darcy's countenance. "And this has distressed you? Did you learn something of your sister you do not like?"

"Nothing objectionable, to be sure—Jane remains as angelic as ever. It is just . . ." Elizabeth paused, struggling to put her feelings into words. "I have always felt myself to be in *Jane's* shadow, for she is everything good and wonderful. But she told Anne last night that she has always felt to be in *mine*."

"And this distresses you?"

Feeling caged, Elizabeth rose from the bench and began pacing in front of it. As she spoke, her hands were moving wildly in the air. "How can Jane possibly feel inadequate next to me? It is entirely unfathomable."

"We are all different in essentials," was Mr. Darcy's reasonable response. "You possess some strengths that your sister does not, and the reverse is true. Do we not all feel inadequate at times, especially when confronted by the weaknesses in our characters?"

"Perhaps we do, Mr. Darcy," replied Elizabeth. "But Jane is so far beyond me—"

Mr. Darcy rose from the bench, the surprise of his sudden action stopping Elizabeth in her pacing. She looked at him, wondering at the tenderness in his expression, the way he stepped forward and captured her hands in his own. Elizabeth did not think she could have pulled away from him if she had tried. She was captivated by his eyes, blue and deep as an ocean, which seemed to dive deeply into her own, seeing into the depths of her soul.

"It seems to me, Miss Bennet, that you have often placed little value on your own contributions to your relationship with your sister. But anyone who sees Miss Bennet in your company must also see the importance she places on you. You may consider your sister to be all that is good, but she is no more perfect than anyone else. Can you not accept that you are just as good as she?"

"I have never lacked confidence, Mr. Darcy." Elizabeth paused and laughed. "I am sure you know this about me. It is not the thought that I lack worth that has unsettled me so. It is that Jane has claimed that she is in my shadow."

Mr. Darcy was silent for a moment, considering his next words. When he did speak, Elizabeth was forced to listen. "When Georgiana was almost imposed upon by Wickham, I felt as if I had failed her. I, who was duty bound to protect her, had almost lost her to a life of misery with a man I openly disdain. But this experience taught me that I was as dependent on her as she is on me. She has struggled with herself, trying to understand she has worth as a person, worth as a sister to a brother who is, after all, much older than she is. And she has said that she often feels like she cannot measure up to me, her elder brother.

"I know our situations are not at all the same, Miss Bennet, but I am trying to say that we should never think our contributions less than they are. My sister provides me much of my joy in life, including a visible reminder of a mother I adored. She is the innocence in a world filled with much sorrow and hardship, and she is the one person who can often pull me from my sometimes black moods. You have much worth, Miss Bennet, not only to Jane and to Anne, but increasingly to Georgiana. You have worth to me. Do not dwell on this. Accept it as your due from a sister who obviously loves you and esteems you beyond price. The fact that such a good woman as your sister esteems you so much is evidence of your estimable nature. The reverse is also true. This is not something that needs to weigh you down. Let it go."

"I will try, Mr. Darcy," Elizabeth found herself saying.

"That is all anyone can ask." He smiled at her. "Now, I know for a fact that Georgiana and Anne will soon wonder where you are. Shall we not return to the house?"

Elizabeth agreed, and they soon found the entrance to Mr. Darcy's house and made their way down the hall. Inside, Elizabeth found a sort of . . . peace—a calmness had come over her. She had not truly been distressed by her ruminations. She had been more shocked to learn of Jane's feelings. But as Mr. Darcy had said, there was no reason to dwell on it or think of it in any way other than to be grateful that she had a wonderful sister who esteemed her so much. That, she decided, was something she would express to Jane when she was once again in her company.

The sound of a voice with which she was not familiar alerted Elizabeth to the presence of at least one visitor in the house. She looked up at Mr. Darcy, wondering if he had known and had been sent to retrieve her—she was not certain any visitor would be so important that her presence would be required.

It appeared Mr. Darcy took her look for the question it was, for he responded: "I was not aware of a caller, Miss Bennet, but it sounds like my aunt. I am certain she wishes to make your acquaintance."

His first words prompted Elizabeth to wonder if Lady Catherine had finally made an appearance in London, but then she realized he had *another* aunt. Although she had never met this one, Elizabeth wondered if *she* would not prove to be the more formidable.

She was given no time to think on the subject, for they entered the room, and Elizabeth soon saw he was correct by the presence of an older woman, who was sitting and speaking in an animated fashion with Georgiana and Anne. She was a tall woman in the manner of Lady Catherine, dark hair greying throughout, but with kindly eyes, wearing an obviously expensive dress. Her eyes, when Elizabeth entered the room, fixed on Elizabeth, seeming to measure her, weigh her, as if trying to determine if Elizabeth was good enough to know her two nieces. Apparently, what she saw was acceptable, for she smiled at them both and gestured them forward while rising to meet them.

"Darcy," said she, regarding him with fond affection, "I see you have brought the young miss of whom I have heard so much. We were about to send a servant to fetch you."

"Aunt Susan," said Darcy, his tone filled with a similar level of affection. "When did you arrive in London?"

"Only last night, Darcy. Hugh has sent me letters, informing me of Anne's situation and her friendship with, I assume, this young lady on your arm. I determined to come immediately, so that I could be introduced, if you would be so kind as to do the honors."

Without hesitation, Mr. Darcy agreed and performed the introductions, and Elizabeth soon found herself seated near the countess's side. "As I have stated, I have heard much of you, Miss Bennet, and it appears the praise has not been overstated."

"I would not be so certain, Lady Susan," replied Elizabeth, feeling unaccountably brave in the presence of this formidable woman. "I believe I have taken the measure of your husband and your younger son, and I can quite confidently state that they are both of mischievous dispositions. They may have told you falsehoods for the simple enjoyment of seeing you shocked by my impertinence."

Though Georgiana's eyes widened at the playful way in which Elizabeth spoke to her aunt, Anne and Lady Susan both laughed. "Now, there is the impertinence I have been told to expect. And it quite as delightful as I suspected it would be!"

"She is a treasure, is she not, Aunt?" asked Anne.

"I can imagine how she livened your life, Anne," replied Lady Susan with evident affection. Then she became serious again. "And I would like to second my husband's apology to you, Anne, for not recognizing the situation and rescuing you. It appears we have much for which to atone."

"Nonsense, Aunt," replied Anne, and the level look Lady Susan gave her suggested that she had never heard Anne speak in such a tone before. "I will tell you what I told my uncle—there is nothing to forgive. I did not even know that I wished to be rescued until Elizabeth showed me how to live."

"Still, it was unconscionable of us." Lady Susan's voice brooked no opposition. "In any case, I believe it is in our power to begin to make amends for our oversight and, indeed, to repay Miss Bennet in some small way."

Before the lady could continue, the door to the sitting-room opened and the housekeeper entered with Jane following behind. She entered and saw Lady Susan, and her face immediately assumed a rosy hue, suggesting embarrassment.

"Jane!" cried Elizabeth, rising and going to her sister, catching her hands. "I am so happy to see you!"

There must have been something in her tone which was different, for Jane cast her a questioning glance, eyes searching Elizabeth's for some explanation. She soon remembered her manners, for she turned to Anne, who had also risen and approached.

"I apologize, Anne—I did not know you were to have visitors today, or I would not have come."

Anne greeted Jane warmly. "Of course, you did not, and you would not have been admitted today, were you not welcome. Come in, Jane, for I should like to introduce you to my aunt."

Jane seemed to understand Anne's meaning, for she paled at the mention of an aunt, though she allowed herself to be led forward. Anne again provided the introductions, and Lady Susan declared herself delighted to make Jane's acquaintance.

"I believe I have heard of you as well, my dear," said Lady Susan, "though my intelligence has only been gained today from Anne and Georgiana. But I am happy to make your acquaintance, as I understand you have become a friend of my nieces."

"And I am happy to make yours," said Jane, speaking quietly as was her wont. "But I think it is Lizzy who has been of great service, to Anne, in particular."

"You are correct." Rather than continue in that vein, Lady Susan seemed to understand the need to change the subject, which she did. "If you will forgive my saying so, though, there is something in the shape of your jaws which suggests familiarity, I might never have thought you sisters. You do not look at all alike."

"Aunt!" protested Anne, but Elizabeth and Jane only shared a smile.

"We have often heard others say the same thing, Lady Susan," replied Elizabeth. "My youngest and eldest siblings resemble each other closely, while we middle three are quite unlike them, though we look like each other."

Lady Susan turned a knowing smile on Mr. Darcy. "That is like your mother and Lady Catherine. Those who were introduced to them could hardly believe that they were related, let alone sisters."

"My mother was slight and blonde," said Mr. Darcy to Jane and Elizabeth. "Georgiana resembles her closely. Lady Catherine is both much larger of stature, dark of hair, and her face does not resemble my mother's at all."

The conversation continued for some moments, and Elizabeth looked on with interest. It seemed like Lady Susan was much more open than Lady Catherine could claim, though Elizabeth suspected that she could be as imperious as Anne's mother. She was friendly and kind, though, two attributes which could not be ascribed to Lady Catherine.

"Miss Bennet, Miss Elizabeth," said Lady Susan at length, "the purpose for my call today was to meet you, though of course I had no notion of meeting you here, Miss Bennet. One of my closest friends, a Lady Harriet, is to host a ball. I am certain Darcy has already received an invitation, and I would like you all to attend, though I suspect he was thinking of declining it."

Mr. Darcy smiled at her words, which were accompanied by a raised eyebrow. "It is likely among the invitations my butler sets out for me, though I have not yet seen it."

"Then you must accept it, Darcy, for everyone in your house, as well as Miss Bennet." Lady Susan turned back to the younger ladies. "I understand you have attended some events these past days since you have arrived in London?"

"I have," replied Elizabeth, intrigued by the welcome and acceptance she received from this woman. "But Jane has been staying with my uncle, and other than a few occasions in which we have met for outings, I do not think Jane has had much opportunity to attend."

"No, I have not," replied Jane. "Please do not feel obliged to include me in the invitation, Lady Susan. Elizabeth is staying with Mr. Darcy — I am only staying with my aunt."

"Oh, I absolutely insist! It is the least I can do." Lady Susan leaned in toward them, showing them a playful grin. "In fact, though Lady Harriet is everything that is lovely, I find most of those who consider themselves to be of high society to be absolute bores. I am sure your presence will make it much more interesting.

"Now," continued the lady, "it is apparent to me that you both dress well, according to your station and situation, and my nieces inform me that you have attended at least one ball, and certain other events. This, however, will be a formal ball, and as such, you will require formal wear of a type you likely have not seen before in your home society. We shall need to shop before the night of the ball, and as it is merely two weeks away we shall be required to do it quickly."

"I am not sure —"

"It will do you no good to try to gainsay me, Miss Elizabeth," replied Lady Susan, and though her voice was firm, the wink she directed at Elizabeth suggested that at least some of her firmness was nothing more than jesting. But Elizabeth did not think they would be able to wriggle out of it either. "We shall go to my modiste to have some appropriate gowns made up for you."

"Elizabeth has already met Madam Fournier, Aunt!" said Georgiana, as she bounced with excitement.

"She has?" asked Lady Susan, turning her gaze on Elizabeth with some interest.

"We had some new gowns made up when we first came to London," replied Anne. "Elizabeth had a few made, but I had little appropriate for society in London."

"I am shocked," murmured Lady Susan in a dry tone. The other ladies laughed.

"Then it is well that she already knows you, Miss Elizabeth," continued Lady Susan.

"She also knows Elizabeth's uncle!"

"Oh?" asked, Lady Susan, turning back to Georgiana, her eyes demanding the story. Georgiana was only too happy to oblige.

"That is quite interesting, indeed," said Lady Susan. She turned back to Elizabeth and Jane. "Do you think your uncle would mind if we visited his warehouses again?" Lady Susan chuckled. "If we could dress you in something spectacular, I am certain it would cause great jealousy in the ladies present. It would turn their thoughts from questions of your origins to your dresses." The lady smiled kindly. "I am certain you are already aware that many look down on those who do not normally attend the season in London. If we can distract them, it would be to your benefit."

"I did not receive any negative attention when I attended the last ball with Mr. Darcy," protested Elizabeth.

"But that was given by my friend's wife, and those who were invited were well known to him," interjected Mr. Darcy. "Lady Susan is quite right. Though your comportment is exemplary, you can hardly hope to avoid impertinent questions, especially from some of those who will attend a ball that Lady Harriet Greenwood hosts, for there will be a much greater variety of people there."

"I am certain my uncle will oblige us," said Jane.

"Excellent. Now, Miss Bennet, if you will speak to your uncle and send a note to your sister to confirm, I would be much obliged. We can then make our plans for our outing. We should not leave it too long, as we must allow time for Madam Fournier to finish our dresses, but a few days should do no harm."

Thus, it was settled. For her part, Elizabeth decided there was no need to continue her protestations, for it appeared like Lady Susan was as accustomed to having her own way as Lady Catherine was.

When her aunt left Darcy house that day, Anne was left with a little bemusement at the expression on the Bennet sisters' faces. Jane, it was clear, had never met someone so forceful as the countess and was taken aback. For Elizabeth's part, Anne thought she was bursting at the seams to make some witty comment. She did not disappoint.

"Your aunt is as much of a force of nature as your mother, is she not?"

"Lizzy!" gasped Jane, turning a censorious look on her sister. Anne, however, just laughed.

"Indeed, she is. But Aunt Susan is much more diplomatic and much less forceful about it than my mother." Anne paused and attempted to give the impression of deep thought—Jane watched her, seeming almost fearful of what she would say, while Elizabeth was not fooled in the slightest. Instead, she watched Anne with amused anticipation.

"In fact, one might almost suggest the difference between them to be Aunt Susan's conviction that she is assisting and doing her best to make others happy—my mother possesses the same conviction, but in her meddling, it does not concern her if those she is 'helping' are made happy in the process."

"Oh, Anne," said Mr. Darcy, shaking his head. His tone might have suggested displeasure, but Anne was certain he was feeling more than a little enjoyment in their banter.

It was clear that Jane did not quite know how to respond, and though Georgiana knew both women intimately, Anne thought it was beyond her to direct any criticism at either. Elizabeth, though was diverted by the hint of sardonic amusement in Anne's observations. And well she should be—Elizabeth was responsible for it, to a certain extent.

"You must not listen to us, Miss Bennet," said Anne. "I *am* still fond of my mother, though considering her behavior, I am not certain she deserves it. My characterization of her is not far off the mark."

"I hope you are reconciled with her someday," replied Jane.

"Thank you," replied Anne. She attempted to give every indication of sanguinity, but inside she was feeling a hint of gloom—she hoped very much her mother would eventually bend her stiff neck, for Anne had no desire to be estranged from her forever.

It was not long before Jane took her leave, and Anne expressed her pleasure at the prospect of seeing her again for dinner only a few days later. At the same time, Georgiana was called away by Mrs. Annesley to spend the rest of the morning in her studies.

"You have invited the Gardiners to dinner again?" asked Darcy, turning his gaze on Anne with mild interest.

"Yes, we have," replied Anne, keeping her voice as nonchalant as she could. "I enjoy their company, and Elizabeth has not had much chance to see her relations. I know you and Fitzwilliam enjoy Mr. Gardiner's company as well."

"We do, indeed," replied Darcy. "I shall be happy to continue my acquaintance with them."

This last he said with a smile at Elizabeth, which was returned in full—one of the first true, warm smiles Anne had ever seen Elizabeth direct at him, though she had been warming to him of late. It was time, Anne decided, to test Darcy's newfound complacency.

"In fact, since we have so many good friends nearby," said Anne, "I took the liberty of inviting Mr. Bingley and his family to dine with us as well. I am quite certain we will be a merry party, indeed."

Anne was quite impressed with her cousin. Darcy did not bat an eyelash, did not so much as blink when she informed him of her plans. What he was thinking, she was not certain, but she thought there was a measure of trepidation in the depths of his eyes.

"The Bingleys?" asked he. "I was not aware you were well acquainted with my friend's sisters, Anne."

"I do not know about *well* acquainted," replied Anne, shrugging at his words. "But you are aware Miss Bingley and Mrs. Hurst came to visit us more than a week ago." Darcy nodded, a little tightly, Anne noticed. "We had an interesting visit, indeed. And then, of course, Miss Bingley visited again the next day, an unlooked-for bit of civility on her part, I assure you."

Anne turned to Elizabeth and winked, and she was gratified when Elizabeth attempted to stifle a giggle. "Did I inform you of Miss Bingley's response to our invitation?"

"Ah, no, Anne, I do not believe you did."

"She seems to think that I have come to her way of thinking," replied Anne.

It was with a great deal of satisfaction that Anne turned to Darcy after she said this, as she had known he would speak up.

"I am sorry, Anne, but you have confused me. You have come to Miss Bingley's way of thinking? To what do you refer?"

"Only that Miss Bingley thinks that I should not have Elizabeth staying here, for she is far too provincial and has misrepresented herself to me."

"Miss Bingley said that to you?" asked Darcy. By this time, he was frowning, his attention turning away from how they would be hosting the Bingleys and the Gardiners at the same time, just as she had intended.

"Not in so many words, I assure you," replied Anne. "But when she came back the next day, it was to make sure I knew of Elizabeth's common origins, the baseness of her character, and the grasping nature of her association with me."

"I fail to see how it is Miss Bingley's concern, even if such charges were true." Darcy turned to Elizabeth and his countenance softened. "It is clear to anyone with eyes to see and wit to understand that Miss Bennet has added immeasurably to our family party. Even if her accusations were true, it is not Miss Bingley's place to say anything."

"I disabused her of that notion quite firmly, Cousin. But it does not change the fact that she came here, filled with stories of Elizabeth's behavior and charges against her character. I dare say she felt assured of the success of her mission." Anne paused and laughed. "In fact, I wonder if she was considering whether I was a good marriage prospect for her brother, for Georgiana, though she is your sister, is still quite young, whereas I am of marriageable age."

Darcy started at the notion, but Elizabeth only giggled and exclaimed: "You may not be far from the truth, Anne. She *did* make it quite clear in her letter to Jane that *she*, at least, expected a *very* close connection between Mr. Bingley and Georgiana in the future. As Mr. Darcy's cousin, you might fill that role admirably and bring her much closer to her own ambitions."

"She said that in a letter to your sister?" asked Darcy, a hint of hysteria entering his voice.

"She did," replied Elizabeth. She had noted what Anne had and was diverted by it, Anne was certain.

"Then I apologize, Miss Bennet. She informed me only that she had written your sister to advise her of our return to London—nothing more. What she states of my sister is most emphatically not true. *If* Bingley and Georgiana were to form an attachment sometime in the future, I would welcome the connection to my dearest friend, but at present she is much too young."

Elizabeth was silent for a few moments, her gaze fixed on Darcy—he seemed to feel it, as Anne sensed more than a hint of nervousness in his manner.

"It is not your fault, Mr. Darcy," replied Elizabeth, though her voice was quiet. "Jane was . . . hurt by Miss Bingley's callousness, and even more so when she visited Miss Bingley when she came to London, and Miss Bingley only returned it after three weeks."

"That is not proper at all, Miss Elizabeth," said Darcy. "Your sister has my sympathies." He paused for a moment, apparently in thought, before he once again fixed his attentions on Elizabeth. "Pardon me for asking such an impertinent question, Miss Bennet, but your sister—she esteems Mr. Bingley?"

"More than any other man of her acquaintance, Mr. Darcy," replied Elizabeth.

Darcy nodded, but it was distracted and thoughtful, and he did not say anything more. For her part, Elizabeth did not say much more herself, and after a few moments, she excused herself to return to her room, leaving Anne behind with Darcy. Initially when she had brought up this subject, Anne had thought Darcy would fight her over her plans for the evening with their friends. But she was certain he would only put up a token resistance now, if that at all.

"I assume this dinner of yours was carefully planned out," said Darcy when Elizabeth had left the room.

"It was," replied Anne, "but not in the manner you think."

Darcy raised an eyebrow, demanding an explanation, and Anne was only too willing to provide it. "The evening was *my* idea and my execution. Elizabeth has known of it, but she only agreed to it after much persuasion."

"That I can well imagine," replied Darcy. "As protective of her sister as she is, I do not doubt she would hesitate before putting her before a man who hurt her so."

"Yes, that is exactly it."

A shake of his head and Darcy focused again on Anne. "I am not certain I agree with your meddling."

"What of *your* meddling?" demanded Anne.

Darcy paled and Anne gave him a grim nod. "Yes, Cousin, I am aware of the role you played in separating Jane and Mr. Bingley. Miss Bingley was eager to crow of it and use it to attempt to persuade me to her point of view. You should be grateful that Elizabeth knows nothing of it. I do not need to describe her probable reaction to the knowledge, should she ever become aware of it."

"Indeed, you do not." Darcy's words were so quiet as to be almost inaudible. "I only thought Miss Bennet did not care for Mr. Bingley as a woman should for a prospective suitor and would accept him for no other reason than that her mother would demand it of her."

That suggestion was worthy of nothing more than a derisive snort from Anne, which she hesitated not to give. "Miss Bennet may appear complying, Darcy, but she is not. In her own way, she possesses a similar measure of strength as Elizabeth. Were you aware that Elizabeth refused Mr. Collins when he proposed?"

Anne almost laughed at the expression of utter horror which came over her cousin. "Mr. Collins?" choked he.

"Yes. *That* Mr. Collins. But Elizabeth refused him and was supported by her father. Elizabeth and Jane have pledged to each other not to marry without love. Elizabeth could not respect Mr. Collins, let alone love him. Given such knowledge, can you imagine Miss Bennet would be coerced into marrying Mr. Bingley if she did not wish it?"

"When you put it that way, it *does* sound silly."

It was the humble way in which Darcy responded which defused

Anne's annoyance.

"There is no way you could have known of their pact, Darcy. It is easy to misread another's character, especially when that person is as closed as Miss Bennet. In the future, I would suggest that you reserve judgment and allow others to make their own decisions without interference.

"And before you say it," said Anne, pre-empting his argument, "the dinner has not been designed to throw Mr. Bingley and Jane together, manipulating them into making a match. I am much more interested in Jane's happiness. We are merely creating a situation whereby his *sisters'* manipulations may be defeated, and they can find their own way without others meddling in their lives. Once they are together in this room, the rest will be up to them."

"Very well," said Darcy. He rose to depart, but before he left the room, he turned and said: "And it was very sage advice you gave me a moment ago, Cousin. You may be assured I will follow it."

Then Darcy let himself out of the room, leaving Anne satisfied. Everything was proceeding according to plan.

Chapter XXVI

It had become clear to Elizabeth that her friend, Anne de Bourgh, was rather devious. Loath though Elizabeth to use such a word to describe a dear friend—which often carried negative connotations—it was no less than the truth. And the night of the dinner with both the Bingley and Gardiner parties more than amply proved this. The first piece of evidence was, of course, the times she gave the two parties.

"Your family will soon be here," said Anne, her voice alive with excitement. "I believe we can expect the Bingley party soon after."

"Miss Bingley will, indeed, wish to make an entrance," replied Elizabeth, amused by her friend's excitement. "No doubt she believes it to be the height of proper behavior to arrive fashionably late."

Anne laughed. "I am sure you are correct. But I have ensured it, for I have given Miss Bingley a time fifteen minutes later than that which I gave your aunt."

"Why?" asked Elizabeth, shocked at her friend's manipulations.

"Because I wish for Jane and the Gardiners to be settled here when Mr. Bingley arrives. It gives the impression, with Jane and the Gardiners already present, that it is *the Bingleys* who are the ones visiting and put the Gardiners at an implied higher level. That is key, not only for Mr. Bingley's perception of Jane, but also for Miss Bingley, though I am sure the woman will miss the subtlety."

"Anne," said Elizabeth in a warning tone, "there was to be no manipulations. I do not wish for Jane's feelings to be bruised again."

"And they will not," replied Anne, the firmness in her tone allowing for now disagreement. "I will do nothing where the two of them are concerned, but can you imagine how Miss Bingley would behave if they were to arrive before your family."

"I can well imagine it," replied Elizabeth with a shake of her head.

"Exactly. Trust me, Elizabeth—I only mean to make it as easy as possible for Jane and her beau."

There was nothing to be said, so Elizabeth kept her peace, though she regarded Anne for some time, watchful for her friend's *other* manipulations, of which she was certain would be many. In due course, the Gardiner party did arrive—met at the door by both Anne and Elizabeth—and were welcomed with their usual anticipation. Mr. Gardiner immediately stood with Mr. Darcy and Colonel Fitzwilliam, and they began to speak, while Anne guided Jane to a nearby position where there were two chairs in close proximity. Elizabeth sat with Georgiana and Mrs. Gardiner, keeping a close eye on Anne, while noting her easy conversation with Jane.

"Is it my imagination, Lizzy," whispered Mrs. Gardiner after a few moments, "or is there something about which you are worried tonight?"

"Worried, no," replied Elizabeth shortly. "But I believe Anne is being clever, and I do not wish for anything to go wrong."

"Clever? In what way?"

Elizabeth would have wished to forgo any discussion of the night's imminent entertainment, but she knew her aunt would likely be cross if she did not warn her in advance. Thus, Elizabeth screwed up her courage and replied.

"You are not to be the only guests tonight. Anne has also invited the Bingley party to dine with us."

Though her eyes widened in response, Mrs. Gardiner essayed a look at Anne, her expression unreadable. For her part, Anne seemed to possess some sort of preternatural notion of what they were discussing, and while Jane was saying something to her, Anne returned Mrs. Gardiner's gaze and responded with a deliberate wink. Mrs. Gardiner could not contain her laughter.

"What a friend you have managed to make, Lizzy!" said Aunt Gardiner. "I never would have suspected this of her."

"Nor would I," replied Elizabeth. She turned to her aunt and said: "I assume Jane still pines after Mr. Bingley?"

"I do not know that 'pine' is precisely the proper word, Lizzy. I am certain she still considers him to be the best man of her acquaintance, but her demeanor has improved substantially since you have come to town. I do not doubt she will be grateful to accept whatever attention he decides to bestow on her." Mrs. Gardiner's gaze swung away from Anne, and Elizabeth felt a faintly severe quality inherent in it. "The unknown in all this is Mr. Bingley. Can I assume you have some indication of his regard? I know you would not wish to injure your sister."

"Nothing obvious," confessed Elizabeth. "But the fact that Miss Bingley has kept her brother away, even to the point of avoiding the same events we have attended, seems telling."

"Might that not be coincidence?"

"I suppose it might. But I do not think it is."

Mrs. Gardiner observed Elizabeth for several more moments before she sighed and turned her attention back to Jane. "I hope it is not, Lizzy. But I will trust you. It seems there is little to be done regardless."

Elizabeth agreed and fell silent, watching the room with care, wondering if they had not made a large mistake in planning this evening. When, at length, the Bingley party did arrive, Jane and the Gardiners had settled in and were speaking with pleasant friendship among themselves, and though they had been a little fluid in their positions and conversations, Anne had stuck close to Jane's side.

The Bingleys' arrival time of thirty minutes after the Gardiners' was not missed by either Anne or Elizabeth, and they shared a look and rolled eyes at Miss Bingley's predictability. They were met at the front of the house by the housekeeper—another manipulation of Anne's—and soon they were shown into the room. The first of the party—Miss Bingley herself—entered the room, a compliment already on the tip of her tongue.

"Miss de Bourgh, we are so happy to be with you tonight," purred Miss Bingley as she stepped into the room. That was, of course, when she noticed those others present, and the color drained from her face like rouge on a woman's cheeks washed away by tears.

"I say, Caroline, why have you stopped in the middle of the doorway?"

When the masculine voice spoke behind her, Miss Bingley's eyes widened in terror, and for a moment, Elizabeth wondered if the woman would attempt to physically prevent her brother from entering the room.

"Come, Caroline, let us enter," came Mr. Bingley's voice again. "I have not seen much of Darcy in the time since we have been back in London."

A grimace settled over Miss Bingley's face, but she did not protest. She stepped forward as if she was meeting a firing squad and turned a glare on Elizabeth, as if it was her fault. Elizabeth only smiled sweetly at her, which further seemed to fuel the woman's anger.

"Darcy!" said Mr. Bingley, stepping into the room with his usual wide grin affixed. "I do not believe I have ever come to town without visiting you for this length of time. How —"

And that was, of course, the exact moment when Mr. Bingley noticed Elizabeth seated close by. He stopped, shocked, his mouth agape, and he blurted: "Miss Elizabeth!" Then, as he moved to greet her, he caught sight of Jane sitting demurely next to Anne. Had Elizabeth not known her sister, she might have thought Jane was terrified of the amiable man. "Miss Bennet!"

Anne rose and approached Mr. Bingley, and she curtseyed to them all — Miss Bingley was still behind her brother, and Mr. and Mrs. Hurst had entered and were watching with something akin to astonishment. "Welcome to Darcy's home. Elizabeth, would you do me the honor of introducing these two gentlemen?" asked Anne, mimicking her words and actions from the first visit Mrs. Hurst and Miss Bingley had made to the house.

"Of course, Anne," said Elizabeth, as she stood and stepped forward to do the honors.

It was clear from Mr. Bingley's demeanor that he was barely aware of her presence. He bowed to Anne's curtsey and spoke to Elizabeth, but as he did so his eyes slid to Jane of their own accord.

"Miss Elizabeth, I am surprised to see you here. I had no notion you would be at Darcy's house tonight, for Caroline did not drop a word of it."

"I am quite as surprised as you, Charles," interjected Miss Bingley's acid tone.

"I have actually been staying at Mr. Darcy's house for some weeks, Mr. Bingley," replied Elizabeth. "I met Anne in Kent and spent some time with her there, before we came to London and Mr. Darcy's house."

"And your sister?" asked Mr. Bingley, his attention now firmly fixed on Jane who blushed and looked down at the hands folded in her lap.

"Jane is staying with my Aunt and Uncle Gardiner," replied Elizabeth. "We have seen much of them since our arrival, however, for which I am grateful. You see, I have been separated from her for some months now."

"Separated?" asked Mr. Bingley, clearly confused.

"Perhaps it would be best to ask Jane yourself," suggested Anne, gesturing toward the chair by Jane which was now empty. "I am certain she would be happy to explain it to you."

Elizabeth frowned at Anne, thinking she was pushing a little more than Elizabeth might have wished, but Mr. Bingley looked at Anne for several moments before nodding. "I believe I would like that very much."

He took himself to Jane's side and sat in the chair, but for a few moments, neither seemed to know quite what to say. Elizabeth watched them with dread, wondering if they would ever work up the courage to speak. Anne, however, only regarded them, complacency in her demeanor. And she was correct—though it took them a few moments to begin speaking, soon they had their heads together and were talking with as much animation as Elizabeth had ever seen in all the times they had been together in Hertfordshire.

"You seem to have been correct, Lizzy," said Aunt Gardiner as Elizabeth sat down once again beside her. "I have rarely seen a man look on a woman with such devotion as Mr. Bingley. I knew the moment he entered the room that all would be well."

"I am glad you had such confidence, Aunt," replied Elizabeth. "I will own to more trepidation."

"Well, if we can keep his sister from interfering, I dare say they shall have their happy ending."

It was a valid concern. Miss Bingley had taken a seat not far from Jane and Mr. Bingley, next to her sister, and she watched the absorbed couple, fuming and disgusted. She made every attempt to hamper their discussion, but when she would say something, both other parties would listen politely, but return to their conversation immediately.

"How wonderful it is to see you, Miss Bennet," said she. "I had no notion you would be here tonight."

"Nor I you, Miss Bingley," replied Jane.

"It seems like Miss de Bourgh planned a larger gathering than either of you had anticipated," replied Mr. Bingley. "I, for one, could not be happier."

Jane blushed while Miss Bingley colored, but Mr. Bingley did not notice, as he had already turned to Jane to speak to her again. For a few moments, Miss Bingley watched them with anger before trying again.

"How long will you be in London, Miss Bennet?"

"Our plans are not fixed, but I do not think it will be much longer. Both Lizzy and I have been from home for some time now, and our father is eager for us to return."

"I see," said Miss Bingley, a slow smile spreading over her face. "And your family and all your *sisters*—they are quite well? I seem to remember their fascination with the officers—I do hope they are still . . . eager for their acquaintance."

"Not having been home in some time I cannot speak with any accuracy," replied Jane, parrying Miss Bingley's attack. "But by all accounts, they are all well, though I have heard that the officers are to decamp for Brighton for the summer."

"That is a *great* pity," sneered Miss Bingley.

"You are to return to Longbourn?" asked Mr. Bingley, focusing on what, to him, must have been the more important subject.

"Indeed, we are," replied Jane. Her sad smile seemed to suggest that she was not confident of his reaction.

"Then that is quite agreeable, indeed!" exclaimed Mr. Bingley. "I do not know of anyone who likes to be in London for the summer. As I have an estate I have leased and have not been to in some time, it is the perfect time for us to retire to the country as well."

The smile ran away from Miss Bingley's face, and her distress was in reverse proportion to Jane's growing happiness. "You are to go to Hertfordshire this summer?" asked Jane, her voice alive with hope.

"Of course," replied Mr. Bingley, the firmness in his tone greater than any Elizabeth had ever heard from the man. "Certain . . . other circumstances have kept me from Hertfordshire these past months, but I have known few happier times than last autumn when we were all there together. I will be very happy to be among the good people of Meryton again."

"Charles," said Miss Bingley, a hint of desperation in her tone, "perhaps—"

"No, Caroline, my decision has been made," replied Mr. Bingley. "I have leased Netherfield and have not been there for some months now. It is time to resume my responsibilities." Mr. Bingley turned back to Jane with a look of infinite tenderness. "If Miss Bennet is to be there as well, that is simply fortunate for me."

Miss Bingley subsided, but not with any grace that Elizabeth could detect. She watched them with annoyance mixed with dread, but when she caught Elizabeth's eyes, her look became one of pure poison.

They went into dinner soon after, and again Elizabeth was heartened by the way that Mr. Bingley insisted upon escorting Jane to dinner, despite whatever protocol dictated, leaving his brother-in-law to escort Anne, while Mr. Darcy escorted Mrs. Hurst. The others all paired up according to their various rankings, but the one who caught Elizabeth's eye was Colonel Fitzwilliam. It was clear that even though he did not know the extent of the histories which were playing out before him, he knew that something was afoot, and he delighted in it accordingly.

"It seems my cousin has done some scheming, Miss Elizabeth," said he as he escorted Elizabeth and Georgiana into the dining room.

"Indeed, she has," replied Elizabeth.

Colonel Fitzwilliam snorted. "I would never have thought she had it in her. I am now wondering if I was too hasty in declaiming any interest in pursuing her as a marriage partner."

Curious, Elizabeth eyed the colonel, not having heard any suggestion of any kind of an attachment between Colonel Fitzwilliam and Anne, but as he did not venture to clarify his remarks, Elizabeth would not ask impertinent questions.

It was after dinner in the music room when Miss Bingley was afforded the opportunity to vent her spleen. Elizabeth and Miss Bingley had taken their turns at the pianoforte—Georgiana could not be prevailed upon to do so, primarily, Elizabeth thought, because of the presence of the Bingley sisters. Jane and Mr. Bingley were seated together again, neither with any attention to spare for anyone else in the room, when Miss Bingley approached Elizabeth and Anne where they were sitting together. Her tone was waspish when she spoke, and Elizabeth was assaulted with the image of a snake, hissing its warning for those unfortunate enough to have crossed its path.

"Miss de Bourgh!" exclaimed she, though in a voice low and cross. "I thought we had come to an agreement. How could you have betrayed me by bringing Miss Bennet again to my brother's attention?"

"What agreement do you call it, Miss Bingley?" asked Anne. Though she asked her question with the razor's edge of displeasure, Elizabeth could tell that she was, in actuality, diverted.

Miss Bingley's lips tightened, and she forced her reply out from between them. "I can see that Miss Eliza has poisoned you against me. I cannot think your lady mother would be happy with your association with the Bennets."

"She would be much less happy with my association with *you*, Miss Bingley."

Miss Bingley gasped, but Anne only regarded her placidly. She had not raised her voice, had shown no signs of displeasure, though her reply certainly suggested it.

"Miss Bingley, let me say that you saw only what you wanted to see. Never did I say that I was willing to throw off the friendship of my dearest companion."

"You implied it," snapped the other woman.

"You were eager to believe any such implication, and this after I told you quite firmly and openly that I was not about to be swayed. If you believed it, then you must have wished violently for it."

Though she clearly wanted to say something further to Anne, Miss Bingley instead chose to focus her vitriol on Elizabeth.

"I suppose you are feeling rather smug in your success, Eliza. You have turned my brother against me, and you think, no doubt, that you have been successful in ensnaring him for your insipid sister. But I am not beaten yet."

"Actually," replied Elizabeth, "I am quite happy for Jane, for I do not think your brother could find a better wife. Of course, I shall have to counsel her to think carefully before she accepts him—socially, it will be a clear step down for her, as he *is* the son of a tradesman. She *is* a gentleman's daughter, after all."

Miss Bingley's eyes bulged at Elizabeth, and Elizabeth wondered if the woman would suffer an apoplexy right there in Darcy's house.

"But love will conquer all, I suppose," continued Elizabeth. "If Jane loves him—a sentiment I have no doubt is returned—then I will advise her to allow her heart free rein. There is nothing to be prized more in marriage than a meeting of like hearts and minds."

"You are a simpleton!" cried Miss Bingley. "I have never heard such drivel."

"Clearly your brother does not agree," said Anne. "In fact, he seems to be quite taken with Jane. And I agree with Elizabeth—I doubt your brother could find a better wife."

Miss Bingley swallowed heavily and turned a sickly smile on Anne. "Perhaps you should speak with your cousin. I have it on good authority that Georgiana thinks more highly of my brother than any other man of her acquaintance."

Unable to help themselves, Elizabeth and Anne exchanged glances and burst into laughter, drawing more than one pair of eyes to them. Mr. Bingley, in particular, smiled, seeming delighted at how his sister was getting on with them. He could not have been more wrong.

"You are sorely mistaken, Miss Bingley," replied Anne. "Georgiana is too young, and she has told me that she enjoys Mr. Bingley's company for the pleasure he brings to her elder brother. She is not in love with him."

There appeared to be nothing more to say. Miss Bingley excused herself and went to sit by her sister on the bench of the pianoforte. Though Mrs. Hurst continued to play, Miss Bingley whispered her poisonous nothings in her sister's ear. Elizabeth did not know what they were saying, but she was certain that now that Jane was before Mr. Bingley, they would not be successful in their schemes again.

It would not be surprising to anyone that Darcy had not anticipated the evening, not knowing what would happen between Miss Bennet and Bingley. Darcy had not been convinced of Miss Bennet's regard for his friend, regardless of what Anne and Miss Elizabeth had told him. But after seeing them together, he could not help but wonder how he could have missed it.

"Do not mope, Darcy," said Fitzwilliam by his side. "Just enjoy the spectacle."

Darcy turned and glared at his cousin. "Were you also aware of this in advance?"

"If you mean Anne's obvious machinations, then no. I also was not aware of the situation between Bingley and Miss Bennet, though I do applaud Anne for her ingenuity. She out-maneuvered Miss Bingley quite spectacularly."

There was nothing to say to that, so Darcy did not even make the attempt. What was more surprising to him was how Miss Bingley clearly thought she could influence him to continue to try to separate Bingley from Miss Bennet.

"Mr. Darcy!" hissed she as she came and stood by him a little later that evening. "I am so distressed at your cousin's actions this evening. Did you not inform her what a mistake it would be to bring Charles and Miss Bennet together again?"

"No, I did not, Miss Bingley," replied Darcy, eschewing any mention of how he had not even known of it himself, aware it would only make him appear foolish. "Anne has been acting as my hostess and, as such, may invite whomever she pleases."

"She has been listening to Eliza too much. Clearly the girl has filled her ears with nonsense. Having the Bennets as relations? It is not to be borne!"

Again, Darcy chose not to reply to her assertion. In fact, he chose not to reply at all. He was, after all, intent upon making those same Bennets *his* relations.

"I am afraid your assistance is going to be more critical than ever now."

"Assistance?" echoed Darcy. "I am afraid I have no notion of what you speak."

Darcy had never seen the exasperation in the woman's glance directed at *him*. "To separate Charles from Jane Bennet again!" Miss Bingley's eyes found Miss Elizabeth, and Darcy was certain she was wishing all manner of calamities on her head. "Look at her, sitting there so smugly, assured of her success, not giving any thought to the ruin of *my family*. How I wish I had never heard the name Bennet!"

Contrary to Miss Bingley's assertions, Darcy could see little other than pleasure in Elizabeth's face as she spoke with animation with Georgiana. She had been a good influence on his dearest sister—Darcy hardly knew how to thank her for bringing Georgiana out of her shell.

"But with your assistance," continued Miss Bingley, turning back to Darcy, "this may all be repaired. I will not have Jane Bennet as a sister—every proper feeling rebels against it."

"I thought you esteemed Miss Bennet," said Darcy, knowing it was untrue.

The woman made a growling sound in her throat. "Jane is, by herself, tolerable. But her family." Disgust rolled off the woman in waves. "I shall not have it!"

"If your brother decides he will marry Miss Bennet, you *shall* have it," replied Darcy. He was at the end of his patience with this woman.

Once again Miss Bingley turned her attention to him. "But you can influence him—I am sure of it. He always listens to you."

"He did when he was uncertain of Miss Bennet's regard," replied Darcy. "Now, I would think no such doubt exists. Furthermore, since *I* am now convinced of it, I will not say anything against his intentions for her. It was the only reason I agreed with you last time."

"But, Mr. Darcy!"

"No, Miss Bingley," replied Darcy. "I will not do it. My only wish is for Bingley to be happy. He is his own man and may make his own decisions. If Miss Bennet is his choice, I will do nothing but wish him every happiness."

Then, certain she was not about to allow the subject to rest, Darcy bowed and moved away. Miss Bingley did not follow him, and for that he was grateful. He had no doubt she would continue to work on her brother, and Darcy, knowing Bingley as he did, had little notion she would be successful. For himself, he was through trying to advise his friend. Not only had he been spectacularly wrong, he knew that Miss Elizabeth wished for her sister's happiness with Bingley. That was enough for Darcy.

When the night was late and the guests were soon to depart, it was left to Hurst to sum up the evening and the previous relationship between the two principles. He had watched them with an almost un-Hurst-like amusement, if one was not familiar with the man and his enjoyment of tweaking his sister's nose. As the night wore on, Darcy began to suspect he would not leave without saying something pointed. In this, Darcy proved to be correct.

"It is about time, Bingley," said Hurst in his rumbling voice which, unusually, carried no hint of being intoxicated. "You have been moping over the girl all winter. It is time you married her and spent the rest of your life happy."

Though it was clear Bingley was shocked at his brother's words, he quickly agreed with them. "Thank you, Hurst—I believe I shall take your advice under consideration."

Miss Bennet blushed, but the way she looked back at Bingley showed she was not displeased. Anything but, in fact.

Chapter XXVII

An expected visitor returned to Darcy house the following morning, and Darcy was not eager to receive him. The previous night at dinner, Bingley had been first surprised by Miss Bennet's presence, and then his attention fixed on her to the exclusion of all else. But Darcy knew that Bingley would realize by the light of day that Darcy must have some knowledge of Miss Bennet's presence in town and would wish to know why Darcy had not mentioned it to him.

And Darcy was correct. The Bingley that strode into his room the following morning had a bounce in his step, a joy in his countenance which had been missing these past months.

"Darcy!" exclaimed he, seeming more pleased to see him than Darcy would have expected. "It is a lovely day, is it not?"

While he restrained himself from shaking his head, Darcy was inordinately amused by what he was seeing. He was also feeling more than a little silly—he had thought that Bingley would overcome his infatuation, as he had so many other times with so many other ladies, but it was clear that Darcy was incorrect in this instance. Miss Bennet's performance from the previous evening, given without any idea that Bingley would be present, had given lie to all Darcy's opinions. He was grateful to be proven wrong, if the old Bingley was to once again make an appearance.

"It is, indeed, my friend," said Darcy, accepting his friend's proffered hand and gesturing to a pair of chairs to the side of his study.

"I am very grateful to you and your cousin, Darcy," said Bingley without preamble. "I do not know how an invitation including both my family and Miss Bennet's came about, but I am delighted regardless. I would never have thought that we would meet in London, in your house, of all places."

"I had considered it possible," confessed Darcy. "I had thought you would visit me before last night, and there was a good chance you would discover that Miss Elizabeth is staying here."

"Yes," replied Bingley. "In fact, I would wonder why you did not tell me of Miss Elizabeth's presence in your house. For that matter, might I assume you knew of Miss Jane Bennet's residence at her uncle's house?"

"I did," said Darcy. There was no point in obfuscating, and Darcy would not have done it even if he thought there was a chance of success. "The reason I did not tell you was because I was still laboring under the misapprehension that Miss Bennet did not care for you as a woman should for a suitor. After last night, it is quite apparent that I was wrong, and I apologize unreservedly for leading you astray."

Bingley regarded Darcy for several moments before he shrugged. "I do not hold it against you, Darcy. I remember well how you convinced me against returning and your reasons for it. You had not spent nearly so much time in her company as I and could not have seen her regard for yourself. Would that I had placed as much confidence in my own observations as I did in yours!

"But all has been put to right now, and I could not be happier. I have come today to let you know that I intend to pursue Miss Bennet. I will pay court to her, follow her to Hertfordshire, if necessary, and I intend to marry her."

"Then I congratulate you, my friend," replied Darcy. "I believe you will do well together."

Bingley paused and then spoke again, his tone far more sardonic than Darcy had ever heard from his friend before. "Do you know that Caroline does not agree with you? She actually continued to question Miss Bennet's feelings for me in the face of what I witnessed last night."

Darcy was far from surprised, but he did not respond directly to Bingley's question. "What of Mrs. Hurst? As I recall, she argued against Miss Bennet as vociferously as Miss Bingley."

A snort escaped Bingley's mouth. "And she likely would still, if not for Hurst. You heard Hurst last night—he has decided that I have been 'mooning after Jane Bennet' these past months. He further claims it is time for me to be happy, and that she is a 'damn fine girl.' I do not know for certain, but I suspect he has forbidden Louisa from attempting to work on me, as she was silent when we discussed it this morning." Bingley paused and laughed. "Can you imagine it? Caroline actually abjured town hours this morning and rose early, all in an attempt to persuade me."

Again, Darcy was not at all surprised, but he could hardly say so to his friend, so he remained silent.

"And Caroline was not content to simply cast aspersions on Miss Bennet's regard for me either. She brought out that old, tired argument about Miss Bennet's social standing and fortune, as if such things would sway me in the slightest, even if her concerns for Miss Bennet's social standing were at all correct."

"They *are* concerns," replied Darcy, feeling obligated to provide a little defense for the absent woman, little though she deserved it. When Bingley's jaw clenched with obstinacy, Darcy held out one hand in surrender. "I am aware that you are not concerned with such things, Bingley, but they should be a consideration in any decision you make—I am not trying to persuade you. I know that your sister sometimes . . . overestimates her position in society."

"That is an understatement," muttered Bingley.

"But she *is* correct about your position in society being affected by the woman you marry. Miss Bennet is unknown in town. A marriage to a woman of some standing would automatically help you be more accepted."

"If one could be convinced to marry me."

"I do not disagree. In addition to this, however, is Miss Bennet's lack of dowry. It will affect your ability to properly dower any daughters you have. However, if you have thought about these things and discarded them, then your sister should have nothing more to say. It is *your* choice, after all. She is dependent upon you—not the reverse."

The expression on Bingley's face became positively devilish. "The very point I made to her."

Darcy was impressed—Bingley had always been intent upon avoiding conflict. The knowledge of this facet of his character had made it easy for Miss Bingley to take far more liberties than she should.

"I informed her that if she did not like my choice of bride, she could live with the Hursts or move into her own establishment. Since Hurst informed her he would not have her poisonous attitude ruining the atmosphere in his home, her only option was her own establishment, which I have no doubt frightens her with thoughts of becoming a spinster. The other option—not an option to Caroline—is to go to our relations in the north. I think that notion frightens her even more."

"That is very well done, Bingley," replied Darcy.

"I knew you would approve. You have been telling me of the need to rein her in for years now, and I have finally seen that you are correct. Caroline will not impede my pursuit of Miss Bennet. If she attempts it, she will remove herself from my house."

"Then I wish you all the luck in the world, Bingley. You know your own mind and may make your own choices—no one else should factor into those decisions."

"And I do not mean to allow them to." Bingley rose. "I am off to the Gardiners' residence, the directions to which I obtained from Mr. Gardiner last night. I will ask Miss Bennet for a courtship this very day."

"That is rather precipitous, even for you, my friend," said Darcy with a laugh. Bingley did not hesitate to join him.

"Perhaps it is. But I do not wish for there to be any ambiguity in my attentions to Miss Bennet. Having been absent these past months, I want her to know that I am serious and that I will not be moved from my course."

After a few more words, Bingley departed, leaving a bemused Darcy standing, watching him go. After all these years of friendship with Bingley, of trying to induce him to seize the reins of his own life and ensure his sister did not rule over him as she sometimes did, it took the admiration of a good woman, now confirmed, to induce him to change. Darcy could not be any happier for his friend. Now it was time to turn his attention to his own happiness. With that in mind, he followed Bingley through the door of his study.

The gardens of Darcy house were the most tranquil location in which Elizabeth could sit and think, and she often took herself there when she was feeling introspective. The morning after the dinner party, Elizabeth had availed herself of the beauty of the small garden, and sat on the bench she favored, her eyes drinking in the sights which surrounded her, enjoying the buzzing of the bees and the chirping of birds.

The previous evening had been stressful, not knowing how Mr.

Bingley would act or whether she and Anne had done right in bringing him together with Jane again. After Mr. Bingley's display, however, Elizabeth could not be happier. It seemed her sister, after the months of heartache and despair, would obtain her heart's desire.

The one matter of which she remained uncertain was Mr. Darcy's reaction to what had happened. He had been quiet and thoughtful the previous evening, and Elizabeth had often seen his eyes on Jane and Mr. Bingley. But he was still difficult to understand; he might have been equally as capable of attempting to warn Mr. Bingley away from Jane as he was to throw his full support behind his friend's transparent attentions. Elizabeth was not certain which, as she was still uncertain of the role he had played in the separation in the first place.

These thoughts, spinning in Elizabeth's mind, were the reason she took a more contrary position when the man appeared in the garden, apparently looking for her, as had happened often of late. Elizabeth was determined to avoid questions concerning his intentions and, instead, focus on Jane and Mr. Bingley.

"Miss Bennet," said he as he approached. "I see you have found your way into the garden yet again."

"I find such places conducive to deep thought, Mr. Darcy," said Elizabeth, her words designed to pique his curiosity.

"Might I sit and discuss these weighty subjects with you, Miss Bennet?"

"Of course, sir. It is, after all, your garden."

"Ah, but I would not impose upon you, even if you are staying in my house."

"Then please, be seated, Mr. Darcy."

He did with alacrity, and when he turned to her, Elizabeth thought he had some specific topic about which he wished to speak. But she was not about to allow him to begin, as she had other matters *she* wished to canvass first.

"I believe last night's dinner party was a success, do you not agree?" asked Elizabeth without preamble.

"Quite a success," replied Mr. Darcy without hesitation. "I was happy to see my friend again, as I have only seen him once since his return to town."

Elizabeth regarded Mr. Darcy with suspicion, certain he was not unaware of it. "I am interested to hear you say it, Mr. Darcy. In fact, I had wondered if you might be less than pleased by the guest list your cousin assembled for the evening."

"Anne has acted as my hostess, freeing Georgiana of the burden," replied Mr. Darcy. "She may invite whomever she pleases." Mr. Darcy paused, and then he turned to regard Elizabeth. For a moment, she thought he was baring his very soul to her. "I will not deny that I was not supportive of Bingley's pursuit of your sister last autumn, Miss Bennet. You are too intelligent to be taken in by any dissembling I might choose to attempt, and I would not wish to do so regardless.

"The fact of the matter was I had concerns about a possible match between them, though I will say that those concerns have been rendered meaningless in light of the events of the past day. But the only objection I raised to Bingley regarding your sister was *her* feelings for him."

"You thought her indifferent?" asked Elizabeth, wondering how he could possibly make such a claim. His next words mollified her to a large extent.

"It seems absurd now, does it not?" Mr. Darcy released a self-deprecating chuckle. "Last night as I watched them, I wondered that I had not seen it before. It is especially incomprehensible when you consider that Miss Bennet's character is much like *mine*—we are both reticent, quiet in company, and neither of us share our feelings with others. I did not see that in her, and I wonder if my powers of observation are completely deficient as a result."

"There are few who can detect Jane's true feelings," said Elizabeth, much appeased by his words. "Not long after your party came to Hertfordshire, Charlotte and I could both see Jane's interest in Mr. Bingley, but we have known her for many years. Charlotte commented that Jane should show her feelings more to leave him in no doubt, but I laughed her opinion away, averring that Mr. Bingley must be a simpleton if he did not recognize them for himself. It appears I was wrong too."

"I think that Bingley *did* understand her feelings. But he has often had a greater reliance on *my* judgment than his own."

"And what role did his sisters play?" asked Elizabeth, certain she knew already. She decided there was no point in belaboring Mr. Darcy's actions and directed the conversation away from them accordingly.

"They were more concerned for your sister's position in society and the extent of her dowry." Mr. Darcy smiled. "But I am certain you already suspected this. Those arguments alone would not have been enough to persuade him, I am sorry to say, so it was my assurances of the tepidity of your sister's feelings which persuaded him."

"You were wrong, Mr. Darcy," said Elizabeth. "That much is

evident. However, as you were acting in the best interest of a very good friend, I find that I can forgive you. I am certain Jane has, and she would not wish for me to hold a grudge."

"Then I am grateful to your sister." Mr. Darcy paused, then he continued in an exaggerated conversational tone. "I do not know if you were aware of his presence, but Bingley visited the house this morning and left no more than fifteen minutes ago, asking for an explanation, which I did not scruple to give."

Elizabeth regarded her companion with interest. "I had not known. I suppose his sisters tried to argue against his pursuit of Jane?"

"Only the younger. The elder was held in check as Hurst decided to support Bingley. Of a greater interest, however, is that Bingley has gone directly to your uncle's house to request a courtship with your sister."

"Oh, that is wonderful news!" cried Elizabeth, clapping her hands. "I always thought his esteem was not lacking. This is a perfect ending to this tale, though it took some twists and turns to arrive here."

"It is not an ending, Miss Bennet. In fact, I believe it is the beginning of the rest of their lives. And I am happy that they are about to obtain it, regardless of any obstacles which presented themselves during the journey."

"Indeed, it is, Mr. Darcy. I could not be any happier."

They sat for some time in the garden, and though not much was said between them, Elizabeth found herself rather more complaisant in Mr. Darcy's company than she thought she might have been upon learning the truth of his interference with respect to Mr. Bingley and Jane. It was the fact that he had owned it himself without disguise, Elizabeth decided—that and his confession that he had been wrong to do so.

"I would have you know, Miss Bennet," said Mr. Darcy after they had sat in that attitude for some time, "that Bingley's happiness is not my only concern."

"Oh?" asked Elizabeth. She had been considering her ever-changing opinion of Mr. Darcy, and his sudden words had taken her by surprise.

"Yes. For you see, though Bingley looks like he is about to find his happiness with *his* Bennet sister, I believe there is still the matter of *my* happiness to consider."

Given what had gone between them in the last weeks, Elizabeth could not fail to understand Mr. Darcy's meaning when he spoke so boldly. She turned to regard him for a long moment, weighing, considering. Mr. Darcy bore it all with patience and an understated measure of hope. Could Elizabeth possibly accept this man's attentions? Had she not despised him only a short time before?

Then it all became so easy. What reason could she possibly have to resist? Had he not shown her, by word and deed, the ardent nature of his regard? And could she state with any measure of truth that she did not return that regard, that he had not stolen her heart in return?

No. Elizabeth would not tell herself such falsehoods. Somehow, he had crept like a thief in the night and stolen her heart. She would not deny herself this happiness.

"Then I wish you the best, Mr. Darcy. I hope you find your happiness."

The expression of heart felt delight which spread over his countenance became him, but if Elizabeth expected a proposal at that moment, she was destined to be disappointed. He spoke with her, softly and with great affection, and Elizabeth knew that he would come to the point when he thought the time was right. And for the moment, Elizabeth was content to receive the attentions of a suitor. The rest would take care of itself at the proper time.

"You appear to be watching something with great interest, Cousin."

Anne did not even turn at the sound of Fitzwilliam's voice, so intent was she on the scene before her, through the window in the corridor which overlooked the gardens at the end of the house. It was, perhaps, an odd sort of place to stand in one attitude, but it was the best vantage point to see the scene playing out below. Anne could not be any happier.

"Interesting," said Fitzwilliam as he looked out himself and saw Darcy and Elizabeth below, sitting together, their hands almost touching where they rested on the bench between them. "It seems to me, Cousin, that you have been indulging in a spot of matchmaking these past weeks."

"Do not say such a thing," said Anne, never taking her eyes from the couple below them. "Matchmaking is such an uncouth word. I have not done anything so gauche as to try to direct Darcy and Elizabeth toward each other."

"Then I would like to know what you call it," replied Fitzwilliam with a soft chuckle.

"I merely corrected Elizabeth's opinion of Darcy as best I could, and when Darcy asked me for my opinion of my mother's designs, I was truthful in stating I had no wish to marry him. The rest they have done themselves."

When Fitzwilliam stared at her with evident skepticism, Anne could only look skyward. She turned and walked away, knowing he would follow her. "You may not have seen it, Fitzwilliam, but Darcy and Elizabeth are well suited. She will give him a sense of liveliness and bring him happiness, while she gains the benefit of his sober nature—which she sometimes lacks, given her fiery personality—and the protection of a good home and a steady protector."

"It does not hurt that he is quite wealthy either."

Taking umbrage at his sardonic tone, Anne whirled on him, jabbing a finger at him and saying: "Do not, even for a moment, suggest that my friend is a fortune hunter, for that could not be further from the truth."

"I am aware of that, Anne," said Fitzwilliam. He was shaking with laughter, likely from the sight of being taken to task by a diminutive woman, when he was a large and brawny man.

"Then why did you suggest it?"

"To see how you would react," replied Fitzwilliam, waggling his eyebrows.

Anne looked skyward and began to walk down the hallway again. "I have suspected Darcy's interest from the beginning and thought he would do well by marrying the girl. The larger issue, I had thought, was Miss Bennet's feelings for Darcy. I did not think they were positive."

"Hence my disabusing her of certain notions and guiding her to a positive opinion of him."

"It seems to me we are once again entering matchmaking territory."

"Believe what you will," replied Anne, uncaring about his opinion. "But I have done nothing more than allow Elizabeth to see him in a way that would change her opinion. For a man I have often thought was stiff and unyielding, Darcy has pursued her in a creditable manner, and he has appeared adept at saying the right thing to her at the right time."

"I could never have imagined it," replied Fitzwilliam. "I understand he did not say much right when he was in Hertfordshire last autumn."

"Much of that may be attributed to what happened with Georgiana and his general worry over her." Anne showed Fitzwilliam a smug smile. "But that has now been overcome. Perhaps now Mother will allow this dream of hers to die and allow me to live my own life."

Fitzwilliam laughed and shook his head. "I knew there had to be some ulterior motive."

"Perhaps there was. But it has all worked out for the best."

Excusing herself, Anne retired to her room, content with her work. Elizabeth would be happy with Darcy, and Anne would finally be allowed to do as she would. She was anticipating it already.

Chapter XXVIII

The following days were magical. Elizabeth laughed and dreamed and talked and jested with Anne and Georgiana, and the three ladies got on famously. Having already made one lifelong friend in Anne, Elizabeth was happy to have made another in Georgiana. Whether they would share a closer relationship, as was becoming increasingly likely, Elizabeth decided not to consider — that would all work itself out in time.

Then there was the matter of Jane, whose winter malaise and heartbreak were now a distant memory. The day after Mr. Bingley's conversation with Mr. Darcy, Jane arrived as early as possible, bursting with the need to share her news, news of which Elizabeth, of course, was already aware.

"He has asked for a courtship, and I have accepted!" exclaimed Jane as soon as she entered the room.

Elizabeth did not hesitate to fly into her sister's arms, exclaiming her joy, and Anne and Georgiana were also quick to close around her, offering their own congratulations and felicitations. Jane accepted them all with a modest air, she who was deserving of all manner of praise, acting as humbly as the poorest woman in the kingdom.

"Though I will declare that I have often found men of the species to be quite dense," said Anne with a mischievous grin, "I am happy Mr. Bingley has proven that he will not be beset in such a way forever. It has taken him long enough to come to such a resolution, but I could not be happier that he has finally arrived at it."

Though Jane thanked Anne with pleasure, and not a little laughter, Elizabeth did not suppose that her sister had not recognized Anne's hand in what had occurred the previous evening.

"I suppose I must thank you for your assistance, Miss de Bourgh," said Jane. She was not prone to teasing as Elizabeth was, but in her words there was an arch quality of which Elizabeth could only approve. "For the first few moments after Mr. Bingley entered the room, I will own that I was considering punishments for you both, but as all has turned out well, I suppose I shall commute your sentences."

Anne laughed heartily, as did Elizabeth. "I wondered what your response would be. But I thought the arrival of Mr. Bingley, and what I thought would be *his* reaction, would more than drive out whatever displeasure you felt for me."

"But how did you know?" Jane's eyes sought Elizabeth's. "I had not thought my sister to be so little worthy of trust."

"If you will excuse Elizabeth," said Anne, "it was largely my doing. I noticed that something was amiss in your manners when we first met, and I pulled the truth from Elizabeth. Being of the same mind as she with respect to Mr. Bingley's likely feelings for you, we agreed we should give you both the opportunity to come to your own conclusions." Anne waved off Jane's next words. "I know you will say that I had never seen you in company before, but Miss Bingley's desire to keep her brother from you was evident, proving *her* understanding of her brother's affections matched Elizabeth's."

"Then I must reiterate my thanks. I hope you are now content."

There was a hint of a challenge in Jane's words, and Anne was happy to respond in the affirmative, as was Elizabeth. Contented with their replies, Jane moved the topic to Mr. Bingley's coming the previous day, how he had declared his love and his intention to demonstrate his constancy, and had asked her for a courtship.

"I almost expected him to propose," said Jane, "and I was of two minds about whether I should accept him. There were . . . concerns, questions I am certain Elizabeth would be only too happy to share, should I ask her."

"Good for you, Jane!" exclaimed Elizabeth. "Mr. Bingley should not be afraid to show his regard for you, and you should not accept him until convinced of it."

"I am very happy for you, Jane," interjected Georgiana. "I thought . . . Well, I was convinced that Miss Bingley wished to have *me* for a sister." Georgiana shuddered to the amusement of them all. "I could never have accepted his proposal, should he have asked."

Though she had known of Miss Bingley's falsehoods, still Jane was shocked at this admission. "You do not think Mr. Bingley would make a good husband?"

"Oh, I believe he would make an excellent husband, Miss Bennet. But I am equally certain Miss Bingley would make a terrible *sister-in-law*!"

For a moment, all three listening to her could not respond, so shocked were they that Georgiana would say such a thing. Then they all burst into laughter—even Jane—and were quickly joined by Georgiana, though hers might have been a little forced.

"Perhaps I should reprimand you for speaking so of Miss Bingley," chortled Anne, "but I am far too diverted to do so. Of more importance, I agree with you far too much!"

Georgiana colored, but she beamed at her cousin. "I know that I should not speak so. But for as long as I have known her, Miss Bingley has praised me, my playing, my taste and judgment—odd, if you consider I was naught but thirteen when I made her acquaintance. And when she praised her brother, noted what a good husband he would make and how he seemed to regard me with such approval, I had the impression she was always on the verge of ordering my wedding clothes for me!"

The ladies erupted in mirth anew, and they continued bantering for some time after. Suffice it to say that Miss Bingley, though they were not mean-spirited in speaking of her, was made to seem ridiculous, a designation Elizabeth thought more than earned.

Two days after the dinner party, the four young ladies boarded a carriage to go shopping with Lady Susan for their evening attire—even Georgiana, who was not at all excited about the prospect of her future coming out, watched them wistfully, no doubt visions of beautiful evenings of wonder, the romance and excitement, catching her in their grip.

Lady Susan was quite impressed by the selection of Mr. Gardiner's stock of fabrics and told him so, displaying no haughtiness of a countess for a tradesman. For his part, Mr. Gardiner responded with pleasure and no improper deference, proving himself to be a gentleman of substance, even if he was a tradesman. The ladies did select two fabrics which pleased them, but they retired to Madam

Fournier's shop with the promise that Mr. Gardiner had made a delivery to her only a few days before, and that it was likely she would still have it among her stock.

Madam Fournier's shop was much as it ever was, but the deference the madam paid to Lady Susan was even in excess of what she had paid to Georgiana as the sister of a wealthy man. They had an agreeable time choosing patterns and colors, adding bits of fluff to their attire, debating over which colors suited whom the best. In the end, Elizabeth was pleased with her selection, though she refused to grant Lady Susan's wish of paying for their purchases.

"My uncle will pay for our gowns," declared Elizabeth when the matter was raised once again by the countess. "I appreciate everything you have done for us and the assistance you have given us, but it is right that our uncle should cover our costs."

"I see you will not be persuaded," replied Lady Susan. "I will retreat from the field, Miss Elizabeth, for I see you are determined to have your way." Then Lady Susan looked on her with a softened expression. "However, I will insist upon treating you all at Gunter's. Surely you cannot deny me such a small pleasure."

It was with a laugh that Elizabeth agreed and allowed the lady her way. They soon said their farewells to Madam Fournier and made their way to Gunter's for their treats. It was during their time there, however, that Elizabeth was made aware of Lady Susan's desire to speak with her alone, and Anne—Elizabeth could not have known how traitorous her friend would prove to be—aided her aunt by starting a conversation with Jane and Georgiana and diverting their attention away.

"It seems, Miss Elizabeth, that you have been quite an influence on my nieces," said Lady Susan. "Anne is almost unrecognizable, and Georgiana, though I will own I saw some improvement before I returned to my husband's estate, seems to have more confidence and ability to speak." She paused and chuckled. "Though I suppose it is possible that it is just the present company which encourages her."

"They are both delightful, and I have been fortunate to make their acquaintance," replied Elizabeth. "I am sure I have done nothing especially noble."

"I heard of how you agreed to attend to Anne at the expense of your visit with your friend. I know of the friendship you offered to Anne, the way you patiently helped her to gain her independence, how you stood up to my sister in the face of her poor behavior." Lady Susan paused and smiled. "If I was not aware that you truly do not think that you deserve such praise, I might accuse you of false modesty."

"Then let us simply say that I was happy to be a friend to Anne," replied Elizabeth. She wondered if she should say what she thought next, but something moved her to candor. "I will own that I did not think much of her when I was first introduced, but I soon learned that impression was mistaken. Anne is as estimable a lady as I have ever met."

Lady Susan's eyes found her niece and she nodded. "I understand what you are saying, Miss Bennet. I believe we all became accustomed to simply thinking there was not much depth to Anne. But we were all so mistaken, and it is humbling to know it took a stranger to our family to see and unlock it. The difference between Anne now and the way she was when I last saw her is nothing less than astonishing."

"I believe it is far more her doing than anything I have done," replied Elizabeth, eager for the conversation to end. Lady Susan seemed to understand and accept this, though her next words were far more shocking.

"Anne has, indeed, changed much, and much must be to her credit. Now, Miss Bennet, what I truly wished to discuss is Darcy's obvious attraction to you."

Uneasy at the lady's motives, Elizabeth could only say. "Mr. Darcy?"

The look the lady directed at her would have cowed grown men. "Do not attempt to suggest you have not seen it. I have known him since he was a boy and am intimately familiar with his ways. I have never seen him look on a woman with such admiration, and I have only been in company with you both once!"

"I am not unaware," replied Elizabeth slowly, not certain how she should respond. "I understand it is not what you would wish. I know Mr. Darcy could have prospects which are far exceed that which I can offer him."

"Do you doubt your own value, Miss Elizabeth?"

"I do not," replied Elizabeth, irked at the suggestion. "I merely say the truth: I do not possess the material advantages that Mr. Darcy has a right to expect in a wife."

"Then I would ask you not to say such things." Lady Susan watched her, a hint of steel in her gaze. "I have long known that Darcy would not be happy simply to marry a woman of fortune or one of standing, not if she was the daughter of the Duke of Devonshire himself. No, Darcy requires something more than that. And though you cannot give him certain benefits by your own admission, you can provide something more than all these things, for he requires a companion, a woman to love, who will love him in turn."

The countess's gaze never wavered. "The question is, Miss Bennet, do you love him?"

It was an impertinent question and in other circumstances Elizabeth would have decried it as such and refused to answer. His other aunt, Lady Catherine de Bourgh, would have insulted her connections and fortune, never considering her compatibility with Mr. Darcy or the state of their mutual affections. But his uncle and aunt had proven themselves of a different sort. It was this knowledge, Lady Susan's open concern for Mr. Darcy, which prompted her to speak.

"I hardly know," said Elizabeth, not knowing how his aunt would interpret her words.

"Is he not a good man? Do you not think you will be happy with him?"

"He *is* a good man. Whether I would be happy with him, I cannot yet say. It was not so long ago that my feelings for him were not positive at all, for various reasons. They have undergone a material change, but can they have changed so far so quickly? I am not certain, though my heart often tells me otherwise."

"He did not make a good initial impression?"

Elizabeth rolled her eyes. "Anything but!"

Using as few words as possible, as well as putting as lighthearted an interpretation on it as she could, Elizabeth told Lady Susan a little of Mr. Darcy's behavior in Meryton. The lady, obviously intimately acquainted with Mr. Darcy as she was, only laughed and shook her head.

"It has ever been thus," said she. "Darcy has always been awkward and hesitant when first meeting people. He often appears to be giving insult, even when none has been intended."

"But once he comes to know you, he is much more at ease," observed Elizabeth quietly.

"Indeed," replied Lady Susan. She was silent a moment before she continued once again. "Miss Elizabeth, you have mentioned those things that you lack, and I have countered with those in your favor. What you do not know is that in her life, Lady Anne Darcy was my closest friend. We knew each other as girls, had our coming out together, married within months of each other. We were inseparable."

Lady Susan fell silent, her mind seemed to be filled with little remembrances of a dear friend long since lost. Clearly the ache had dulled with the years, but it had never quite left her. Elizabeth could understand it quite well—she had been quite close to her grandmother before the elderly lady had passed away, and the pain of loss had never quite left her.

"Let me inform you that Darcy's mother wished for her son to be happy, in whatever way most suited him," continued the lady at length. "As he was still a young boy when she passed, I am not certain that she had thought much of his marriage, or any other such weighty subjects. But in the time she had, she was beloved of her husband, a sentiment she returned, and she raised him to be a good man, but also to be as happy as life will allow.

"In all honesty, I think that Darcy has forgotten much of the second part of Lady Anne's life lessons. It is clear, however, that meeting you has rekindled that desire to find a lady who did not see him as a conquest first and foremost. In you, he has found a woman he believes can make him happy. I could wish for nothing more for him. So you see, I am not opposed to his attentions to you—far from it, in fact."

"And you do not think that I will face challenges in London society? I am not known to any of them; will they not resent me accordingly?"

"My dear, they would all resent the new Mrs. Darcy regardless, for the simple fact he did not choose any of them. But I am confident in your abilities—I know you will meet them all with fortitude and determination. There is also my support to consider, and though I do not boast, I do not wield an inconsequential measure of influence. With our support, I dare say you will be well in our society."

"Thank you, Lady Susan," replied Elizabeth. "But I would caution you not to place the cart before the horse—Mr. Darcy has not proposed to me."

"No," replied Lady Susan. "But he will. Of that, I am convinced."

Lady Susan Fitzwilliam was quite happy with Miss Elizabeth Bennet. There was something refreshing and genuine about the girl, especially when compared with most of the debutantes these days, who were, in Lady Susan's mind, less than impressive. Having two daughters herself, Lady Susan had always striven to raise them to not only be proper, demure, and kind ladies, but she had also taught them to use their intelligence and try to be something more than just a simpering debutant. In that, she thought she had been successful—they were both good women, both had made good marriages, and both were in demand by others in society for their characters, rather than just their connections.

Miss Elizabeth was not the most beautiful of specimens, thought

Lady Susan as she observed the girl speaking with the others her age. She was certainly not so lovely as her elder sister. But that did not mean her beauty was insufficient; in fact, when Lady Susan observed her, watched her as she spoke with animation, her eyes alight with happiness and mirth, she was not surprised Darcy had been captivated. They would make a good match, she was certain of it. The censure of the ton might last for some little time, but it would not be long before Miss Elizabeth herself won over all but the proudest and most disagreeable, and who cared what *they* thought anyway!

When they had finished their treats, the five ladies rose and made their way out to the sidewalk, their outing for the day completed. While she watched them, Lady Susan thought of the spectacle these ladies would create when they appeared at the ball her friend was hosting. She could hardly wait to savor those delights—society, even that of the upper classes, too often descended into boredom and ennui.

It was while they were walking down the street toward their carriage that they were accosted by a pair of ladies Lady Susan had never met, but had heard much of. She prepared to be amused all over again. Though the elder was largely silent, the younger more than made up for her lack.

"Dear Georgiana!" exclaimed the woman. "And A . . . Miss de Bourgh, of course! How very fortunate we are to find you here today!"

It was not difficult for Lady Susan to see the distaste in her youngest niece's countenance upon being waylaid by the loud lady, though she was certain the woman did not notice it at all. What was more interesting was how she had ignored Miss Bennet and Miss Elizabeth, especially since, by all accounts, the lady's brother was now in a courtship with Miss Bennet! Had the woman no sense?

"Miss Bingley," replied Anne. "Mrs. Hurst. We are happy to see you. In fact, we were just speaking of you, were we not Elizabeth?"

Lady Susan did not miss the exasperated look Miss Elizabeth directed at Anne, and she wondered at it. Miss Bingley, however, turned to Miss Elizabeth as if noticing her for the first time, and her lip curled with a sneer.

"Miss Eliza Bennet. And, of course, my dear Jane." Though Miss Bingley's countenance softened a little when she mentioned the elder sister, there was still a coldness in her tone Lady Susan found less than amusing. The Bingleys did not inhabit a high position in society, it was true, but Miss Bingley would need to be more welcoming of Miss Bennet if she did not wish to spawn rumors about a break in the family.

Then Miss Bingley's gimlet eyes swung back to Miss Elizabeth, and they became flinty and frigid. "I see you are still staying at Mr. Darcy's house, Miss Eliza. Have you forsaken scampering around the countryside, or do you use Hyde Park as your own personal wilderness? It is far too well manicured to provide the mud your petticoats require, but the Serpentine would do well enough to make them sodden."

"I feel no need to wade in the Serpentine," replied Miss Elizabeth, seemingly more amused by the other woman's vitriol than offended by it. "But, yes, I do walk in Hyde Park as often as I can, though Mr. Darcy's garden at the back of his house also has beauties to explore. I have found another lover of nature, as Mr. Darcy has often walked with me."

The flaring of Miss Bingley's nostrils confirmed her affront. This was a woman who, though Lady Susan had never met her, had been intent upon becoming the next mistress of Pemberley for some time. Had Lady Susan ever been inclined to doubt her nephew's words, Miss Bingley's behavior was more than proof enough.

"Excuse me, Anne," said Lady Susan, stepping forward, intent upon preventing Miss Bingley of making a spectacle of them all, "but perhaps you would be so good as to introduce me to your friend?"

"Of course, Aunt," replied Anne. The amusement in her tone suggested that she expected to be vastly diverted by what was to follow. For Miss Bingley's part, she started and stared at Lady Susan, seeming to notice her for the first time. Lady Susan had often met the Miss Bingleys of the world, and as a group they seemed to have a specific quality—that of an almost occult sense of where to find one of higher status. For Miss Bingley to have missed the fact that Lady Susan was with them was unusual, to say the least.

When the introductions were complete, Lady Susan directed a long look at Miss Bingley, wondering how open she should be with the girl. Moreover, she wondered if any advice she gave would be heeded. It was evident that Miss Bingley kept her own counsel with respect to her behavior, much to her own detriment.

Lady Susan withstood Miss Bingley's flattery for several moments—*of course* she could not be happier to make the acquaintance of Miss de Bourgh's esteemed aunt, she was certain they would be excellent friends, and so many other things that Lady Susan had heard more times than she could count. At length, they began making their way down the street to where their conveyance waited, and the sisters were eager to accompany them.

She might have been content to observe the woman's ridiculous behavior in silent amusement, but then Miss Bingley decided to send another barb in Miss Elizabeth's direction, and it raised Lady Susan's ire. She could not help but respond.

"On the contrary, Miss Bingley," said Lady Susan in response to Miss Bingley's insinuation that Lady Susan could not be sanguine about her nieces' association with the Bennet sisters, "I am quite happy with both Miss Bennet *and* Miss Elizabeth. They have become excellent friends to my nieces and, I dare say, will become excellent friends of *mine*."

It was to Miss Bingley's credit that her smile did not slip a jot. But Lady Susan was not finished with her. She stopped walking, forcing Miss Bingley to halt along with her, though the woman was not as confident as she had been only a moment before.

"Miss Bingley, let us speak plainly. In the short time that we have been together today, you have not only ignored the woman your brother is courting, but you have also attempted to disparage a good young woman of whom I think highly, and you have done so twice. I cannot account for such incivility."

Though she paled, Miss Bingley was clearly no coward. She shot an aggrieved look at the sisters who had continued some little distance ahead—along with Mrs. Hurst, who was looking back, her anxiety evident.

"It does not follow that I agree with my brother's pursuit of Miss Bennet, and I still have hope that I may convince him to end his fascination before it is too late. As for Miss Elizabeth . . ." Miss Bingley's nose wrinkled as if a skunk had crossed her path. "She is the most impertinent, improper woman I have ever had the displeasure to meet." Miss Bingley's eyes sought Lady Susan's. "I am sure you must agree with me."

"Your confidence is misplaced," replied Lady Susan shortly. The smile ran away from Miss Bingley's face. "Perhaps you do not recall, but in the past few moments I have praised Miss Elizabeth and her sister highly. In fact, I find both ladies delightful.

"Regardless of what *you* think of them," said Lady Susan, allowing her expression to turn harsh, "you invite gossip if you treat the object of your brother's affections in such a way, and the manner in which you attempted to insult Miss Elizabeth is ridiculous. I do not know if you intended your words to be subtle, but your attacks were anything but, which shows a measure of desperation, in my experience."

Miss Bingley's eyes were wide, as if she had never expected to be called out for her behavior. Lady Susan had just about had enough of this woman's company, and she did not hesitate to finish stating her criticisms, so she could return to that which was more agreeable.

"I am aware of your ambitions, Miss Bingley. Darcy is too, I might add. My advice to you is to cease making a fool of yourself—your wishes shall never be, for Darcy has no interest in you."

"I assure you, my lady—"

"And *I* assure *you* that you are wasting your time. If Darcy wished to have you for a wife, he would have proposed long ago. Please do yourself a favor and cease to make a spectacle of yourself. Your attacks against Miss Elizabeth will not be tolerated again in my presence. If you choose to continue to treat Miss Bennet as you have, that is your choice, but I would advise you against it. It does not take much to start tongues wagging in London."

So saying, Lady Susan motioned toward the party, now waiting beside the carriage, and she began to walk, forcing Miss Bingley to scurry along beside her. It was not long before they had taken their leave of the Bingley sisters, but though the other ladies pressed her for an account of her conversation with Miss Bingley, Lady Susan decided she had said enough of the woman.

Later, when she had returned to her home, Lady Susan was forced to confess that she had enjoyed plucking Miss Bingley's feathers. There were few things as satisfying as pricking the conceit of a supercilious woman and exposing all her pretentions for what they were.

Chapter XXIX

While Elizabeth was enjoying herself at Mr. Darcy's house, she knew that her time there was drawing to a close. As it stood, she had been away from home for three months, and Jane for more than five. Though their mother was eager for them to stay in London—much easier for them to find husbands there, to her mother's thinking—Mr. Bennet was becoming more insistent about their return. This was made even more evident the day before the ball.

As Jane was to attend, and their aunt and uncle would not, it had been decided that she would spend a few nights at Darcy house. Elizabeth could not have been more excited about her sister's coming, and when Jane arrived, she was quick to grasp her by the hand and show her to her room, chattering the entire way.

"Oh, it is good to have you here, Jane!" said Elizabeth, as her sister's personal effects were placed in her room. "I have so missed being with you!"

"I am happy to be here," replied Jane in her usually calm manner. "And I believe Mr. Bingley will be by later to thank Mr. Darcy for the invitation to the ball."

Elizabeth looked at her sister, uncertain to what she was referring. Jane noticed it and said: "We will be attending a high society event,

Lizzy, given by an earl and his wife. Mr. Bingley told me that he and his sisters rarely receive invitations to similar events, and when they do, it is always due to Mr. Darcy's influence. Even so, he thinks this will be the most important event he has ever attended."

"Well, well," said Elizabeth, "it appears Miss Bingley is not nearly so high and mighty as she might have thought. Do you know if the invitation has been extended to include his sisters?"

Though at one time Jane might have been inclined to chastise Elizabeth for speaking in such a manner, it was clear her eyes had been opened, for she ignored the first part of Elizabeth's statement. "They have been invited. However, Mr. Bingley has warned his sisters about what is expected of them when they attend, and Mr. Hurst has supported him."

"And the punishment if they step out of line?"

This time Jane did roll her eyes. "Oh, Lizzy; it is not kind to be so gleeful at Miss Bingley's expense."

"Not kind, perhaps, but she is eminently deserving."

Jane did not disagree. "I know not what Mr. Hurst has told his wife, though I believe she is of a more complying disposition than her sister. Miss Bingley, however, has been told that she will be sent to the north. As I understand it, she does not like it there. She visited me once these past days, and she was very kind and attentive."

When Elizabeth cast her a significant look, Jane only shook her head. "I am aware of Miss Bingley's character, Elizabeth. You have no need to worry for me."

"I have no doubt of your discernment, dearest," said Elizabeth, kissing her sister's cheek. "But I have great faith in your ability to forgive and to attribute others' actions to pure motives."

"I will not be used again."

It was the tone with which her sister spoke that reassured Elizabeth she was saying nothing but the truth. After Jane was settled, they returned to the sitting-room to attend their hosts, and there Elizabeth discovered she had received a letter. She knew from its thinness that it was from her father—his letters always had been known for their brevity—and the writing on the front confirmed it.

"Well?" asked Anne when Elizabeth had read it. "What does it say? Or is it a private communication from a gentleman which requires discretion?"

Georgiana giggled, but Elizabeth only shook her head at her friend. "It is not private. It is from my father and, as I suspected, he is now insisting that we return home. I am afraid that Jane and I will need to return to Hertfordshire after the ball."

The expression Anne turned on her was unreadable for a long moment, then she shrugged. "It matters little at this point. Since Mr. Bingley is courting our Jane, I suspect he will simply follow her to Hertfordshire, and since he and Darcy are close friends, I have no doubt an invitation will be speedily issued thereafter. Thus, you may both continue your courtships in Hertfordshire!"

"Anne!" exclaimed Elizabeth.

But Anne only laughed. "Do not deny it, Elizabeth. It is nothing less than the truth."

Further protestation would only fuel Anne's desire to tease, and Elizabeth was not about to grant her friend any further ammunition to use against her. She contented herself with a glare at her friend—which was not at all efficacious, as far as she could detect—and turned the subject to other matters.

Before they could continue, however, the opening door caught their attention, and the housekeeper entered the room with a visitor following behind. Shocked, Elizabeth rose, noting that Anne had risen along with her.

"There you are, Anne."

It was Lady Catherine.

Stunned at the sudden appearance of her mother, Anne regarded her, noting the expression of haughty disinterest which was plastered on her face. She carried herself with the bearing of a queen, walking with a straight back and a regal air which seemed to suggest to anyone watching that she was a general inspecting her troops. As was her wont, she entered and, choosing a high-backed chair which was most like her favorite at Rosings, she sat and gazed out over them all.

"Mother," said Anne, hating herself for the hint of a tremor in her voice. "I had not expected to see you here." Anne felt she her nervousness in a creditable manner—it would not do to show weakness to one such as her mother, who could sense it as a wolf smelled blood.

"No, it appears you did not." Lady Catherine looked out over them all. "Sit up straight, Georgiana, and do not slouch."

Though Anne could not see anything wrong with Georgiana's posture, the girl jerked and attempted to sit up straighter. She had always been intimidated by Lady Catherine.

"I see Miss Elizabeth Bennet is still here with you." Lady Catherine's feelings about Elizabeth's presence were not clearly seen in her manner, but she gave Anne no time to think on the matter. "And I see you have another guest at present. I suspect that it is one of Miss Bennet's sisters. Would you do the honor of introducing me?"

"Of course, Mother," said Anne, uncertain what to make of her mother's behavior. "This is Jane Bennet, Elizabeth's elder sister. Jane, this is my mother, Lady Catherine de Bourgh."

"I am happy to make your acquaintance, Lady Catherine," said Jane, dropping into a respectful curtsey.

Nodding, though not losing her regal nature, Lady Catherine replied: "I see, now, that your sister's praise of you is not the idle boasting of a beloved sibling, Miss Bennet. Have you been here for long?"

"I just came this morning, your ladyship," replied Jane. "Your sister, Lady Susan, has kindly agreed to include me in an invitation to a ball to be held tomorrow at the home of one of her friends."

"I see." Her mother was silent for a moment, and Anne wondered what she was thinking. Then her eyes found Elizabeth again, and Anne thought she detected a hint of tightening around them. "And you, Miss Elizabeth?"

Elizabeth was quite obviously not certain what was being asked of her, and she did not hesitate to say it. "I am sorry, your ladyship, but I do not understand your question. Perhaps if you restated it?"

"I am merely inquiring as to your presence here. Have you stayed with my nephew the entire time since you left my house?"

"Yes, she has, Mother," replied Anne, more than a hint of a challenge in her tone.

"You may allow Miss Elizabeth to make her own reply, Anne." She turned her attention back to Elizabeth. "I hope you understand the superior circumstances in which you have been housed, Miss Elizabeth, not to mention the condescension with which my sister has favored you."

"Indeed, I do," replied Elizabeth. "Mr. Darcy has a lovely house, and all your relations have been nothing but welcoming and kind. I could ask for nothing more."

"Of course," replied Lady Catherine. "I would have expected nothing less."

"I will own to some surprise at your coming here, Mother," said Anne, not willing to allow this interrogation to proceed any further. "I believe my uncle made it quite clear that you were to remain at Rosings unless certain conditions were met. I will repeat—your coming was quite unexpected, and I find myself wondering why you have come.

Will you not explain?"

"My brother does not control my actions," said Lady Catherine. Her displeasure was evident, but rather than cow her as it might have in the past, Anne only found her annoyance rising.

"No, I dare say he does not. But if you mean to restate those opinions you previously espoused, then you have wasted your time coming here, for I shall not be moved."

"I see your defiance has grown to much greater proportions than the last time I saw you," said Lady Catherine, her nose wrinkled and her tone cross. "I begin to suspect that it was always there, though hidden. I previously thought that it was brought on by your association with . . . other persons. Now I am not certain."

"There is much about me you do not understand," replied Anne, and even she was surprised by the bitterness in her voice. "Be that as it may, I would appreciate it if you would state the reason for your visit."

It was a surprise when her mother paused and darted a look at the other three ladies in the room. Normally she could be counted on to speak in a forthright fashion without delay.

"Your companions will leave us now so that we may speak privately." Lady Catherine turned to the other three women. "You may wait in the music room and return to attend me when Anne and I have completed our discussion."

Georgiana almost jumped from her seat in her eagerness to be out of Lady Catherine's company, but Miss Bennet was much slower. Elizabeth, though she rose, turned to Anne, a question in her eyes. Though Anne had little wish to speak with her mother alone, a look at the woman seemed to suggest a hint of pleading in her eyes, though Anne could not be certain. She doubted her mother would ever humble herself enough to beg for an audience with her, but perhaps some good could come of this.

"Very well, Mother," said Anne, nodding slightly to Elizabeth. Ever the good friend and supporter, Elizabeth's eyebrow rose, and though Anne would have preferred to have her friend here, she thought it unlikely that her mother would speak in a candid fashion if they were not alone. And Anne was no longer the quiet, accepting woman she had been before. If her mother meant to intimidate her, she would discover that to her detriment.

The Bennet sisters filed from the room, leaving Anne alone with her mother, and when the door closed behind them, Anne turned and quite deliberately raised an eyebrow. Lady Catherine saw it and huffed with irritation. But rather than speak, she began to study Anne, observing her dress, her hair, her countenance, her eyes drawing a line from Anne's head to her feet. This Anne bore with patience—it was like her mother, but also subtly different in a manner she could not quite determine.

"It seems as if you are at least taking care for your health," said Lady Catherine at length. "I almost might have expected Miss Elizabeth to drag you from here to there, putting you at risk in her eagerness to traipse all over the city. But I suppose being in London, she can hardly walk with such impunity as she does in the country."

"You are correct, Mother," replied Anne. "Elizabeth must take more care here than she would at her father's home. But you are incorrect in the other part. I frequently walk with Elizabeth now, and though I cannot state with any truth that I am as strong as she, I have made great strides."

Her mother's mouth opened, Anne thought to deliver a stinging rebuke, but she seemed to think better of it. Instead, she leaned forward and gazed into Anne's face, peering with great concentration.

"There seems to be some truth to your assertion," said Lady Catherine, though her voice was soft and hesitant.

"And your Cousin Darcy? Are you getting on well with him?"

"That is where you need to cease speaking, Mother," said Anne. "I will not marry my cousin. If you attempt to try to browbeat us into accepting your decrees, then you might as well have remained in Kent."

As if she were swallowing bile, Lady Catherine paused and shook her head. "I did not come to speak of that."

"Then why did you come?" asked Anne. "And what is the meaning of your question?"

"I . . ." Lady Catherine fell silent, and Anne had the impression she was searching for the proper words. "When you left . . . left me in Kent, I . . ." Lady Catherine growled, a frustrated tone. "It led me to introspection. I realized that you had not truly known your cousin that well and what I took for a closeness between you was nothing more than an attempt to convince myself. I wondered if you truly knew him well at all."

Anne pondered how to respond to her mother. She was essentially correct, and Anne wished to ensure she understood it. But her mother's manners, the stops and starts, the hesitation—none of these had ever been a part of her character as long as Anne could remember. Whether it meant she was softening her stance, Anne could not be certain, but she did not wish to say something she should not and ruin what seemed to be a more conciliatory stance from her mother.

"I did not know him well," replied Anne, deciding that simple honesty was best for the present. "We have attended to that deficiency here in London. I now understand Darcy better than I ever did before."

"And what is your conclusion?"

Anne laughed. "My conclusion is that he is the same man I had thought him to be. But you should also know that I have also determined, more than I ever had before, that though he is a good man whom any woman would be fortunate to have as a husband, he is not for me. We are too similar. We do not suit."

Rather than begin to demand Anne's compliance as she might have done in the past, Lady Catherine nodded slowly, her gaze introspective. "I will own that I had . . . hoped you might have changed your mind. But I am not surprised."

"You are not?"

Lady Catherine shook her head. "No. When you left Rosings, I was confronted for the first time with a daughter who was not the person I thought her to be. You . . . you reminded me of myself, to be honest—nothing I said had any effect, and you dictated to me, rather than the reverse."

"I had my convictions, Mother," replied Anne. "Elizabeth helped me to understand myself, to *know* who I am. I am greatly indebted to her."

A great sigh was Lady Catherine's response, and she attempted to smile, an expression Anne had rarely seen on her mother's countenance. "It appears we have much for which to be thankful. Miss Bennet . . ." Her mother paused and shook her head. "I was not convinced, you know, when we asked her to come to Rosings."

"Of that, I am aware. You did it because I demanded it of you."

"Yes," replied her mother. "But I did not understand what you needed, I fear. I only knew what I wished for your future to be. I still wish it, if I am to be honest, but I will . . . attempt to respect your wishes. I do not wish to continue with this distance between us. You are my flesh and blood, and I wish to be your mother."

By the time Lady Catherine finished speaking, her voice was so soft Anne was forced to strain to hear her.

"I wish it too, Mother," said Anne. "I never wished to be estranged from you. I . . . I want to be your friend and your daughter, not your subject."

Lady Catherine winced at the last word, but she did not try to deny it. "Then shall we start anew?"

Her expression was so hopeful, it was almost pathetic, coming from a woman who never pleaded. A lifetime of being in this woman's company came rushing back to Anne, and she remembered how they had often been quite companionable in each other's company.

But Anne was not about to allow her mother back into her life without a clear understanding as to what role she would play in it.

"I would like that very much, Mother," replied Anne. "But there are a few things you should understand first. I have become independent, largely through Elizabeth's assistance. I will not take kindly to your directing me or demanding that I obey your edicts. I have become aware of my capabilities, and I promise I will not go beyond them."

A slow nod was her mother's response. "Very well. I hope you will not be upset if I express concern when I feel it?"

It was the fact that her mother had phrased it as a question that told Anne she was intent on being agreeable. "That would be fine, Mother. I do not think anyone would reject words meant in such a spirit."

Lady Catherine nodded, her confidence seeming to have been restored. Then the smile ran away from her face when Anne made her next point.

"Another thing you should know, Mother, is that Darcy has been all but courting Elizabeth since we came to his house. Not only do I approve of this, but I am hoping he will eventually come to the point and propose to her."

"But—" Lady Catherine composed herself and did not continue with whatever angry rant she had been about to unleash. Anne nodded to herself, relieved that her mother could restrain herself when necessary. When she spoke, there was a diffidence in her voice, though it was coupled—in an odd fashion—with a large measure of her usual imperious surety.

"If you are not to marry Darcy, then he requires a woman of society, one who will be a credit to his name and provide useful connections to increase the family's influence. Miss Bennet . . ."

She paused and seemed to sense Anne's refusal to hear anything against her friend.

"Miss Bennet *is* a good sort of girl," continued Lady Catherine after a moment's hesitance. "She is also a gentlewoman, which is something, I suppose. But she also possesses ties to trade and from what Mr. Collins says, a most improper family."

"And Mr. Collins is, himself, the very model of propriety."

A laugh actually escaped Lady Catherine's mouth at Anne's jibe. "I suppose you are correct." She then became serious. "Anne, surely you understand that a marriage to Miss Bennet would make it very difficult for Darcy. She will be censured and slighted, and her acceptance will be dearly bought. Perhaps I could find another man amongst my acquaintances willing to take her on? She is not bereft of attractions. She might do for the wife of a second son, or a parson, perhaps."

"No, Mother," replied Anne, shaking her head. "It is Elizabeth whom Darcy chooses. He can hardly take his eyes off her, and he treats her as if she was Aphrodite in the flesh. Darcy will not be moved. He only wishes to be happy.

"And I think you underestimate Elizabeth's capabilities." Anne smiled, filled with mirth at the way her friend would no doubt deal with the naysayers. "Elizabeth is well able to handle any critical comments others make of her, and as my aunt and uncle have welcomed her—and I suspect they know of Darcy's interest—I expect they will help ease her acceptance."

"Hugh has welcomed her?"

"As has Aunt Susan, as evidenced by the invitation to the ball tomorrow night. Please, Mother—allow Darcy this happiness. She will be a good wife to him, and he is nothing less than besotted with her."

It was quite obviously very hard for her. She did not say anything for a few moments, but Anne could see the struggle it was for her to overcome a lifetime of opinions. In some ways, Anne had it easier than her mother—she had never been much in society, had only her mother's commentary on the importance of rank. She had never seen much value in it.

"Very well, Anne," said Lady Catherine, though it was clear she was still unhappy. "I will say nothing to Miss Bennet or Darcy about his attentions. In the end, I doubt he would listen to me regardless."

"True, Mother." Anne smiled and stood. "Now, can I assume you have come with the intention of staying?"

"I have."

"Good. Then let us see you to a room and make sure you are settled. You should also attend the ball with us tomorrow, as it will do you good to once again be among society."

She did not say anything, but Lady Catherine followed readily as Anne departed from the room. There were no embraces, no affectionate smiles—Anne had not expected any, as her mother was simply not that sort of person. Perhaps there might be in the future.

Anne hoped there would be—she would wish to have a true and loving relationship with her mother, if it was at all attainable.

The sudden arrival of Lady Catherine to his home was not at all welcome to Darcy. The lady had a propensity to make herself disagreeable to all and sundry, to insert her opinion where it was least wanted, and she held a grudge against Miss Bennet which Darcy could not tolerate. He had been at his club that morning, discussing the situation with Bingley, and they had agreed that they would remove to Hertfordshire if the Bennet sisters should be called home. Given what he knew of Mr. Bennet and what Miss Elizabeth had said, Darcy suspected it would not be long before they were.

To arrive home and discover the presence of his aunt was disagreeable, and Darcy waited for the inevitable arguments and fights which would result from her disapproval of everything which was happening in Darcy's home. Only they did not come.

"Mother has apologized and wishes to join our party, Darcy," said Anne, as she informed him of her conversation with her mother and what had been decided.

"That is quite surprising," said Darcy after hearing her account. "I had not thought she would capitulate so easily."

"Nor had I," replied Anne. "I suppose it became rather lonely at Rosings."

But Darcy had another concern. "What of my attentions to Miss Elizabeth?"

Anne laughed, far from the response Darcy had expected. "You have finally confessed it!"

"I confessed it many days ago, to Miss Elizabeth, at least. She is the only one for whom I was concerned."

"I suppose that is true," replied Anne, still chuckling. "For the present, you may rest your concerns. I informed my mother of your attentions and told her I would not take kindly to any interference."

"I cannot imagine she took that well."

"In fact, one of the reasons she came was to ensure you made a marriage with the right kind of woman, now that I am no longer a consideration."

Darcy thought his eyes might pop out of his head in response to that revelation, but Anne only laughed again. "I *think* I have managed to sway her, Cousin."

"Has the woman no sense at all?" muttered Darcy, shaking his head. "I have spent my entire adult life endeavoring to avoid marrying an heiress."

"And one heiress in particular," replied Anne.

"I am glad you are so diverted by all of this," said Darcy, feeling more than a little cross.

"I have no choice. If I was not, I might find my mother's actions offensive. I wish to have a relationship with my mother, but I do not wish to have it on *her* terms."

It was with a newfound sense of admiration for his cousin that Darcy thought of their conversation. Miss Elizabeth had helped her, it was true, but Anne had firmly taken the reins of her own life with a determination to live it as best she could, and Darcy was happy that she had.

Lady Catherine's behavior for the rest of the day was indicative of her evident desire to please her daughter, yet her conflicting opinion of Miss Elizabeth and even more, he thought, her disapproval of any marriage between those of dissimilar ranks clearly made it difficult for her. She said very little, instead choosing to carefully watch the interactions of them all, but as she was not accustomed to hiding her thoughts, they were painfully plain for all who desired to see. When the evening had ended, the four ladies went off to their rooms for the evening, Lady Catherine also retiring to her own, while Darcy and Fitzwilliam went to his study for a nightcap. They did not stay long, however, as Darcy wished to retire himself, while Fitzwilliam took himself to the billiard room for a short time. What Darcy did not expect was to see Lady Catherine again that night.

After he walked to the upper floor where the family apartments were located, Darcy had been able to hear soft sounds of laughter emanating from behind one of the doors. Though none of their words could be understood, the clear bursts of laughter were easy to hear. Darcy smiled, once again thinking of the blessings he had received lately, when his eyes found a silent form standing in the corridor. It was Lady Catherine.

The lady was as Darcy had never seen her before—she was standing stock still, her eyes fixed on the door to Georgiana's room, an earnest expression filling her countenance, quite a difference from her usually haughty superiority. One arm was folded across her midsection, while the elbow of the other rested on her arm, her hand rising to her chin in thought. And every time a new burst of laughter made its way through the door, her brows furrowed further, as if she was attempting to puzzle out a particularly difficult riddle.

"Step forward, Darcy," said she, though she did not turn and look at him. "I heard you climbing the stairs."

"I had not meant to attempt silence," replied Darcy. "I was only surprised to see you here."

Lady Catherine sniffed, though her usual arrogance was lacking. "This is Georgiana's room, is it not?"

"It is. I see the ladies have gathered again to exchange confidences. Georgiana, Anne, and Miss Elizabeth have done so several times since Miss Elizabeth came to stay here. I suppose Miss Bennet's presence made such a gathering necessary tonight."

For a long moment Lady Catherine's only response was a grunt. Darcy decided to allow her to speak on her own, for he could not suppose she did not have something to say. Her earnest expression informed him that her thoughts were not at all what they might normally have consisted.

"Anne tells me you have been courting Miss Elizabeth."

Darcy smiled at her mention of the fiery, beautiful woman he intended to make his wife. "Courting is perhaps not the correct word, for I have not spoken with her father or her uncle. I suppose calling on her is not quite correct either, as she is living under my roof. But if you mean it in the sense that I esteem her and wish to make her my wife, then she is not incorrect."

Finally, Lady Catherine turned to look at him. "I will own that I cannot understand the power she possesses over you.

"Oh, she is pretty enough," continued Lady Catherine when Darcy tried to respond, "and she is intelligent, but she is far too outspoken and displays a distressing lack of deference."

"That is precisely what I find irresistible about her."

Lady Catherine's eyes found Darcy's, and she frowned, attempting to understand his words. Darcy was more than happy to assist.

"I have had enough of deference, Lady Catherine. Had I wanted deference, I could have married my friend Bingley's sister, for she supplied that in abundance. So could many other ladies of the ton."

"Tell me you did not contemplate such a thing!" exclaimed Lady Catherine.

Chuckling, and shaking his head, Darcy said: "Not Miss Bingley, though I likely would not have been deterred by her position in society had I any attraction for her."

"Do not attempt to jest about such things."

"I assure you I do not. I care little for the strictures of society in this matter, Lady Catherine. Caroline Bingley at least has a substantial dowry, which would have appeased some, had I chosen to offer for her. Unfortunately for her ambitions, she possesses other qualities—such as her flattering deference to anything I say—which made a marriage between us impossible.

"What I am trying to inform you, Lady Catherine, is the list of qualities I desire in a wife does not begin and end with dowry and connections—in fact, they are two minor considerations on that list. Of much more importance are love, compatibility, intelligence, independence, integrity, and many other qualities which Miss Elizabeth personifies. If she does not have a large dowry, I can more than make up for that lack, and her lack of connections is refreshing, for it means that she has not been corrupted by society."

"It seems you have given this much thought, if nothing else," said Lady Catherine, a hint of irritability evident in her voice.

"I have, though I will own that when I first met her, I was blinded to her worth and my thoughts were much the same as yours." Laughter once again rang out from behind Georgiana's door, and Darcy turned and smiled at it, gesturing with one hand. "Think of the wonders Miss Elizabeth has done for your daughter. Consider also my own sister, who was quiet as a mouse when she arrived, and now she laughs heartily in Miss Elizabeth's presence. Can you truly say this is not a worthy woman? Have we as a family not already gained from her presence?"

"I suppose when you put it that way . . . ."

"I do," replied Darcy.

"Then you mean to pursue her, regardless of what I say."

"You or anyone else."

"Then I suppose I have no choice but to accept it." A wry smile Darcy had never seen from his aunt appeared on her face. "But do not expect acceptance to come easily. I will try to remain civil to her and her family, but if I should slip, I would ask you do not hold it against me."

Before Darcy could reply, Lady Catherine turned on her heel and walked to her room, the door shutting behind her. Darcy could hardly believe the conversation he had just had with her, so surreal had it been.

But he also had hope. Lady Catherine's arrival had been a serious concern in his pursuit of Miss Elizabeth, but now it seemed that concern had been neutralized. It was a thoughtful—and grateful—Darcy that made his way to his room for the night.

Chapter XXX

The following morning, Elizabeth awoke refreshed and calm, with none of the thoughts which had so unsettled her in recent days and weeks swirling through her head. Her friendship with Anne, her growing love for Georgiana, and the presence of her dearest friend and sister after so long a separation had acted like a balm to her soul. Thoughts of Mr. Darcy and his avowed intentions persisted, but she was willing to simply allow the future to flow as it would. The lack of such weighty thoughts made her lethargic, whereas most mornings she was awake immediately and eager to meet the day.

It was a day of preparation, for three of the young ladies would be attending a ball far finer than any they had hitherto attended, and they were looking forward to it and dreading it in equal measure. As a result, most of their preparations were undertaken more carefully than they might have in other circumstances, and it showed in the radiance of their countenances, the expert and complex manner in which their maids styled their hair, and the fineness of their new ball gowns.

The one who was not to be attending, Georgiana, was more despondent about it than Elizabeth might have thought, given what she knew of the reticent and shy girl. It seemed that Georgiana had grown much these past weeks.

"I *do* wish I could attend," said she, for what seemed like the hundredth time that day. "Even if I was unable to dance, I am sure the spectacle would have been quite beyond anything I have ever before seen."

Elizabeth, whose hair was being pinned up by Tilly, looked at her friend in the mirror and smiled. "In another two years, you will be coming out yourself and will be the most sought-after girl in society. You would not wish to spoil it by attending early, in a situation where you will not be able to make the most of it."

"That is easy for you to say, Elizabeth, for you are able to attend tonight, and you came out at the age of fifteen."

"Which is much too young," said Elizabeth, "even in a small country society. Trust me, Georgiana—it is better for *you* that you wait patiently, learn everything you can, and enter society when you are ready."

"You should listen to Elizabeth," said Anne, who was seated nearby on Elizabeth's bed. "A few weeks ago, you were eager to remain away from society forever."

"And a part of me still is," said Georgiana. Then she smiled shyly at Elizabeth. "I can wait. And in the end, I care nothing for being sought after, or any such nonsense. I only wish to find someone to love."

"Then you are already wise beyond your years," replied Elizabeth.

When their preparations were complete, Elizabeth entered the carriage with the others who were to attend—which included Colonel Fitzwilliam, who was resplendent in his regimentals—and they made the short journey to the site of the ball, a house in the Mayfair district which was a little closer to Hyde Park and on a different street from Mr. Darcy's house.

"We might simply have walked here!" exclaimed Elizabeth, when the carriage rolled to a stop only moments later.

"Please do not say such a thing in the dance, Miss Elizabeth," said Lady Catherine. "It is customary to arrive in a carriage. Such comments will only show your country manners and nature."

"I fully agree with her," said Anne, shooting her mother a glance. "Perhaps we should walk home after."

"If you can walk after hours of dancing, I will be happy to escort you," said Mr. Darcy.

Fitzwilliam chuckled and nodded, noting: "Darcy speaks the truth. Most attendees will end the amusement exhausted. That is one reason why everyone arrives in a carriage."

"I meant no disrespect toward Miss Elizabeth," said Lady Catherine. "But society can be harsh, especially to those who make comments which are unexpected or are considered to be lacking in polish."

"I thank you, Lady Catherine," said Elizabeth, eager to avoid an argument. "I will attempt to rein in my tongue."

The line of carriages was not long, and they were soon able to disembark, though Darcy told them with some amusement that it was because they had arrived on time, and that most of the attendees would be fashionably late. Shuddering at the thought of the crush which would ensue, Elizabeth allowed herself to be led into the entrance hall where the family was lined up to greet them.

Lady Harriet Greenwood was a woman of about Lady Susan's age, but whereas Lady Susan was tall and handsome, Lady Harriet was short and plump, not at all handsome, but with a motherly demeanor, which instantly put others at ease. Her husband—Lord Edgar Greenwood, Earl of Stoneway—was, by contrast, tall and austere, seeming almost as Mr. Darcy had during his time in Hertfordshire the previous autumn. As Darcy's aunt and uncle were also present, the Bennet sisters and Anne were introduced and welcomed by the other couple, and it was obvious to Elizabeth that the acceptance of the Matlocks smoothed Elizabeth and Jane's way.

With the greetings and introductions complete, the friends entered the ballroom and obtained some punch from the nearby refreshment tables. The musicians had begun to play, though their early offerings consisted of soft prelude music, interspersed with the sounds of instruments receiving minute tuning adjustments. It was a small stringed orchestra, and though Elizabeth had always thought the musicians which were hired for the assemblies in Meryton were nothing wanting, it was obvious these were a cut above.

Slowly the hall began to fill, and there were many who were known to Colonel Fitzwilliam and Mr. Darcy, and even a few to Lady Catherine as well. Lord and Lady Matlock soon joined them, and even more introductions were given, and Elizabeth was amused to see the looks of interest Anne received, but also the ones she and Jane garnered as well.

"How shall I remember so many names?" asked Anne after they had been introduced to, it seemed, several hundred previously unknown people.

Elizabeth turned to her with amusement. "I do not think it is required to remember them all. In fact, I think they will be quite eager to remind you of their names and situations—especially the young men I saw watching you!"

"I fear Miss Elizabeth is correct," said a scowling Lady Catherine. "There was far too much interest, and much of it from those you should not even consider."

"Have no fear, Mother," said Anne. "I do not consider any of them at present. I am just newly into society—I have no intention of surrendering my independence so quickly."

Lady Catherine glanced at her daughter, but she did not respond. Anne had already turned her attention back to Elizabeth.

"And what of the young men I saw watching you with interest?"

"They were mostly watching Jane," replied Elizabeth. "Unfortunately, they are destined to be disappointed."

Her eyes found Jane, who stood with Mr. Bingley—he having arrived some moments before—and her attention was fixed on him to the exclusion of all others. Beyond them stood Mr. Hurst, Mrs. Hurst, and Miss Bingley, and though the former two looked about with some astonishment, the latter was watching Mr. Darcy as if he was a heavily laden banquet table and she, a famished woman.

"You may deny it," said Anne, "but a fair few of them watched *you* with interest."

"Then they will be disappointed when they learn of my situation," replied Elizabeth with little interest. "I am not concerned about their attention."

"Especially not when you are receiving the attentions of my cousin," said Anne with a sly look at Mr. Darcy.

Elizabeth decided it would be prudent to ignore her. They stood there for some time speaking amongst themselves, but before long, the music began for the opening dance, and Elizabeth noted the couples assembling on the dance floor. She also noticed the approach of Mr. Darcy and his cousin, who gallantly bowed before them and entreated them to dance.

Feeling unaccountably shy—she had wondered why Mr. Darcy, if his interest was as profound as he averred, had not previously secured her first sets—Elizabeth accepted his hand while Anne accepted Colonel Fitzwilliam's, and they made their way to where the other couples were gathering. Within moments the set started, and they began to move in the complex steps with which Elizabeth was so familiar.

"You once told me you talk as a rule when you are dancing," said Mr. Darcy, wasting no time in opening his mouth. "Can I expect the same behavior now that we are in a ballroom in London?"

Though distracted momentarily by the sight of Jane dancing with Mr. Bingley for the first time since November, Elizabeth answered: "I am at your disposal, Mr. Darcy. Anything you wish to speak of, I am more than happy to answer."

"Even books? Or does your stricture against them still stand?"

Elizabeth laughed. "I suppose I could relax it, if you wish. But I shall warn you, Mr. Darcy, that you should not expect any insightful comments or opinions should you insist. There is too much else occurring to do the subject any justice."

"Then I shall leave the topic to you, Miss Elizabeth," replied Mr. Darcy. The intensity in his gaze quite took her breath away. "Or perhaps we should simply stare at each other like besotted fools. It would give society much of which to speak, do you not think?"

Feeling her cheeks heating, Elizabeth nonetheless managed to respond. "I doubt they would take much notice of *my* behavior, Mr. Darcy."

"On the contrary, Miss Bennet, I believe you and your sister are quite the curiosity. You are known, for example, to have arrived in my company and that of Lady Catherine and the earl's second son, and you were welcomed with open arms by no less than two earls and their wives, one of whom is Lady Catherine's brother. I am afraid the days of your relative obscurity are at an end."

A single glance about the room informed Elizabeth that it was nothing less than the truth. A few in attendance were looking at Jane and Mr. Bingley—though she noticed that most of these were young men—many more were watching herself and Mr. Darcy. Elizabeth thought their gazes suggested curiosity, some were mixed with anger, while others held disdain. It appeared like everything she had been told about what to expect was true, and she wondered if she would escape unscathed.

"There is no need to worry, Miss Elizabeth." The sound of Mr. Darcy's voice, so gentle and affectionate that it felt like a caress, drew her eyes back to him, and they were immediately caught in the trap of his gaze. She thought she might have been caught there an eternity, had he not spoken again soon after, breaking the spell. "You need not concern yourself for their opinion, and there are only a few who will dare to speak their feelings aloud. The recommendation of both the Earls of Matlock and Stoneway are not inconsequential, and the Darcy name is not without weight."

"I am not concerned, Mr. Darcy," replied Elizabeth, holding her head high. "My courage is no brittle thing, I assure you."

"I would not have thought it was. But anyone can be disconcerted by such attention if they are not accustomed to it. I believe if Georgiana was here to witness the interest in you, she would wish she was back at home safe in bed."

Elizabeth laughed. "I have no doubt you are correct, sir."

They continued through the sets and when they were completed, they changed partners, Elizabeth dancing with Colonel Fitzwilliam and Mr. Darcy, with Anne. But though Elizabeth soon was engaged by a dizzying succession of young men eager to partner a young lady unknown to them, she found her eyes darting back to find Mr. Darcy time and time again throughout the evening. And her inability to keep her eyes from him for long told her much that was hidden before. Somehow, her heart had softened toward him and made him agreeable in her eyes. Her ultimate acceptance of his offer, should he make one, was all but assured. There could never be more love in her heart than what she now felt for Mr. Darcy.

For Darcy, the evening was more tolerable than similar evenings in the past—or at least it was in some ways. The cream of society was there that evening—though there were some Lady Harriet would not invite—and Darcy found himself enjoying it more, and it was mostly due to Miss Elizabeth's presence. On the other hand, however, it was difficult watching as Miss Elizabeth was escorted to the dance floor by what seemed like every man in attendance.

But it also informed Darcy of her ability to be at ease in any situation, for she was happy and friendly with all, no matter what strata of society they inhabited or their behavior toward her. Darcy could almost imagine the day when she would be mistress of *his* home, making their guests welcome in the same manner in which she moved in society that evening.

There was one, he noted, who was not enjoying the evening nearly so much, and though Darcy did not like the woman, he was able to feel a little sympathy for her. The Bingleys had rarely attended a function of this nature before—those events to which they had been previously invited had tended to inhabit a tier lower than a ball given at an earl's residence. And on those occasions, Miss Bingley had used her brother's connection with Darcy to secure dance partners, helped in no small measure by the obligation Darcy had always felt to dance with his sister's friend.

But as he had not danced with her this evening, she stood most of the evening by the side of the dance floor, watching the dancers, and alternately casting some desperate glances in his direction. Her only partners thus far had been Bingley, Hurst, and one other young man with whom Darcy was not at all acquainted. Darcy did not wish to give the woman false hope, and moreover, he did not like the way she treated Miss Elizabeth, so he had come with the express purpose of refusing to dance with her.

As the evening wore on, however, his heart was softened a little toward her. She was not a malicious woman, he decided — or perhaps she was at times. But she was more single-minded, haughty, and determined to have him for a husband, than hateful. She had gone too far in her attempts to discredit Miss Elizabeth and reach for that which she would never obtain, it was true, and Darcy was angered because of it. But that did not change the fact that she *did* have much to offer to the right man; that man, however, was not he, and he would not have her misunderstand his feelings.

Pity for the woman's plight finally won Darcy over, and he approached the sisters, asking them in turn if they would favor him with a dance. The relief in Miss Bingley's eyes was quite beyond anything Darcy had ever witnessed in her. Their dances at previous events had been characterized by her desire to keep his attention by constant commentary, but on this evening, she was all but silent, regarding him with more than a hint of speculation. Darcy could not state the content of her thoughts with any accuracy, and he decided that he truly had no desire to know. If she was content to be silent, then he had no reason to complain.

Thus, it was a surprise when, after they had started dancing the second of the set, she spoke up, saying: "There was never a chance of eliciting a proposal from you, was there?"

"I am afraid not," said Darcy, not wishing to crush the woman's spirit, but unwilling to lie to her. "There was never any attraction between us, and I cannot propose to a woman without already possessing an affection for her."

Miss Bingley tilted her head to the side, regarding him as if she did not know him. "I would not have imagined it, Mr. Darcy. I have been taught that marriages are undertaken for financial gain and connections."

"Can you honestly state you would have brought me the required connections?"

Though she colored, Miss Bingley did not look away. "I have always understood my background would be a hindrance. I thought your friendship with Charles and my dowry would be enough to overcome it."

"Then I am afraid you did not understand me," replied Darcy. "Such considerations must be pondered, but they are not of utmost importance to me."

Miss Bingley nodded, and they were separated by the dance. When they came together again, she appeared introspective again. "That explains why Miss Elizabeth was able to gain your attention. I never would have thought that acting in a contrary fashion, arguing with and teasing a man would be a successful method with which to capture a husband. And that says nothing about her own lack of connections or a suitable dowry."

"It is when a man is subjected to nothing more than sycophancy and deference," replied Darcy. It was clear Miss Bingley understood his reference quite well, for she blushed and her gaze found the floor. "I wish for a partner, Miss Bingley—not a subject."

The woman nodded, and when she raised her head to look at him again, he could tell she was trying to put a brave face on her disappointment. "Then I hope you will be happy, sir."

Darcy accepted her words for the peace offering they were, and they fell silent. When the sets were finished, Darcy escorted her back to the side of the room and claimed her sister's hand, leading her to the dance floor. He was pleased to note that Miss Bingley was quickly claimed by another gentleman and was situated a few couples to his left. Perhaps she would find enjoyment this evening after all.

After supper—Darcy again partnered Miss Elizabeth for the preceding set, causing more whispers to soar through the ballroom—Darcy found himself standing close to Anne and Lady Catherine, who were seated, watching the dancers. As with the previous ball they had attended, Anne had become fatigued toward the end of the evening and was now sitting out, intent upon not overtaxing her strength. Lady Susan was also nearby, and the three ladies were speaking in low tones. When Lady Susan beckoned Darcy over to them, it was with a clearly observed sense of amusement, and he fully expected to be teased by his female relations.

"I am feeling rather gratified at the Miss Bennets' success tonight," said Lady Susan when he had joined them. "I had thought they would garner some interest, but I dare say neither has sat out the entire evening.

"It is obvious that Mr. Bingley has not missed that fact either," said Anne.

Darcy followed her gaze, and he noted where Bingley stood by the dance floor, his eyes affixed upon Jane Bennet, who was dancing with one of Darcy's school friends. Bingley was also acquainted with the man in a passing fashion and should have known that Miss Bennet was in no danger, but he had been thus the entire night, only dancing a few times, watching Miss Bennet carefully when she was escorted by some other man. It was vastly different from Bingley's normally amiable behavior.

"I do not think Darcy has missed it either," continued Anne, darting a mischievous glance his way.

"I have not. But I have seen Miss Elizabeth in other venues, and I am aware of her character. She is enjoying herself. But she has not been affected by any of them."

"That is my opinion too," replied Lady Susan. "At first, I wondered, but it is clear she is only speaking of superficial topics."

"The girl is far too open," groused Lady Catherine. "She bares herself to ridicule by being so unguarded."

"She is fine, Catherine," replied Lady Susan. "She is still perhaps a little unpolished, but I have no doubt she will make a splash in society. I, for one, cannot wait. Look at all the young ladies who are watching her with envy! I have never been so diverted at the sight of so many disappointed, haughty young women!"

"That is what worries me," said Anne, glancing over to where her aunt had pointed.

It was true that there did appear to be many disappointed young ladies, and Darcy had had his share of fluttering eyelashes, simpering laughs, and coquettish glances throughout the evening, but in truth, as his attentions had been fixed on Miss Elizabeth, he had not given them much notice. It was a refreshing change, indeed.

"They will hold their tongues," replied Lady Susan, her sniff of derision informing them of her opinion of their displeasure. "Our greeting of the Bennet sisters was calculated to encourage decorum. Few will wish to anger the houses of Matlock and Stoneway over a woman they will fool themselves into believing is not a threat to their ambitions."

"Are you not a little overconfident, Lady Susan?" asked Darcy. In reality, he was more than a little amused, as his aunt seemed determined to have Miss Elizabeth as a niece.

"Not at all," replied Lady Susan, turning a smug gaze on Darcy. "Given the way you have been looking at each other tonight, I am confident an engagement announcement will be forthcoming before long. I only wish you would teach my second son what you have learned—he seems content to remain a bachelor for the rest of his life."

Darcy's eyes found Fitzwilliam where he danced with some miss with whom Darcy was not acquainted, and the roguish grin with which he favored her suggested he was behaving at his most outrageous.

"If you will forgive me, Aunt Susan," replied Darcy, "I will leave your son to his own devices. He will settle down at a time of his own choosing, I am certain."

Though Lady Susan's glance suggested annoyance, she was too happy about the developments concerning Miss Elizabeth to dwell on it. For his part, Darcy spent the rest of the evening watching her, content to see her brightly shining countenance as she dazzled young man after young man. By now Darcy was confident in her affections, and knew that she was just being herself. Had he waited longer, they might have been challengers for her favor. But there was no one left on the field, and if they attempted to enter it, he knew they would be required to retreat. It was only a matter of time before he would be able to make her his alone.

Chapter XXXI

*I*t was, by far, the most enjoyable night of society Elizabeth had ever spent, but by the time the end had arrived, she found she was, as Mr. Darcy had suggested, quite exhausted and quite willing to allow the carriage to take them the short distance back to his house. She could never have imagined the evening would proceed in such an agreeable manner, but she was happy she had had a taste of that society. Not all those to whom she had been introduced had been agreeable—in fact, some of the young women had been condescending, and some of the men she thought would be best to avoid altogether. But overall, Lady Susan had eased her introduction into her world, and Elizabeth had no cause to think it had been anything but a success.

The residents of Darcy house slept late the next morning and rose after they had regained some of their vigor. When they had made their way down to the visiting rooms, they were met by an obviously annoyed Georgiana.

"I have been waiting patiently for some details of last night's amusement!" cried the girl, apparently desperate to hear the news.

"I told you they would be late and would arise late," replied Mrs. Annesley, her tone slightly chiding. "Had you concentrated on your lessons, you might have been able to keep your excitement under control."

Georgiana's rolled eyes—carefully where her companion could not see them—spoke to her thoughts for the reprimand. Instead, she looked at Elizabeth, a glare reminiscent of those she had often seen from Mr. Darcy demanding she speak. Elizabeth laughed and obliged, and the young ladies spent some minutes regaling her with tales of what they had done and with whom they had danced. The girl was shining with anticipation and Elizabeth thought Mr. Darcy might have a hard time holding her eagerness in check. It was a circumstance which could hardly have been fathomed only a few months earlier.

Throughout that day and the next, Elizabeth spent every moment she could with Anne and Georgiana, knowing that her time with them was rapidly coming to a close. Even Lady Catherine, who still looked on Elizabeth with exasperation at times, seemed affected by this coming separation. At times, Elizabeth thought it would become quite maudlin, for they all seemed to feel it.

"Oh, that is enough already!" laughed Anne after Georgiana had told Elizabeth how much she would miss her several times over. "We shall not be separated very long at all!"

Georgiana turned to Anne and regarded her with confusion for some moments, before it was replaced with excitement. "Are we to go to Hertfordshire? Are we to see Elizabeth and Jane again?"

"Yes, my dear Cousin, we are," replied Anne, smiling at Georgiana's obvious enthusiasm.

"I am so happy!" cried Georgiana, throwing herself into Elizabeth's arms. "I shall meet your sisters, and we shall have so much fun!"

"Perhaps . . ." said Lady Catherine, regarding Georgiana with a pensive frown, but she trailed off. "Well, I suppose it is unavoidable, if we are to go to Hertfordshire." She cast a stern frown on Georgiana. "But you must remember your station, Georgiana, and not allow the behavior of young ladies of a lesser station to influence yours."

"Oh, Mother," said Anne, shaking her head. "I cannot think they can be all that much different."

"In fact, Lady Catherine is not incorrect in this instance," said Elizabeth, suppressing a wince. "My younger sisters are . . . exuberant, and they do not appreciate being checked. I think they could both do with a little of Georgiana's reserve."

"Then I will be happy to share it with them!" exclaimed Georgiana.

Elizabeth could only laugh. "Let us then hope *they* will emulate *you*!"

Lady Catherine watched Elizabeth with unconcealed annoyance, and Elizabeth was certain the lady was determined to take her younger sisters in hand once they were within range of her influence. Far from being exasperated with her ladyship's presumption, Elizabeth thought her younger sisters could do with a little of Lady Catherine's severity. They had certainly never listened to their elder sisters, and heaven knew their mother never acted to check their behavior!

The preparations for an imminent departure gained a much more festive air; had Elizabeth not known otherwise, she might have thought that Georgiana expected to leave for Hertfordshire at the same time as Elizabeth herself left. As it was, Elizabeth was quite happy to see the girl so enthusiastic, though she was not certain how Mr. Darcy felt about the prospect of his sister's pending corruption at the hands of her youngest sisters.

"I am quite happy for her to make your sisters' acquaintances," said Mr. Darcy when Elizabeth playfully raised the subject with him later that day. "Though you, Anne, and your sister have been an excellent influence on my sister, I cannot help but think she would benefit from an acquaintance with those of her own age."

"You do not worry about her being afflicted by their high spirits?"

Mr. Darcy only smiled. "I hope Georgiana knows what is acceptable and what is not. It *is* possible they will also benefit from her demeanor. And I am certain my aunt will have something to say, should they get out of hand."

Elizabeth could not help the laughter which bubbled up, and Mr. Darcy laughed along with her. She wondered at it, however, for she could not have imagined Mr. Darcy willingly allowing his sister in company with hers not long ago. She did not make that observation, however, for she did not wish to offend him, though she was certain he would allow the truth of it.

"How are your own preparations?" asked Mr. Darcy. "Are you anticipating your return?"

"I am, though perhaps not as much as I might have thought." Elizabeth paused and considered the matter for some moments. "I have . . . been away from home for some time now, and though I cannot quite put my finger on it, something has . . . changed."

The nod with which Mr. Darcy favored her informed Elizabeth that he understood her perfectly, perhaps better than she understood herself. "Is it like your world has expanded and Longbourn has not grown with it?"

A frown found Elizabeth's face as she thought about it, before nodding slowly. "Perhaps that is it, though I will always love my childhood home."

"As is proper." Mr. Darcy paused, though his gaze never wavered. "Miss Bennet, though you are to leave my house, we will be in company again soon, for as you know, Bingley cannot be away from your sister for more than a few days!"

Elizabeth laughed. "I think you must be correct."

"I have given this matter much thought, and I would like to obtain your permission to call on you when you return to your home."

Though thrilled with his request, Elizabeth saw a prime opportunity to tease him. "I must own to being impressed, Mr. Darcy. I had not thought you would ride all the way from London only to call on me."

"Minx!" exclaimed Mr. Darcy. "You know I intend to join Bingley at Netherfield when he goes, though I *would* be willing to show my devotion to call on you from London if necessary. But three miles, I believe, is no true measure, so I will need to show that devotion in other ways, if you will allow it."

"You know how my mother will react when she realizes it, do you not?"

"I am counting on it." The smile he showed her was roguish. "She will be my most ardent supporter, I am certain."

"Now that is not fair, Mr. Darcy!" protested Elizabeth.

"No, but it should inform you how serious I am about my intentions."

"I never doubted them."

Then, in a movement so unexpected and firm, Mr. Darcy leaned down and kissed her. It was nothing more than an instant, but it left Elizabeth aching for so much more. But he was not willing to press his luck, though he did lean his forehead against hers once he had accomplished his objective.

"I am sorry for my impulsive action, Miss Bennet, but it seemed the only way to silence you."

Elizabeth laughed. "It seems to have been effective, though I will thank you not to take this means of winning arguments *all* the time."

Then, realizing what she had said, Elizabeth colored, and her eyes sought the floor beneath their feet.

"I believe, Miss Bennet," said Mr. Darcy, drawing her eyes back to him, "that when all is said and done, we will find that *I* am far more in *your* power than the reverse. And I would not have it any other way."

* * *

And so it was that the eldest Bennet sisters returned to their home soon after, and Mr. Darcy's words about Mr. Bingley's inability to part from Miss Bennet were proven, for the combined Bingley and Darcy party followed only three short days after. And though Mrs. Bennet was ecstatic to have Mr. Bingley returned to her eldest and most deserving daughter, she was unable to make out the presence of not only Mr. Darcy, but also his sister, his aunt, and his cousin.

For Elizabeth herself, though she was happy to be home, she soon realized that she had become more accustomed to the softness and quietude of Mr. Darcy's house, and the much more frenetic pace of Longbourn was suddenly taxing on her nerves. Mr. Bennet was happy to see Jane and Elizabeth return, and he commented more than once on how agreeable he found their presence. What was not so agreeable was Elizabeth's reaction upon learning the family's most recent news when she arrived home.

"Lizzy!" exclaimed Lydia almost as soon as they walked through the door. "You must congratulate me, for I am to go to Brighton for the summer."

"You, go to Brighton?" asked Elizabeth, perplexed at the very notion.

"Yes, for you see I have been invited by Harriet Forster, my particular friend and the colonel's wife. I am to enjoy Brighton's charms and to become the favorite of all the officers."

"Is it not unfair, Lizzy?" asked Kitty, who was obviously near to tears. "I am two years older—should I not have been invited as well?"

"Oh, who would wish to invite *you*?" demanded Lydia, her voice laden with derision. "*I* am Harriet's particular friend. She does not like you nearly so well as she likes me!"

"Do not be unkind to your sister, Lydia," said Elizabeth. "Are you certain of this?"

"Of course, I am!" exclaimed Lydia, her affront obvious. "You and Jane have had all the fun, though I cannot imagine a visit to Kent to see *Mr. Collins* would be agreeable. It is now my turn. Papa has already given his consent."

And laughing, Lydia went skipping off to demand Jane's congratulations. Elizabeth watched her go, wondering how such an empty-headed girl could possibly be trusted with naught but Mrs. Harriet Forster as a chaperon, a girl who was as silly and ridiculous as Lydia was herself. The more she thought about it, the more Elizabeth realized she must make the attempt to convince her father against sending her.

Unfortunately, Mr. Bennet was quite insensible to the notion that Lydia's going would do anything other than secure their peace.

"Of course, I have given my consent," said he when Elizabeth raised the subject. "Would you expect me to subject the entire family to her tantrums all summer if she is prevented?"

"I would expect that she would be taken in hand before she ruins us all," replied Elizabeth, with perhaps more passion than tact.

Mr. Bennet, far from taking offense, only laughed. "You should not concern yourself, Lizzy. These officers are not fools—none of them will wish to be saddled with a silly, dowerless girl who will bring them nothing but headaches. Lydia will be quite safe, and will have the added benefit of making herself ridiculous and realizing the reality of her own insignificance in a distant place where it will not affect her family."

Though Elizabeth was not at all in agreement with her father's assertion, there was nothing she could say to convince him, and she was forced to retreat from the field in defeat. Elizabeth had always known of her father's lackadaisical style of caring for his daughters—she knew he loved them, but the level of involvement which would be required to change Lydia's habits was far beyond that which he was willing to exert himself.

Lydia was as unkind in the last days before she departed as she had been when Elizabeth first discovered the change in her status, and Kitty bore the brunt of it. Elizabeth attempted to console her sister, and in response, she found a little improvement in Kitty's spirits.

"You do not think Brighton will be as fun as Lydia claims?" asked Kitty in response to Elizabeth's gentle words.

"I do not," said Elizabeth. "The colonel will be busy with his duties, and though Lydia will have Mrs. Forster with her and the officers not far away, I am certain her boasts of parties and balls every day are nothing more than wishful thinking."

"I suppose," replied Kitty, though Elizabeth could readily see she was not convinced.

"Besides," continued Elizabeth, "when Mr. Bingley comes, Mr. Darcy and his sister and cousin will be accompanying them. Anne is a treasure, but I think you will enjoy Georgiana's company especially. She is a wonderful young woman and will require someone her own age to welcome her into the neighborhood."

"Truly?" asked Kitty, her eyes wide.

"Yes. But you will be required to improve your behavior. Georgiana is a proper young lady, and she is not yet out. She will appreciate your friendship, but her aunt, Lady Catherine de Bourgh, will not appreciate your animal spirits."

"I will try," said Kitty. It was clear she was excited about the prospect of meeting such an elegant young lady, and as such, Elizabeth merely had to remind her of Georgiana's coming, and Kitty would think of her behavior and try to do better.

Thus it was that Lydia departed for Brighton the same day that the Netherfield party arrived in the area, and as Elizabeth would have expected, Mr. Bingley wasted no time in calling on the Bennets to once again put himself in Jane's company, so they arrived only hours after Lydia's departure. He was welcomed with the civility and excitement Elizabeth might have expected from her mother, but she was surprised to discover that Lady Catherine's presence had an unexpected benefit: her mother, never having been in company with the daughter of an earl before, was so astonished and overcome that she was much quieter in the lady's presence.

All the ladies were introduced to the Bennets, and Kitty and Georgiana became friends quickly, as Elizabeth might have expected. What was unexpected, however, was Mary's affinity for Georgiana's company, which Elizabeth attributed to the girls' common interest in music—Mary was soon to leave with the Gardiners for their tour to the north, but just on the basis of a few days, Elizabeth thought she and Georgiana would end as lifelong friends. Anne and Lady Catherine spoke kindly to all, and though it was quite obviously hard for Lady Catherine, even Elizabeth, who suspected the lady's true feelings, could hardly detect them, for she was kind to Mrs. Bennet. In fact, Elizabeth thought Lady Catherine came to possess an exasperated sort of fondness for her mother, though her attempts to correct Mrs. Bennet's behavior were doomed to failure. Mrs. Bennet was too set in her ways, which might be a blessing, as Lady Catherine's ideas of proper behavior were often laughable.

The Netherfield party once again settled into Mr. Bingley's home, and they were welcomed by all the neighborhood, much to the delight of many. Among the most vocal of those who made the Bingleys feel welcome again was Sir William, who never lost an opportunity to be civil. Elizabeth was happy to note that Mr. Darcy was much more able to bear the man's effusions with patience than he had been the previous autumn. Mr. Bingley, of course, was as happy and amiable as ever, and even his sisters were better behaved, though Miss Bingley still had a low tolerance for Meryton society.

What had happened to the young woman Elizabeth could not quite be certain, for her cutting remarks and snide superiority were a thing of the past. Or perhaps it was more accurate to say that she concealed her emotions much better, for Elizabeth did not think her opinion was any better than it was before. She was perfectly polite to Elizabeth, giving her every appearance of civility, seemingly intent upon maintaining her ability to claim an acquaintance with Mr. Darcy. Whether that would result in an advantageous marriage, Elizabeth did not know, but at least her days of open hostility were at an end.

In due course Mr. Bingley proposed to Jane and was accepted, and soon after that, Mr. Darcy asked for Elizabeth's hand with the same result. The raptures of Mrs. Bennet on such occasions might be guessed, but as she was quite in awe of Lady Catherine, she was at least able to temper her enthusiasm to a certain extent—that was to say she only called for her smelling salts once before she sat down to begin planning a wedding fine enough to satisfy a man of Mr. Darcy's position in society. In this she eagerly involved Lady Catherine, and though the lady was not nearly so enthusiastic about the match as was Mrs. Bennet, she seemed to take some solace in having some say in the arrangements. And though Elizabeth and Mr. Darcy—and Jane and Mr. Bingley, for they were to be married in a joint ceremony—would have preferred simple and elegant arrangements, they decided it was better to simply allow the two ladies—and Lady Susan when she arrived—to have their own way.

Lydia, of course, was enjoying herself in Brighton during this time. And perhaps she was enjoying herself a little too much, given the reports she gleefully sent back whenever she had the chance. As the summer wore on and the wedding approached, however, Mr. Bennet began to talk about calling his youngest daughter home so she could be present. Soon, unfortunately, her return became necessary.

On a beautiful August morning only a week before her wedding, Elizabeth was called into her father's study. She had spent many pleasant hours in the room since her return when Mr. Darcy was not available, sitting with the parent with whom she had always been close, reminiscing, speaking of the imminent changes facing the family. This, however, was not to be a discussion so benign.

"Sit down, Lizzy," said Mr. Bennet. He rubbed a weary hand over his eyes, and brandished a letter. "It seems you were more correct than I had thought with respect to your sister's determination to ruin us."

"What has she done?" asked Elizabeth. Though her voice was calm, her hands were clenched into fists; she knew Mr. Darcy would not forsake her, regardless of what Lydia had done, but she would never forgive Lydia if she did something to tarnish the old and respected name she was soon to take for her own.

"Oh, nothing so dreadful, I suppose," replied Mr. Bennet with a smile Elizabeth knew to be forced. "It appears Forster caught her with a young man of the regiment—Mr. Denny, to be precise—engaged in amorous activities."

"And you call this not dreadful?" exclaimed Elizabeth. It was nearly a shriek.

Mr. Bennet chuckled and shook his head. "From what the colonel said in his letter, I believe they were both still fully clothed. It was nothing more than a kiss, from what I understand."

"That is bad enough!" said Elizabeth.

"I am sorry to make such a gauche reference, Lizzy," said Mr. Bennet. "Colonel Forster is sending my wayward daughter home with an escort to avoid any further trouble, which is actually rather convenient, for it saves me the trouble of retrieving her myself."

"And when is she expected?"

"This very afternoon, unless they are delayed. The reason I called you in is to discuss what to do with her. Your mother, as you know, is busy with your wedding, and cannot be counted on to control Lydia regardless. I expect your sister will be offended by her ill use, claiming that she would have been married before you and Jane had the colonel only let her be."

"That is Lydia, without a doubt," said Elizabeth quietly.

"As your young man and his family will be here this afternoon, I thought it might be best to sequester Lydia until I can ensure she will not embarrass us all with her antics. I thought to ask for your opinion on how it might be done."

"I am certain I do not know," said Elizabeth. She paused, considering the matter. "You know Lydia will be loud and obnoxious, as she usually is, and I cannot imagine being confined to her room will check her tantrums to any great extent."

"I suppose not. Still, I shall do my best to ensure she is as well behaved as possible."

And with that Elizabeth was forced to be content. But contentment was a state which was elusive, for as the time approached for Lydia to arrive, Elizabeth became nervous, and all the things Lady Catherine likely thought about her family were no more than an hour or two away from being proven correct.

"What is it, Elizabeth?" asked Anne. Elizabeth, even amid her worries, had noted her friend's growing understanding of her perturbation of mind, and she had wondered when Anne would ask her about it. Elizabeth attempted to demur, but Anne was not about to allow it.

"It is obvious something is bothering you," said Anne, her stern tone demanding answers. "Surely you may share it with me."

Elizabeth sighed, knowing that Anne could be as inexorable as Lady Catherine when she put her mind to it. "My youngest sister is to return home today," said Elizabeth with a sigh. "Apparently, she has had some . . . trouble in Brighton and is not likely to behave well when she arrives."

Contrary to Elizabeth's expectation, Anne only laughed. "Then I am certain we shall weather the storm. You need not worry for our opinions, Elizabeth. You will find that we Fitzwilliams are a hardy lot—we shall not be frightened away by a spoiled child."

Unbeknownst to Elizabeth, there was another who overheard their conversation, and when the carriage was sighted and Mr. Bennet made his way out to greet it, Elizabeth followed along with Anne. She did not realize it until she made her presence known, but their eavesdropper also made her way outside at the same time.

The complaints began as soon as the carriage stopped, and Lydia made her way—reluctantly—from the coach to stand in front of them. She blamed the Forsters, the officers, and even her sisters who had been left behind in Hertfordshire for her near disgrace. Even Mary did not escape her censure, and she was not due to return with the Gardiners for another few days! In short, everyone was to blame except for Lydia herself.

Elizabeth attempted to speak to her sister to quiet her, but she was the only one who tried. Mr. Bennet was shaking his head and giving directions for her luggage to be brought into the house, and even Anne was watching Lydia, eyes wide, no doubt understanding for the first time what Elizabeth had informed her of Lydia's behavior. That was when the other made herself known.

"Miss Lydia Bennet!" Lady Catherine's voice cracked like a whip, and for the first time since descending from the carriage, Lydia ceased speaking, staring at Lady Catherine with her mouth wide open.

"That is much better," said Lady Catherine, but while her voice was quieter, the authority inherent in it was not diminished at all. "You are quite the most ill-mannered, childish young lady I have ever met! What is the meaning of this?"

With obvious affront, Lydia sucked in a breath to unleash a torrent of abuse on the lady, when Lady Catherine stepped up to her and directed a glare so fierce at her that Lydia stepped back in alarm. "Children, Miss Lydia, are to be seen and not heard, and you are most definitely a child who has not learned to behave herself. Now, you will pick up your reticule and march inside the house to your room, and there I shall attend you as you are bathing and preparing for dinner. I will explain to you *exactly* how you shall behave, and if you put one foot out of line, it shall go very ill for you. Am I clear?"

A mutinous glint appeared in Lydia's eyes, and she cast a glance at her father. But Mr. Bennet, far from being offended by this obvious usurpation of his authority, instead looked on with amusement, and when Lydia looked at him, he only shook his head and turned his attention to the disposition of the carriage and Lydia's trunks. She made one more futile gesture at asserting her independence, but it was ruthlessly quashed by Lady Catherine once again.

"Now, Miss Lydia." And so saying, Lady Catherine grasped the girl by the arm and marched her into the house and up the stairs. Elizabeth might have expected Lydia to complain the entire way, but she made not a sound.

By her side, Anne burst into laughter, and though she was still concerned about Lydia's ability to be fractious, Elizabeth joined in, releasing the tension she had been feeling all day.

"I had not thought to find a useful purpose for my mother's imperious nature," chortled Anne, "but in this case, I must own she has outdone herself."

"If anyone possesses the means to be more stubborn than my sister, I must confess that person to be your mother!" replied Elizabeth.

When they descended the stairs that evening for dinner, Lady Catherine stayed by Lydia's side to ensure her good behavior. It was the quietest Elizabeth had ever seen her sister, and though she was not certain this would be a permanent improvement, anything was better than she had been before. And though Lydia would have times where her true nature shone forth, Elizabeth was continually astonished at the change Lady Catherine was able to effect in her sister. Lydia would never be a quiet, proper lady like Georgiana, but she eventually grew to the point where she did not continually embarrass her sisters.

The season for their courtship was a happy one for Elizabeth, and she truly came to love Mr. Darcy more and more each day. When the day arrived that she was to resign the name of her birth in favor of her new husband's, she was able to do so without any hint of concern or hesitation, for he was truly the best man she had ever known.

"This is the happiest day of my life, Mrs. Darcy," said Mr. Darcy.

"It is for me too," replied Elizabeth, feeling overwhelmed by a ceremony that, even now only minutes after, she could remember but little.

"How long shall we stay for the wedding breakfast?"

Elizabeth playfully swatted him. "Shall we offend our family by leaving so early?"

"If it means I am to be alone with you at last, my dear, then I am happy to offend anyone."

With a laugh, Elizabeth steered her husband back to her mother's guests, who were arriving from the chapel. "We will be able to leave soon enough, Husband. For now, let us give them whatever attention we can spare."

And Mr. Darcy did so with as much grace as an impatient man could muster. But in this instance, Elizabeth could not fault his lack of civility. In fact, she was feeling a little impatient herself.

It was spring, and the flowers were in bloom. It was a time Anne loved, for she had so often been denied the simple pleasure of watching an industrious bee, making its way from flower to flower, or the feeling of the wind on her face. Elizabeth's entrance into her life the year before had been both boon and blessing, neither of which Anne had never thought she would receive. To top it off, she was once again visiting her dearest friend and could not be happier.

This bench on which she sat, the bench Elizabeth so favored whenever she was in London, was in such a peaceful locale that Anne had taken to sitting here, thinking about the changes her life had seen. She was hardly the same woman, she knew, and she owed much of it to her dearest friend and now cousin. She had been truly blessed.

The spring was the first time since the previous summer that the Darcys had been in town, for after their wedding, they had returned to London for a period of only three days, after which they had departed for Pemberley, where they had spent the winter after a short journey to the Darcy family lodge in the Lake Country. Though she might have thought a newly married couple would prefer to remain alone throughout the winter, the Darcys had hosted the Bennets, the Fitzwilliams, the de Bourgh's, and even Mr. and Mrs. Collins for the Christmas season, and laughter and joy had abounded at Pemberley. She was a good mistress of Darcy's estates, thought Anne, as Anne had always known she would be.

Those days had not been without their trials, however. Anne had taken to Elizabeth's sisters and family without reservation, amused at their differing characters and not put off by their sometimes less than proper behavior. But her mother still struggled at times, though she was perfectly polite. Miss Lydia, in particular, still tried all their nerves, though the girl had made a little improvement. But she was obviously fearful of Lady Catherine, for all it took was a glare, and Lydia would cease whatever objectionable behavior in which she was engaged. Georgiana still got on famously with Miss Kitty and Miss Mary, and while Mrs. Bennet remained her exuberant self, there was no harm in her. As for Mr. Bennet, there were few men as eager to avoid society as he—not even Darcy was so taciturn—but his sense of humor was diverting, and Anne found many similarities between him and his second daughter.

They had returned to London for the season, though the Bennets returned to Hertfordshire, and though Darcy was his usual self when it came to socializing, Elizabeth was fond of society, and he indulged her whenever he could. The Bingleys, though they did not live in nearly so fashionable a neighborhood, were also nearby, giving both Elizabeth and Anne another dear friend with whom they could face society.

As for Mr. Bingley's sisters, well, they were present, and while the elder was now with child and was to return to her husband's estate before long, the younger was not nearly so objectionable as she had been before. She had a suitor now, or so Anne understood, a circumstance which was a relief to Mr. Bingley. For his sake, Anne hoped Miss Bingley succeeded in eliciting a proposal and that Miss Bingley would be induced to accept.

"Anne?" a voice called from the doorway, and Anne turned and smiled at the approaching figure of her closest friend. "I thought I might find you here."

"Yes, I believe I have usurped your favorite place in London!" said Anne in a teasing tone.

"Perhaps you have," replied Elizabeth. "But I am not averse to sharing it, I assure you."

Elizabeth came and sat next to Anne, and for a short time they sat in companionable silence, watching the world pass them by in their idyllic retreat.

"Shall you come into the house now?" asked Elizabeth, turning to Anne after a time. "If I am not very much mistaken, Mr. Ashdown should be visiting soon. I sure he will after the attention he paid to you last night."

"I will not be the subject of your teasing," said Anne, attempting to display a mock displeasure with her friend.

Elizabeth only raised an eyebrow. "After all the teasing to which you subjected *me*, I should think you would expect it."

"Perhaps I should," replied Anne with a laugh. "But that does not mean I will accept it."

"You *do* like him very well, do you not?" asked Elizabeth.

"I do not object to his attentions," said Anne. "We shall simply need to see."

"Then you may keep your secrets. But you must inform me as soon as there are any developments."

"I surely shall."

Together they rose and made their way back into the house. For Anne, it felt like she was home, a home she had never had before. And it was in a large part due to this wonderful woman whose arm she was holding. Elizabeth Darcy was her companion, her friend, her confidante, and was quite the best person Anne had ever known.

The End

PLEASE ENJOY THE FOLLOWING EXCERPT FROM THE UPCOMING NOVEL ON TIDES OF FATE, BOOK THREE OF THE EARTH AND SKY TRILOGY.

Wisteria was much as Terrace remembered. She was heavyset, though not quite overweight, with the brown hair and eyes of her people, and though her younger sister was delicate and slender, Wisteria was rather like a battering ram in comparison. She was not unattractive, but Terrace knew many men would be put off by her plainer features and the contemptuous curl of her lips. If, indeed, they had not already been put off by her domineering manner and poisonous tongue. With some interest, Terrace noted a few pockmarked scars on Wisteria's face, including one—quite deep—just under her left eye. Terrace wondered whether she had been in a battle of some kind.

There were a number of noble men and women standing by in the room, gazing on Terrace, as though wondering what she would do. Wisteria held her hand out to a nearby servant, who placed a goblet in her hand, backing away deferentially, almost genuflecting before the woman.

Terrace watched this scene with shock. Groundbreathers had never required such strong obeisance from their subjects. Most of those who lived in the castle were Groundbreathers themselves, descended from the same people who had originally been blessed by Terrain. Tillman's requirements for respect had been almost perfunctory in nature, though Sequoia had always been more stringent. But even *that* imperious woman, who Terrace knew to be a good person at heart, had not acted the way her oldest daughter did. The girl almost seemed to think that she was Terrain himself.

"Welcome, Aunt," Wisteria said, her contemptuous amusement not hidden when she paused to drink deeply from the goblet that had been provided to her. "To what do I owe the honor of this unannounced visit?"

"I am sure you understand exactly why I am here, Wisteria. I wish to know what happened to my brother, and I want to know what you have done with River."

Wisteria cocked her head to the side. "You were informed, were you not?"

"I was. But I would hear it from you nonetheless."

Wisteria shrugged. "It is as you were told. There was an attempt to take over the castle, and my father was an unfortunate casualty."

"You speak of him as if he was nothing more than a Groundwalker," Terrace spat. "He was *king* of our people!"

"You had best moderate your tone," the chamberlain said. "Your niece is to be addressed with the respect she deserves and referred to as 'Your Majesty.'"

"I changed her soiled linens when she was a child and swatted her bottom when she misbehaved," Terrace snapped. "You had best mind your manners, or my niece will need a new toady to do her bidding."

The man stiffened at the insult, but Terrace's glare must have been fierce enough that he knew better than to speak any further. The sullen glare he directed at her, however, informed Terrace that she had made an enemy. But she did not fear what a man who kissed her niece's feet could do, and she turned her stony gaze back on Wisteria.

"Well, Wisteria?" Terrace prompted. "I am waiting for your answer."

"I do not make light of my father's death," Wisteria responded. "I mourn his passing as much as anyone, but as *I* am the eldest and the leadership of our people must be maintained, I have put my personal feelings aside for the good of the people and so that I might act in obedience to Terrain."

Terrace glared at her niece. Wisteria had rarely been obedient to anyone, and Terrace had always thought her devotion to the earth god to be little more than superficial.

"Where is River?" Terrace asked, deciding a different tack was required. "Where are Sequoia and Tierra?"

Watching for Wisteria's reaction as she was, Terrace was not surprised when an expression of almost insane revulsion crossed the young woman's face. Wisteria had always hated Tierra with an antipathy so deep that Terrace suspected Wisteria would not shed a tear if Tierra fell over dead.

"My mother disappeared in the chaos," Wisteria replied, though her short tone indicated her patience was being exhausted. "As for River and *Tierra*, they are safe at present. That is all you need to know."

"River is my daughter, and I demand—"

"You are in a position to demand nothing!"

Aunt and niece glared at each other, neither giving an inch. Wisteria stared with cold eyes, her gaze almost seeming to bore through Terrace as though she were not even there. Belatedly, Terrace realized that this woman now held absolute power over the castle and its surrounding environs. These strange Iron Swords guaranteed that.

Wisteria would not be loved by her people. She did not have the ability to inspire such loyalty. Rather, she would rule by fear and her implacable will. Judging by the atmosphere in the throne room, she had already made a start down that path.

It was time to take greater care. Terrace could not do anything from the inside of a cell, and Wisteria would have no compunction about incarcerating her own aunt if her displeasure grew too great.

"I am merely concerned over my daughter," Terrace said. Her attempt at a conciliatory tone was likely an abject failure, but Terrace thought Wisteria would care more about outward respect than inner feelings.

"I know you are concerned," Wisteria replied, her grating attempt at a soothing tone nearly causing Terrace to grimace, "but at present, you must trust me. River will be returned to you, and I promise you she has not been harmed."

Terrace did not miss how Wisteria did not even attempt to mollify her concerning the fate of Tierra. "And when will that be?"

Again, Wisteria's composure cracked, though she controlled her tone. "That is yet to be determined. I will keep you informed of her status. At present, I believe it would be best to return to your home."

Though it galled Terrace to be forced to retreat in such a manner, there was nothing more to be done. "Very well. But I must insist you inform me the moment there is any news."

Terrace inclined her head in farewell and turned to leave, but she was arrested by the sound of Wisteria's voice.

"Aunt, I am afraid I must ask you to remember that my father is dead . . . and *I* am now the queen. My father's reign was marred by laxness, not only in the manner in which his subjects were allowed to behave, but also in . . . other matters that he championed before his death. I have restored the order of our kingdom now. I require all my subjects to behave properly, as our god would require it. I will not hesitate to enforce my dictates. Am I understood?"

Once again, Wisteria and Terrace stared at each other, Terrace searching for any hint of weakness. If there was any, it was well-hidden, for Wisteria's expression was unreadable. It appeared Tillman was correct after all. He had often mentioned his concerns over the fitness of his daughter to rule when he passed away, and Terrace could see nothing before her but the realization of those fears. Wisteria was not to be trifled with, and if she were not stopped, then she had the potential to become the worst despot in the history of their people.

"Perfectly," Terrace replied.

"Excellent! Then we shall see each other anon. Changes are coming,

Aunt, and we must do our part to bring about our god's designs."

Terrace nodded and turned to leave the room, her retinue trailing behind her. She did not understand what Wisteria meant concerning Terrain, but she feared it nonetheless. It was at times like this that she wished Heath was still with her. He had always known what to do, and he had possessed an instinctual ability to read others and determine their motivations with a single glance. Terrace missed him; she had loved and cherished him, and theirs had been a marriage of the hearts.

But there was no point in dwelling on her loss. Terrace had to take action. First, Terrace needed to try to find Sequoia. She was the key. If Terrace could find Sequoia, then Tierra and River could be located afterward.

But first, Terrace needed to involve Basil. As it was his fiancée who was missing, Basil had a direct interest in the matter, and Terrace would not leave him out of it.

And so Terrace departed the castle. But it would not be for the last time. She was now convinced that Wisteria had played a part in Tillman's demise. Terrace meant to find out what had happened to her brother. Wisteria would be held responsible, even if she had only failed to act to save him.

FROM ONE GOOD SONNET PUBLISHING

http://onegoodsonnet.com/

FOR READERS WHO ENJOYED
THE COMPANION

Chaos Comes to Kent
Mr. Collins invites his cousin to stay at his parsonage and the Bennets go to Kent and are introduced to an amiable Lady Catherine de Bourgh. When Mr. Darcy and his cousin, Colonel Fitzwilliam, visit Lady Catherine at the same time, they each begin to focus on a Bennet sister, prodded by well-meaning relations, but spurred on by their own feelings.

Coincidence
Fitzwilliam Darcy finds Miss Elizabeth Bennet visiting her friend, Mrs. Collins, in Kent, only to realize that she detests him. It is not long before he is bewitched by her all over again, and he resolves to change her opinion of him and win her at all costs. Though she only wishes to visit her friend, Elizabeth Bennet is soon made uncomfortable by the presence of Mr. Darcy, who always seems to be near. As their acquaintance deepens, them much learn ore about each other in order to find their happiness.

In the Wilds of Derbyshire
Elizabeth Bennet goes to her uncle's estate in Derbyshire after Jane's marriage to Mr. Bingley, feeling there is nothing left for her in Meryton. She quickly becomes close to her young cousin and uncle, though her aunt seems to hold a grudge against her. She also meets the handsome Mr. Fitzwilliam Darcy, and she realizes that she can still have everything she has ever wished to have. But there are obstacles she must overcome . . . .

My Brother's Keeper
When Fitzwilliam Darcy accompanies Charles Bingley to Netherfield, he is accompanied by George Wickham, a friend of many years. At first, Darcy does not see Elizabeth Bennet for the jewel she is, but his eyes are soon opened to her true worth. As Darcy and Elizabeth grow closer and love begins to blossom between them, the actions of a scoundrel threaten their happiness. All is in the balance when one who they call friend is forced to make a decision which will affect their felicity.

The Angel of Longbourn
When Elizabeth Bennet finds Fitzwilliam Darcy unconscious and suffering from a serious illness, the Bennets quickly return him to their house, where they care for him like he is one of their own. Mr. Darcy soon forms an attachment with the young woman he comes to view as his personal angel. But the course of true love cannot proceed smoothly, for others have an interest in Darcy for their own selfish reasons…

For more details, visit
http://www.onegoodsonnet.com/genres/pride-and-prejudice-variations

Also by One Good Sonnet Publishing

The Smothered Rose Trilogy

Book 1: Thorny

In this retelling of "Beauty and the Beast," a spoiled boy who is forced to watch over a flock of sheep finds himself more interested in catching the eye of a girl with lovely ground-trailing tresses than he is in protecting his charges. But when he cries "wolf" twice, a determined fairy decides to teach him a lesson once and for all.

Book 2: Unsoiled

When Elle finds herself practically enslaved by her stepmother, she scarcely has time to even clean the soot off her hands before she collapses in exhaustion. So when Thorny tries to convince her to go on a quest and leave her identity as Cinderbella behind her, she consents. Little does she know that she will face challenges such as a determined huntsman, hungry dwarves, and powerful curses . . . .

Book 3: Roseblood

Both Elle and Thorny are unhappy with the way their lives are going, and the revelations they have had about each other have only served to drive them apart. What is a mother to do? Reunite them, of course. Unfortunately, things are not quite so simple when a magical lettuce called "rapunzel" is involved.

If you're a fan of thieves with a heart of gold, then you don't want to Miss . . .

THE PRINCES AND THE PEAS
A TALE OF ROBIN HOOD

A NOVEL OF THIEVES, ROYALTY, AND IRREPRESSIBLE LEGUMES

BY LELIA EYE

An infamous thief faces his greatest challenge yet when he is pitted against forty-nine princes and the queen of a kingdom with an unnatural obsession with legumes. Sleeping on top of a pea hidden beneath a pile of mattresses? Easy. Faking a singing contest? He could do that in his sleep. But stealing something precious out from under "Old Maid" Marian's nose . . . now that is a challenge that even the great Robin Hood might not be able to surmount.

When Robin Hood comes up with a scheme that involves disguising himself as a prince and participating in a series of contests for a queen's hand, his Merry Men provide him their support. Unfortunately, however, Prince John attends the contests with the Sheriff of Nottingham in tow, and as all of the Merry Men know, Robin Hood's pride will never let him remain inconspicuous. From sneaking peas onto his neighbors' plates to tweaking the noses of prideful men like the queen's chamberlain, Robin Hood is certain to make an impression on everyone attending the contests. But whether he can escape from the kingdom of Clorinda with his prize in hand before his true identity comes to light is another matter entirely.

About the Author

Jann Rowland

Jann Rowland is a Canadian who enjoys reading and sports, and dabbles a little in music, taking pleasure in singing and playing the piano.

Though Jann did not start writing until his mid-twenties, writing has grown from a hobby to an all-consuming passion. His interest in Jane Austen stems from his university days when he took a class in which *Pride and Prejudice* was required reading. However, his first love is fantasy fiction, which he hopes to pursue writing in the future.

He now lives in Alberta with his wife of more than twenty years and his three children.

For more information on Jann Rowland, please visit: http://onegoodsonnet.com.

Manufactured by Amazon.ca
Bolton, ON